SCRIBNER REPRINT EDITIONS

THE NOVELS AND TALES OF
HENRY JAMES

New York Edition

VOLUME XX

THE WINGS
OF THE DOVE

VOLUME II

HENRY JAMES

AUGUSTUS M. KELLEY • PUBLISHERS
FAIRFIELD 1976

Re-issued 1976 by

Augustus M. Kelley, Publishers

Fairfield, New Jersey 07006

By arrangement with CHARLES SCRIBNER'S SONS

Library of Congress Cataloging in Publication Data

James, Henry, 1843-1916.
  The wings of the dove.

  (Scribner reprint editions)
  Reprint of the ed. published by Scribner, New York,
which was issued as v. 19-20 of The novels and tales of
Henry James.
  I. Title.
PZ3.J234No7 vol. 19-20   [PS2116]   813'.4   71-158798
ISBN 0-678-02819-2 (v. 19)
ISBN 0-678-02820-6 (v. 20)

PRINTED IN THE UNITED STATES OF AMERICA
by SENTRY PRESS, NEW YORK, N. Y. 10013
Bound by A. HOROWITZ & SON, FAIRFIELD, N. J.

THE WINGS OF THE DOVE
VOLUME II

BOOK SIXTH

THE WINGS OF THE DOVE

I

"I SAY, you know, Kate—you *did* stay!" had been
Merton Densher's punctual remark on their adventure after they had, as it were, got out of it; an observation which she not less promptly, on her side, let
him see that she forgave in him only because he was a
man. She had to recognise, with whatever disappointment, that it was doubtless the most helpful he could
make in this character. The fact of the adventure
was flagrant between them; they had looked at each
other, on gaining the street, as people look who have
just rounded together a dangerous corner, and there
was therefore already enough unanimity sketched out
to have lighted, for her companion, anything equi-
vocal in her action. But the amount of light men *did*
need!— Kate could have been eloquent at this moment about that. What, however, on his seeing more,
struck him as most distinct in her was her sense that,
reunited after his absence and having been now half
the morning together, it behooved them to face without delay the question of handling their immediate
future. That it would require some handling, that
they should still have to deal, deal in a crafty manner,
with difficulties and delays, was the great matter he
had come back to, greater than any but the refreshed
consciousness of their personal need of each other.

3

This need had had twenty minutes, the afternoon before, to find out where it stood, and the time was fully accounted for by the charm of the demonstration. He had arrived at Euston at five, having wired her from Liverpool the moment he landed, and she had quickly decided to meet him at the station, whatever publicity might attend such an act. When he had praised her for it on alighting from his train she had answered frankly enough that such things should be taken at a jump. She did n't care to-day who saw her, and she profited by it for her joy. To-morrow, inevitably, she should have time to think and then, as inevitably, would become a baser creature, a creature of alarms and precautions. It was none the less for to-morrow at an early hour that she had appointed their next meeting, keeping in mind for the present a particular obligation to show at Lancaster Gate by six o'clock. She had given, with imprecations, her reason — people to tea, eternally, and a promise to Aunt Maud; but she had been liberal enough on the spot and had suggested the National Gallery for the morning quite as with an idea that had ripened in expectancy. They might be seen there too, but nobody would know them; just as, for that matter, now, in the refreshment-room to which they had adjourned, they would incur the notice but, at the worst, of the unacquainted. They would "have something" there for the facility it would give. Thus had it already come up for them again that they had no place of convenience.

He found himself on English soil with all sorts of feelings, but he had n't quite faced having to reckon

with a certain ruefulness in regard to that subject as
one of the strongest. He was aware later on that there
were questions his impatience had shirked; whereby
it actually rather smote him, for want of preparation
and assurance, that he had nowhere to "take" his
love. He had taken it thus, at Euston — and on
Kate's own suggestion — into the place where people
had beer and buns, and had ordered tea at a small
table in the corner; which, no doubt, as they were
lost in the crowd, did well enough for a stop-gap. It
perhaps did as well as her simply driving with him
to the door of his lodging, which had had to figure as
the sole device of his own wit. That wit, the truth
was, had broken down a little at the sharp prevision
that once at his door they would have to hang back.
She would have to stop there, would n't come in with
him, could n't possibly; and he should n't be able to
ask her, would feel he could n't without betraying a
deficiency of what would be called, even at their advanced stage, respect for her: that again was all that
was clear except the further fact that it was madden-
ing. Compressed and concentrated, confined to a
single sharp pang or two, but none the less in wait for
him there on the Euston platform and lifting its head
as that of a snake in the garden, was the disconcerting
sense that "respect," in their game, seemed somehow
— he scarce knew what to call it — a fifth wheel to
the coach. It was properly an inside thing, not an
outside, a thing to make love greater, not to make
happiness less. They had met again for happiness,
and he distinctly felt, during his most lucid moment
or two, how he must keep watch on anything that

5

really menaced that boon. If Kate had consented to drive away with him and alight at his house there would probably enough have occurred for them, at the foot of his steps, one of those strange instants between man and woman that blow upon the red spark, the spark of conflict, ever latent in the depths of passion. She would have shaken her head — oh sadly, divinely — on the question of coming in; and he, though doing all justice to her refusal, would have yet felt his eyes reach further into her own than a possible word at such a time could reach. This would have meant the suspicion, the dread of the shadow, of an adverse will. Lucky therefore in the actual case that the scant minutes took another turn and that by the half-hour she did in spite of everything contrive to spend with him Kate showed so well how she could deal with things that maddened. She seemed to ask him, to beseech him, and all for his better comfort, to leave her, now and henceforth, to treat them in her own way.

She had still met it in naming so promptly, for their early convenience, one of the great museums; and indeed with such happy art that his fully seeing where she had placed him had n't been till after he left her. His absence from her for so many weeks had had such an effect upon him that his demands, his desires had grown; and only the night before, as his ship steamed, beneath summer stars, in sight of the Irish coast, he had felt all the force of his particular necessity. He had n't in other words at any point doubted he was on his way to say to her that really their mistake must end. Their mistake was to have believed that they

could hold out — hold out, that is, not against Aunt
Maud, but against an impatience that, prolonged and
exasperated, made a man ill. He had known more
than ever, on their separating in the court of the station, how ill a man, and even a woman, could feel
from such a cause; but he struck himself as also knowing that he had already suffered Kate to begin finely
to apply antidotes and remedies and subtle sedatives.
It had a vulgar sound — as throughout, in love, the
names of things, the verbal terms of intercourse, were,
compared with love itself, horribly vulgar; but it was
as if, after all, he might have come back to find himself "put off," though it would take him of course a
day or two to see. His letters from the States had
pleased whom it concerned, though not so much as he
had meant they should; and he should be paid according to agreement and would now take up his money.
It was n't in truth very much to take up, so that he
had n't in the least come back flourishing a cheque-
book; that new motive for bringing his mistress to
terms he could n't therefore pretend to produce. The
ideal certainty would have been to be able to present
a change of prospect as a warrant for the change of
philosophy, and without it he should have to make
shift but with the pretext of the lapse of time. The
lapse of time — not so many weeks after all, she might
always of course say — could n't at any rate have
failed to do something for him; and that consideration
it was that had just now tided him over, all the more
that he had his vision of what it had done personally
for Kate. This had come out for him with a splen-
dour that almost scared him even in their small cor-

ner of the room at Euston — almost scared him because it just seemed to blaze at him that waiting was
the game of dupes. Not yet had she been so the creature he had originally seen; not yet had he felt so
soundly safely sure. It was all there for him, playing
on his pride of possession as a hidden master in a
great dim church might play on the grandest organ.
His final sense was that a woman could n't be like
that and then ask of one the impossible.

She had been like that afresh on the morrow; and
so for the hour they had been able to float in the mere
joy of contact — such contact as their situation in
pictured public halls permitted. This poor makeshift for closeness confessed itself in truth, by twenty
small signs of unrest even on Kate's part, inadequate;
so little could a decent interest in the interesting place
presume to remind them of its claims. They had met
there in order not to meet in the streets and not again,
with an equal want of invention and of style, at a
railway-station; not again, either, in Kensington
Gardens, which, they could easily and tacitly agree,
would have had too much of the taste of their old
frustrations. The present taste, the taste that morning in the pictured halls, had been a variation; yet
Densher had at the end of a quarter of an hour fully
known what to conclude from it. This fairly con-
soled him for their awkwardness, as if he had been
watching it affect her. She might be as nobly charming as she liked, and he had seen nothing to touch her
in the States; she could n't pretend that in such conditions as those she herself *believed* it enough to ap-
pease him. She could n't pretend she believed he

would believe it enough to render her a like service. It was n't enough for that purpose — she as good as showed him it was n't. That was what he could be glad, by demonstration, to have brought her to. He would have said to her had he put it crudely and on the spot: "*Now* am I to understand you that you consider this sort of thing can go on?" It would have been open to her, no doubt, to reply that to have him with her again, to have him all kept and treasured, so still, under her grasping hand, as she had held him in their yearning interval, was a sort of thing that he must allow her to have no quarrel about; but that would be a mere gesture of her grace, a mere sport of her subtlety. She knew as well as he what they wanted; in spite of which indeed he scarce could have said how beautifully he might n't once more have named it and urged it if she had n't, at a given moment, blurred, as it were, the accord. They had soon seated themselves for better talk, and so they had remained a while, intimate and superficial. The immediate things to say had been many, for they had n't exhausted them at Euston. They drew upon them freely now, and Kate appeared quite to forget — which was prodigiously becoming to her — to look about for surprises. He was to try afterwards, and try in vain, to remember what speech or what silence of his own, what natural sign of the eyes or accidental touch of the hand, had precipitated for her, in the midst of this, a sudden different impulse. She had got up, with inconsequence, as if to break the charm, though he was n't aware of what he had done at the moment to make the charm a danger. She had patched it up agreeably enough the next minute by some odd remark about some picture, to which he had n't so much as replied; it being quite independently of this that he had himself exclaimed on the dreadful closeness of the rooms. He had observed that they must go out again to breathe; and it was as if their common consciousness, while they passed into another part, was that of persons who, infinitely engaged together, had been startled and were trying to look natural. It was probably while they were so occupied — as the young man subsequently reconceived — that they had stumbled upon his little New York friend. He thought of her for some reason as little, though she was of about Kate's height, to which, any more than to any other felicity in his mistress, he had never applied the diminutive.

What was to be in the retrospect more distinct to him was the process by which he had become aware that Kate's acquaintance with her was greater than he had gathered. She had written of it in due course as a new and amusing one, and he had written back that he had met over there, and that he much liked, the young person; whereupon she had answered that he must find out about her at home. Kate, in the event, however, had not returned to that, and he had of course, with so many things to find out about, been otherwise taken up. Little Miss Theale's individual history was not stuff for his newspaper; besides which, moreover, he was seeing but too many little Miss Theales. They even went so far as to impose themselves as one of the groups of social phenomena that fell into the scheme of his public letters. For this group in especial perhaps — the irrepressible, the supereminent. young persons — his best pen was ready. Thus it was that there could come back to him in London, an hour or two after their luncheon with the American pair, the sense of a situation for which Kate had n't wholly prepared him. Possibly indeed as marked as this was his recovered perception that preparations, of more than one kind, had been exactly what, both yesterday and to-day, he felt her as having in hand. That appearance in fact, if he dwelt on it, so ministered to apprehension as to require some brushing away. He shook off the suspicion to some extent, on their separating first from their hostesses and then from each other, by the aid of a long and rather aimless walk. He was to go to the office later, but he had the next two or three hours, and he gave himself as a pretext that he had eaten much too much. After Kate had asked him to put her into a cab — which, as an announced, a resumed policy on her part, he found himself deprecating — he stood a while by a corner and looked vaguely forth at his London. There was always doubtless a moment for the absentee recaptured — *the* moment, that of the reflux of the first emotion — at which it was beyond disproof that one was back. His full parenthesis was closed, and he was once more but a sentence, of a sort, in the general text, the text that, from his momentary street-corner, showed as a great grey page of print that somehow managed to be crowded without being "fine." The grey, however, was more or less the blur of a point of view not yet quite seized again; and there would be colour enough to come out. He was

11

back, flatly enough, but back to possibilities and prospects, and the ground he now somewhat sightlessly covered was the act of renewed possession.

He walked northward without a plan, without suspicion, quite in the direction his little New York friend, in her restless ramble, had taken a day or two before. He reached, like Milly, the Regent's Park; and though he moved further and faster he finally sat down, like Milly, from the force of thought. For him too in this position, be it added — and he might positively have occupied the same bench — various troubled fancies folded their wings. He had no more yet said what he really wanted than Kate herself had found time. She should hear enough of that in a couple of days. He had practically not pressed her as to what most concerned them; it had seemed so to concern them during these first hours but to hold each other, spiritually speaking, close. This at any rate was palpable, that there were at present more things rather than fewer between them. The explanation about the two ladies would be part of the lot, yet could wait with all the rest. They were not meanwhile certainly what most made him roam — the missing explanations were n't. That was what she had so often said before, and always with the effect of suddenly breaking off: "Now please call me a good cab." Their previous encounters, the times when they had reached in their stroll the south side of the park, had had a way of winding up with this special irrelevance. It was effectively what most divided them, for he would generally, but for her reasons, have been able to jump in with her. What did she think he wished to do to her? — it was a question he had had occasion to put. A small matter, however, doubtless — since, when it came to that, they did n't depend on cabs good or bad for the sense of union: its importance was less from the particular loss than as a kind of irritating mark of her expertness. This expertness, under providence, had been great from the first, so far as joining him was concerned; and he was critical only because it had been still greater, even from the first too, in respect to leaving him. He had put the question to her again that afternoon, on the repetition of her appeal — had asked her once more what she supposed he wished to do. He recalled, on his bench in the Regent's Park, the freedom of fancy, funny and pretty, with which she had answered; recalled the moment itself, while the usual hansom charged them, during which he felt himself, disappointed as he was, grimacing back at the superiority of her very "humour," in its added grace of gaiety, to the celebrated solemn American. Their fresh appointment had been at all events by that time made, and he should see what her choice in respect to it — a surprise as well as a relief — would do toward really simplifying. It meant either new help or new hindrance, though it took them at least out of the streets. And her naming this privilege had naturally made him ask if Mrs. Lowder knew of his return.

"Not from me," Kate had replied. "But I shall speak to her now." And she had argued, as with rather a quick fresh view, that it would now be quite easy. "We've behaved for months so properly that I've margin surely for my mention of you. You'll

13

come to see *her*, and she'll leave you with me; she'll show her good nature, and her lack of betrayed fear, in that. With her, you know, you've never broken, quite the contrary, and she likes you as much as ever. We're leaving town; it will be the end; just now therefore it's nothing to ask. I'll ask to-night," Kate had wound up, "and if you'll leave it to me — my cleverness, I assure you, has grown infernal — I'll make it all right."

He had of course thus left it to her and he was wondering more about it now than he had wondered there in Brook Street. He repeated to himself that if it was n't in the line of triumph it was in the line of muddle. This indeed, no doubt, was as a part of his wonder for still other questions. Kate had really got off without meeting his little challenge about the terms of their intercourse with her dear Milly. Her dear Milly, it was sensible, *was* somehow in the picture. Her dear Milly, popping up in his absence, occupied — he could n't have said quite why he felt it — more of the foreground than one would have expected her in advance to find clear. She took up room, and it was almost as if room had been made for her. Kate had appeared to take for granted he would know why it had been made; but that was just the point. It was a foreground in which he himself, in which his connexion with Kate, scarce enjoyed a space to turn round. But Miss Theale was perhaps at the present juncture a possibility of the same sort as the softened, if not the squared, Aunt Maud. It might be true of her also that if she were n't a bore she'd be a convenience. It rolled over him of a sudden, after he had resumed his walk, that this might easily be what Kate had meant. The charming girl adored her — Densher had for himself made out that — and would protect, would lend a hand, to their interviews. These might take place, in other words, on her premises, which would remove them still better from the streets. *That* was an explanation which did hang together. It was impaired a little, of a truth, by this fact that their next encounter was rather markedly not to depend upon her. Yet this fact in turn would be accounted for by the need of more preliminaries. One of the things he conceivably should gain on Thursday at Lancaster Gate would be a further view of that propriety.

II

I⊤ was extraordinary enough that he should actually
be finding himself, when Thursday arrived, none so
wide of the mark. Kate had n't come all the way to
this for him, but she had come to a good deal by the
end of a quarter of an hour. What she had begun
with was her surprise at her appearing to have left
him on Tuesday anything more to understand. The
parts, as he now saw, under her hand, did fall more or
less together, and it was n't even as if she had spent
the interval in twisting and fitting them. She was
bright and handsome, not fagged and worn, with the
general clearness; for it certainly stuck out enough
that if the American ladies themselves were n't to be
squared, which was absurd, they fairly imposed the
necessity of trying Aunt Maud again. One could n't
say to them, kind as she had been to them: "We'll
meet, please, whenever you'll let us, at your house;
but we count on you to help us to keep it secret."
They must in other terms inevitably speak to Aunt
Maud — it would be of the last awkwardness to ask
them not to: Kate had embraced all this in her choice
of speaking first. What Kate embraced altogether
was indeed wonderful to-day for Densher, though he
perhaps struck himself rather as getting it out of her
piece by piece than as receiving it in a steady light.
He had always felt, however, that the more he asked
of her the more he found her prepared, as he imaged

it, to hand out. He had said to her more than once even before his absence: "You keep the key of the cupboard, and I foresee that when we're married you'll dole me out my sugar by lumps." She had replied that she rejoiced in his assumption that sugar would be his diet, and the domestic arrangement so prefigured might have seemed already to prevail. The supply from the cupboard at this hour was doubtless, of a truth, not altogether cloyingly sweet; but it met in a manner his immediate requirements. If her explanations at any rate prompted questions the questions no more exhausted them than they exhausted her patience. And they were naturally, of the series, the simpler; as for instance in his taking it from her that Miss Theale then could do nothing for them. He frankly brought out what he had ventured to think possible. "If we can't meet here and we've really exhausted the charms of the open air and the crowd, some such little raft in the wreck, some occasional opportunity like that of Tuesday, has been present to me these two days as better than nothing. But if our friends are so accountable to this house of course there's no more to be said. And it's one more nail, thank God, in the coffin of our odious delay." He was but too glad without more ado to point the moral. "Now I hope you see we can't work it anyhow."

If she laughed for this — and her spirits seemed really high — it was because of the opportunity that, at the hotel, he had most shown himself as enjoying. "Your idea's beautiful when one remembers that you had n't a word except for Milly." But she was as beautifully good-humoured. "You might of course get used to her — you *will*. You're quite right — so long as they're with us or near us." And she put it, lucidly, that the dear things couldn't *help*, simply as charming friends, giving them a lift. "They'll speak to Aunt Maud, but they won't shut their doors to us: that would be another matter. A friend always helps — and she's a friend." She had left Mrs. Stringham by this time out of the question; she had reduced it to Milly. "Besides, she particularly likes us. She particularly likes *you*. I say, old boy, make something of that." He felt her dodging the ultimatum he had just made sharp, his definite reminder of how little, at the best, they could work it; but there were certain of his remarks — those mostly of the sharper penetration — that it had been quite her practice from the first not formally, not reverently to notice. She showed the effect of them in ways less trite. This was what happened now: he didn't think in truth that she wasn't really minding. She took him up, none the less, on a minor question. "You say we can't meet here, but you see it's just what we do. What could be more lovely than this?"

It wasn't to torment him — that again he didn't believe; but he had to come to the house in some discomfort, so that he frowned a little at her calling it thus a luxury. Wasn't there an element in it of coming back into bondage? The bondage might be veiled and varnished, but he knew in his bones how little the very highest privileges of Lancaster Gate could ever be a sign of their freedom. They were upstairs, in one of the smaller apartments of state, a room arranged as a boudoir, but visibly unused — it defied familiarity — and furnished in the ugliest of blues. He had immediately looked with interest at the closed doors, and Kate had met his interest with the assurance that it was all right, that Aunt Maud did them justice — so far, that was, as this particular time was concerned; that they should be alone and have nothing to fear. But the fresh allusion to this that he had drawn from her acted on him now more directly, brought him closer still to the question. They *were* alone — it *was* all right: he took in anew the shut doors and the permitted privacy, the solid stillness of the great house. They connected themselves on the spot with something made doubly vivid in him by the whole present play of her charming strong will. What it amounted to was that he could n't have her — hanged if he could! — evasive. He could n't and he would n't — would n't have her inconvenient and elusive. He did n't want her deeper than himself, fine as it might be as wit or as character; he wanted to keep her where their communications would be straight and easy and their intercourse independent. The effect of this was to make him say in a moment: "Will you take me just as I am?"

She turned a little pale for the tone of truth in it — which qualified to his sense delightfully the strength of her will; and the pleasure he found in this was not the less for her breaking out after an instant into a strain that stirred him more than any she had ever used with him. "Ah do let me try myself! I assure you I see my way — so don't spoil it: wait for me and give me time. Dear man," Kate said, "only believe in me, and it will be beautiful."

He had n't come back to hear her talk of his believing in her as if he did n't; but he had come back — and it all was upon him now — to seize her with a sudden intensity that her manner of pleading with him had made, as happily appeared, irresistible. He laid strong hands upon her to say, almost in anger, "Do you love me, love me, love me?" and she closed her eyes as with the sense that he might strike her but that she could gratefully take it. Her surrender was her response, her response her surrender; and, though scarce hearing what she said, he so profited by these things that it could for the time be ever so intimately appreciable to him that he was keeping her. The long embrace in which they held each other was the rout of evasion, and he took from it the certitude that what she had from him was real to her. It was stronger than an uttered vow, and the name he was to give it in afterthought was that she had been sublimely sincere. *That* was all he asked — sincerity making a basis that would bear almost anything. This settled so much, and settled it so thoroughly, that there was nothing left to ask her to swear to. Oaths and vows apart, now they could talk. It seemed in fact only now that their questions were put on the table. He had taken up more expressly at the end of five minutes her plea for her own plan, and it was marked that the difference made by the passage just enacted was a difference in favour of her choice of means. Means had somehow suddenly become a detail — her province and her care; it had grown more consistently vivid that her intelligence was one with her passion. "I certainly don't want," he said — and he could say it

20

with a smile of indulgence — "to be all the while bringing it up that I don't trust you."

"I should hope not! What do you think I want to do?"

He had really at this to make out a little what he thought, and the first thing that put itself in evidence was of course the oddity, after all, of their game, to which he could but frankly allude. "We're doing, at the best, in trying to temporise in so special a way, a thing most people would call us fools for." But his visit passed, all the same, without his again attempting to make "just as he was" serve. He had no more money just as he was than he had had just as he had been, or than he should have, probably, when it came to that, just as he always would be; whereas she, on her side, in comparison with her state of some months before, had measureably more to relinquish. He easily saw how their meeting at Lancaster Gate gave more of an accent to that quantity than their meeting at stations or in parks; and yet on the other hand he could n't urge this against it. If Mrs. Lowder was indifferent her indifference added in a manner to what Kate's taking him as he was would call on her to sacrifice. Such in fine was her art with him that she seemed to put the question of their still waiting into quite other terms than the terms of ugly blue, of florid Sèvres, of complicated brass, in which their boudoir expressed it. She said almost all in fact by saying, on this article of Aunt Maud, after he had once more pressed her, that when he should see her, as must inevitably soon happen, he would understand. "Do you mean," he asked at this, "that there's any *definite* sign of her coming round? I'm not talking," he explained, "of mere hypocrisies in her, or mere brave duplicities. Remember, after all, that supremely clever as we are, and as strong a team, I admit, as there is going — remember that she can play with us quite as much as we play with her."

"She does n't want to play with *me*, my dear," Kate lucidly replied; "she does n't want to make me suffer a bit more than she need. She cares for me too much, and everything she does or does n't do has a value. *This* has a value — her being as she has been about us to-day. I believe she's in her room, where she's keeping strictly to herself while you're here with me. But that is n't 'playing' — not a bit."

"What is it then," the young man returned — "from the moment it is n't her blessing and a cheque?"

Kate was complete. "It's simply her absence of smallness. There *is* something in her above trifles. She *generally* trusts us; she does n't propose to hunt us into corners; and if we frankly ask for a thing — why," said Kate, "she shrugs, but she lets it go. She has really but one fault — she's indifferent, on such ground as she has taken about us, to details. However," the girl cheerfully went on, "it is n't in detail we fight her."

"It seems to me," Densher brought out after a moment's thought of this, "that it's in detail we deceive her" — a speech that, as soon as he had uttered it, applied itself for him, as also visibly for his companion, to the afterglow of their recent embrace.

Any confusion attaching to this adventure, however, dropped from Kate, whom, as he could see with

22

sacred joy, it must take more than that to make com-
punctious. "I don't say we can do it again. I mean,"
she explained, "meet here."

Densher indeed had been wondering where they
could do it again. If Lancaster Gate was so limited
that issue reappeared. "I may n't come back at all?"

"Certainly — to see her. It's she, really," his
companion smiled, "who's in love with you."

But it made him — a trifle more grave — look at
her a moment. "Don't make out, you know, that
every one's in love with me."

She hesitated. "I don't say every one."

"You said just now Miss Theale."

"I said she liked you — yes."

"Well, it comes to the same thing." With which,
however, he pursued: "Of course I ought to thank
Mrs. Lowder in person. I mean for *this* — as from
myself."

"Ah but, you know, not too much!" She had an
ironic gaiety for the implications of his "this," besides
wishing to insist on a general prudence. "She'll
wonder what you're thanking her for!"

Densher did justice to both considerations. "Yes,
I can't very well tell her all."

It was perhaps because he said it so gravely that
Kate was again in a manner amused. Yet she gave
out light. "You can't very well 'tell' her anything,
and that does n't matter. Only be nice to her. Please
her; make her see how clever you are — only without
letting her see that you're trying. If you're charming
to her you've nothing else to do."

But she oversimplified too. "I can be 'charming'

23

to her, so far as I see, only by letting her suppose I give you up — which I'll be hanged if I do! It *is*," he said with feeling, "a game."

"Of course it's a game. But she'll never suppose you give me up — or I give *you* — if you keep reminding her how you enjoy our interviews."

"Then if she has to see us as obstinate and constant," Densher asked, "what good does it do?"

Kate was for a moment checked. "What good does what — ?"

"Does my pleasing her — does anything. I *can't*," he impatiently declared, "please her."

Kate looked at him hard again, disappointed at his want of consistency; but it appeared to determine in her something better than a mere complaint. "Then *I* can! Leave it to me." With which she came to him under the compulsion, again, that had united them shortly before, and took hold of him in her urgency to the same tender purpose. It was her form of entreaty renewed and repeated, which made after all, as he met it, their great fact clear. And it somehow clarified *all* things so to possess each other. The effect of it was that, once more, on these terms, he could only be generous. He had so on the spot then left everything to her that she reverted in the course of a few moments to one of her previous — and as positively seemed — her most precious ideas. "You accused me just now of saying that Milly's in love with you. Well, if you come to that, I do say it. So there you are. That's the good she'll do us. It makes a basis for her seeing you — so that she'll help us to go on."

Densher stared — she was wondrous all round. "And what sort of a basis does it make for my seeing *her?*"

"Oh I don't mind!" Kate smiled.

"Don't mind my leading her on?"

She put it differently. "Don't mind her leading *you.*"

"Well, she won't — so it's nothing not to mind. But how can that 'help,'" he pursued, "with what she knows?"

"What she knows? That need n't prevent."

He wondered. "Prevent her loving us?"

"Prevent her helping you. She's *like* that," Kate Croy explained.

It took indeed some understanding. "Making nothing of the fact that I love another?"

"Making everything," said Kate. "To console you."

"But for what?"

"For not getting your other."

He continued to stare. "But how does she know — ?"

"That you *won't* get her? She does n't; but on the other hand she does n't know you will. Meanwhile she sees you baffled, for she knows of Aunt Maud's stand. *That*" — Kate was lucid — "gives her the chance to be nice to you."

"And what does it give *me*," the young man none the less rationally asked, "the chance to be? A brute of a humbug to her?"

Kate so possessed her facts, as it were, that she smiled at his violence. "You'll extraordinarily like her. She's exquisite. And there are reasons. I mean others."

"What others?"

"Well, I'll tell you another time. Those I give you," the girl added, "are enough to go on with."

"To go on to what?"

"Why, to seeing her again — say as soon as you can: which, moreover, on all grounds, is no more than decent of you."

He of course took in her reference, and he had fully in mind what had passed between them in New York. It had been no great quantity, but it had made distinctly at the time for his pleasure; so that anything in the nature of an appeal in the name of it could have a slight kindling consequence. "Oh I shall naturally call again without delay. Yes," said Densher, "her being in love with me is nonsense; but I must, quite independently of that, make every acknowledgement of favours received."

It appeared practically all Kate asked. "Then you see. I shall meet you there."

"I don't quite see," he presently returned, "why she should wish to receive *you* for it."

"She receives me for myself — that is for *her* self. She thinks no end of me. That I should have to drum it into you!"

Yet still he didn't take it. "Then I confess she's beyond me."

Well, Kate could but leave it as she saw it. "She regards me as already — in these few weeks — her dearest friend. It's quite separate. We're in, she and I, ever so deep." And it was to confirm this that, as if it had flashed upon her that he was somewhere at sea, she threw out at last her own real light. "She does n't of course know I care for *you*. She thinks I care so little that it's not worth speaking of." That he *had* been somewhere at sea these remarks made quickly clear, and Kate hailed the effect with surprise. "Have you been supposing that she does know —?"

"About our situation? Certainly, if you're such friends as you show me — and if you have n't otherwise represented it to her." She uttered at this such a sound of impatience that he stood artlessly vague. "You *have* denied it to her?"

She threw up her arms at his being so backward. "'Denied it'? My dear man, we've never spoken of you."

"Never, never?"

"Strange as it may appear to your glory — never."

He could n't piece it together. "But won't Mrs. Lowder have spoken?"

"Very probably. But of *you*. Not of me."

This struck him as obscure. "How does she know me but as part and parcel of you?"

"How?" Kate triumphantly asked. "Why exactly to make nothing of it, to have nothing to do with it, to stick consistently to her line about it. Aunt Maud's line is to keep all reality out of our relation — that is out of my being in danger from you — by not having so much as suspected or heard of it. She'll get rid of it, as she believes, by ignoring it and sinking it — if she only does so hard enough. Therefore *she*, in her manner, 'denies' it if you will. That's how she knows you otherwise than as part and parcel of me.

She won't for a moment have allowed either to Mrs. Stringham or to Milly that I've in any way, as they say, distinguished you."

"And you don't suppose," said Densher, "that they must have made it out for themselves?"

"No, my dear, I don't; not even," Kate declared, "after Milly's so funnily bumping against us on Tuesday."

"She doesn't see from *that* — ?"

"That you're, so to speak, mad about me. Yes, she sees, no doubt, that you regard me with a complacent eye — for you show it, I think, always too much and too crudely. But nothing beyond that. *I* don't show it too much; I don't perhaps — to please you completely where others are concerned — show it enough."

"Can you show it or not as you like?" Densher demanded.

It pulled her up a little, but she came out resplendent. "Not where *you* are concerned. Beyond seeing that you're rather gone," she went on, "Milly only sees that I'm decently good to you."

"Very good indeed she must think it!"

"Very good indeed then. She easily sees me," Kate smiled, "as very good indeed."

The young man brooded. "But in a sense to take some explaining."

"Then I explain." She was really fine; it came back to her essential plea for her freedom of action and his beauty of trust. "I mean," she added, "I *will* explain."

"And what will *I* do?"

28

"Recognise the difference it must make if she thinks." But here in truth Kate faltered. It was his silence alone that, for the moment, took up her apparent meaning; and before he again spoke she had returned to remembrance and prudence. They were now not to forget that, Aunt Maud's liberality having put them on their honour, they must n't spoil their case by abusing it. He must leave her in time; they should probably find it would help them. But she came back to Milly too. "Mind you go to see her."

Densher still, however, took up nothing of this. "Then I may come again?"

"For Aunt Maud — as much as you like. But we can't again," said Kate, "play her *this* trick. I can't see you here alone."

"Then where?"

"Go to see Milly," she for all satisfaction repeated.

"And what good will that do me?"

"Try it and you'll see."

"You mean you'll manage to be there?" Densher asked. "Say you are, how will that give us privacy?"

"Try it — you'll see," the girl once more returned. "We must manage as we can."

"That's precisely what *I* feel. It strikes me we might manage better." His idea of this was a thing that made him an instant hesitate; yet he brought it out with conviction. "Why won't you come to *me*?"

It was a question her troubled eyes seemed to tell him he was scarce generous in expecting her definitely to answer, and by looking to him to wait at least she appealed to something that she presently made him feel as his pity. It was on that special shade of tenderness that he thus found himself thrown back; and while he asked of his spirit and of his flesh just what concession they could arrange she pressed him yet again on the subject of her singular remedy for their embarrassment. It might have been irritating had she ever struck him as having in her mind a stupid corner. "You'll see," she said, "the difference it will make."

Well, since she wasn't stupid she was intelligent; it was he who was stupid — the proof of which was that he would do what she liked. But he made a last effort to understand, her allusion to the "difference" bringing him round to it. He indeed caught at something subtle but strong even as he spoke. "Is what you meant a moment ago that the difference will be in her being made to believe you hate me?"

Kate, however, had simply, for this gross way of putting it, one of her more marked shows of impatience; with which in fact she sharply closed their discussion. He opened the door on a sign from her, and she accompanied him to the top of the stairs with an air of having so put their possibilities before him that questions were idle and doubts perverse. "I verily believe I *shall* hate you if you spoil for me the beauty of what I see!"

III

HE was really, notwithstanding, to hear more from her of what she saw; and the very next occasion had for him still other surprises than that. He received from Mrs. Lowder on the morning after his visit to Kate the telegraphic expression of a hope that he might be free to dine with them that evening; and his freedom affected him as fortunate even though in some degree qualified by her missive. "Expecting American friends whom I'm so glad to find you know!" His knowledge of American friends was clearly an accident of which he was to taste the fruit to the last bitterness. This apprehension, however, we hasten to add, enjoyed for him, in the immediate event, a certain merciful shrinkage; the immediate event being that, at Lancaster Gate, five minutes after his due arrival, prescribed him for eight-thirty, Mrs. Stringham came in alone. The long daylight, the postponed lamps, the habit of the hour, made dinners late and guests still later; so that, punctual as he was, he had found Mrs. Lowder alone, with Kate herself not yet in the field. He had thus had with her several bewildering moments — bewildering by reason, fairly, of their tacit invitation to him to be supernaturally simple. This was exactly, goodness knew, what he wanted to be; but he had never had it so largely and freely — *so* supernaturally simply, for that matter — imputed to him as of easy achievement.

31

It was a particular in which Aunt Maud appeared to offer herself as an example, appeared to say quite agreeably: "What I want of you, don't you see? is to be just exactly as *I* am." The quantity of the article required was what might especially have caused him to stagger — he liked so, in general, the quantities in which Mrs. Lowder dealt. He would have liked as well to ask her how feasible she supposed it for a poor young man to resemble her at any point; but he had after all soon enough perceived that he was doing as she wished by letting his wonder show just a little as silly. He was conscious moreover of a small strange dread of the results of discussion with her — strange, truly, because it was her good nature, not her asperity, that he feared. Asperity might have made him angry — in which there was always a comfort; good nature, in his conditions, had a tendency to make him ashamed — which Aunt Maud indeed, wonderfully, liking him for himself, quite struck him as having guessed. To spare him therefore she also avoided discussion; she kept him down by refusing to quarrel with him. This was what she now proposed to him to enjoy, and his secret discomfort was his sense that on the whole it was what would best suit him. Being kept down was a bore, but his great dread, verily, was of being ashamed, which was a thing distinct; and it mattered but little that he was ashamed of that too.

It was of the essence of his position that in such a house as this the tables could always be turned on him. "What do you offer, what do you offer?" — the place, however muffled in convenience and decorum, constantly hummed for him with that thick irony. The irony was a renewed reference to obvious bribes, and he had already seen how little aid came to him from denouncing the bribes as ugly in form. That was what the precious metals — they alone — could afford to be; it was vain enough for him accordingly to try to impart a gloss to his own comparative brummagem. The humiliation of this impotence was precisely what Aunt Maud sought to mitigate for him by keeping him down; and as her effort to that end had doubtless never yet been so visible he had probably never felt so definitely placed in the world as while he waited with her for her half-dozen other guests. She welcomed him genially back from the States, as to his view of which her few questions, though not coherent, were comprehensive, and he had the amusement of seeing in her, as through a clear glass, the outbreak of a plan and the sudden consciousness of a curiosity. She became aware of America, under his eyes, as a possible scene for social operations; the idea of a visit to the wonderful country had clearly but just occurred to her, yet she was talking of it, at the end of a minute, as her favourite dream. He did n't believe in it, but he pretended to; this helped her as well as anything else to treat him as harmless and blameless. She was so engaged, with the further aid of a complete absence of allusions, when the highest effect was given her method by the beautiful entrance of Kate. The method therefore received support all round, for no young man could have been less formidable than the person to the relief of whose shyness her niece ostensibly came. The ostensible, in Kate, struck him altogether, on this occasion, as prodigious; while scarcely less prodigious, for that matter, was his own reading, on the spot, of the relation between his companions — a relation lighted for him by the straight look, not exactly loving nor lingering, yet searching and soft, that, on the part of their hostess, the girl had to reckon with as she advanced. It took her in from head to foot, and in doing so it told a story that made poor Densher again the least bit sick: it marked so something with which Kate habitually and consummately reckoned.

That was the story — that she was always, for her beneficent dragon, under arms; living up, every hour, but especially at festal hours, to the "value" Mrs. Lowder had attached to her. High and fixed, this estimate ruled on each occasion at Lancaster Gate the social scene; so that he now recognised in it something like the artistic idea, the plastic substance, imposed by tradition, by genius, by criticism, in respect to a given character, on a distinguished actress. As such a person was to dress the part, to walk, to look, to speak, in every way to express, the part, so all this was what Kate was to do for the character she had undertaken, under her aunt's roof, to represent. It was made up, the character, of definite elements and touches — things all perfectly ponderable to criticism; and the way for her to meet criticism was evidently at the start to be sure her make-up had had the last touch and that she looked at least no worse than usual. Aunt Maud's appreciation of that to-night was indeed managerial, and the performer's own contribution fairly that of the faultless soldier on parade. Densher saw himself for the moment as in his purchased stall

at the play; the watchful manager was in the depths
of a box and the poor actress in the glare of the footlights. But she *passed*, the poor performer — he could
see how she always passed; her wig, her paint, her
jewels, every mark of her expression impeccable, and
her entrance accordingly greeted with the proper
round of applause. Such impressions as we thus note
for Densher come and go, it must be granted, in very
much less time than notation demands; but we may
none the less make the point that there was, still further, time among them for him to feel almost too
scared to take part in the ovation. He struck himself
as having lost, for the minute, his presence of mind —
so that in any case he only stared in silence at the
older woman's technical challenge and at the younger
one's disciplined face. It was as if the drama — it
thus came to him, for the fact of a drama there was
no blinking — was between *them*, them quite pre-
ponderantly; with Merton Densher relegated to mere
spectatorship, a paying place in front, and one of the
most expensive. This was why his appreciation had
turned for the instant to fear — had just turned, as
we have said, to sickness; and in spite of the fact that
the disciplined face did offer him over the footlights,
as he believed, the small gleam, fine faint but exquisite, of a special intelligence. So might a practised
performer, even when raked by double-barrelled
glasses, seem to be all in her part and yet convey a
sign to the person in the house she loved best.

The drama, at all events, as Densher saw it, meanwhile went on — amplified soon enough by the advent
of two other guests, stray gentlemen both, stragglers

in the rout of the season, who visibly presented themselves to Kate during the next moments as subjects
for a like impersonal treatment and sharers in a like
usual mercy. At opposite ends of the social course,
they displayed, in respect to the "figure" that each,
in his way, made, one the expansive, the other the
contractile effect of the perfect white waistcoat. A
scratch company of two innocuous youths and a paci-
fied veteran was therefore what now offered itself to
Mrs. Stringham, who rustled in a little breathless and
full of the compunction of having had to come alone.
Her companion, at the last moment, had been indisposed — positively not well enough, and so had
packed her off, insistently, with excuses, with wild
regrets. This circumstance of their charming friend's
illness was the first thing Kate took up with Densher
on their being able after dinner, without bravado, to
have ten minutes "naturally," as she called it —
which was n't what *he* did — together; but it was already as if the young man had, by an odd impression,
throughout the meal, not been wholly deprived of
Miss Theale's participation. Mrs. Lowder had made
dear Milly the topic, and it proved, on the spot, a
topic as familiar to the enthusiastic younger as to
the sagacious older man. Any knowledge they might
lack Mrs. Lowder's niece was moreover alert to
supply, while Densher himself was freely appealed to
as the most privileged, after all, of the group. Was n't
it he who had in a manner invented the wonderful
creature — through having seen her first, caught her
in her native jungle? Had n't he more or less paved
the way for her by his prompt recognition of her

rarity, by preceding her, in a friendly spirit — as he had the "ear" of society — with a sharp flashlight or two?

He met, poor Densher, these enquiries as he could, listening with interest, yet with discomfort; wincing in particular, dry journalist as he was, to find it seemingly supposed of him that he had put his pen — oh his "pen!" — at the service of private distinction. The ear of society? — they were talking, or almost, as if he had publicly paragraphed a modest young lady. They dreamt dreams, in truth, he appeared to perceive, that fairly waked *him* up, and he settled himself in his place both to resist his embarrassment and to catch the full revelation. His embarrassment came naturally from the fact that if he could claim no credit for Miss Theale's success, so neither could he gracefully insist on his not having been concerned with her. What touched him most nearly was that the occasion took on somehow the air of a commemorative banquet, a feast to celebrate a brilliant if brief career. There was of course more said about the heroine than if she had n't been absent, and he found himself rather stupefied at the range of Milly's triumph. Mrs. Lowder had wonders to tell of it; the two wearers of the waistcoat, either with sincerity or with hypocrisy, professed in the matter an equal expertness; and Densher at last seemed to know himself in presence of a social "case." It was Mrs. Stringham, obviously, whose testimony would have been most invoked had n't she been, as her friend's representative, rather confined to the function of inhaling the incense; so that Kate, who treated her beautifully, smiling at her, cheering and consoling her across the table, appeared benevolently both to speak and to interpret for her. Kate spoke as if she would n't perhaps understand *their* way of appreciating Milly, but would let them none the less, in justice to their good will, express it in their coarser fashion. Densher himself was n't unconscious in respect to this of a certain broad brotherhood with Mrs. Stringham; wondering indeed, while he followed the talk, how it might move American nerves. He had only heard of them before, but in his recent tour he had caught them in the remarkable fact, and there was now a moment or two when it came to him that he had perhaps — and not in the way of an escape — taken a lesson from them.

They quivered, clearly, they hummed and drummed, they leaped and bounded in Mrs. Stringham's typical organism — this lady striking him as before all things excited, as, in the native phrase, keyed-up, to a perception of more elements in the occasion than he was himself able to count. She was accessible to sides of it, he imagined, that were as yet obscure to him; for, though she unmistakeably rejoiced and soared, he none the less saw her at moments as even more agitated than pleasure required. It was a state of emotion in her that could scarce represent simply an impatience to report at home. Her little dry New England brightness — he had "sampled" all the shades of the American complexity, if complexity it were — had its actual reasons for finding relief most in silence; so that before the subject was changed he perceived (with surprise at the others) that they had given her enough of it. He had quite had enough of it himself

by the time he was asked if it were true that their
friend had really not made in her own country the
mark she had chalked so large in London. It was
Mrs. Lowder herself who addressed him that enquiry;
while he scarce knew if he were the more impressed
with her launching it under Mrs. Stringham's nose
or with her hope that he would allow to London the
honour of discovery. The less expansive of the white
waistcoats propounded the theory that they saw in
London — for all that was said — much further than
in the States: it would n't be the first time, he urged,
that they had taught the Americans to appreciate
(especially when it was funny) some native product.
He did n't mean that Miss Theale was funny —
though she was weird, and this was precisely her
magic; but it might very well be that New York, in
having her to show, had n't been aware of its luck.
There *were* plenty of people who were nothing over
there and yet were awfully taken up in England; just
as — to make the balance right, thank goodness —
they sometimes sent out beauties and celebrities who
left the Briton cold. The Briton's temperature in
truth was n't to be calculated — a formulation of the
matter that was not reached, however, without producing in Mrs. Stringham a final feverish sally. She
announced that if the point of view for a proper admiration of her young friend *had* seemed to fail a little
in New York, there was no manner of doubt of her
having carried Boston by storm. It pointed the moral
that Boston, for the finer taste, left New York nowhere; and the good lady, as the exponent of this
doctrine — which she set forth at a certain length —

made, obviously, to Densher's mind, her nearest approach to supplying the weirdness in which Milly's absence had left them deficient. She made it indeed effective for him by suddenly addressing him. "You know nothing, sir — but not the least little bit — about my friend."

He had n't pretended he did, but there was a purity of reproach in Mrs. Stringham's face and tone, a purity charged apparently with solemn meanings; so that for a little, small as had been his claim, he could n't but feel that she exaggerated. He wondered what she did mean, but while doing so he defended himself. "I certainly don't know enormously much — beyond her having been most kind to me, in New York, as a poor bewildered and newly landed alien, and my having tremendously appreciated it." To which he added, he scarce knew why, what had an immediate success. "Remember, Mrs. Stringham, that you were n't then present."

"Ah there you are!" said Kate with much gay expression, though what it expressed he failed at the time to make out.

"You were n't present *then*, dearest," Mrs. Lowder richly concurred. "You don't know," she continued with mellow gaiety, "how far things may have gone."

It made the little woman, he could see, really lose her head. She had more things in that head than any of them in any other; unless perhaps it were Kate, whom he felt as indirectly watching him during this foolish passage, though it pleased him — and because of the foolishness — not to meet her eyes. He met Mrs. Stringham's, which affected him: with her he

could on occasion clear it up — a sense produced by
the mute communion between them and really the
beginning, as the event was to show, of something
extraordinary. It was even already a little the effect
of this communion that Mrs. Stringham perceptibly
faltered in her retort to Mrs. Lowder's joke. "Oh it's
precisely my point that Mr. Densher *can't* have had
vast opportunities." And then she smiled at him. "I
was n't away, you know, long."

It made everything, in the oddest way in the world,
immediately right for him. "And I was n't *there* long,
either." He positively saw with it that nothing for
him, so far as she was concerned, would again be
wrong. "She's beautiful, but I don't say she's easy
to know."

"Ah she's a thousand and one things!" replied
the good lady, as if now to keep well with him.

He asked nothing better. "She was off with you to
these parts before I knew it. I myself was off too —
away off to wonderful parts, where I had endlessly
more to see."

"But you did n't forget her!" Aunt Maud interposed with almost menacing archness.

"No, of course I did n't forget her. One does n't
forget such charming impressions. But I never," he
lucidly maintained, "chattered to others about her."

"She'll thank you for that, sir," said Mrs. Stringham with a flushed firmness.

"Yet does n't silence in such a case," Aunt Maud
blandly enquired, "very often quite prove the depth
of the impression?"

He would have been amused, had n't he been

slightly displeased, at all they seemed desirous to fasten on him. "Well, the impression was as deep as you like. But I really want Miss Theale to know," he pursued for Mrs. Stringham, "that I don't figure by any consent of my own as an authority about her."

Kate came to his assistance — if assistance it was — before their friend had had time to meet this charge. "You're right about her not being easy to know. One *sees* her with intensity — sees her more than one sees almost any one; but then one discovers that that isn't knowing her and that one may know better a person whom one doesn't 'see,' as I say, half so much."

The discrimination was interesting, but it brought them back to the fact of her success; and it was at that comparatively gross circumstance, now so fully placed before them, that Milly's anxious companion sat and looked — looked very much as some spectator in an old-time circus might have watched the oddity of a Christian maiden, in the arena, mildly, caressingly, martyred. It was the nosing and fumbling not of lions and tigers but of domestic animals let loose as for the joke. Even the joke made Mrs. Stringham uneasy, and her mute communion with Densher, to which we have alluded, was more and more determined by it. He wondered afterwards if Kate had made this out; though it was not indeed till much later on that he found himself, in thought, dividing the things she might have been conscious of from the things she must have missed. If she actually missed, at any rate, Mrs. Stringham's discomfort, that but showed how her own idea held her. Her own idea was, by insisting on the fact of the girl's prominence as a feature of the season's end, to keep Densher in relation, for the rest of them, both to present and to past. "It's everything that has happened *since* that makes you naturally a little shy about her. You don't know what has happened since, but we do; we've seen it and followed it; we've a little been *of* it." The great thing for him, at this, as Kate gave it, *was* in fact quite irresistibly that the case was a real one — the kind of thing that, when one's patience was shorter than one's curiosity, one had vaguely taken for possible in London, but in which one had never been even to this small extent concerned. The little American's sudden social adventure, her happy and, no doubt, harmless flourish, had probably been favoured by several accidents, but it had been favoured above all by the simple spring-board of the scene, by one of those common caprices of the numberless foolish flock, gregarious movements as inscrutable as ocean-currents. The huddled herd had drifted to her blindly — it might as blindly have drifted away. There had been of course a signal, but the great reason was probably the absence at the moment of a larger lion. The bigger beast would come and the smaller would then incontinently vanish. It was at all events characteristic, and what was of the essence of it was grist to his scribbling mill, matter for his journalising hand. That hand already, in intention, played over it, the "motive," as a sign of the season, a feature of the time, of the purely expeditious and rough-and-tumble nature of the social boom. The boom as in *itself* required — that would be the note; the subject of the process a comparatively minor question. Anything was boomable enough when nothing else was more so: the author of the "rotten" book, the beauty who was no beauty, the heiress who was only that, the stranger who was for the most part saved from being inconveniently strange but by being inconveniently familiar, the American whose Americanism had been long desperately discounted, the creature in fine as to whom spangles or spots of any sufficiently marked and exhibited sort could be loudly enough predicated.

So he judged at least, within his limits, and the idea that what he had thus caught in the fact was the trick of fashion and the tone of society went so far as to make him take up again his sense of independence. He had supposed himself civilised; but if this was civilisation —! One could smoke one's pipe outside when twaddle was within. He had rather avoided, as we have remarked, Kate's eyes, but there came a moment when he would fairly have liked to put it, across the table, to her: "I say, light of my life, is *this* the great world?" There came another, it must be added — and doubtless as a result of something that, over the cloth, did hang between them — when she struck him as having quite answered: "Dear no — for what do you take me? Not the least little bit: only a poor silly, though quite harmless, imitation." What she might have passed for saying, however, was practically merged in what she did say, for she came overtly to his aid, very much as if guessing some of his thoughts. She enunciated, to relieve his bewilderment, the obvious truth that you could n't leave London for three

months at that time of the year and come back to
find your friends just where they were. As they had
of course been jigging away they might well be so red
in the face that you would n't know them. She reconciled in fine his disclaimer about Milly with that
honour of having discovered her which it was vain for
him modestly to shirk. He *had* unearthed her, but it
was they, all of them together, who had developed
her. She was always a charmer, one of the greatest
ever seen, but she was n't the person he had
"backed."

Densher was to feel sure afterwards that Kate had
had in these pleasantries no conscious, above all no
insolent purpose of making light of poor Susan Shepherd's property in their young friend — which property, by such remarks, was very much pushed to the
wall; but he was also to know that Mrs. Stringham
had secretly resented them, Mrs. Stringham holding
the opinion, of which he was ultimately to have a
glimpse, that all the Kate Croys in Christendom were
but dust for the feet of her Milly. That, it was true,
would be what she must reveal only when driven to
her last entrenchments and well cornered in her passion — the rare passion of friendship, the sole passion
of her little life save the one other, more imperturbably cerebral, that she entertained for the art of Guy
de Maupassant. She slipped in the observation that
her Milly was incapable of change, was just exactly,
on the contrary, the same Milly; but this made little
difference in the drift of Kate's contention. She was
perfectly kind to Susie: it was as if she positively
knew her as handicapped for any disagreement by

feeling that she, Kate, had "type," and by being committed to admiration of type. Kate had occasion subsequently — she found it somehow — to mention to our young man Milly's having spoken to her of this view on the good lady's part. She would like — Milly had had it from her — to put Kate Croy in a book and see what she could so do with her. "Chop me up fine or serve me whole" — it was a way of being got at that Kate professed she dreaded. It would be Mrs. Stringham's, however, she understood, because Mrs. Stringham, oddly, felt that with such stuff as the strange English girl was made of, stuff that (in spite of Maud Manningham, who was full of sentiment) she had never known, there was none other to be employed. These things were of later evidence, yet Densher might even then have felt them in the air. They were practically in it already when Kate, waiving the question of her friend's chemical change, wound up with the comparatively unobjectionable proposition that he must now, having missed so much, take them all up, on trust, further on. He met it peacefully, a little perhaps as an example to Mrs. Stringham — "Oh as far on as you like!" This even had its effect: Mrs. Stringham appropriated as much of it as might be meant for herself. The nice thing about her was that she could measure how much; so that by the time dinner was over they had really covered ground.

IV

THE younger of the other men, it afterwards appeared, was most in his element at the piano; so that they had coffee and comic songs upstairs — the gentlemen, temporarily relinquished, submitting easily in this interest to Mrs. Lowder's parting injunction not to sit too tight. Our especial young man sat tighter when restored to the drawing-room; he made it out perfectly with Kate that they might, off and on, foregather without offence. He had perhaps stronger needs in this general respect than she; but she had better names for the scant risks to which she consented. It was the blessing of a big house that intervals were large and, of an August night, that windows were open; whereby, at a given moment, on the wide balcony, with the songs sufficiently sung, Aunt Maud could hold her little court more freshly. Densher and Kate, during these moments, occupied side by side a small sofa — a luxury formulated by the latter as the proof, under criticism, of their remarkably good conscience. "To seem not to know each other — once you're here — would be," the girl said, "to overdo it"; and she arranged it charmingly that they *must* have some passage to put Aunt Maud off the scent. She would be wondering otherwise what in the world they found their account in. For Densher, none the less, the profit of snatched moments, snatched contacts, was partial and poor; there were in particu-

lar at present more things in his mind than he could
bring out while watching the windows. It was true, on
the other hand, that she suddenly met most of them
— and more than he could see on the spot — by coming out for him with a reference to Milly that was not
in the key of those made at dinner. "She's not a bit
right, you know. I mean in health. Just see her to-
night. I mean it looks grave. For you she would
have come, you know, if it had been at all possible."

He took this in such patience as he could muster.
"What in the world's the matter with her?"

But Kate continued without saying. "Unless indeed your being here has been just a reason for her
funking it."

"What in the world's the matter with her?" Densher asked again.

"Why just what I've told you — that she likes you
so much."

"Then why should she deny herself the joy of
meeting me?"

Kate cast about — it would take so long to explain.
"And perhaps it's true that she *is* bad. She easily
may be."

"Quite easily, I should say, judging by Mrs.
Stringham, who's visibly preoccupied and worried."

"Visibly enough. Yet it may n't," said Kate, "be
only for that."

"For what then?"

But this question too, on thinking, she neglected.
"Why, if it's anything real, does n't that poor lady
go home? She'd be anxious, and she has done all
she need to be civil."

"I think," Densher remarked, "she has been quite beautifully civil."

It made Kate, he fancied, look at him the least bit harder; but she was already, in a manner, explaining. "Her preoccupation is probably on two different heads. One of them would make her hurry back, but the other makes her stay. She's commissioned to tell Milly all about you."

"Well then," said the young man between a laugh and a sigh, "I'm glad I felt, downstairs, a kind of 'drawing' to her. Was n't I rather decent to her?"

"Awfully nice. You've instincts, you fiend. It's all," Kate declared, "as it should be."

"Except perhaps," he after a moment cynically suggested, "that she is n't getting much good of me now. Will she report to Milly on *this?*" And then as Kate seemed to wonder what "this" might be: "On our present disregard for appearances."

"Ah leave appearances to me!" She spoke in her high way. "I'll make them all right. Aunt Maud, moreover," she added, "has her so engaged that she won't notice." Densher felt, with this, that his companion had indeed perceptive flights he could n't hope to match — had for instance another when she still subjoined: "And Mrs. Stringham's appearing to respond just in order to make that impression."

"Well," Densher dropped with some humour, "life's very interesting! I hope it's really as much so for you as you make it for others; I mean judging by what you make it for me. You seem to me to represent it as thrilling for *ces dames*, and in a different way for each: Aunt Maud, Susan Shepherd, Milly. But

49

what *is*," he wound up, "the matter? Do you mean she's as ill as she looks?"

Kate's face struck him as replying at first that his derisive speech deserved no satisfaction; then she appeared to yield to a need of her own — the need to make the point that "as ill as she looked" was what Milly scarce could be. If she had been as ill as she looked she could scarce be a question with them, for her end would in that case be near. She believed herself nevertheless — and Kate could n't help believing her too — seriously menaced. There was always the fact that they had been on the point of leaving town, the two ladies, and had suddenly been pulled up. "We bade them good-bye — or all but — Aunt Maud and I, the night before Milly, popping so very oddly into the National Gallery for a farewell look, found you and me together. They were then to get off a day or two later. But they've not got off — they're not getting off. When I see them — and I saw them this morning — they have showy reasons. They do mean to go, but they've postponed it." With which the girl brought out: "They've postponed it for *you*." He protested so far as a man might without fatuity, since a protest was itself credulous; but Kate, as ever, understood herself. "You've made Milly change her mind. She wants not to miss you — though she wants also not to show she wants you; which is why, as I hinted a moment ago, she may consciously have hung back to-night. She does n't know when she may see you again — she does n't know she ever may. She does n't see the future. It has opened out before her in these last weeks as a dark confused thing."

Densher wondered. "After the tremendous time you've all been telling me she has had?"

"That's it. There's a shadow across it."

"The shadow, you consider, of some physical break-up?"

"Some physical break-down. Nothing less. She's scared. She has so much to lose. And she wants more."

"Ah well," said Densher with a sudden strange sense of discomfort, "could n't one say to her that she can't have everything?"

"No — for one would n't want to. She really," Kate went on, "has been somebody here. Ask Aunt Maud — you may think me prejudiced," the girl oddly smiled. "Aunt Maud will tell you — the world's before her. It has all come since you saw her, and it's a pity you 've missed it, for it certainly would have amused you. She has really been a perfect success — I mean of course so far as possible in the scrap of time — and she has taken it like a perfect angel. If you can imagine an angel with a thumping bank-account you 'll have the simplest expression of the kind of thing. Her fortune's absolutely huge; Aunt Maud has had all the facts, or enough of them, in the last confidence, from 'Susie,' and Susie speaks by book. Take them then, in the last confidence, from *me*. There she is." Kate expressed above all what it most came to. "It's open to her to make, you see, the very greatest marriage. I assure you we 're not vulgar about her. Her possibilities are quite plain."

Densher showed he neither disbelieved nor grudged them. "But what good then on earth can I do her?"

Well, she had it ready. "You can console her."

"And for what?"

"For all that, if she's stricken, she must see swept away. I shouldn't care for her if she hadn't so much," Kate very simply said. And then as it made him laugh not quite happily: "I shouldn't trouble about her if there were one thing she did have." The girl spoke indeed with a noble compassion. "She has nothing."

"Not all the young dukes?"

"Well we must see — see if anything can come of them. She at any rate does love life. To have met a person like you," Kate further explained, "is to have felt you become, with all the other fine things, a part of life. Oh she has you arranged!"

"*You* have, it strikes me, my dear" — and he looked both detached and rueful. "Pray what am I to do with the dukes?"

"Oh the dukes will be disappointed!"

"Then why shan't I be?"

"You'll have expected less," Kate wonderfully smiled. "Besides, you *will* be. You'll have expected enough for that."

"Yet it's what you want to let me in for?"

"I want," said the girl, "to make things pleasant for her. I use, for the purpose, what I have. You're what I have of most precious, and you're therefore what I use most."

He looked at her long. "I wish I could use *you* a little more." After which, as she continued to smile at him, "Is it a bad case of lungs?" he asked.

Kate showed for a little as if she wished it might be.

"Not lungs, I think. Is n't consumption, taken in time, now curable?"

"People are, no doubt, patched up." But he wondered. "Do you mean she has something that's past patching?" And before she could answer: "It's really as if her appearance put her outside of such things — being, in spite of her youth, that of a person who has been through all it's conceivable she should be exposed to. She affects one, I should say, as a creature saved from a shipwreck. Such a creature may surely, in these days, on the doctrine of chances, go to sea again with confidence. She has *had* her wreck — she has met her adventure."

"Oh I grant you her wreck!" — Kate was all response so far. "But do let her have still her adventure. There are wrecks that are not adventures."

"Well — if there be also adventures that are not wrecks!" Densher in short was willing, but he came back to his point. "What I mean is that she has none of the effect — on one's nerves or whatever—of an invalid."

Kate on her side did this justice. "No — that's the beauty of her."

"The beauty — ?"

"Yes, she's so wonderful. She won't show for that, any more than your watch, when it's about to stop for want of being wound up, gives you convenient notice or shows as different from usual. She won't die, she won't live, by inches. She won't smell, as it were, of drugs. She won't taste, as it were, of medicine. No one will know."

"Then what," he demanded, frankly mystified

53

now, "are we talking about? In what extraordinary state *is* she?"

Kate went on as if, at this, making it out in a fashion for herself. "I believe that if she's ill at all she's very ill. I believe that if she's bad she's not a *little* bad. I can't tell you why, but that's how I see her. She'll really live or she'll really not. She'll have it all or she'll miss it all. Now I don't think she'll have it all."

Densher had followed this with his eyes upon her, her own having thoughtfully wandered, and as if it were more impressive than lucid. "You 'think' and you 'don't think,' and yet you remain all the while without an inkling of her complaint?"

"No, not without an inkling; but it's a matter in which I don't want knowledge. She moreover herself does n't want one to want it: she has, as to what may be preying upon her, a kind of ferocity of modesty, a kind of — I don't know what to call it — intensity of pride. And then and then —" But with this she faltered.

"And then what?"

"I'm a brute about illness. I hate it. It's well for you, my dear," Kate continued, "that you're as sound as a bell."

"Thank you!" Densher laughed. "It's rather good then for yourself too that you're as strong as the sea."

She looked at him now a moment as for the selfish gladness of their young immunities. It was all they had together, but they had it at least without a flaw — each had the beauty, the physical felicity, the personal virtue, love and desire of the other. Yet it was as if that very consciousness threw them back the next moment into pity for the poor girl who had everything else in the world, the great genial good they, alas, did n't have, but failed on the other hand of this. "How we're talking about her!" Kate compunctiously sighed. But there were the facts. "From illness I keep away."

"But you don't — since here you are, in spite of all you say, in the midst of it."

"Ah I'm only watching —!"

"And putting me forward in your place? Thank you!"

"Oh," said Kate, "I'm breaking you in. Let it give you the measure of what I shall expect of you. One can't begin too soon."

She drew away, as from the impression of a stir on the balcony, the hand of which he had a minute before possessed himself; and the warning brought him back to attention. "You have n't even an idea if it's a case for surgery?"

"I dare say it may be; that is that if it comes to anything it may come to that. Of course she's in the highest hands."

"The doctors are after her then?"

"She's after *them* — it's the same thing. I think I'm free to say it now — she sees Sir Luke Strett."

It made him quickly wince. "Ah fifty thousand knives!" Then after an instant: "One seems to guess."

Yes, but she waved it away. "Don't guess. Only do as I tell you."

For a moment now, in silence, he took it all in, might have had it before him. "What you want of me then is to make up to a sick girl."

"Ah but you admit yourself that she does n't affect you as sick. You understand moreover just how much — and just how little."

"It 's amazing," he presently answered, "what you think I understand."

"Well, if you 've brought me to it, my dear," she returned, "that has been your way of breaking *me* in. Besides which, so far as making up to her goes, plenty of others will."

Densher for a little, under this suggestion, might have been seeing their young friend on a pile of cushions and in a perpetual tea-gown, amid flowers and with drawn blinds, surrounded by the higher nobility. "Others can follow their tastes. Besides, others are free."

"But so are you, my dear!"

She had spoken with impatience, and her suddenly quitting him had sharpened it; in spite of which he kept his place, only looking up at her. "You 're prodigious!"

"Of course I 'm prodigious!" — and, as immediately happened, she gave a further sign of it that he fairly sat watching. The door from the lobby had, as she spoke, been thrown open for a gentleman who, immediately finding her within his view, advanced to greet her before the announcement of his name could reach her companion. Densher none the less felt himself brought quickly into relation; Kate's welcome to the visitor became almost precipitately an

56

appeal to her friend, who slowly rose to meet it. "I
don't know whether you know Lord Mark." And
then for the other party: "Mr. Merton Densher —
who has just come back from America."

"Oh!" said the other party while Densher said
nothing — occupied as he mainly was on the spot with
weighing the sound in question. He recognised it in
a moment as less imponderable than it might have
appeared, as having indeed positive claims. It
was n't, that is, he knew, the "Oh!" of the idiot,
however great the superficial resemblance: it was that
of the clever, the accomplished man; it was the very
specialty of the speaker, and a deal of expensive train-
ing and experience had gone to producing it. Densher
felt somehow that, as a thing of value accidentally
picked up, it would retain an interest of curiosity.
The three stood for a little together in an awkwardness to which he was conscious of contributing his
share; Kate failing to ask Lord Mark to be seated,
but letting him know that he would find Mrs. Lowder, with some others, on the balcony.

"Oh and Miss Theale I suppose? — as I seemed
to hear outside, from below, Mrs. Stringham's unmistakeable voice."

"Yes, but Mrs. Stringham's alone. Milly's un-
well," the girl explained, "and was compelled to disappoint us."

"Ah 'disappoint' — rather!" And, lingering a
little, he kept his eyes on Densher. "She is n't really
bad, I trust?"

Densher, after all he had heard, easily supposed
him interested in Milly; but he could imagine him

also interested in the young man with whom he had
found Kate engaged and whom he yet considered
without visible intelligence. That young man con-
cluded in a moment that he was doing what he wanted,
satisfying himself as to each. To this he was aided
by Kate, who produced a prompt: "Oh dear no; I
think not. I've just been reassuring Mr. Densher,"
she added — "who's as concerned as the rest of us.
I've been calming his fears."

"Oh!" said Lord Mark again—and again it was
just as good. That was for Densher, the latter could
see, or think he saw. And then for the others: "*My*
fears would want calming. We must take great care
of her. This way?"

She went with him a few steps, and while Densher,
hanging about, gave them frank attention, presently
paused again for some further colloquy. What passed
between them their observer lost, but she was presently with him again, Lord Mark joining the rest.
Densher was by this time quite ready for her. "It's
he who's your aunt's man?"

"Oh immensely."

"I mean for *you*."

"That's what I mean too," Kate smiled. "There
he is. Now you can judge."

"Judge of what?"

"Judge of him."

"Why should I judge of him?" Densher asked.
"I've nothing to do with him."

"Then why do you ask about him?"

"To judge of you — which is different."

Kate seemed for a little to look at the difference. "To take the measure, do you mean, of my danger?"

He hesitated; then he said: "I'm thinking, I dare say, of Miss Theale's. How does your aunt reconcile his interest in her —?"

"With his interest in me?"

"With her own interest in you," Densher said while she reflected. "If that interest — Mrs. Lowder's — takes the form of Lord Mark, hasn't he rather to look out for the forms *he* takes?"

Kate seemed interested in the question, but "Oh he takes them easily," she answered. "The beauty is that she doesn't trust him."

"That Milly doesn't?"

"Yes — Milly either. But I mean Aunt Maud. Not really."

Densher gave it his wonder. "Takes him to her heart and yet thinks he cheats?"

"Yes," said Kate — "that's the way people are. What they think of their enemies, goodness knows, is bad enough; but I'm still more struck with what they think of their friends. Milly's own state of mind, however," she went on, "is lucky. That's Aunt Maud's security, though she doesn't yet fully recognise it — besides being Milly's own."

"You conceive it a real escape then not to care for him?"

She shook her head in beautiful grave deprecation. "You oughtn't to make me say too much. But I'm glad I don't."

"Don't say too much?"

"Don't care for Lord Mark."

"Oh!" Densher answered with a sound like his lordship's own. To which he added: "You absolutely hold that that poor girl does n't?"

"Ah you know what I hold about that poor girl!" It had made her again impatient.

Yet he stuck a minute to the subject. "You scarcely call him, I suppose, one of the dukes."

"Mercy, no — far from it. He's not, compared with other possibilities, 'in' it. Milly, it's true," she said, to be exact, "has no natural sense of social values, does n't in the least understand our differences or know who's who or what's what."

"I see. That," Densher laughed, "is her reason for liking *me*."

"Precisely. She does n't resemble me," said Kate, "who at least know what I lose."

Well, it had all risen for Densher to a considerable interest. "And Aunt Maud — why should n't *she* know? I mean that your friend there is n't really anything. Does she suppose him of ducal value?"

"Scarcely; save in the sense of being uncle to a duke. That's undeniably something. He's the best moreover we can get."

"Oh, oh!" said Densher; and his doubt was not all derisive.

"It is n't Lord Mark's grandeur," she went on without heeding this; "because perhaps in the line of that alone — as he has no money — more could be done. But she's not a bit sordid; she only counts with the sordidness of others. Besides, he's grand enough, with a duke in his family and at the other end of the string. *The* thing's his genius."

"And do you believe in that?"

"In Lord Mark's genius?" Kate, as if for a more final opinion than had yet been asked of her, took a moment to think. She balanced indeed so that one would scarce have known what to expect; but she came out in time with a very sufficient "Yes!"

"Political?"

"Universal. I don't know at least," she said, "what else to call it when a man's able to make himself without effort, without violence, without machinery of any sort, so intensely felt. He has somehow an effect without his being in any traceable way a cause."

"Ah but if the effect," said Densher with conscious superficiality, "isn't agreeable —?"

"Oh but it is!"

"Not surely for every one."

"If you mean not for you," Kate returned, "you may have reasons — and men don't count. Women don't know if it's agreeable or not."

"Then there you are!"

"Yes, precisely — that takes, on his part, genius."

Densher stood before her as if he wondered what everything she thus promptly, easily and above all amusingly met him with, would have been found, should it have come to an analysis, to "take." Something suddenly, as if under a last determinant touch, welled up in him and overflowed — the sense of his good fortune and her variety, of the future she promised, the interest she supplied. "All women but you are stupid. How can I look at another? You're different and different — and then you're different again. No marvel Aunt Maud builds on you — ex-

cept that you 're so much too good for what she builds
for. Even 'society' won't know how good for it you
are; it's too stupid, and you're beyond it. You'd
have to pull it uphill—it's you yourself who are at the
top. The women one meets — what are they but
books one has already read? You're a whole library
of the unknown, the uncut." He almost moaned, he
ached, from the depth of his content. "Upon my
word I've a subscription!"

She took it from him with her face again giving out
all it had in answer, and they remained once more
confronted and united in their essential wealth of life.
"It's you who draw me out. I exist in you. Not in
others."

It had been, however, as if the thrill of their association itself pressed in him, as great felicities do, the
sharp spring of fear. "See here, you know: don't,
don't —!"

"Don't what?"

"Don't fail me. It would kill me."

She looked at him a minute with no response but
her eyes. "So you think you'll kill *me* in time to
prevent it?" She smiled, but he saw her the next
instant as smiling through tears; and the instant after
this she had got, in respect to the particular point,
quite off. She had come back to another, which was
one of her own; her own were so closely connected
that Densher's were at best but parenthetic. Still
she had a distance to go. "You do then see your
way?" She put it to him before they joined — as was
high time — the others. And she made him understand she meant his way with Milly.

He had dropped a little in presence of the explanation; then she had brought him up to a sort of recognition. He could make out by this light something of what he saw, but a dimness also there was, undispelled since his return. "There's something you must definitely tell me. If our friend knows that all the while — ?"

She came straight to his aid, formulating for him his anxiety, though quite to smooth it down. "All the while she and I here were growing intimate, you and I were in unmentioned relation? If she knows that, yes, she knows our relation must have involved your writing to me."

"Then how could she suppose you were n't answering?"

"She does n't suppose it."

"How then can she imagine you never named her?"

"She does n't. She knows now I did name her. I've told her everything. She's in possession of reasons that will perfectly do."

Still he just brooded. "She takes things from you exactly as I take them?"

"Exactly as you take them."

"She's just such another victim?"

"Just such another. You're a pair."

"Then if anything happens," said Densher, "we can console each other?"

"Ah something *may* indeed happen," she returned, "if you'll only go straight!"

He watched the others an instant through the window. "What do you mean by going straight?"

"Not worrying. Doing as you like. Try, as I've told you before, and you'll see. You'll have me perfectly, always, to refer to."

"Oh rather, I hope! But if she's going away?"

It pulled Kate up but a moment. "I'll bring her back. There you are. You won't be able to say I have n't made it smooth for you."

He faced it all, and certainly it was queer. But it was n't the queerness that after another minute was uppermost. He was in a wondrous silken web, and it *was* amusing. "You spoil me!"

He was n't sure if Mrs. Lowder, who at this juncture reappeared, had caught his word as it dropped from him; probably not, he thought, her attention being given to Mrs. Stringham, with whom she came through and who was now, none too soon, taking leave of her. They were followed by Lord Mark and by the other men, but two or three things happened before any dispersal of the company began. One of these was that Kate found time to say to him with furtive emphasis: "You must go now!" Another was that she next addressed herself in all frankness to Lord Mark, drew near to him with an almost reproachful "Come and talk to *me!*" — a challenge resulting after a minute for Densher in a consciousness of their installation together in an out-of-the-way corner, though not the same he himself had just occupied with her. Still another was that Mrs. Stringham, in the random intensity of her farewells, affected him as looking at him with a small grave intimation, something into which he afterwards read the meaning that if he had happened to desire a few words with her after dinner he would have found her ready. This impression was naturally light, but it just left him with the sense of something by his own act overlooked, unappreciated. It gathered perhaps a slightly sharper shade from the mild formality of her "Good-night, sir!" as she passed him; a matter as to which there was now nothing more to be done, thanks to the alertness of the young man he by this time had appraised as even more harmless than himself. This personage had forestalled him in opening the door for her and was evidently — with a view, Densher might have judged, to ulterior designs on Milly — proposing to attend her to her carriage. What further occurred was that Aunt Maud, having released her, immediately had a word for himself. It was an imperative "Wait a minute," by which she both detained and dismissed him; she was particular about her minute, but he had n't yet given her, as happened, a sign of withdrawal.

"Return to our little friend. You 'll find her really interesting."

"If you mean Miss Theale," he said, "I shall certainly not forget her. But you must remember that, so far as her 'interest' is concerned, I myself discovered, I — as was said at dinner — invented her."

"Well, one seemed rather to gather that you had n't taken out the patent. Don't, I only mean, in the press of other things, too much neglect her."

Affected, surprised by the coincidence of her appeal with Kate's, he asked himself quickly if it might n't help him with her. He at any rate could but try. "You 're all looking after my manners. That 's exactly, you know, what Miss Croy has been saying to

65

me. *She* keeps me up — she has had so much to say about them."

He found pleasure in being able to give his hostess an account of his passage with Kate that, while quite veracious, might be reassuring to herself. But Aunt Maud, wonderfully and facing him straight, took it as if her confidence were supplied with other props. If she saw his intention in it she yet blinked neither with doubt nor with acceptance; she only said imperturbably: "Yes, she'll herself do anything for her friend; so that she but preaches what she practises."

Densher really quite wondered if Aunt Maud knew how far Kate's devotion went. He was moreover a little puzzled by this special harmony; in face of which he quickly asked himself if Mrs. Lowder had bethought herself of the American girl as a distraction for him, and if Kate's mastery of the subject were therefore but an appearance addressed to her aunt. What might really *become* in all this of the American girl was therefore a question that, on the latter contingency, would lose none of its sharpness. However, questions could wait, and it was easy, so far as he understood, to meet Mrs. Lowder. "It isn't a bit, all the same, you know, that I resist. I find Miss Theale charming."

Well, it was all she wanted. "Then don't miss a chance."

"The only thing is," he went on, "that she's — naturally now — leaving town and, as I take it, going abroad."

Aunt Maud looked indeed an instant as if she herself had been dealing with this difficulty. "She won't go," she smiled in spite of it, "till she has seen you. Moreover, when she does go —" She paused, leaving him uncertain. But the next minute he was still more at sea. "We shall go too."

He gave a smile that he himself took for slightly strange. "And what good will that do *me?*"

"We shall be near them somewhere, and you'll come out to us."

"Oh!" he said a little awkwardly.

"I'll see that you do. I mean I'll write to you."

"Ah thank you, thank you!" Merton Densher laughed. She was indeed putting him on his honour, and his honour winced a little at the use he rather helplessly saw himself suffering her to believe she could make of it. "There are all sorts of things," he vaguely remarked, "to consider."

"No doubt. But there's above all the great thing."

"And pray what's that?"

"Why the importance of your not losing the occasion of your life. I'm treating you handsomely, I'm looking after it for you. I *can* — I can smooth your path. She's charming, she's clever and she's good. And her fortune's a real fortune."

Ah there she was, Aunt Maud! The pieces fell together for him as he felt her thus buying him off, and buying him — it would have been funny if it hadn't been so grave — with Miss Theale's money. He ventured, derisive, fairly to treat it as extravagant. "I'm much obliged to you for the handsome offer —"

"Of what doesn't belong to me?" She wasn't abashed. "I don't say it does — but there's no reason it shouldn't to *you*. Mind you, moreover" —

she kept it up — "I'm not one who talks in the air. And you owe me something — if you want to know why."

Distinct he felt her pressure; he felt, given her basis, her consistency; he even felt, to a degree that was immediately to receive an odd confirmation, her truth. Her truth, for that matter, was that she believed him bribeable: a belief that for his own mind as well, while they stood there, lighted up the impossible. What then in this light did Kate believe him? But that was n't what he asked aloud. "Of course I know I owe you thanks for a deal of kind treatment. Your inviting me for instance to-night —!"

"Yes, my inviting you to-night's a part of it. But you don't know," she added, "how far I've gone for you."

He felt himself red and as if his honour were colouring up; but he laughed again as he could. "I see how far you're going."

"I'm the most honest woman in the world, but I've nevertheless done for you what was necessary." And then as her now quite sombre gravity only made him stare: "To start you it *was* necessary. From *me* it has the weight." He but continued to stare, and she met his blankness with surprise. "Don't you understand me? I've told the proper lie for you." Still he only showed her his flushed strained smile; in spite of which, speaking with force and as if he must with a minute's reflexion see what she meant, she turned away from him. "I depend upon you now to make me right!"

The minute's reflexion he was of course more free

to take after he had left the house. He walked up the Bayswater Road, but he stopped short, under the murky stars, before the modern church, in the middle of the square that, going eastward, opened out on his left. He had had his brief stupidity, but now he understood. She had guaranteed to Milly Theale through Mrs. Stringham that Kate did n't care for him. She had affirmed through the same source that the attachment was only his. He made it out, he made it out, and he could see what she meant by its starting him. She had described Kate as merely compassionate, so that Milly might be compassionate too. "Proper" indeed it was, her lie — the very properest possible and the most deeply, richly diplomatic. So Milly was successfully deceived.

V

To see her alone, the poor girl, he none the less promptly felt, was to see her after all very much on the old basis, the basis of his three visits in New York; the new element, when once he was again face to face with her, not really amounting to much more than a recognition, with a little surprise, of the positive extent of the old basis. Everything but that, everything embarrassing fell away after he had been present five minutes: it was in fact wonderful that their excellent, their pleasant, their permitted and proper and harmless American relation — the legitimacy of which he could thus scarce express in names enough — should seem so unperturbed by other matters. They had both since then had great adventures — such an adventure for him was his mental annexation of her country; and it was now, for the moment, as if the greatest of them all were this acquired consciousness of reasons other than those that had already served. Densher had asked for her, at her hotel, the day after Aunt Maud's dinner, with a rich, that is with a highly troubled, preconception of the part likely to be played for him at present, in any contact with her, by Kate's and Mrs. Lowder's so oddly conjoined and so really superfluous attempts to make her interesting. She had been interesting enough without them — that appeared to-day to come back to him; and, admirable and beautiful as was the charitable zeal of the two

ladies, it might easily have nipped in the bud the
germs of a friendship inevitably limited but still perfectly open to him. What had happily averted the
need of his breaking off, what would as happily continue to avert it, was his own good sense and good
humour, a certain spring of mind in him which ministered, imagination aiding, to understandings and allowances and which he had positively never felt such
ground as just now to rejoice in the possession of.
Many men — he practically made the reflexion —
would n't have taken the matter that way, would have
lost patience, finding the appeal in question irrational,
exorbitant; and, thereby making short work with it,
would have let it render any further acquaintance
with Miss Theale impossible. He had talked with
Kate of this young woman's being "sacrificed," and
that would have been one way, so far as he was concerned, to sacrifice her. Such, however, had not been
the tune to which his at first bewildered view had,
since the night before, cleared itself up. It was n't so
much that he failed of being the kind of man who
"chucked," for he knew himself as the kind of man
wise enough to mark the case in which chucking
might be the minor evil and the least cruelty. It was
that he liked too much every one concerned willingly
to show himself merely impracticable. He liked Kate,
goodness knew, and he also clearly enough liked
Mrs. Lowder. He liked in particular Milly herself;
and had n't it come up for him the evening before
that he quite liked even Susan Shepherd? He had
never known himself so generally merciful. It was a
footing, at all events, whatever accounted for it, on

which he should surely be rather a muff not to manage by one turn or another to escape disobliging. Should he find he could n't work it there would still be time enough. The idea of working it crystallised before him in such guise as not only to promise much interest — fairly, in case of success, much enthusiasm; but positively to impart to failure an appearance of barbarity.

Arriving thus in Brook Street both with the best intentions and with a margin consciously left for some primary awkwardness, he found his burden, to his great relief, unexpectedly light. The awkwardness involved in the responsibility so newly and so ingeniously traced for him turned round on the spot to present him another face. This was simply the face of his old impression, which he now fully recovered — the impression that American girls, when, rare case, they had the attraction of Milly, were clearly the easiest people in the world. Had what had happened been that this specimen of the class was from the first so committed to ease that nothing subsequent *could* ever make her difficult? That affected him now as still more probable than on the occasion of the hour or two lately passed with her in Kate's society. Milly Theale had recognised no complication, to Densher's view, while bringing him, with his companion, from the National Gallery and entertaining them at luncheon; it was therefore scarce supposable that complications had become so soon too much for her. His pretext for presenting himself was fortunately of the best and simplest; the least he could decently do, given their happy acquaintance, was to call with an enquiry after learning that she had been prevented by illness from meeting him at dinner. And then there was the beautiful accident of her other demonstration; he must at any rate have given a sign as a sequel to the hospitality he had shared with Kate. Well, he was giving one now — such as it was; he was finding her, to begin with, accessible, and very naturally and prettily glad to see him. He had come, after luncheon, early, though not so early but that she might already be out if she were well enough; and she was well enough and yet was still at home. He had an inner glimpse, with this, of the comment Kate would have made on it; it was n't absent from his thought that Milly would have been at home by *her* account because expecting, after a talk with Mrs. Stringham, that a certain person might turn up. He even — so pleasantly did things go — enjoyed freedom of mind to welcome, on that supposition, a fresh sign of the beautiful hypocrisy of women. He went so far as to enjoy believing the girl *might* have stayed in for him; it helped him to enjoy her behaving as if she had n't. She expressed, that is, exactly the right degree of surprise; she did n't a bit overdo it: the lesson of which was, perceptibly, that, so far as his late lights had opened the door to any want of the natural in their meetings, he might trust her to take care of it for him as well as for herself.

She had begun this, admirably, on his entrance, with her turning away from the table at which she had apparently been engaged in letter-writing; it was the very possibility of his betraying a concern for her as one of the afflicted that she had within the first minute conjured away. She was never, never — did

73

he understand? — to be one of the afflicted for him;
and the manner in which he understood it, something
of the answering pleasure that he could n't help knowing he showed, constituted, he was very soon after to
acknowledge, something like a start for intimacy.
When things like that could pass people had in truth
to be equally conscious of a relation. It soon made
one, at all events, when it did n't find one made. She
had let him ask — there had been time for that, his
allusion to her friend's explanatory arrival at Lancaster Gate without her being inevitable; but she had
blown away, and quite as much with the look in her
eyes as with the smile on her lips, every ground for
anxiety and every chance for insistence. How was
she? — why she was as he thus saw her and as she
had reasons of her own, nobody else's business, for
desiring to appear. Kate's account of her as too proud
for pity, as fiercely shy about so personal a secret,
came back to him; so that he rejoiced he could take a
hint, especially when he wanted to. The question the
girl had quickly disposed of — "Oh it was nothing:
I'm all right, thank you!" — was one he was glad
enough to be able to banish. It was n't at all, in spite
of the appeal Kate had made to him on it, his affair;
for his interest had been invoked in the name of compassion, and the name of compassion was exactly
what he felt himself at the end of two minutes forbidden so much as to whisper. He had been sent to
see her in order to be sorry for her, and how sorry he
might be, quite privately, he was yet to make out.
Did n't that signify, however, almost not at all? —
inasmuch as, whatever his upshot, he was never to

give her a glimpse of it. Thus the ground was unexpectedly cleared; though it was not till a slightly longer time had passed that he read clear, at first with amusement and then with a strange shade of respect, what had most operated. Extraordinarily, quite amazingly, he began to see that if his pity had n't had to yield to still other things it would have had to yield quite definitely to her own. That was the way the case had turned round: he had made his visit to be sorry for her, but he would repeat it — if he did repeat it — in order that she might be sorry for him. His situation made him, she judged — when once one liked him — a subject for that degree of tenderness: he felt this judgement in her, and felt it as something he should really, in decency, in dignity, in common honesty, have very soon to reckon with.

Odd enough was it certainly that the question originally before him, the question placed there by Kate, should so of a sudden find itself quite dislodged by another. This other, it was easy to see, came straight up with the fact of her beautiful delusion and her wasted charity; the whole thing preparing for him as pretty a case of conscience as he could have desired, and one at the prospect of which he was already wincing. If he was interesting it was because he was unhappy; and if he was unhappy it was because his passion for Kate had spent itself in vain; and if Kate was indifferent, inexorable, it was because she had left Milly in no doubt of it. That above all was what came up for him — how clear an impression of this attitude, how definite an account of his own failure, Kate must have given her friend. His immediate

75

quarter of an hour there with the girl lighted up for him almost luridly such an inference; it was almost as if the other party to their remarkable understanding had been with them as they talked, had been hovering about, had dropped in to look after her work. The value of the work affected him as different from the moment he saw it so expressed in poor Milly. Since it was false that he was n't loved, so his right was quite quenched to figure on that ground as important; and if he did n't look out he should find himself appreciating in a way quite at odds with straightness the good faith of Milly's benevolence. *There* was the place for scruples; there the need absolutely to mind what he was about. If it was n't proper for him to enjoy consideration on a perfectly false footing, where was the guarantee that, if he kept on, he might n't soon himself pretend to the grievance in order not to miss the sweet? Consideration — from a charming girl — was soothing on whatever theory; and it did n't take him far to remember that he had himself as yet done nothing deceptive. It was Kate's description of him, his defeated state, it was none of his own; his responsibility would begin, as he might say, only with acting it out. The sharp point was, however, in the difference between acting and not acting: this difference in fact it was that made the case of conscience. He saw it with a certain alarm rise before him that everything was acting that was not speaking the particular word. "If you like me because you think *she* does n't, it is n't a bit true: she *does* like me awfully!" — that would have been the particular word; which there were at the same time but too palpably such difficulties about his uttering. Would n't it be virtually as indelicate to challenge her as to leave her deluded ? — and this quite apart from the exposure, so to speak, of Kate, as to whom it would constitute a kind of betrayal. Kate's design was something so extraordinarily special to Kate that he felt himself shrink from the complications involved in judging it. Not to give away the woman one loved, but to back her up in her mistakes — once they had gone a certain length — that was perhaps chief among the inevitabilities of the abjection of love. Loyalty was of course supremely prescribed in presence of any design on her part, however roundabout, to do one nothing but good.

Densher had quite to steady himself not to be awe-struck at the immensity of the good his own friend must on all this evidence have wanted to do him. Of one thing indeed meanwhile he was sure: Milly Theale would n't herself precipitate his necessity of intervention. She would absolutely never say to him: "*Is* it so impossible she shall ever care for you seriously?" — without which nothing could well be less delicate than for him aggressively to set her right. Kate would be free to do that if Kate, in some prudence, some contrition, for some better reason in fine, should revise her plan; but he asked himself what, failing this, *he* could do that would n't be after all more gross than doing nothing. This brought him round again to the acceptance of the fact that the poor girl liked him. She put it, for reasons of her own, on a simple, a beautiful ground, a ground that already supplied her with the pretext she required. The

ground was there, that is, in the impression she had
received, retained, cherished; the pretext, over and
above it, was the pretext for acting on it. That she
now believed as she did made her sure at last that she
might act; so that what Densher therefore would have
struck at would be the root, in her soul, of a pure
pleasure. It positively lifted its head and flowered, this
pure pleasure, while the young man now sat with her,
and there were things she seemed to say that took the
words out of his mouth. These were not all the things
she did say; they were rather what such things meant
in the light of what he knew. Her warning him for
instance off the question of how she was, the quick
brave little art with which she did that, represented to
his fancy a truth she did n't utter. "I 'm well for *you*
— that 's all you have to do with or need trouble
about: I shall never be anything so horrid as ill for
you. So there you are; worry about me, spare me,
please, as little as you can. Don't be afraid, in short,
to ignore my 'interesting' side. It is n't, you see,
even now while you sit here, that there are n't lots of
others. Only do *them* justice and we shall get on
beautifully." This was what was folded finely up in
her talk — all quite ostensibly about her impressions
and her intentions. She tried to put Densher again on
his American doings, but he would n't have that to-
day. As he thought of the way in which, the other
afternoon, before Kate, he had sat complacently
"jawing," he accused himself of excess, of having
overdone it, having made — at least apparently —
more of a "set" at their entertainer than he was at all
events then intending. He turned the tables, drawing

her out about London, about her vision of life there, and only too glad to treat her as a person with whom he could easily have other topics than her aches and pains. He spoke to her above all of the evidence offered him at Lancaster Gate that she had come but to conquer; and when she had met this with full and gay assent — "How could I help being the feature of the season, the what-do-you-call-it, the theme of every tongue ?" — they fraternised freely over all that had come and gone for each since their interrupted encounter in New York.

At the same time, while many things in quick succession came up for them, came up in particular for Densher, nothing perhaps was just so sharp as the odd influence of their present conditions on their view of their past ones. It was as if they had n't known how "thick" they had originally become, as if, in a manner, they had really fallen to remembrance of more passages of intimacy than there had in fact at the time quite been room for. They were in a relation now so complicated, whether by what they said or by what they did n't say, that it might have been seeking to justify its speedy growth by reaching back to one of those fabulous periods in which prosperous states place their beginnings. He recalled what had been said at Mrs. Lowder's about the steps and stages, in people's careers, that absence caused one to miss, and about the resulting frequent sense of meeting them further on; which, with some other matters also recalled, he took occasion to communicate to Milly. The matters he could n't mention mingled themselves with those he did; so that it would doubtless have been hard to say which of the two groups now played most of a part. He was kept face to face with this young lady by a force absolutely resident in their situation and operating, for his nerves, with the swiftness of the forces commonly regarded by sensitive persons as beyond their control. The current thus determined had positively become for him, by the time he had been ten minutes in the room, something that, but for the absurdity of comparing the very small with the very great, he would freely have likened to the rapids of Niagara. An uncriticised acquaintance between a clever young man and a responsive young woman could do nothing more, at the most, than go, and his actual experiment went and went and went. Nothing probably so conduced to make it go as the marked circumstance that they had spoken all the while not a word about Kate; and this in spite of the fact that, if it were a question for them of what had occurred in the past weeks, nothing had occurred comparable to Kate's predominance. Densher had but the night before appealed to her for instruction as to what he must do about her, but he fairly winced to find how little this came to. She had foretold him of course how little; but it was a truth that looked different when shown him by Milly. It proved to him that the latter had in fact been dealt with, but it produced in him the thought that Kate might perhaps again conveniently be questioned. He would have liked to speak to her before going further — to make sure she really meant him to succeed quite so much. With all the difference that, as we say, came up for him, it came up afresh, naturally, that he might make his visit brief and never renew it; yet the strangest thing of all was that the argument against that issue would have sprung precisely from the beautiful little eloquence involved in Milly's avoidances.

Precipitate these well might be, since they emphasised the fact that she was proceeding in the sense of the assurances she had taken. Over the latter she had visibly not hesitated, for had n't they had the merit of giving her a chance? Densher quite saw her, felt her take it; the chance, neither more nor less, of help rendered him according to her freedom. It was what Kate had left her with: "Listen to him, *I?* Never! So do as you like." What Milly "liked" was to do, it thus appeared, as she was doing: our young man's glimpse of which was just what would have been for him not less a glimpse of the peculiar brutality of shaking her off. The choice exhaled its shy fragrance of heroism, for it was not aided by any question of parting with Kate. She would be charming to Kate as well as to Kate's adorer; she would incur whatever pain could dwell for her in the sight — should she continue to be exposed to the sight — of the adorer thrown with the adored. It would n't really have taken much more to make him wonder if he had n't before him one of those rare cases of exaltation — food for fiction, food for poetry — in which a man's fortune with the woman who does n't care for him is positively promoted by the woman who does. It was as if Milly had said to herself: "Well, he can at least meet her in my society, if that's anything to him; so that my line can only be to make my society attractive." She certainly could n't have made a different impression if she *had* so reasoned. All of which, none the less, did n't prevent his soon enough saying to her, quite as if she were to be whirled into space: "And now, then, what becomes of you? Do you begin to rush about on visits to country-houses?"

She disowned the idea with a headshake that, put on what face she would, could n't help betraying to him something of her suppressed view of the possibility — ever, ever perhaps — of any such proceedings. They were n't at any rate for her now. "Dear no. We go abroad for a few weeks somewhere of high air. That has been before us for many days; we 've only been kept on by last necessities here. However, everything 's done and the wind 's in our sails."

"May you scud then happily before it! But when," he asked, "do you come back?"

She looked ever so vague; then as if to correct it: "Oh when the wind turns. And what do you do with your summer?"

"Ah I spend it in sordid toil. I drench it with mercenary ink. My work in your country counts for play as well. You see what 's thought of the pleasure your country can give. My holiday 's over."

"I 'm sorry you had to take it," said Milly, "at such a different time from ours. If you could but have worked while we 've been working —"

"I might be playing while you play? Oh the distinction is n't so great with me. There 's a little of each for me, of work and of play, in either. But you and Mrs. Stringham, with Miss Croy and Mrs. Lowder — you all," he went on, "have been given up, like navvies or niggers, to real physical toil. Your rest is something you've earned and you need. My labour's comparatively light."

"Very true," she smiled; "but all the same I like mine."

"It does n't leave you 'done'?"

"Not a bit. I don't get tired when I'm interested. Oh I could go far."

He bethought himself. "Then why don't you? — since you've got here, as I learn, the whole place in your pocket."

"Well, it's a kind of economy — I'm saving things up. I've enjoyed so what you speak of — though your account of it's fantastic — that I'm watching over its future, that I can't help being anxious and careful. I want — in the interest itself of what I've had and may still have — not to make stupid mistakes. The way not to make them is to get off again to a distance and see the situation from there. I shall keep it fresh," she wound up as if herself rather pleased with the ingenuity of her statement — "I shall keep it fresh, by that prudence, for my return."

"Ah then you *will* return? Can you promise one that?"

Her face fairly lighted at his asking for a promise; but she made as if bargaining a little. "Is n't London rather awful in winter?"

He had been going to ask her if she meant for the invalid; but he checked the infelicity of this and took the enquiry as referring to social life. "No — I like it, with one thing and another; it's less of a mob than later on; and it would have for *us* the merit — should you come here then — that we should probably see more of you. So do reappear for us — if it is n't a question of climate."

She looked at that a little graver. "If what is n't a question — ?"

"Why the determination of your movements. You spoke just now of going somewhere for that."

"For better air?" — she remembered. "Oh yes, one certainly wants to get out of London in August."

"Rather, of course!" — he fully understood. "Though I'm glad you've hung on long enough for me to catch you. Try us at any rate," he continued, "once more."

"Whom do you mean by 'us'?" she presently asked.

It pulled him up an instant — representing, as he saw it might have seemed, an allusion to himself as conjoined with Kate, whom he was proposing not to mention any more than his hostess did. But the issue was easy. "I mean all of us together, every one you'll find ready to surround you with sympathy."

It made her, none the less, in her odd charming way, challenge him afresh. "Why do you say sympathy?"

"Well, it's doubtless a pale word. What we *shall* feel for you will be much nearer worship."

"As near then as you like!" With which at last Kate's name was sounded. "The people I'd most come back for are the people you know. I'd do it for Mrs. Lowder, who has been beautifully kind to me."

"So she has to *me*," said Densher. "I feel," he added as she at first answered nothing, "that, quite contrary to anything I originally expected, I've made a good friend of her."

"*I* did n't expect it either — its turning out as it has. But I did," said Milly, "with Kate. I shall come back for her too. I 'd do anything" — she kept it up — "for Kate."

Looking at him as with conscious clearness while she spoke, she might for the moment have effectively laid a trap for whatever remains of the ideal straightness in him were still able to pull themselves together and operate. He was afterwards to say to himself that something had at that moment hung for him by a hair. "Oh I know what one would do for Kate!" — it had hung for him by a hair to break out with that, which he felt he had really been kept from by an element in his consciousness stronger still. The proof of the truth in question was precisely in his silence; resisting the impulse to break out was what he *was* doing for Kate. This at the time moreover came and went quickly enough; he was trying the next minute but to make Milly's allusion. easy for herself. "Of course I know what friends you are — and of course I understand," he permitted himself to add, "any amount of devotion to a person so charming. That 's the good turn then she 'll do us all — I mean her working for your return."

"Oh you don't know," said Milly, "how much I 'm really on her hands."

He could but accept the appearance of wondering how much he might show he knew. "Ah she 's very masterful."

"She 's great. Yet I don't say she bullies me."

85

"No — that's not the way. At any rate it is n't hers," he smiled. He remembered, however, then that an undue acquaintance with Kate's ways was just what he must n't show; and he pursued the subject no further than to remark with a good intention that had the further merit of representing a truth: "I don't feel as if I knew her — really to call know."

"Well, if you come to that, I don't either!" she laughed. The words gave him, as soon as they were uttered, a sense of responsibility for his own; though during a silence that ensued for a minute he had time to recognise that his own contained after all no element of falsity. Strange enough therefore was it that he could go too far — if it *was* too far — without being false. His observation was one he would perfectly have made to Kate herself. And before he again spoke, and before Milly did, he took time for more still — for feeling how just here it was that he must break short off if his mind was really made up not to go further. It was as if he had been at a corner — and fairly put there by his last speech; so that it depended on him whether or no to turn it. The silence, if prolonged but an instant, might even have given him a sense of her waiting to see what he would do. It was filled for them the next thing by the sound, rather voluminous for the August afternoon, of the approach, in the street below them, of heavy carriage-wheels and of horses trained to "step." A rumble, a great shake, a considerable effective clatter, had been apparently succeeded by a pause at the door of the hotel, which was in turn accompanied by a due display of diminished prancing and stamping. "You've a visitor,"

Densher laughed, "and it must be at least an ambassador."

"It's only my own carriage; it does that — is n't it wonderful? — every day. But we find it, Mrs. Stringham and I, in the innocence of our hearts, very amusing." She had got up, as she spoke, to assure herself of what she said; and at the end of a few steps they were together on the balcony and looking down at her waiting chariot, which made indeed a brave show. "Is it very awful?"

It was to Densher's eyes — save for its absurd heaviness — only pleasantly pompous. "It seems to me delightfully rococo. But how do I know? You're mistress of these things, in contact with the highest wisdom. You occupy a position, moreover, thanks to which your carriage — well, by this time, in the eye of London, also occupies one." But she was going out, and he must n't stand in her way. What had happened the next minute was first that she had denied she was going out, so that he might prolong his stay; and second that she had said she would go out with pleasure if he would like to drive — that in fact there were always things to do, that there had been a question for her to-day of several in particular, and that this in short was why the carriage had been ordered so early. They perceived, as she said these things, that an enquirer had presented himself, and, coming back, they found Milly's servant announcing the carriage and prepared to accompany her. This appeared to have for her the effect of settling the matter — on the basis, that is, of Densher's happy response. Densher's happy response, however, had as yet hung fire, the process we have described in him operating by this time with extreme intensity. The system of not pulling up, not breaking off, had already brought him headlong, he seemed to feel, to where they actually stood; and just now it was, with a vengeance, that he must do either one thing or the other. He had been waiting for some moments, which probably seemed to him longer than they were; this was because he was anxiously watching himself wait. He could n't keep that up for ever; and since one thing or the other was what he must do, it was for the other that he presently became conscious of having decided. If he had been drifting it settled itself in the manner of a bump, of considerable violence, against a firm object in the stream. "Oh yes; I 'll go with you with pleasure. It 's a charming idea."

She gave no look to thank him — she rather looked away; she only said at once to her servant, "In ten minutes"; and then to her visitor, as the man went out, "We 'll go somewhere — I shall like that. But I must ask of you time — as little as possible — to get ready." She looked over the room to provide for him, keep him there. "There are books and things — plenty; and I dress very quickly." He caught her eyes only as she went, on which he thought them pretty and touching.

Why especially touching at that instant he could certainly scarce have said; it was involved, it was lost in the sense of her wishing to oblige him. Clearly what had occurred was her having wished it so that she had made him simply wish, in civil acknowledgement, to oblige *her;* which he had now fully done by

88

turning his corner. He was quite round it, his corner, by the time the door had closed upon her and he stood there alone. Alone he remained for three minutes more — remained with several very living little matters to think about. One of these was the phenomenon — typical, highly American, he would have said — of Milly's extreme spontaneity. It was perhaps rather as if he had sought refuge — refuge from another question — in the almost exclusive contemplation of this. Yet this, in its way, led him nowhere; not even to a sound generalisation about American girls. It was spontaneous for his young friend to have asked him to drive with her alone — since she had n't mentioned her companion; but she struck him after all as no more advanced in doing it than Kate, for instance, who was n't an American girl, might have struck him in not doing it. Besides, Kate *would* have done it, though Kate was n't at all, in the same sense as Milly, spontaneous. And then in addition Kate *had* done it — or things very like it. Furthermore he was engaged to Kate — even if his ostensibly not being put her public freedom on other grounds. On all grounds, at any rate, the relation between Kate and freedom, between freedom and Kate, was a different one from any he could associate or cultivate, as to anything, with the girl who had just left him to prepare to give herself up to him. It had never struck him before, and he moved about the room while he thought of it, touching none of the books placed at his disposal. Milly was forward, as might be said, but not advanced; whereas Kate was backward — backward still, comparatively, as an English girl — and yet advanced in a high degree. However — though this did n't straighten it out — Kate was of course two or three years older; which at their time of life considerably counted.

Thus ingeniously discriminating, Densher continued slowly to wander; yet without keeping at bay for long the sense of having rounded his corner. He had so rounded it that he felt himself lose even the option of taking advantage of Milly's absence to retrace his steps. If he might have turned tail, vulgarly speaking, five minutes before, he could n't turn tail now; he must simply wait there with his consciousness charged to the brim. Quickly enough moreover that issue was closed from without; in the course of three minutes more Miss Theale's servant had returned. He preceded a visitor whom he had met, obviously, at the foot of the stairs and whom, throwing open the door, he loudly announced as Miss Croy. Kate, on following him in, stopped short at sight of Densher — only, after an instant, as the young man saw with free amusement, not from surprise and still less from discomfiture. Densher immediately gave his explanation — Miss Theale had gone to prepare to drive — on receipt of which the servant effaced himself.

"And you 're going with her?" Kate asked.

"Yes — with your approval; which I 've taken, as you see, for granted."

"Oh," she laughed, "my approval's complete!" She was thoroughly consistent and handsome about it.

"What I mean is of course," he went on — for he

was sensibly affected by her gaiety — "at your so lively instigation."

She had looked about the room — she might have been vaguely looking for signs of the duration, of the character of his visit, a momentary aid in taking a decision. "Well, instigation then, as much as you like." She treated it as pleasant, the success of her plea with him; she made a fresh joke of this direct impression of it. "So much so as that? Do you know I think I won't wait?"

"Not to see her — after coming?"

"Well, with you in the field —! I came for news of her, but she must be all right. If she *is* —"

But he took her straight up. "Ah how do I know?" He was moved to say more. "It's not *I* who am responsible for her, my dear. It seems to me it's you." She struck him as making light of a matter that had been costing him sundry qualms; so that they could n't both be quite just. Either she was too easy or he had been too anxious. He did n't want at all events to feel a fool for that. "I'm doing nothing — and shall not, I assure you, do anything but what I'm told."

Their eyes met with some intensity over the emphasis he had given his words; and he had taken it from her the next moment that he really need n't get into a state. What in the world was the matter? She asked it, with interest, for all answer. "Isn't she better — if she's able to see you?"

"She assures me she's in perfect health."

Kate's interest grew. "I knew she would." On which she added: "It won't have been really for illness that she stayed away last night."

"For what then?"

"Well — for nervousness."

"Nervousness about what?"

"Oh you know!" She spoke with a hint of impatience, smiling however the next moment. "I've told you that."

He looked at her to recover in her face what she had told him; then it was as if what he saw there prompted him to say: "What have you told *her?*"

She gave him her controlled smile, and it was all as if they remembered where they were, liable to surprise, talking with softened voices, even stretching their opportunity, by such talk, beyond a quite right feeling. Milly's room would be close at hand, and yet they were saying things —! For a moment, none the less, they kept it up. "Ask *her,* if you like; you're free — she'll tell you. Act as you think best; don't trouble about what you think I may or mayn't have told. I'm all right with her," said Kate. "So there you are."

"If you mean *here* I am," he answered, "it's unmistakeable. If you also mean that her believing in you is all I have to do with you're so far right as that she certainly does believe in you."

"Well then take example by her."

"She's really doing it for you," Densher continued. "She's driving me out for you."

"In that case," said Kate with her soft tranquillity, "you can do it a little for *her.* I'm not afraid," she smiled.

He stood before her a moment, taking in again the face she put on it and affected again, as he had already so often been, by more things in this face and in her whole person and presence than he was, to his relief, obliged to find words for. It was n't, under such impressions, a question of words. "I do nothing for any one in the world but you. But for you I'll do anything."

"Good, good," said Kate. "That's how I like you."

He waited again an instant. "Then you swear to it?"

"To 'it'? To what?"

"Why that you do 'like' me. Since it's all for that, you know, that I'm letting you do — well, God knows what with me."

She gave at this, with a stare, a disheartened gesture — the sense of which she immediately further expressed. "If you don't believe in me then, after all, had n't you better break off before you've gone further?"

"Break off with you?"

"Break off with Milly. You might go now," she said, "and I'll stay and explain to her why it is."

He wondered — as if it struck him. "What would you say?"

"Why that you find you can't stand her, and that there's nothing for me but to bear with you as I best may."

He considered of this. "How much do you abuse me to her?"

"Exactly enough. As much as you see by her attitude."

Again he thought. "It does n't seem to me I ought to mind her attitude."

"Well then, just as you like. I'll stay and do my best for you."

He saw she was sincere, was really giving him a chance; and that of itself made things clearer. The feeling of how far he had gone came back to him not in repentance, but in this very vision of an escape; and it was not of what he had done, but of what Kate offered, that he now weighed the consequence. "Won't it make her — her not finding me here — be rather more sure there's something between us?"

Kate thought. "Oh I don't know. It will of course greatly upset her. But you need n't trouble about that. She won't die of it."

"Do you mean she *will?*" Densher presently asked.

"Don't put me questions when you don't believe what I say. You make too many conditions."

She spoke now with a shade of rational weariness that made the want of pliancy, the failure to oblige her, look poor and ugly; so that what it suddenly came back to for him was his deficiency in the things a man of any taste, so engaged, so enlisted, would have liked to make sure of being able to show — imagination, tact, positively even humour. The circumstance is doubtless odd, but the truth is none the less that the speculation uppermost with him at this juncture was: "What if I should begin to bore this creature?" And that, within a few seconds, had translated itself. "If you'll swear again you love me —!"

She looked about, at door and window, as if he were asking for more than he said. "Here? There's nothing between us here," Kate smiled.

"Oh *is n't* there?" Her smile itself, with this, had so settled something for him that he had come to her pleadingly and holding out his hands, which she immediately seized with her own as if both to check him and to keep him. It was by keeping him thus for a minute that she did check him; she held him long enough, while, with their eyes deeply meeting, they waited in silence for him to recover himself and renew his discretion. He coloured as with a return of the sense of where they were, and that gave her precisely one of her usual victories, which immediately took further form. By the time he had dropped her hands he had again taken hold, as it were, of Milly's. It was not at any rate with Milly he had broken. "I'll do all you wish," he declared as if to acknowledge the acceptance of his condition that he had practically, after all, drawn from her — a declaration on which she then, recurring to her first idea, promptly acted.

"If you *are* as good as that I go. You'll tell her that, finding you with her, I would n't wait. Say that, you know, from yourself. She'll understand."

She had reached the door with it — she was full of decision; but he had before she left him one more doubt. "I don't see how she can understand enough, you know, without understanding too much."

"You don't need to see."

He required then a last injunction. "I must simply go it blind?"

"You must simply be kind to her."

"And leave the rest to you?"

"Leave the rest to *her*," said Kate disappearing.

It came back then afresh to that, as it had come

95

before. Milly, three minutes after Kate had gone, returned in her array — her big black hat, so little superstitiously in the fashion, her fine black garments throughout, the swathing of her throat, which Densher vaguely took for an infinite number of yards of priceless lace, and which, its folded fabric kept in place by heavy rows of pearls, hung down to her feet like the stole of a priestess. He spoke to her at once of their friend's visit and flight. "She had n't known she 'd find me," he said — and said at present without difficulty. He had so rounded his corner that it was n't a question of a word more or less.

She took this account of the matter as quite sufficient; she glossed over whatever might be awkward. "I 'm sorry — but I of course often see *her*." He felt the discrimination in his favour and how it justified Kate. This was Milly's tone when the matter was left to her. Well, it should now be wholly left.

BOOK SEVENTH

I

WHEN Kate and Densher abandoned her to Mrs.
Stringham on the day of her meeting them together
and bringing them to luncheon, Milly, face to face
with that companion, had had one of those moments
in which the warned, the anxious fighter of the battle
of life, as if once again feeling for the sword at his
side, carries his hand straight to the quarter of his
courage. She laid hers firmly on her heart, and the
two women stood there showing each other a strange
front. Susan Shepherd had received their great doctor's visit, which had been clearly no small affair for
her; but Milly had since then, with insistence, kept
in place, against communication and betrayal, as she
now practically confessed, the barrier of their invited
guests. "You've been too dear. With what I see
you're full of you treated them beautifully. *Is n't*
Kate charming when she wants to be?"

Poor Susie's expression, contending at first, as in
a high fine spasm, with different dangers, had now
quite let itself go. She had to make an effort to reach
a point in space already so remote. "Miss Croy? Oh
she was pleasant and clever. She knew," Mrs. Stringham added. "She knew."

Milly braced herself — but conscious above all, at
the moment, of a high compassion for her mate. She
made her out as struggling — struggling in all her
nature against the betrayal of pity, which in itself,

given her nature, could only be a torment. Milly gathered from the struggle how much there was of the pity, and how therefore it was both in her tenderness and in her conscience that Mrs. Stringham suffered. Wonderful and beautiful it was that this impression instantly steadied the girl. Ruefully asking herself on what basis of ease, with the drop of their barrier, they were to find themselves together, she felt the question met with a relief that was almost joy. The basis, the inevitable basis, was that she was going to be sorry for Susie, who, to all appearance, had been condemned in so much more uncomfortable a manner to be sorry for *her*. Mrs. Stringham's sorrow would hurt Mrs. Stringham, but how could her own ever hurt? She had, the poor girl, at all events, on the spot, five minutes of exaltation in which she turned the tables on her friend with a pass of the hand, a gesture of an energy that made a wind in the air. "Kate knew," she asked, "that you were full of Sir Luke Strett?"

"She spoke of nothing, but she was gentle and nice; she seemed to want to help me through." Which the good lady had no sooner said, however, than she almost tragically gasped at herself. She glared at Milly with a pretended pluck. "What I mean is that she saw one had been taken up with something. When I say she knows I should say she's a person who guesses." And her grimace was also, on its side, heroic. "But *she* does n't matter, Milly."

The girl felt she by this time could face anything. "Nobody matters, Susie. Nobody." Which her next words, however, rather contradicted. "Did he take it ill that I was n't here to see him? Was n't it really just what he wanted — to have it out, so much more simply, with *you?*"

"We did n't have anything 'out,' Milly," Mrs. Stringham delicately quavered.

"Did n't he awfully like you," Milly went on, "and did n't he think you the most charming person I could possibly have referred him to for an account of me? Did n't you hit it off tremendously together and in fact fall quite in love, so that it will really be a great advantage for you to have me as a common ground? You 're going to make, I can see, no end of a good thing of me."

"My own child, my own child!" Mrs. Stringham pleadingly murmured; yet showing as she did so that she feared the effect even of deprecation.

"Is n't he beautiful and good too himself? — altogether, whatever he may say, a lovely acquaintance to have made? You 're just the right people for me — I see it now; and do you know what, between you, you must do?" Then as Susie still but stared, wonderstruck and holding herself: "You must simply see me through. Any way you choose. Make it out together. I, on my side, will be beautiful too, and we 'll be — the three of us, with whatever others, oh as many as the case requires, any one you like! — a sight for the gods. I 'll be as easy for you as carrying a feather." Susie took it for a moment in such silence that her young friend almost saw her — and scarcely withheld the observation — as taking it for "a part of the disease." This accordingly helped Milly to be, as she judged, definite and wise. "He 's at any rate

awfully interesting, is n't he? — which is so much to
the good. We have n't at least — as we might have,
with the way we tumbled into it — got hold of one of
the dreary."

"Interesting, dearest?" — Mrs. Stringham felt
her feet firmer. "I don't know if he's interesting or
not; but I do know, my own," she continued to
quaver, "that he's just as much interested as you
could possibly desire."

"Certainly — that's it. Like all the world."

"No, my precious, not like all the world. Very
much more deeply and intelligently."

"Ah there you are!" Milly laughed. "That's the
way, Susie, I want you. So 'buck' up, my dear.
We'll have beautiful times with him. Don't worry."

"I'm not worrying, Milly." And poor Susie's face
registered the sublimity of her lie.

It was at this that, too sharply penetrated, her
companion went to her, met by her with an embrace
in which things were said that exceeded speech. Each
held and clasped the other as if to console her for this
unnamed woe, the woe for Mrs. Stringham of learning the torment of helplessness, the woe for Milly
of having *her*, at such a time, to think of. Milly's
assumption was immense, and the difficulty for her
friend was that of not being able to gainsay it without
bringing it more to the proof than tenderness and
vagueness could permit. Nothing in fact came to the
proof between them but that they could thus cling
together — except indeed that, as we have indicated,
the pledge of protection and support was all the
younger woman's own. "I don't ask you," she pre-

sently said, "what he told you for yourself, nor what
he told you to tell me, nor how he took it, really, that
I had left him to you, nor what passed between you
about me in any way. It wasn't to get that out of you
that I took my means to make sure of your meeting
freely — for there are things I don't want to know. I
shall see him again and again and shall know more
than enough. All I do want is that you shall see me
through on *his* basis, whatever it is; which it's enough
— for the purpose — that you yourself should know:
that is with him to show you how. I'll make it charming for you — that's what I mean; I'll keep you up
to it in such a way that half the time you won't know
you're doing it. And for that you're to rest upon me.
There. It's understood. We keep each other going,
and you may absolutely feel of me that I shan't break
down. So, with the way you have n't so much as a
dig of the elbow to fear, how could you be safer?"

"He told me I *can* help you — of course he told
me that," Susie, on her side, eagerly contended.
"Why should n't he, and for what else have I come
out with you? But he told me nothing dreadful —
nothing, nothing, nothing," the poor lady passion-
ately protested. "Only that you must do as you like
and as he tells you — which *is* just simply to do as
you like."

"I must keep in sight of him. I must from time to
time go to him. But that's of course doing as I like.
It's lucky," Milly smiled, "that I like going to him."

Mrs. Stringham was here in agreement; she gave
a clutch at the account of their situation that most
showed it as workable. "That's what *will* be charm-

ing for me, and what I'm sure he really wants of me
— to help you to do as you like."

"And also a little, won't it be," Milly laughed,
"to save me from the consequences? Of course,"
she added, "there must first *be* things I like."

"Oh I think you'll find some," Mrs. Stringham
more bravely said. "I think there *are* some — as for
instance just this one. I mean," she explained,
"really having us so."

Milly thought. "Just as if I wanted you comfortable about *him*, and him the same about you? Yes
— I shall get the good of it."

Susan Shepherd appeared to wander from this
into a slight confusion. "Which of them are you talking of?"

Milly wondered an instant — then had a light.
"I'm not talking of Mr. Densher." With which
moreover she showed amusement. "Though if you
can be comfortable about Mr. Densher too so much
the better."

"Oh you meant Sir Luke Strett? Certainly he's
a fine type. Do you know," Susie continued, "whom
he reminds me of? Of *our* great man — Dr. Buttrick
of Boston."

Milly recognised Dr. Buttrick of Boston, but she
dropped him after a tributary pause. "What do you
think, now that you've seen him, of Mr. Densher?"

It was not till after consideration, with her eyes
fixed on her friend's, that Susie produced her answer.
"I think he's very handsome."

Milly remained smiling at her, though putting on
a little the manner of a teacher with a pupil. "Well,

that will do for the first time. I *have* done," she went
on, "what I wanted."

"Then that's all *we* want. You see there are plenty
of things."

Milly shook her head for the "plenty." "The best
is not to know — that includes them all. I don't — I
don't know. Nothing about anything — except that
you're *with* me. Remember that, please. There
won't be anything that, on my side, for you, I shall
forget. So it's all right."

The effect of it by this time was fairly, as intended,
to sustain Susie, who dropped in spite of herself into
the reassuring. "Most certainly it's all right. I think
you ought to understand that he sees no reason —"

"Why I should n't have a grand long life?" Milly
had taken it straight up, as to understand it and for
a moment consider it. But she disposed of it otherwise. "Oh of course I know *that*." She spoke as if
her friend's point were small.

Mrs. Stringham tried to enlarge it. "Well, what
I mean is that he did n't say to me anything that he
has n't said to yourself."

"Really? — I would in his place!" She might
have been disappointed, but she had her good humour. "He tells me to *live*" — and she oddly limited
the word.

It left Susie a little at sea. "Then what do you
want more?"

"My dear," the girl presently said, "I don't 'want,'
as I assure you, anything. Still," she added, "I *am*
living. Oh yes, I'm living."

It put them again face to face, but it had wound

Mrs. Stringham up. "So am I then, you'll see!" —
she spoke with the note of her recovery. Yet it was
her wisdom now — meaning by it as much as she did
— not to say more than that. She had risen by Milly's
aid to a certain command of what was before them;
the ten minutes of their talk had in fact made her
more distinctly aware of the presence in her mind of
a new idea. It was really perhaps an old idea with a
new value; it had at all events begun during the last
hour, though at first but feebly, to shine with a special
light. That was because in the morning darkness
had so suddenly descended — a sufficient shade of
night to bring out the power of a star. The dusk
might be thick yet, but the sky had comparatively
cleared; and Susan Shepherd's star from this time
on continued to twinkle for her. It was for the moment, after her passage with Milly, the one spark
left in the heavens. She recognised, as she continued
to watch it, that it had really been set there by Sir
Luke Strett's visit and that the impressions immediately following had done no more than fix it. Milly's
reappearance with Mr. Densher at her heels — or, so
oddly perhaps, at Miss Croy's heels, Miss Croy being
at Milly's — had contributed to this effect, though it
was only with the lapse of the greater obscurity that
Susie made that out. The obscurity had reigned during the hour of their friends' visit, faintly clearing indeed while, in one of the rooms, Kate Croy's remarkable advance to her intensified the fact that Milly and
the young man were conjoined in the other. If it
hadn't acquired on the spot all the intensity of which
it was capable, this was because the poor lady still sat

in her primary gloom, the gloom the great benignant doctor had practically left behind him.

The intensity the circumstance in question *might* wear to the informed imagination would have been sufficiently revealed for us, no doubt — and with other things to our purpose — in two or three of those confidential passages with Mrs. Lowder that she now permitted herself. She had n't yet been so glad that she believed in her old friend; for if she had n't had, at such a pass, somebody or other to believe in she should certainly have stumbled by the way. Discretion had ceased to consist of silence; silence was gross and thick, whereas wisdom should taper, however tremulously, to a point. She betook herself to Lancaster Gate the morning after the colloquy just noted; and there, in Maud Manningham's own sanctum, she gradually found relief in giving an account of herself. An account of herself was one of the things that she had long been in the habit of expecting herself regularly to give — the regularity depending of course much on such tests of merit as might, by laws beyond her control, rise in her path. She never spared herself in short a proper sharpness of conception of how she had behaved, and it was a statement that she for the most part found herself able to make. What had happened at present was that nothing, as she felt, was left of her to report to; she was all too sunk in the inevitable and the abysmal. To give an account of herself she must give it to somebody else, and her first instalment of it to her hostess was that she must please let her cry. She could n't cry, with Milly in observation, at the hotel, which she had accordingly left for that purpose; and the power happily came to her with the good opportunity. She cried and cried at first — she confined herself to that; it was for the time the best statement of her business. Mrs. Lowder moreover intelligently took it as such, though knocking off a note or two more, as she said, while Susie sat near her table. She could resist the contagion of tears, but her patience did justice to her visitor's most vivid plea for it. "I shall never be able, you know, to cry again — at least not ever with *her ;* so I must take it out when I can. Even if she does herself it won't be for me to give away; for what would that be but a confession of despair? I'm not with her for that — I'm with her to be regularly sublime. Besides, Milly won't cry herself."

"I'm sure I hope," said Mrs. Lowder, "that she won't have occasion to."

"She won't even if she does have occasion. She won't shed a tear. There's something that will prevent her."

"Oh!" said Mrs. Lowder.

"Yes, her pride," Mrs. Stringham explained in spite of her friend's doubt, and it was with this that her communication took consistent form. It had never been pride, Maud Manningham had hinted, that kept *her* from crying when other things made for it; it had only been that these same things, at such times, made still more for business, arrangements, correspondence, the ringing of bells, the marshalling of servants, the taking of decisions. "I might be crying now," she said, "if I were n't writing letters" — and this quite without harshness for her anxious companion, to whom she allowed just the administrative margin for difference. She had interrupted her no more than she would have interrupted the piano-tuner. It gave poor Susie time; and when Mrs. Lowder, to save appearances and catch the post, had, with her addressed and stamped notes, met at the door of the room the footman summoned by the pressure of a knob, the facts of the case were sufficiently ready for her. It took but two or three, however, given their importance, to lay the ground for the great one — Mrs. Stringham's interview of the day before with Sir Luke, who had wished to see her about Milly.

"He had wished it himself?"

"I think he was glad of it. Clearly indeed he was. He stayed a quarter of an hour. I could see that for *him* it was long. He's interested," said Mrs. Stringham.

"Do you mean in her case?"

"He says it *is n't* a case."

"What then is it?"

"It is n't, at least," Mrs. Stringham explained, "the case she believed it to be — thought it at any rate *might* be — when, without my knowledge, she went to see him. She went because there was something she was afraid of, and he examined her thoroughly — he has made sure. She's wrong — she has n't what she thought."

"And what did she think?" Mrs. Lowder demanded.

"He did n't tell me."

"And you did n't ask?"

"I asked nothing," said poor Susie — "I only took what he gave me. He gave me no more than he had to — he was beautiful," she went on. "He *is*, thank God, interested."

"He must have been interested in *you*, dear," Maud Manningham observed with kindness.

Her visitor met it with candour. "Yes, love, I think he *is*. I mean that he sees what he can do with me."

Mrs. Lowder took it rightly. "For *her*."

"For her. Anything in the world he will or he must. He can use me to the last bone, and he likes at least that. He says the great thing for her is to be happy."

"It 's surely the great thing for every one. Why, therefore," Mrs. Lowder handsomely asked, "should we cry so hard about it ?"

"Only," poor Susie wailed, "that it 's so strange, so beyond us. I mean if she can't be."

"She must be." Mrs. Lowder knew no impossibles. "She *shall* be."

"Well — if you 'll help. He thinks, you know, we *can* help."

Mrs. Lowder faced a moment, in her massive way, what Sir Luke Strett thought. She sat back there, her knees apart, not unlike a picturesque ear-ringed matron at a market-stall; while her friend, before her, dropped their items, tossed the separate truths of the matter one by one, into her capacious apron. "But is that all he came to you for—to tell you she must be happy ?"

"That she must be *made* so — that 's the point. It seemed enough, as he told me," Mrs. Stringham went on; "he makes it somehow such a grand possible affair."

"Ah well, if he makes it possible!"

"I mean especially he makes it grand. He gave it to me, that is, as *my* part. The rest's his own."

"And what's the rest?" Mrs. Lowder asked.

"I don't know. *His* business. He means to keep hold of her."

"Then why do you say it isn't a 'case'? It must be very much of one."

Everything in Mrs. Stringham confessed to the extent of it. "It's only that it isn't *the* case she herself supposed."

"It's another?"

"It's another."

"Examining her for what she supposed he finds something else?"

"Something else."

"And what does he find?"

"Ah," Mrs. Stringham cried, "God keep me from knowing!"

"He didn't tell you that?"

But poor Susie had recovered herself. "What I mean is that if it's there I shall know in time. He's considering, but I can trust him for it — because he does, I feel, trust me. He's considering," she repeated.

"He's in other words not sure?"

"Well, he's watching. I think that's what he means. She's to get away now, but to come back to him in three months."

"Then I think," said Maud Lowder, "that he ought n't meanwhile to scare us."

It roused Susie a little, Susie being already enrolled in the great doctor's cause. This came out at least in her glimmer of reproach. "Does it scare us to enlist us for her happiness?"

Mrs. Lowder was rather stiff for it. "Yes; it scares *me*. I'm always scared — I may call it so — till I understand. What happiness is he talking about?"

Mrs. Stringham at this came straight. "Oh you know!"

She had really said it so that her friend had to take it; which the latter in fact after a moment showed herself as having done. A strange light humour in the matter even perhaps suddenly aiding, she met it with a certain accommodation. "Well, say one seems to see. The point is —!" But, fairly too full now of her question, she dropped.

"The point is will it *cure?*"

"Precisely. Is it absolutely a remedy — *the* specific?"

"Well, I should think we might know!" Mrs. Stringham delicately declared.

"Ah but we have n't the complaint."

"Have you never, dearest, been in love?" Susan Shepherd enquired.

"Yes, my child; but not by the doctor's direction."

Maud Manningham had spoken perforce with a break into momentary mirth, which operated — and happily too — as a challenge to her visitor's spirit. "Oh of course we don't ask his leave to fall. But it's something to know he thinks it good for us."

"My dear woman," Mrs. Lowder cried, "it strikes me we know it without him. So that when *that's* all he has to tell us —!"

"Ah," Mrs. Stringham interposed, "it is n't 'all.' I feel Sir Luke will have more; he won't have put me off with anything inadequate. I'm to see him again; he as good as told me that he'll wish it. So it won't be for nothing."

"Then what will it be for? Do you mean he has somebody of his own to propose? Do you mean you told him nothing?"

Mrs. Stringham dealt with these questions. "I showed him I understood him. That was all I could do. I did n't feel at liberty to be explicit; but I felt, even though his visit so upset me, the comfort of what I had from you night before last."

"What I spoke to you of in the carriage when we had left her with Kate?"

"You had *seen*, apparently, in three minutes. And now that he's here, now that I've met him and had my impression of him, I feel," said Mrs. Stringham, "that you've been magnificent."

"Of course I've been magnificent. When," asked Maud Manningham, "was I anything else? But Milly won't be, you know, if she marries Merton Densher."

"Oh it's always magnificent to marry the man one loves. But we're going fast!" Mrs. Stringham woefully smiled.

"The thing *is* to go fast if I see the case right. What had I after all but my instinct of that on coming back with you, night before last, to pick up Kate? I felt what I felt — I knew in my bones the man had returned."

"That's just where, as I say, you're magnificent. But wait," said Mrs. Stringham, "till you've seen him."

"I shall see him immediately" — Mrs. Lowder took it up with decision. "What *is* then," she asked, "your impression?"

Mrs. Stringham's impression seemed lost in her doubts. "How can he ever care for her?"

Her companion, in her companion's heavy manner, sat on it. "By being put in the way of it."

"For God's sake then," Mrs. Stringham wailed, "*put* him in the way! You have him, one feels, in your hand."

Maud Lowder's eyes at this rested on her friend's. "Is that your impression of him?"

"It's my impression, dearest, of you. You handle every one."

Mrs. Lowder's eyes still rested, and Susan Shepherd now felt, for a wonder, not less sincere by seeing that she pleased her. But there was a great limitation. "I don't handle Kate."

It suggested something that her visitor had n't yet had from her — something the sense of which made Mrs. Stringham gasp. "Do you mean Kate cares for *him?*"

That fact the lady of Lancaster Gate had up to this moment, as we know, enshrouded, and her friend's quick question had produced a change in her face. She blinked — then looked at the question hard; after which, whether she had inadvertently betrayed herself or had only reached a decision and then been affected by the quality of Mrs. Stringham's surprise, she accepted all results. What took place in her for Susan Shepherd was not simply that she made the best of them, but that she suddenly saw more in them to her purpose than she could have imagined. A certain impatience in fact marked in her this transition: she had been keeping back, very hard, an important truth, and would n't have liked to hear that she had n't concealed it cleverly. Susie nevertheless felt herself pass as not a little of a fool with her for not having thought of it. What Susie indeed, however, most thought of at present, in the quick, new light of it, was the wonder of Kate's dissimulation. She had time for that view while she waited for an answer to her cry. "Kate thinks she cares. But she's mistaken. And no one knows it." These things, distinct and responsible, were Mrs. Lowder's retort. Yet they were n't all of it. "*You* don't know it — that must be your line. Or rather your line must be that you deny it utterly."

"Deny that she cares for him?"

"Deny that she so much as thinks that she does. Positively and absolutely. Deny that you've so much as heard of it."

Susie faced this new duty. "To Milly, you mean — if she asks?"

"To Milly, naturally. No one else *will* ask."

"Well," said Mrs. Stringham after a moment, "Milly won't."

Mrs. Lowder wondered. "Are you sure?"

"Yes, the more I think of it. And luckily for *me*. I lie badly."

"*I* lie well, thank God," Mrs. Lowder almost snorted, "when, as sometimes will happen, there's nothing else so good. One must always do the best. But without lies then," she went on, "perhaps we can work it out." Her interest had risen; her friend saw her, as within some minutes, more enrolled and inflamed — presently felt in her what had made the difference. Mrs. Stringham, it was true, descried this at the time but dimly; she only made out at first that Maud had found a reason for helping her. The reason was that, strangely, she might help Maud too, for which she now desired to profess herself ready even to lying. What really perhaps most came out for her was that her hostess was a little disappointed at her doubt of the social solidity of this appliance; and that in turn was to become a steadier light. The truth about Kate's delusion, as her aunt presented it, the delusion about the state of her affections, which might be removed — this was apparently the ground on which they now might more intimately meet. Mrs. Stringham saw herself recruited for the removal of Kate's delusion — by arts, however, in truth, that she as yet quite failed to compass. Or was it perhaps to be only for the removal of Mr. Densher's ? — success in which indeed might entail other successes. Before that job, unfortunately, her heart had already failed. She felt that she believed in her bones what Milly believed, and what would now make working for Milly such a dreadful upward tug. All this within her was confusedly present — a cloud of questions out of which

Maud Manningham's large seated self loomed, however, as a mass more and more definite, taking in fact
for the consultative relation something of the form of
an oracle. From the oracle the sound did come — or
at any rate the sense did, a sense all accordant with
the insufflation she had just seen working. "Yes," the
sense was, "I'll help you for Milly, because if that
comes off I shall be helped, by its doing so, for Kate"
— a view into which Mrs. Stringham could now sufficiently enter. She found herself of a sudden, strange
to say, quite willing to operate to Kate's harm, or at
least to Kate's good as Mrs. Lowder with a noble
anxiety measured it. She found herself in short not
caring what became of Kate — only convinced at
bottom of the predominance of Kate's star. Kate
was n't in danger, Kate was n't pathetic; Kate Croy,
whatever happened, would take care of Kate Croy.
She saw moreover by this time that her friend was
travelling even beyond her own speed. Mrs. Lowder
had already, in mind, drafted a rough plan of action,
a plan vividly enough thrown off as she said : "You
must stay on a few days, and you must immediately,
both of you, meet him at dinner." In addition to
which Maud claimed the merit of having by an instinct
of pity, of prescient wisdom, done much, two nights
before, to prepare that ground. "The poor child,
when I was with her there while you were getting
your shawl, quite gave herself away to me."

"Oh I remember how you afterwards put it to me.
Though it was nothing more," Susie did herself the
justice to observe, "than what I too had quite felt."

But Mrs. Lowder fronted her so on this that she

wondered what she had said. "I suppose I ought
to be edified at what you can so beautifully give up."

"Give up?" Mrs. Stringham echoed. "Why, I
give up nothing — I cling."

Her hostess showed impatience, turning again with
some stiffness to her great brass-bound cylinder-desk
and giving a push to an object or two disposed there.
"*I* give up then. You know how little such a person
as Mr. Densher was to be my idea for her. You know
what I've been thinking perfectly possible."

"Oh you've been great" — Susie was perfectly
fair. "A duke, a duchess, a princess, a palace : you've
made me believe in them too. But where we break
down is that *she* does n't believe in them. Luckily
for her — as it seems to be turning out — she does
n't want them. So what's one to do? I assure you
I've had many dreams. But I've only one dream
now."

Mrs. Stringham's tone in these last words gave so
fully her meaning that Mrs. Lowder could but show
herself as taking it in. They sat a moment longer
confronted on it. "Her having what she does want?"

"If it *will* do anything for her."

Mrs. Lowder seemed to think what it might do;
but she spoke for the instant of something else. "It
does provoke me a bit, you know — for of course I'm
a brute. And I had thought of all sorts of things.
Yet it does n't prevent the fact that we must be
decent."

"We must take her" — Mrs. Stringham carried
that out — "as she is."

"And we must take Mr. Densher as *he* is." With

which Mrs. Lowder gave a sombre laugh. "It's a pity he is n't better!"

"Well, if he were better," her friend rejoined, "you'd have liked him for your niece; and in that case Milly would interfere. I mean," Susie added, "interfere with *you*."

"She interferes with me as it is — not that it matters now. But I saw Kate and her — really as soon as you came to me — set up side by side. I saw your girl — I don't mind telling you — helping my girl; and when I say that," Mrs. Lowder continued, "you'll probably put in for yourself that it was part of the reason of my welcome to you. So you see what I give up. I do give it up. But when I take that line," she further set forth, "I take it handsomely. So good-bye to it all. Good-day to Mrs. Densher! Heavens!" she growled.

Susie held herself a minute. "Even as Mrs. Densher my girl will be somebody."

"Yes, she won't be nobody. Besides," said Mrs. Lowder, "we're talking in the air."

Her companion sadly assented. "We're leaving everything out."

"It's nevertheless interesting." And Mrs. Lowder had another thought. "*He's* not quite nobody either." It brought her back to the question she had already put and which her friend had n't at the time dealt with. "What in fact do you make of him?"

Susan Shepherd, at this, for reasons not clear even to herself, was moved a little to caution. So she remained general. "He's charming."

She had met Mrs. Lowder's eyes with that extreme pointedness in her own to which people resort when they are not quite candid — a circumstance that had its effect. "Yes; he's charming."

The effect of the words, however, was equally marked; they almost determined in Mrs. Stringham a return of amusement. "I thought you did n't like him!"

"I don't like him for Kate."

"But you don't like him for Milly either."

Mrs. Stringham rose as she spoke, and her friend also got up. "I like him, my dear, for myself."

"Then that's the best way of all."

"Well, it's one way. He's not good enough for my niece, and he's not good enough for you. One's an aunt, one's a wretch and one's a fool."

"Oh *I'm* not — not either," Susie declared.

But her companion kept on. "One lives for others. *You* do that. If I were living for myself I should n't at all mind him."

But Mrs. Stringham was sturdier. "Ah if I find him charming it's however I'm living."

Well, it broke Mrs. Lowder down. She hung fire but an instant, giving herself away with a laugh. "Of course he's all right in himself."

"That's all I contend," Susie said with more reserve; and the note in question — what Merton Densher was "in himself" — closed practically, with some inconsequence, this first of their councils.

II

It had at least made the difference for them, they could feel, of an informed state in respect to the great doctor, whom they were now to take as watching, waiting, studying, or at any rate as proposing to himself some such process before he should make up his mind. Mrs. Stringham understood him as considering the matter meanwhile in a spirit that, on this same occasion, at Lancaster Gate, she had come back to a rough notation of before retiring. She followed the course of his reckoning. If what they had talked of *could* happen — if Milly, that is, could have her thoughts taken off herself — it would n't do any harm and might conceivably do much good. If it could n't happen — if, anxiously, though tactfully working, they themselves, conjoined, could do nothing to contribute to it — they would be in no worse a box than before. Only in this latter case the girl would have had her free range for the summer, for the autumn; she would have done her best in the sense enjoined on her, and, coming back at the end to her eminent man, would — besides having more to show him — find him more ready to go on with her. It was visible further to Susan Shepherd — as well as being ground for a second report to her old friend — that Milly did her part for a working view of the general case, inasmuch as she mentioned frankly and promptly that she meant to go and say good-bye to Sir

Luke Strett and thank him. She even specified what she was to thank him for, his having been so easy about her behaviour.

"You see I did n't know that — for the liberty I took — I should n't afterwards get a stiff note from him."

So much Milly had said to her, and it had made her a trifle rash. "Oh you 'll never get a stiff note from him in your life."

She felt her rashness, the next moment, at her young friend's question. "Why not, as well as any one else who has played him a trick?"

"Well, because he does n't regard it as a trick. He could understand your action. It 's all right, you see."

"Yes — I do see. It *is* all right. He 's easier with me than with any one else, because that 's the way to let me down. He 's only making believe, and I 'm not worth hauling up."

Rueful at having provoked again this ominous flare, poor Susie grasped at her only advantage. "Do you really accuse a man like Sir Luke Strett of trifling with you?"

She could n't blind herself to the look her companion gave her — a strange half-amused perception of what she made of it. "Well, so far as it 's trifling with me to pity me so much."

"He does n't pity you," Susie earnestly reasoned. "He just — the same as any one else — likes you."

"He has no business then to like me. He 's not the same as any one else."

"Why not, if he wants to work for you?"

Milly gave her another look, but this time a wonderful smile. "Ah there you are!" Mrs. Stringham coloured, for there indeed she was again. But Milly let her off. "Work for me, all the same — work for me! It's of course what I want." Then as usual she embraced her friend. "I'm not going to be as nasty as this to *him*."

"I'm sure I hope not!" — and Mrs. Stringham laughed for the kiss. "I've no doubt, however, he'd take it from you! It's *you*, my dear, who are not the same as any one else."

Milly's assent to which, after an instant, gave her the last word. "No, so that people can take anything from me." And what Mrs. Stringham did indeed resignedly take after this was the absence on her part of any account of the visit then paid. It was the beginning in fact between them of an odd independence — an independence positively of action and custom — on the subject of Milly's future. They went their separate ways with the girl's intense assent; this being really nothing but what she had so wonderfully put in her plea for after Mrs. Stringham's first encounter with Sir Luke. She fairly favoured the idea that Susie had or was to have other encounters — private pointed personal; she favoured every idea, but most of all the idea that she herself was to go on as if nothing were the matter. Since she was to be worked for that would be her way; and though her companions learned from herself nothing of it this was in the event her way with her medical adviser. She put her visit to him on the simplest ground; she had come just to tell him how touched she had been by his good nature. That required little explaining, for, as Mrs. Stringham had said, he quite understood he could but reply that it was all right.

"I had a charming quarter of an hour with that clever lady. You've got good friends."

"So each one of them thinks of all the others. But so I also think," Milly went on, "of all of them together. You're excellent for each other. And it's in that way, I dare say, that you're best for me."

There came to her on this occasion one of the strangest of her impressions, which was at the same time one of the finest of her alarms — the glimmer of a vision that if she should go, as it were, too far, she might perhaps deprive their relation of facility if not of value. Going too far was failing to try at least to remain simple. He would be quite ready to hate her if she did, by heading him off at every point, embarrass his exercise of a kindness that, no doubt, rather constituted for him a high method. Susie would n't hate her, since Susie positively wanted to suffer for her; Susie had a noble idea that she might somehow so do her good. Such, however, was not the way in which the greatest of London doctors was to be expected to wish to do it. He would n't have time even should he wish; whereby, in a word, Milly felt herself intimately warned. Face to face there with her smooth strong director, she enjoyed at a given moment quite such another lift of feeling as she had known in her crucial talk with Susie. It came round to the same thing; him too she would help to help her if that could possibly be; but if it could n't possibly be she would assist also to make this right.

It would n't have taken many minutes more, on the
basis in question, almost to reverse for her their characters of patient and physician. What *was* he in fact
but patient, what was she but physician, from the
moment she embraced once for all the necessity,
adopted once for all the policy, of saving him alarms
about her subtlety? She would leave the subtlety to
him: he would enjoy his use of it, and she herself, no
doubt, would in time enjoy his enjoyment. She went
so far as to imagine that the inward success of these
reflexions flushed her for the minute, to his eyes, with
a certain bloom, a comparative appearance of health;
and what verily next occurred was that he gave colour
to the presumption. "Every little helps, no doubt!"
— he noticed good-humouredly her harmless sally.
"But, help or no help, you're looking, you know,
remarkably well."

"Oh I thought I was," she answered; and it was
as if already she saw his line. Only she wondered
what he would have guessed. If he had guessed anything at all it would be rather remarkable of him.
As for what there *was* to guess, he could n't — if this
was present to him — have arrived at it save by his
own acuteness. That acuteness was therefore immense; and if it supplied the subtlety she thought of
leaving him to, his portion would be none so bad.
Neither, for that matter, would hers be — which she
was even actually enjoying. She wondered if really
then there might n't be something for her. She
had n't been sure in coming to him that she was
"better," and he had n't used, he would be awfully
careful not to use, that compromising term about her;

in spite of all of which she would have been ready to say, for the amiable sympathy of it, "Yes, I *must* be," for he had this unaided sense of something that had happened to her. It was a sense unaided, because who could have told him of anything? Susie, she was certain, had n't yet seen him again, and there were things it was impossible she could have told him the first time. Since such was his penetration, therefore, why should n't she gracefully, in recognition of it, accept the new circumstance, the one he was clearly wanting to congratulate her on, as a sufficient cause? If one nursed a cause tenderly enough it might produce an effect; and this, to begin with, would be a way of nursing. "You gave me the other day," she went on, "plenty to think over, and I 've been doing that — thinking it over—quite as you 'll have probably wished me. I think I must be pretty easy to treat," she smiled, "since you 've already done me so much good."

The only obstacle to reciprocity with him was that he looked in advance so closely related to all one's possibilities that one missed the pleasure of really improving it. "Oh no, you 're extremely difficult to treat. I 've need with you, I assure you, of all my wit."

"Well, I mean I do come up." She had n't meanwhile a bit believed in his answer, convinced as she was that if she *had* been difficult it would be the last thing he would have told her. "I 'm doing," she said, "as I like."

"Then it 's as *I* like. But you must really, though we 're having such a decent month, get straight

away." In pursuance of which, when she had replied
with promptitude that her departure — for the Tyrol
and then for Venice — was quite fixed for the four-
teenth, he took her up with alacrity. "For Venice?
That's perfect, for we shall meet there. I've a dream
of it for October, when I'm hoping for three weeks
off; three weeks during which, if I can get them clear,
my niece, a young person who has quite the whip
hand of me, is to take me where she prefers. I heard
from her only yesterday that she expects to prefer
Venice."

"That's lovely then. I shall expect you there. And
anything that, in advance or in any way, I can do for
you —!"

"Oh thank you. My niece, I seem to feel, does for
me. But it will be capital to find you there."

"I think it ought to make you feel," she said after
a moment, "that I *am* easy to treat."

But he shook his head again; he would n't have it.
"You 've not come to that *yet*."

"One has to be so bad for it?"

"Well, I don't think I've ever come to it — to
'ease' of treatment. I doubt if it's possible. I've not,
if it is, found any one bad enough. The ease, you see,
is for *you*."

"I see — I see."

They had an odd friendly, but perhaps the
least bit awkward pause on it; after which Sir Luke
asked: "And that clever lady — she goes with
you?"

"Mrs. Stringham? Oh dear, yes. She 'll stay with
me, I hope, to the end."

He had a cheerful blankness. "To the end of what?"

"Well — of everything."

"Ah then," he laughed, "you're in luck. The end of everything is far off. This, you know, I'm hoping," said Sir Luke, "is only the beginning." And the next question he risked might have been a part of his hope. "Just you and she together?"

"No, two other friends; two ladies of whom we've seen more here than of any one and who are just the right people for us."

He thought a moment. "You'll be four women together then?"

"Ah," said Milly, "we're widows and orphans. But I think," she added as if to say what she saw would reassure him, "that we shall not be unattractive, as we move, to gentlemen. When you talk of 'life' I suppose you mean mainly gentlemen."

"When I talk of 'life,'" he made answer after a moment during which he might have been appreciating her raciness — "when I talk of life I think I mean more than anything else the beautiful show of it, in its freshness, made by young persons of your age. So go on as you are. I see more and more *how* you are. You can't," he went so far as to say for pleasantness, "better it."

She took it from him with a great show of peace. "One of our companions will be Miss Croy, who came with me here first. It's in *her* that life is splendid; and a part of that is even that she's devoted to me. But she's above all magnificent in herself. So that if you'd like," she freely threw out, "to see *her* —"

"Oh I shall like to see any one who's devoted to you, for clearly it will be jolly to be 'in' it. So that if she's to be at Venice I *shall* see her?"

"We must arrange it — I shan't fail. She more-over has a friend who may also be there" — Milly found herself going on to this. "He's likely to come, I believe, for he always follows her."

Sir Luke wondered. "You mean they're lovers?"

"*He* is," Milly smiled; "but not she. She does n't care for him."

Sir Luke took an interest. "What's the matter with him?"

"Nothing but that she does n't like him."

Sir Luke kept it up. "Is he all right?"

"Oh he's very nice. Indeed he's remarkably so."

"And he's to be in Venice?"

"So she tells me she fears. For if he is there he'll be constantly about with her."

"And she'll be constantly about with you?"

"As we're great friends — yes."

"Well then," said Sir Luke, "you won't be four women alone."

"Oh no; I quite recognise the chance of gentle-men. But he won't," Milly pursued in the same wondrous way, "have come, you see, for *me*."

"No — I see. But can't you help him?"

"Can't *you*?" Milly after a moment quaintly asked. Then for the joke of it she explained. "I'm putting you, you see, in relation with my entourage."

It might have been for the joke of it too, by this time, that her eminent friend fell in. "But if this gentleman *is n't* of your 'entourage'? I mean if he's of — what do you call her ? — Miss Croy's. Unless indeed you also take an interest in him."

"Oh certainly I take an interest in him!"

"You think there may be then some chance for him ?"

"I like him," said Milly, "enough to hope so."

"Then that's all right. But what, pray," Sir Luke next asked, "have I to do with him ?"

"Nothing," said Milly, "except that if you're to be there, so may he be. And also that we shan't in that case be simply four dreary women."

He considered her as if at this point she a little tried his patience. "*You're* the least 'dreary' woman I've ever, ever seen. Ever, do you know ? There's no reason why you should n't have a really splendid life."

"So every one tells me," she promptly returned.

"The conviction — strong already when I had seen you once — is strengthened in me by having seen your friend. There's no doubt about it. The world's before you."

"What did my friend tell you ?" Milly asked.

"Nothing that would n't have given you pleasure. We talked about you — and freely. I don't deny that. But it shows me I don't require of you the impossible."

She was now on her feet. "I think I know what you require of me."

"Nothing, for you," he went on, "*is* impossible. So go on." He repeated it again — wanting her so to feel that to-day he saw it. "You're all right."

"Well," she smiled — "keep me so."

"Oh you'll get away from me."

BOOK SEVENTH

"Keep me, keep me," she simply continued with her gentle eyes on him.

She had given him her hand for good-bye, and he thus for a moment did keep her. Something then, while he seemed to think if there were anything more, came back to him; though something of which there was n't too much to be made. "Of course if there's anything I *can* do for your friend: I mean the gentleman you speak of — ?" He gave out in short that he was ready.

"Oh Mr. Densher?" It was as if she had forgotten.

"Mr. Densher — is that his name?"

"Yes — but his case is n't so dreadful." She had within a minute got away from that.

"No doubt — if *you* take an interest." She had got away, but it was as if he made out in her eyes — though they also had rather got away — a reason for calling her back. "Still, if there's anything one can do — ?"

She looked at him while she thought, while she smiled. "I'm afraid there's really nothing one can do."

III

NOT yet so much as this morning had she felt herself sink into possession; gratefully glad that the warmth of the Southern summer was still in the high florid rooms, palatial chambers where hard cool pavements took reflexions in their lifelong polish, and where the sun on the stirred sea-water, flickering up through open windows, played over the painted "subjects" in the splendid ceilings — medallions of purple and brown, of brave old melancholy colour, medals as of old reddened gold, embossed and beribboned, all toned with time and all flourished and scolloped and gilded about, set in their great moulded and figured concavity (a nest of white cherubs, friendly creatures of the air) and appreciated by the aid of that second tier of smaller lights, straight openings to the front, which did everything, even with the Baedekers and photographs of Milly's party dreadfully meeting the eye, to make of the place an apartment of state. This at last only, though she had enjoyed the palace for three weeks, seemed to count as effective occupation; perhaps because it was the first time she had been alone — really to call alone — since she had left London, it ministered to her first full and unembarrassed sense of what the great Eugenio had done for her. The great Eugenio, recommended by granddukes and Americans, had entered her service during the last hours of all — had crossed from Paris, after

multiplied *pourparlers* with Mrs. Stringham, to whom
she had allowed more than ever a free hand, on purpose to escort her to the Continent and encompass her
there, and had dedicated to her, from the moment of
their meeting, all the treasures of his experience. She
had judged him in advance — polyglot and universal,
very dear and very deep — as probably but a swindler
finished to the finger-tips; for he was for ever carrying
one well-kept Italian hand to his heart and plunging
the other straight into her pocket, which, as she had
instantly observed him to recognise, fitted it like a
glove. The remarkable thing was that these elements
of their common consciousness had rapidly gathered
into an indestructible link, formed the ground of a
happy relation; being by this time, strangely, grotesquely, delightfully, what most kept up confidence
between them and what most expressed it.

She had seen quickly enough what was happening
— the usual thing again, yet once again. Eugenio
had, in an interview of five minutes, understood her,
had got hold, like all the world, of the idea not so much
of the care with which she must be taken up as of the
care with which she must be let down. All the world
understood her, all the world had got hold; but for
nobody yet, she felt, would the idea have been so
close a tie or won from herself so patient a surrender.
Gracefully, respectfully, consummately enough —
always with hands in position and the look, in his
thick neat white hair, smooth fat face and black professional, almost theatrical eyes, as of some famous
tenor grown too old to make love, but with an art still
to make money — did he on occasion convey to her

that she was, of all the clients of his glorious career, the one in whom his interest was most personal and paternal. The others had come in the way of business, but for her his sentiment was special. Confidence rested thus on her completely believing that: there was nothing of which she felt more sure. It passed between them every time they conversed; he was abysmal, but this intimacy lived on the surface. He had taken his place already for her among those who were to see her through, and meditation ranked him, in the constant perspective, for the final function, side by side with poor Susie — whom she was now pitying more than ever for having to be herself so sorry and to say so little about it. Eugenio had the general tact of a residuary legatee — which was a character that could be definitely worn; whereas she could see Susie, in the event of her death, in no character at all, Susie being insistently, exclusively concerned in her mere makeshift duration. This principle, for that matter, Milly at present, with a renewed flare of fancy, felt she should herself have liked to believe in. Eugenio had really done for her more than he probably knew — he did n't after all know everything — in having, for the wind-up of the autumn, on a weak word from her, so admirably, so perfectly established her. Her weak word, as a general hint, had been : "At Venice, please, if possible, no dreadful, no vulgar hotel; but, if it can be at all managed — you know what I mean — some fine old rooms, wholly independent, for a series of months. Plenty of them too, and the more interesting the better: part of a palace, historic and picturesque, but strictly inodorous, where we shall

be to ourselves, with a cook, don't you know? —
with servants, frescoes, tapestries, antiquities, the
thorough make-believe of a settlement."

The proof of how he better and better understood
her was in all the place; as to his masterly acquisition
of which she had from the first asked no questions.
She had shown him enough what she thought of it,
and her forbearance pleased him; with the part of the
transaction that mainly concerned her she would soon
enough become acquainted, and his connexion with
such values as she would then find noted could scarce
help growing, as it were, still more residuary. Charming people, conscious Venice-lovers, evidently, had
given up their house to her, and had fled to a distance, to other countries, to hide their blushes alike
over what they had, however briefly, alienated, and
over what they had, however durably, gained. They
had preserved and consecrated, and she now — her
part of it was shameless — appropriated and enjoyed.
Palazzo Leporelli held its history still in its great lap,
even like a painted idol, a solemn puppet hung about
with decorations. Hung about with pictures and
relics, the rich Venetian past, the ineffaceable character, was here the presence revered and served: which
brings us back to our truth of a moment ago — the
fact that, more than ever, this October morning,
awkward novice though she might be, Milly moved
slowly to and fro as the priestess of the worship. Certainly it came from the sweet taste of solitude, caught
again and cherished for the hour; always a need of
her nature, moreover, when things spoke to her with
penetration. It was mostly in stillness they spoke to

135

her best; amid voices she lost the sense. Voices had surrounded her for weeks, and she had tried to listen, had cultivated them and had answered back; these had been weeks in which there were other things they might well prevent her from hearing. More than the prospect had at first promised or threatened she had felt herself going on in a crowd and with a multiplied escort; the four ladies pictured by her to Sir Luke Strett as a phalanx comparatively closed and detached had in fact proved a rolling snowball, condemned from day to day to cover more ground. Susan Shepherd had compared this portion of the girl's excursion to the Empress Catherine's famous progress across the steppes of Russia; improvised settlements appeared at each turn of the road, villagers waiting with addresses drawn up in the language of London. Old friends in fine were in ambush, Mrs. Lowder's, Kate Croy's, her own; when the addresses were n't in the language of London they were in the more insistent idioms of American centres. The current was swollen even by Susie's social connexions; so that there were days, at hotels, at Dolomite picnics, on lake steamers, when she could almost repay to Aunt Maud and Kate with interest the debt contracted by the London "success" to which they had opened the door.

Mrs. Lowder's success and Kate's, amid the shock of Milly's and Mrs. Stringham's compatriots, failed but little, really, of the concert-pitch; it had gone almost as fast as the boom, over the sea, of the last great native novel. Those ladies were "so different" — different, observably enough, from the ladies so

appraising them; it being throughout a case mainly
of ladies, of a dozen at once sometimes, in Milly's
apartment, pointing, also at once, that moral and
many others. Milly's companions were acclaimed
not only as perfectly fascinating in themselves, the
nicest people yet known to the acclaimers, but as obvious helping hands, socially speaking, for the eccen-
tric young woman, evident initiators and smoothers
of her path, possible subduers of her eccentricity.
Short intervals, to her own sense, stood now for great
differences, and this renewed inhalation of her native
air had somehow left her to feel that she already, that
she mainly, struck the compatriot as queer and dis-
sociated. She moved such a critic, it would appear,
as to rather an odd suspicion, a benevolence induced
by a want of complete trust: all of which showed her
in the light of a person too plain and too ill-clothed
for a thorough good time, and yet too rich and too
befriended — an intuitive cunning within her man-
aging this last — for a thorough bad one. The compatriots, in short, by what she made out, approved
her friends for their expert wisdom with her; in spite
of which judicial sagacity it was the compatriots who
recorded themselves as the innocent parties. She saw
things in these days that she had never seen before,
and she could n't have said why save on a principle
too terrible to name; whereby she saw that neither
Lancaster Gate was what New York took it for, nor
New York what Lancaster Gate fondly fancied it in
coquetting with the plan of a series of American visits.
The plan might have been, humorously, on Mrs.
Lowder's part, for the improvement of her social

position — and it had verily in that direction lights
that were perhaps but half a century too prompt; at
all of which Kate Croy assisted with the cool controlled facility that went so well, as the others said,
with her particular kind of good looks, the kind that
led you to expect the person enjoying them *would*
dispose of disputations, speculations, aspirations, in
a few very neatly and brightly uttered words, so simplified in sense, however, that they sounded, even
when guiltless, like rather aggravated slang. It wasn't
that Kate had n't pretended too that *she* should like
to go to America; it was only that with this young
woman Milly had constantly proceeded, and more
than ever of late, on the theory of intimate confes-
sions, private frank ironies that made up for their
public grimaces and amid which, face to face, they
wearily put off the mask.

These puttings-off of the mask had finally quite
become the form taken by their moments together,
moments indeed not increasingly frequent and not
prolonged, thanks to the consciousness of fatigue
on Milly's side whenever, as she herself expressed it,
she got out of harness. They flourished their masks,
the independent pair, as they might have flourished
Spanish fans; they smiled and sighed on removing
them; but the gesture, the smiles, the sighs, strangely
enough, might have been suspected the greatest reality
in the business. Strangely enough, we say, for the
volume of effusion in general would have been found
by either on measurement to be scarce proportional
to the paraphernalia of relief. It was when they called
each other's attention to their ceasing to pretend, it

was then that what they were keeping back was most in the air. There was a difference, no doubt, and mainly to Kate's advantage: Milly did n't quite see what her friend could keep back, was possessed of, in fine, that would be so subject to retention; whereas it was comparatively plain sailing for Kate that poor Milly had a treasure to hide. This was not the treasure of a shy, an abject affection — concealment, on that head, belonging to quite another phase of such states; it was much rather a principle of pride relatively bold and hard, a principle that played up like a fine steel spring at the lightest pressure of too near a footfall. Thus insuperably guarded was the truth about the girl's own conception of her validity; thus was a wondering pitying sister condemned wistfully to look at her from the far side of the moat she had dug round her tower. Certain aspects of the connexion of these young women show for us, such is the twilight that gathers about them, in the likeness of some dim scene in a Maeterlinck play; we have positively the image, in the delicate dusk, of the figures so associated and yet so opposed, so mutually watchful: that of the angular pale princess, ostrich-plumed, black-robed, hung about with amulets, reminders, relics, mainly seated, mainly still, and that of the upright restless slow-circling lady of her court who exchanges with her, across the black water streaked with evening gleams, fitful questions and answers. The upright lady, with thick dark braids down her back, drawing over the grass a more embroidered train, makes the whole circuit, and makes it again, and the broken talk, brief and sparingly allusive, seems more to cover than to free their sense. This is because, when it fairly comes to not having others to consider, they meet in an air that appears rather anxiously to wait for their words. Such an impression as that was in fact grave, and might be tragic; so that, plainly enough, systematically at last, they settled to a care of what they said.

There could be no gross phrasing to Milly, in particular, of the probability that if she was n't so proud she might be pitied with more comfort — more to the person pitying; there could be no spoken proof, no sharper demonstration than the consistently considerate attitude, that this marvellous mixture of her weakness and of her strength, her peril, if such it were, and her option, made her, kept her, irresistibly interesting. Kate's predicament in the matter was, after all, very much Mrs. Stringham's own, and Susan Shepherd herself indeed, in our Maeterlinck picture, might well have hovered in the gloaming by the moat. It may be declared for Kate, at all events, that her sincerity about her friend, through this time, was deep, her compassionate imagination strong; and that these things gave her a virtue, a good conscience, a credibility for herself, so to speak, that were later to be precious to her. She grasped with her keen intelligence the logic of their common duplicity, went unassisted through the same ordeal as Milly's other hushed follower, easily saw that for the girl to be explicit was to betray divinations, gratitudes, glimpses of the felt contrast between her fortune and her fear — all of which would have contradicted her systematic bravado. That was it, Kate wonderingly

saw: to recognise was to bring down the avalanche —
the avalanche Milly lived so in watch for and that
might be started by the lightest of breaths; though
less possibly the breath of her own stifled plaint than
that of the vain sympathy, the mere helpless gaping
inference of others. With so many suppressions as
these, therefore, between them, their withdrawal together to unmask had to fall back, as we have hinted,
on a nominal motive — which was decently represented by a joy at the drop of chatter. Chatter had in
truth all along attended their steps, but they took the
despairing view of it on purpose to have ready, when
face to face, some view or other of something. The
relief of getting out of harness — that was the moral
of their meetings; but the moral of this, in turn, was
that they could n't so much as ask each other why
harness need be worn. Milly wore it as a general
armour.

She was out of it at present, for some reason, as she
had n't been for weeks; she was always out of it, that
is, when alone, and her companions had never yet so
much as just now affected her as dispersed and suppressed. It was as if still again, still more tacitly and
wonderfully, Eugenio had understood her, taking it
from her without a word and just bravely and bril-
liantly in the name, for instance, of the beautiful day:
"Yes, get me an hour alone; take them off — I don't
care where; absorb, amuse, detain them; drown
them, kill them if you will: so that I may just a little,
all by myself, see where I am." She was conscious of
the dire impatience of it, for she gave up Susie as well
as the others to him — Susie who would have drowned

her very self for her; gave her up to a mercenary monster through whom she thus purchased respites. Strange were the turns of life and the moods of weakness; strange the flickers of fancy and the cheats of hope; yet lawful, all the same — were n't they? — those experiments tried with the truth that consisted, at the worst, but in practising on one's self. She was now playing with the thought that Eugenio might *inclusively* assist her: he had brought home to her, and always by remarks that were really quite soundless, the conception, hitherto ungrasped, of some complete use of her wealth itself, some use of it as a counter-move to fate. It had passed between them as preposterous that with so much money she should just stupidly and awkwardly *want* — any more want a life, a career, a consciousness, than want a house, a carriage or a cook. It was as if she had had from him a kind of expert professional measure of what he was in a position, at a stretch, to undertake for her; the thoroughness of which, for that matter, she could closely compare with a looseness on Sir Luke Strett's part that — at least in Palazzo Leporelli when mornings were fine — showed as almost amateurish. Sir Luke had n't said to her "Pay enough money and leave the rest to *me*" — which was distinctly what Eugenio did say. Sir Luke had appeared indeed to speak of purchase and payment, but in reference to a different sort of cash. Those were amounts not to be named nor reckoned, and such moreover as she was n't sure of having at her command. Eugenio — this was the difference — could name, could reckon, and prices of *his* kind were things she had never suf-

fered to scare her. She had been willing, goodness
knew, to pay enough for anything, for everything, and
here was simply a new view of the sufficient quantity.
She amused herself — for it came to that, since Eugenio was there to sign the receipt — with possibilities of meeting the bill. She was more prepared than
ever to pay enough, and quite as much as ever to pay
too much. What else — if such were points at which
your most trusted servant failed — was the use of
being, as the dear Susies of earth called you, a princess
in a palace ?

She made now, alone, the full circuit of the place,
noble and peaceful while the summer sea, stirring
here and there a curtain or an outer blind, breathed
into its veiled spaces. She had a vision of clinging to
it; that perhaps Eugenio could manage. She was *in* it,
as in the ark of her deluge, and filled with such a tenderness for it that why should n't this, in common
mercy, be warrant enough ? She would never, never
leave it — she would engage to that; would ask nothing more than to sit tight in it and float on and on.
The beauty and intensity, the real momentary relief
of this conceit, reached their climax in the positive
purpose to put the question to Eugenio on his return
as she had not yet put it; though the design, it must be
added, dropped a little when, coming back to the great
saloon from which she had started on her pensive
progress, she found Lord Mark, of whose arrival in
Venice she had been unaware, and who had now —
while a servant was following her through empty
rooms — been asked, in her absence, to wait. He had
waited then, Lord Mark, he was waiting — oh un-

mistakeably; never before had he so much struck her as the man to do that on occasion with patience, to do it indeed almost as with gratitude for the chance, though at the same time with a sort of notifying firmness. The odd thing, as she was afterwards to recall, was that her wonder for what had brought him was not immediate, but had come at the end of five minutes; and also, quite incoherently, that she felt almost as glad to see him, and almost as forgiving of his interruption of her solitude, as if he had already been in her thought or acting at her suggestion. He was somehow, at the best, the end of a respite; one might like him very much and yet feel that his presence tempered precious solitude more than any other known to one: in spite of all of which, as he was neither dear Susie, nor dear Kate, nor dear Aunt Maud, nor even, for the least, dear Eugenio in person, the sight of him did no damage to her sense of the dispersal of her friends. She had n't been so thoroughly alone with him since those moments of his showing her the great portrait at Matcham, the moments that had exactly made the high-water-mark of her security, the moments during which her tears themselves, those she had been ashamed of, were the sign of her consciously rounding her protective promontory, quitting the blue gulf of comparative ignorance and reaching her view of the troubled sea. His presence now referred itself to his presence then, reminding her how kind he had been, altogether, at Matcham, and telling her, unexpectedly, at a time when she could particularly feel it, that, for such kindness and for the beauty of what they remembered together, she had n't lost him —

quite the contrary. To receive him handsomely, to
receive him there, to see him interested and charmed,
as well, clearly, as delighted to have found her without some other person to spoil it — these things were
so pleasant for the first minutes that they might have
represented on her part some happy foreknowledge.

She gave an account of her companions while he on
his side failed to press her about them, even though
describing his appearance, so unheralded, as the
result of an impulse obeyed on the spot. He had been
shivering at Carlsbad, belated there and blue, when
taken by it; so that, knowing where they all were, he
had simply caught the first train. He explained how
he had known where they were; he had heard — what
more natural? — from their friends, Milly's and his.
He mentioned this betimes, but it was with his mention, singularly, that the girl became conscious of her
inner question about his reason. She noticed his
plural, which added to Mrs. Lowder or added to
Kate; but she presently noticed also that it did n't
affect her as explaining. Aunt Maud had written to
him, Kate apparently — and this was interesting —
had written to him; but their design presumably
had n't been that he should come and sit there as if
rather relieved, so far as *they* were concerned, at post-
ponements. He only said "Oh!" and again "Oh!"
when she sketched their probable morning for him,
under Eugenio's care and Mrs. Stringham's —
sounding it quite as if any suggestion that he should
overtake them at the Rialto or the Bridge of Sighs
would leave him temporarily cold. This precisely it
was that, after a little, operated for Milly as an ob-

scure but still fairly direct check to confidence. He had known where they all were from the others, but it was not for the others that, in his actual dispositions, he had come. That, strange to say, was a pity; for, stranger still to say, she could have shown him more confidence if he himself had had less intention. His intention so chilled her, from the moment she found herself divining it, that, just for the pleasure of going on with him fairly, just for the pleasure of their remembrance together of Matcham and the Bronzino, the climax of her fortune, she could have fallen to pleading with him and to reasoning, to undeceiving him in time. There had been, for ten minutes, with the directness of her welcome to him and the way this clearly pleased him, something of the grace of amends made, even though he could n't know it — amends for her not having been originally sure, for instance at that first dinner of Aunt Maud's, that he was adequately human. That first dinner of Aunt Maud's added itself to the hour at Matcham, added itself to other things, to consolidate, for her present benevolence, the ease of their relation, making it suddenly delightful that he had thus turned up. He exclaimed, as he looked about, on the charm of the place: "What a temple to taste and an expression of the pride of life, yet, with all that, what a jolly *home !*" — so that, for his entertainment, she could offer to walk him about though she mentioned that she had just been, for her own purposes, in a general prowl, taking everything in more .susceptibly than before. He embraced her offer without a scruple and seemed to rejoice that he was to find her susceptible.

IV

SHE could n't have said what it was, in the conditions, that renewed the whole solemnity, but by the
end of twenty minutes a kind of wistful hush had fallen
upon them, as before something poignant in which her
visitor also participated. That was nothing verily but
the perfection of the charm — or nothing rather but
their excluded disinherited state in the presence of it.
The charm turned on them a face that was cold in its
beauty, that was full of a poetry never to be theirs,
that spoke with an ironic smile of a possible but
forbidden life. It all rolled afresh over Milly: "Oh
the impossible romance —!" The romance for
her, yet once more, would be to sit there for ever,
through all her time, as in a fortress; and the idea
became an image of never going down, of remaining aloft in the divine dustless air, where she would
hear but the plash of the water against stone. The
great floor on which they moved was at an altitude,
and this prompted the rueful fancy. "Ah not to go
down — never, never to go down!" she strangely
sighed to her friend.

"But why should n't you," he asked, "with that
tremendous old staircase in your court? There ought
of course always to be people at top and bottom, in
Veronese costumes, to watch you do it."

She shook her head both lightly and mournfully
enough at his not understanding. "Not even for

147

people in Veronese costumes. I mean that the positive beauty is that one need n't go down. I don't move in fact," she added — "now. I 've not been out, you know. I stay up. That 's how you happily found me."

Lord Mark wondered — he was, oh yes, adequately human. "You don't go about?"

She looked over the place, the storey above the apartments in which she had received him, the sala corresponding to the sala below and fronting the great canal with its gothic arches. The casements between the arches were open, the ledge of the balcony broad, the sweep of the canal, so overhung, admirable, and the flutter toward them of the loose white curtain an invitation to she scarce could have said what. But there was no mystery after a moment; she had never felt so invited to anything as to make that, and that only, just where she was, her adventure. It would be — to this it kept coming back — the adventure of not stirring. "I go about just here."

"Do you mean," Lord Mark presently asked, "that you 're really not well?"

They were at the window, pausing, lingering, with the fine old faded palaces opposite and the slow Adriatic tide beneath; but after a minute, and before she answered, she had closed her eyes to what she saw and unresistingly dropped her face into her arms, which rested on the coping. She had fallen to her knees on the cushion of the window-place, and she leaned there, in a long silence, with her forehead down. She knew that her silence was itself too straight an

answer, but it was beyond her now to say that she
saw her way. She would have made the question
itself impossible to others — impossible for example
to such a man as Merton Densher; and she could
wonder even on the spot what it was a sign of in her
feeling for Lord Mark that from his lips it almost
tempted her to break down. This was doubtless really
because she cared for him so little; to let herself go
with him thus, suffer his touch to make her cup overflow, would be the relief — since it was actually, for
her nerves, a question of relief — that would cost her
least. If he had come to her moreover with the intention she believed, or even if this intention had but
been determined in him by the spell of their situation,
he must n't be mistaken about her value — for what
value did she now have? It throbbed within her as
she knelt there that she had none at all; though, holding herself, not yet speaking, she tried, even in the
act, to recover what might be possible of it. With
that there came to her a light: would n't her value,
for the man who should marry her, be precisely in the
ravage of her disease? *She* might n't last, but her
money would. For a man in whom the vision of her
money should be intense, in whom it should be most
of the ground for "making up" to her, any prospect-
ive failure on her part to be long for this world might
easily count as a positive attraction. Such a man,
proposing to please, persuade, secure her, appro-
priate her for such a time, shorter or longer, as nature and the doctors should allow, would make the
best of her, ill, damaged, disagreeable though she
might be, for the sake of eventual benefits: she being

149

clearly a person of the sort esteemed likely to do the handsome thing by a stricken and sorrowing husband.

She had said to herself betimes, in a general way, that whatever habits her youth might form, that of seeing an interested suitor in every bush should certainly never grow to be one of them — an attitude she had early judged as ignoble, as poisonous. She had had accordingly in fact as little to do with it as possible and she scarce knew why at the present moment she should have had to catch herself in the act of imputing an ugly motive. It did n't sit, the ugly motive, in Lord Mark's cool English eyes; the darker side of it at any rate showed, to her imagination, but briefly. Suspicion moreover, with this, simplified itself: there was a beautiful reason — indeed there were two — why her companion's motive should n't matter. One was that even should he desire her without a penny she would n't marry him for the world; the other was that she felt him, after all, perceptively, kindly, very pleasantly and humanly, concerned for her. They were also two things, his wishing to be well, to be very well, with her, and his beginning to feel her as threatened, haunted, blighted; but they were melting together for him, making him, by their combination, only the more sure that, as he probably called it to himself, he liked her. That was presently what remained with her — his really doing it; and with the natural and proper incident of being conciliated by her weakness. Would she really have had him — she could ask herself that — disconcerted or disgusted by it? If he could only be touched

enough to do what she preferred, not to raise, not to
press any question, he might render her a much better service than by merely enabling her to refuse him.
Again, again it was strange, but he figured to her for
the moment as the one safe sympathiser. It would
have made her worse to talk to others, but she was n't
afraid with him of how he might wince and look pale.
She would keep him, that is, her one easy relation—
in the sense of easy for himself. Their actual outlook
had meanwhile such charm, what surrounded them
within and without did so much toward making ap-
preciative stillness as natural as at the opera, that
she could consider she had n't made him hang on
her lips when at last, instead of saying if she were
well or ill, she repeated: "I go about here. I don't
get tired of it. I never should — it suits me so. I
adore the place," she went on, "and I don't want in
the least to give it up."

"Neither should I if I had your luck. Still, with
that luck, for one's *all* —! Should you positively like
to live here?"

"I think I should like," said poor Milly after an
instant, "to die here."

Which made him, precisely, laugh. That was what
she wanted — when a person did care: it was the
pleasant human way, without depths of darkness.
"Oh it's not good enough for *that!* That requires
picking. But can't you keep it? It is, you know, the
sort of place to see you in; you carry out the note,
fill it, people it, quite by yourself, and you might do
much worse — I mean for your friends — than show
yourself here a while, three or four months, every

year. But it's not my notion for the rest of the time. One has quite other uses for you."

"What sort of a use for me is it," she smilingly enquired, "to kill me?"

"Do you mean we should kill you in England?"

"Well, I've seen you and I'm afraid. You're too much for me—too many. England bristles with questions. This is more, as you say there, my form."

"Oho, oho!"—he laughed again as if to humour her. "Can't you then buy it—for a price? Depend upon it they'll treat for money. That is for money enough."

"I've exactly," she said, "been wondering if they won't. I think I shall try. But if I get it I shall cling to it." They were talking sincerely. "It will be my life—paid for as that. It will become my great gilded shell; so that those who wish to find me must come and hunt me up."

"Ah then you *will* be alive," said Lord Mark.

"Well, not quite extinct perhaps, but shrunken, wasted, wizened; rattling about here like the dried kernel of a nut."

"Oh," Lord Mark returned, "we, much as you mistrust us, can do better for you than that."

"In the sense that you'll feel it better for me really to have it over?"

He let her see now that she worried him, and after a look at her, of some duration, without his glasses —which always altered the expression of his eyes— he re-settled the nippers on his nose and went back to the view. But the view, in turn, soon enough released him. "Do you remember something I said to

152

you that day at Matcham — or at least fully meant to ?"

" Oh yes, I remember everything at Matcham. It's another life."

"Certainly it will be — I mean the kind of thing: what I then wanted it to represent for you. Matcham, you know," he continued, "is symbolic. I think I tried to rub that into you a little."

She met him with the full memory of what he had tried — not an inch, not an ounce of which was lost to her. "What I meant is that it seems a hundred years ago."

"Oh for me it comes in better. Perhaps a part of what makes me remember it," he pursued, "is that I was quite aware of what might have been said about what I was doing. I wanted you to take it from me that I should perhaps be able to look after you — well, rather better. Rather better, of course, than certain other persons in particular."

" Precisely—than Mrs. Lowder, than Miss Croy, even than Mrs. Stringham."

"Oh Mrs. Stringham's all right!" Lord Mark promptly amended.

. It amused her even with what she had else to think of; and she could show him at all events how little, in spite of the hundred years, she had lost what he alluded to. The way he was with her at this moment made in fact the other moment so vivid as almost to start again the tears it had started at the time. "You could do so much for me, yes. I perfectly understood you."

"I wanted, you see," he despite this explained,

"to *fix* your confidence. I mean, you know, in the right place."

"Well, Lord Mark, you did — it's just exactly now, my confidence, where you put it then. The only difference," said Milly, "is that I seem now to have no use for it. Besides," she then went on, "I do seem to feel you disposed to act in a way that would undermine it a little."

He took no more notice of these last words than if she had n't said them, only watching her at present as with a gradual new light. "Are you *really* in any trouble?"

To this, on her side, she gave no heed. Making out his light was a little a light for herself. "Don't say, don't try to say, anything that's impossible. There are much better things you can do."

He looked straight at it and then straight over it. "It's too monstrous that one can't ask you as a friend what one wants so to know."

"What is it you want to know?" She spoke, as by a sudden turn, with a slight hardness. "Do you want to know if I'm badly ill?"

The sound of it in truth, though from no raising of her voice, invested the idea with a kind of terror, but a terror all for others. Lord Mark winced and flushed — clearly could n't help it; but he kept his attitude together and spoke even with unwonted vivacity. "Do you imagine I can see you suffer and not say a word?"

"You won't see me suffer — don't be afraid. I shan't be a public nuisance. That's why I should have liked *this:* it's so beautiful in itself and yet it's out of the gangway. You won't know anything about anything," she added; and then as if to make with decision an end: "And you *don't!* No, not even you." He faced her through it with the remains of his expression, and she saw him as clearly — for *him* — bewildered; which made her wish to be sure not to have been unkind. She would be kind once for all; that would be the end. "I'm very badly ill."

"And you don't do anything?"

"I do everything. Everything's *this,*" she smiled. "I'm doing it now. One can't do more than live."

"Ah than live in the right way, no. But is *that* what you do? Why have n't you advice?"

He had looked about at the rococo elegance as if there were fifty things it did n't give her, so that he suggested with urgency the most absent. But she met his remedy with a smile. "I've the best advice in the world. I'm acting under it now. I act upon it in receiving you, in talking with you thus. One can't, as I tell you, do more than live."

"Oh live!" Lord Mark ejaculated.

"Well, it's immense for *me.*" She finally spoke as if for amusement; now that she had uttered her truth, that he had learnt it from herself as no one had yet done, her emotion had, by the fact, dried up. There she was; but it was as if she would never speak again. "I shan't," she added, "have missed everything."

"Why should you have missed *anything?*" She felt, as he sounded this, to what, within the minute, he had made up his mind. "You're the person in the world for whom that's least necessary; for whom one would call it in fact most impossible; for whom 'missing' at all will surely require an extraordinary amount of misplaced good will. Since you believe in advice, for God's sake take *mine*. I know what you want."

Oh she knew he would know it. But she had brought it on herself — or almost. Yet she spoke with kindness. "I think I want not to be too much worried."

"You want to be adored." It came at last straight. "Nothing would worry you less. I mean as I shall do it. It *is* so" — he firmly kept it up. "You're not loved enough."

"Enough for what, Lord Mark?"

"Why to get the full good of it."

Well, she didn't after all mock at him. "I see what you mean. That full good of it which consists in finding one's self forced to love in return." She had grasped it, but she hesitated. "Your idea is that I might find myself forced to love *you?*"

"Oh 'forced' — !" He was so fine and so expert, so awake to anything the least ridiculous, and of a type with which the preaching of passion somehow so ill consorted — he was so much all these things that he had absolutely to take account of them himself. And he did so, in a single intonation, beautifully. Milly liked him again, liked him for such shades as that, liked him so that it was woeful to see him spoiling it, and still more woeful to have to rank him among those minor charms of existence that she gasped at moments to remember she must give up. "Is it inconceivable to you that you might try?"

"To be so favourably affected by you —?"

"To believe in me. To believe in me," Lord Mark repeated.

Again she hesitated. "To 'try' in return for your trying?"

"Oh I should n't have to!" he quickly declared. The prompt neat accent, however, his manner of disposing of her question, failed of real expression, as he himself the next moment intelligently, helplessly, almost comically saw — a failure pointed moreover by the laugh into which Milly was immediately startled. As a suggestion to her of a healing and uplifting passion it *was* in truth deficient; it would n't do as the communication of a force that should sweep them both away. And the beauty of him was that he too, even in the act of persuasion, of self-persuasion, could understand that, and could thereby show but the better as fitting into the pleasant commerce of prosperity. The way she let him see that she looked at him was a thing to shut him out, of itself, from services of danger, a thing that made a discrimination against him never yet made — made at least to any consciousness of his own. Born to float in a sustaining air, this would be his first encounter with a judgement formed in the sinister light of tragedy. The gathering dusk of *her* personal world presented itself to him, in her eyes, as an element in which it was vain for him to pretend he could find himself at home, since it was charged with depressions and with dooms, with the chill of the losing game. Almost without her needing to speak, and simply by the fact that there could be, in such a case, no decent

substitute for a felt intensity, he had to take it from
her that practically he was afraid — whether afraid to
protest falsely enough, or only afraid of what might be
eventually disagreeable in a compromised alliance,
being a minor question. She believed she made out
besides, wonderful girl, that he had never quite expected to have to protest about anything beyond his
natural convenience — more, in fine, than his disposition and habits, his education as well, his personal *moyens*, in short, permitted. His predicament
was therefore one he could n't like, and also one she
willingly would have spared him had n't he brought
it on himself. No man, she was quite aware, could
enjoy thus having it from her that he was n't good
for what she would have called her reality. It would
n't have taken much more to enable her positively to
make out in him that he was virtually capable of hint-
ing — had his innermost feeling spoken — at the propriety rather, in his interest, of some cutting down,
some dressing up, of the offensive real. He would meet
that halfway, but the real must also meet *him*. Milly's
sense of it for herself, which was so conspicuously,
so financially supported, could n't, or would n't, so
accommodate him, and the perception of that fairly
showed in his face after a moment like the smart of a
blow. It had marked the one minute during which he
could again be touching to her. By the time he had
tried once more, after all, to insist, he had quite ceased
to be so.

By this time she had turned from their window to
make a diversion, had walked him through other
rooms, appealing again to the inner charm of the

place, going even so far for that purpose as to point afresh her independent moral, to repeat that if one only had such a house for one's own and loved it and cherished it enough, it would pay one back in kind, would close one in from harm. He quite grasped for the quarter of an hour the perch she held out to him — grasped it with one hand, that is, while she felt him attached to his own clue with the other; he was by no means either so sore or so stupid, to do him all justice, as not to be able to behave more or less as if nothing had happened. It was one of his merits, to which she did justice too, that both his native and his acquired notion of behaviour rested on the general assumption that nothing — nothing to make a deadly difference for him — ever *could* happen. It was, socially, a working view like another, and it saw them easily enough through the greater part of the rest of their adventure. Downstairs again, however, with the limit of his stay in sight, the sign of his smarting, when all was said, reappeared for her — breaking out moreover, with an effect of strangeness, in another quite possibly sincere allusion to her state of health. He might for that matter have been seeing what he could do in the way of making it a grievance that she should snub him for a charity, on his own part, exquisitely roused. "It's true, you know, all the same, and I don't care a straw for your trying to freeze one up." He seemed to show her, poor man, bravely, how little he cared. "Everybody knows affection often makes things out when indifference does n't notice. And that's why I know that *I* notice."

"Are you sure you've got it right?" the girl smiled.

"I thought rather that affection was supposed to be blind."

"Blind to faults, not to beauties," Lord Mark promptly returned.

"And are my extremely private worries, my entirely domestic complications, which I'm ashamed to have given you a glimpse of — are they beauties?"

"Yes, for those who care for you — as every one does. Everything about you is a beauty. Besides which I don't believe," he declared, "in the seriousness of what you tell me. It's too absurd you should have *any* trouble about which something can't be done. If you can't get the right thing, who *can*, in all the world, I should like to know? You're the first young woman of your time. I mean what I say." He looked, to do him justice, quite as if he did; not ardent, but clear — simply so competent, in such a position, to compare, that his quiet assertion had the force not so much perhaps of a tribute as of a warrant. "We're all in love with you. I'll put it that way, dropping any claim of my own, if you can bear it better. I speak as one of the lot. You were n't born simply to torment us — you were born to make us happy. Therefore you must listen to us."

She shook her head with her slowness, but this time with all her mildness. "No, I must n't listen to you — that's just what I must n't do. The reason is, please, that it simply kills me. I must be as attached to you as you will, since you give that lovely account of yourselves. I give you in return the fullest possible belief of what it would be —" And

she pulled up a little. "I give and give and give —
there you are; stick to me as close as you like and see
if I don't. Only I can't listen or receive or accept
— I can't *agree*. I can't make a bargain. I can't
really. You must believe that from me. It's all I've
wanted to say to you, and why should it spoil anything?"

He let her question fall — though clearly, it might
have seemed, because, for reasons or for none, there
was so much that *was* spoiled. "You want somebody of your own." He came back, whether in good
faith or in bad, to that; and it made her repeat her
headshake. He kept it up as if his faith were of
the best. "You want somebody, you want somebody."

She was to wonder afterwards if she had n't been
at this juncture on the point of saying something
emphatic and vulgar — "Well, I don't at all events
want *you!*" What somehow happened, nevertheless,
the pity of it being greater than the irritation — the
sadness, to her vivid sense, of his being so painfully
astray, wandering in a desert in which there was
nothing to nourish him — was that his error amounted
to positive wrongdoing. She was moreover so acquainted with quite another sphere of usefulness
for him that her having suffered him to insist almost
convicted her of indelicacy. Why had n't she stopped
him off with her first impression of his purpose?
She could do so now only by the allusion she had been
wishing not to make. "Do you know I don't think
you're doing very right? — and as a thing quite apart,
I mean, from my listening to you. That's not right

either — except that I'm *not* listening. You ought n't
to have come to Venice to see *me* — and in fact you've
not come, and you must n't behave as if you had.
You've much older friends than I, and ever so much
better. Really, if you've come at all, you can only
have come — properly, and if I may say so honour-
ably — for the best friend, as I believe her to be, that
you have in the world."

When once she had said it he took it, oddly enough,
as if he had been more or less expecting it. Still, he
looked at her very hard, and they had a moment of
this during which neither pronounced a name, each
apparently determined that the other should. It was
Milly's fine coercion, in the event, that was the
stronger. "Miss Croy?" Lord Mark asked.

It might have been difficult to make out that she
smiled. "Mrs. Lowder." He did make out something, and then fairly coloured for its attestation of
his comparative simplicity. "I call *her* on the whole
the best. I can't imagine a man's having a better."

Still with his eyes on her he turned it over. "Do
you want me to marry Mrs. Lowder?"

At which it seemed to her that it was he who was
almost vulgar! But she would n't in any way have
that. "You know, Lord Mark, what I mean. One
is n't in the least turning you out into the cold world.
There's no cold world for you at all, I think," she
went on; "nothing but a very warm and watchful
and expectant world that's waiting for you at any
moment you choose to take it up."

He never budged, but they were standing on the
polished concrete and he had within a few minutes

possessed himself again of his hat. "Do you want me to marry Kate Croy?"

"Mrs. Lowder wants it — I do no wrong, I think, in saying that; and she understands moreover that you know she does."

Well, he showed how beautifully he could take it; and it was n't obscure to her, on her side, that it was a comfort to deal with a gentleman. "It's ever so kind of you to see such opportunities for me. But what's the use of my tackling Miss Croy?"

Milly rejoiced on the spot to be so able to point out. "Because she's the handsomest and cleverest and most charming creature I ever saw, and because if I were a man I should simply adore her. In fact I do as it is." It was a luxury of response.

"Oh, my dear lady, plenty of people adore her. But that can't further the case of *all*."

"Ah," she went on, "I know about 'people.' If the case of one's bad, the case of another's good. I don't see what you have to fear from any one else," she said, "save through your being foolish, this way, about *me*."

So she said, but she was aware the next moment of what he was making of what she did n't see. "Is it your idea — since we 're talking of these things in these ways — that the young lady you describe in such superlative terms is to be had for the asking?"

"Well, Lord Mark, try. She *is* a great person. But don't be humble." She was almost gay.

It was this apparently, at last, that was too much for him. "But don't you really *know*?"

As a challenge, practically, to the commonest intelligence she could pretend to, it made her of course wish to be fair. "I 'know,' yes, that a particular person 's very much in love with her."

"Then you must know by the same token that she 's very much in love with a particular person."

"Ah I beg your pardon!" — and Milly quite flushed at having so crude a blunder imputed to her. "You 're wholly mistaken."

"It 's not true?"

"It 's not true."

His stare became a smile. "Are you very, very sure?"

"As sure as one can be" — and Milly's manner could match it — "when one has every assurance. I speak on the best authority."

He hesitated. "Mrs. Lowder's?"

"No. I don't call Mrs. Lowder's the best."

"Oh I thought you were just now saying," he laughed, "that everything about her 's so good."

"Good for you" — she was perfectly clear. "For you," she went on, "let her authority be the best. She does n't believe what you mention, and you must know yourself how little she makes of it. So you can take it from her. *I* take it —" But Milly, with the positive tremor of her emphasis, pulled up.

"You take it from Kate?"

"From Kate herself."

"That she 's thinking of no one at all?"

"Of no one at all." Then, with her intensity, she went on. "She has given me her word for it."

"Oh!" said Lord Mark. To which he next added: "And what do you call her word?"

It made Milly, on her side, stare — though perhaps partly but with the instinct of gaining time for the consciousness that she was already a little further "in" than she had designed. "Why, Lord Mark, what should *you* call her word?"

"Ah I'm not obliged to say. I've not asked her. You apparently have."

Well, it threw her on her defence — a defence that she felt, however, especially as of Kate. "We're very intimate,"she said in a moment; "so that, without prying into each other's affairs, she naturally tells me things."

Lord Mark smiled as at a lame conclusion. "You mean then she made you of her own movement the declaration you quote?"

Milly thought again, though with hindrance rather than help in her sense of the way their eyes now met — met as for their each seeing in the other more than either said. What she most felt that she herself saw was the strange disposition on her companion's part to disparage Kate's veracity. She could be only concerned to "stand up" for that.

"I mean what I say: that when she spoke of her having no private interest —"

"She took her oath to you?" Lord Mark interrupted.

Milly did n't quite see why he should so catechise her; but she met it again for Kate. "She left me in no doubt whatever of her being free."

At this Lord Mark did look at her, though he continued to smile. "And thereby in no doubt of *your* being too?" It was as if as soon as he had said it, however, he felt it as something of a mistake, and she could n't herself have told by what queer glare at him she had instantly signified that. He at any rate gave her glare no time to act further; he fell back on the spot, and with a light enough movement, within his rights. "That's all very well, but why in the world, dear lady, should she be swearing to you?"

She had to take this "dear lady" as applying to herself; which disconcerted her when he might now so gracefully have used it for the aspersed Kate. Once more it came to her that she must claim her own part of the aspersion. "Because, as I've told you, we're such tremendous friends."

"Oh," said Lord Mark, who for the moment looked as if that might have stood rather for an absence of such rigours. He was going, however, as if he had in a manner, at the last, got more or less what he wanted. Milly felt, while he addressed his next few words to leave-taking, that she had given rather more than she intended or than she should be able, when once more getting herself into hand, theoretically to defend. Strange enough in fact that he had had from her, about herself — and, under the searching spell of the place, infinitely straight — what no one else had had: neither Kate, nor Aunt Maud, nor Merton Densher, nor Susan Shepherd. He had made her within a minute, in particular, she was aware, lose her presence of mind, and she now wished he would take himself off, so that she might either recover it or bear the loss better in solitude. If he paused, however, she almost at the same time saw, it was because of his watching the approach, from the end of the sala, of one of the gondoliers, who, whatever excursions were appointed for the party with the attendance of the others, always, as the most decorative, most sashed and starched, remained at the palace on the theory that she might whimsically want him — which she never, in her caged freedom, had yet done. Brown Pasquale, slipping in white shoes over the marble and suggesting to her perpetually charmed vision she could scarce say what, either a mild Hindoo, too noiseless almost for her nerves, or simply a barefooted seaman on the deck of a ship — Pasquale offered to sight a small salver, which he obsequiously held out to her with its burden of a visiting-card. Lord Mark — and as if also for admiration of him — delayed his departure to let her receive it; on which she read it with the instant effect of another blow to her presence of mind. This precarious quantity was indeed now so gone that even for dealing with Pasquale she had to do her best to conceal its disappearance. The effort was made, none the less, by the time she had asked if the gentleman were below and had taken in the fact that he had come up. He had followed the gondolier and was waiting at the top of the staircase.

"I'll see him with pleasure." To which she added for her companion, while Pasquale went off: "Mr. Merton Densher."

"Oh!" said Lord Mark — in a manner that, making it resound through the great cool hall, might have carried it even to Densher's ear as a judgement of his identity heard and noted once before.

BOOK EIGHTH

I

Densher became aware, afresh, that he disliked his hotel — and all the more promptly that he had had occasion of old to make the same discrimination. The establishment, choked at that season with the polyglot herd, cockneys of all climes, mainly German, mainly American, mainly English, it appeared as the corresponding sensitive nerve was touched, sounded loud and not sweet, sounded anything and everything but Italian, but Venetian. The Venetian was all a dialect, he knew; yet it was pure Attic beside some of the dialects at the bustling inn. It made, "abroad," both for his pleasure and his pain that he had to feel at almost any point how he had been through everything before. He had been three or four times, in Venice, during other visits, through this pleasant irritation of paddling away — away from the concert of false notes in the vulgarised hall, away from the amiable American families and overfed German porters. He had in each case made terms for a lodging more private and not more costly, and he recalled with tenderness these shabby but friendly asylums, the windows of which he should easily know again in passing on canal or through campo. The shabbiest now failed of an appeal to him, but he found himself at the end of forty-eight hours forming views in respect to a small independent *quartiere*, far down the Grand Canal, which he had once occupied for a month with a sense of pomp and circumstance and yet also with a growth of initiation into the homelier Venetian mysteries. The humour of those days came back to him for an hour, and what further befell in this interval, to be brief, was that, emerging on a traghetto in sight of the recognised house, he made out on the green shutters of his old, of his young windows the strips of white pasted paper that figure in Venice as an invitation to tenants. This was in the course of his very first walk apart, a walk replete with impressions to which he responded with force. He had been almost without cessation, since his arrival, at Palazzo Leporelli, where, as happened, a turn of bad weather on the second day had kept the whole party continuously at home. The episode had passed for him like a series of hours in a museum, though without the fatigue of that; and it had also resembled something that he was still, with a stirred imagination, to find a name for. He might have been looking for the name while he gave himself up, subsequently, to the ramble — he saw that even after years he could n't lose his way — crowned with his stare across the water at the little white papers.

He was to dine at the palace in an hour or two, and he had lunched there, at an early luncheon, that morning. He had then been out with the three ladies, the three being Mrs. Lowder, Mrs. Stringham and Kate, and had kept afloat with them, under a sufficient Venetian spell, until Aunt Maud had directed him to leave them and return to Miss Theale. Of two circumstances connected with this disposition of his person he was even now not unmindful; the first being that the lady of Lancaster Gate had addressed him with high publicity and as if expressing equally the sense of her companions, who had not spoken, but who might have been taken — yes, Susan Shepherd quite equally with Kate — for inscrutable parties to her plan. What he could as little contrive to forget was that he had, before the two others, as it struck him — that was to say especially before Kate — done exactly as he was bidden; gathered himself up without a protest and retraced his way to the palace. Present with him still was the question of whether he looked a fool for it, of whether the awkwardness he felt as the gondola rocked with the business of his leaving it — they could but make, in submission, for a landing-place that was none of the best — had furnished his friends with such entertainment as was to cause them, behind his back, to exchange intelligent smiles. He had found Milly Theale twenty minutes later alone, and he had sat with her till the others returned to tea. The strange part of this was that it had been very easy, extraordinarily easy. He knew it for strange only when he was away from her, because when he was away from her he was in contact with particular things that made it so. At the time, in her presence, it was as simple as sitting with his sister might have been, and not, if the point were urged, very much more thrilling. He continued to see her as he had first seen her — that remained ineffaceably behind. Mrs. Lowder, Susan Shepherd, his own Kate, might, each in proportion, see her as a princess, as an angel, as a star, but for himself, luckily, she had n't as yet complications to any point of discomfort: the princess, the angel, the star, were muffled over, ever so lightly and brightly, with the little American girl who had been kind to him in New York and to whom certainly — though without making too much of it for either of them — he was perfectly willing to be kind in return. She appreciated his coming in on purpose, but there was nothing in that — from the moment she was always at home — that they could n't easily keep up. The only note the least bit high that had even yet sounded between them was this admission on her part that she found it best to remain within. She would n't let him call it keeping quiet, for she insisted that her palace — with all its romance and art and history — had set up round her a whirl-wind of suggestion that never dropped for an hour. It was n't therefore, within such walls, confinement, it was the freedom of all the centuries: in respect to which Densher granted good-humouredly that they were then blown together, she and he, as much as she liked, through space.

Kate had found on the present occasion a moment to say to him that he suggested a clever cousin calling on a cousin afflicted, and bored for his pains; and though he denied on the spot the "bored" he could so far see it as an impression he might make that he wondered if the same image would n't have occurred to Milly. As soon as Kate appeared again the differ-ence came up — the oddity, as he then instantly felt it, of his having sunk so deep. It was sinking because it was all doing what Kate had conceived for him; it was n't in the least doing — and that had been his notion of his life — anything he himself had con-

ceived. The difference, accordingly, renewed, sharp,
sore, was the irritant under which he had quitted the
palace and under which he was to make the best of
the business of again dining there. He said to himself
that he must make the best of everything; that was in
his mind, at the traghetto, even while, with his preoccupation about changing quarters, he studied,
across the canal, the look of his former abode. It had
done for the past, would it do for the present? would
it play in any manner into the general necessity of
which he was conscious? That necessity of making
the best was the instinct — as he indeed himself knew
— of a man somehow aware that if he let go at one
place he should let go everywhere. If he took off his
hand, the hand that at least helped to hold it together,
the whole queer fabric that built him in would fall
away in a minute and admit the light. It was really a
matter of nerves; it was exactly because he was nervous that he *could* go straight; yet if that condition
should increase he must surely go wild. He was walking in short on a high ridge, steep down on either side,
where the proprieties — once he could face at all remaining there — reduced themselves to his keeping
his head. It was Kate who had so perched him, and
there came up for him at moments, as he found himself planting one foot exactly before another, a sensible sharpness of irony as to her management of him.
It was n't that she had put him in danger — to be in
real danger with her would have had another quality.
There glowed for him in fact a kind of rage at what
he was n't having; an exasperation, a resentment, begotten truly by the very impatience of desire, in respect

to his postponed and relegated, his so extremely man-
ipulated state. It was beautifully done of her, but
what was the real meaning of it unless that he was perpetually bent to her will? His idea from the first,
from the very first of his knowing her, had been to be,
as the French called it, *bon prince* with her, mindful
of the good humour and generosity, the contempt, in
the matter of confidence, for small outlays and small
savings, that belonged to the man who was n't generally afraid. There were things enough, goodness knew
— for it was the moral of his plight — that he could
n't afford; but what had had a charm for him if not
the notion of living handsomely, to make up for it, in
another way? of not at all events reading the romance
of his existence in a cheap edition. All he had originally felt in her came back to him, was indeed actually as present as ever — how he had admired and
envied what he called to himself her pure talent for
life, as distinguished from his own, a poor weak thing
of the occasion, amateurishly patched up; only it
irritated him the more that this was exactly what was
now, ever so characteristically, standing out in her.

It was thanks to her pure talent for life, verily,
that he was just where he was and that he was above
all just *how* he was. The proof of a decent reaction
in him against so much passivity was, with no great
richness, that he at least knew — knew, that is, how
he was, and how little he liked it as a thing accepted
in mere helplessness. He was, for the moment, wistful
— that above all described it; that was so large a part
of the force that, as the autumn afternoon closed in,
kept him, on his traghetto, positively throbbing with

his question. His question connected itself, even while he stood, with his special smothered soreness, his sense almost of shame; and the soreness and the shame were less as he let himself, with the help of the conditions about him, regard it as serious. It was born, for that matter, partly of the conditions, those conditions that Kate had so almost insolently braved, had been willing, without a pang, to see him ridiculously — ridiculously so far as just complacently — exposed to. How little it *could* be complacently he was to feel with the last thoroughness before he had moved from his point of vantage. His question, as we have called it, was the interesting question of whether he had really no will left. How could he know — that was the point — without putting the matter to the test? It had been right to be *bon prince*, and the joy, something of the pride, of having lived, in spirit, handsomely, was even now compatible with the impulse to look into their account; but he held his breath a little as it came home to him with supreme sharpness that, whereas he had done absolutely everything that Kate had wanted, she had done nothing whatever that he had. So it was in fine that his idea of the test by which he must try that possibility kept referring itself, in the warm early dusk, the approach of the Southern night — "conditions" these, such as we just spoke of — to the glimmer, more and more ghostly as the light failed, of the little white papers on his old green shutters. By the time he looked at his watch he had been for a quarter of an hour at this post of observation and reflexion; but by the time he walked away again he had found his answer to the idea that had grown so importunate. Since a proof of his will was wanted it was indeed very exactly in wait for him — it lurked there on the other side of the Canal. A ferryman at the little pier had from time to time accosted him; but it was a part of the play of his nervousness to turn his back on that facility. He would go over, but he walked, very quickly, round and round, crossing finally by the Rialto. The rooms, in the event, were unoccupied; the ancient padrona was there with her smile all a radiance but her recognition all a fable; the ancient rickety objects too, refined in their shabbiness, amiable in their decay, as to which, on his side, demonstrations were tenderly veracious; so that before he took his way again he had arranged to come in on the morrow.

He was amusing about it that evening at dinner — in spite of an odd first impulse, which at the palace quite melted away, to treat it merely as matter for his own satisfaction. This need, this propriety, he had taken for granted even up to the moment of suddenly perceiving, in the course of talk, that the incident would minister to innocent gaiety. Such was quite its effect, with the aid of his picture — an evocation of the quaint, of the humblest rococo, of a Venetian interior in the true old note. He made the point for his hostess that her own high chambers, though they were a thousand grand things, were n't really this; made it in fact with such success that she presently declared it his plain duty to invite her on some near day to tea. She had expressed as yet — he could feel it as felt among them all — no such clear wish to go anywhere, not even to make an effort for a parish feast, or an autumn sunset, nor to descend her staircase for Titian or

Gianbellini. It was constantly Densher's view that, as between himself and Kate, things were understood without saying, so that he could catch in her, as she but too freely could in him, innumerable signs of it, the whole soft breath of consciousness meeting and promoting consciousness. This view was so far justified to-night as that Milly's offer to him of her company was to his sense taken up by Kate in spite of her doing nothing to show it. It fell in so perfectly with what she had desired and foretold that she was—and this was what most struck him—sufficiently gratified and blinded by it not to know, from the false quality of his response, from his tone and his very look, which for an instant instinctively sought her own, that he had answered inevitably, almost shamelessly, in a mere time-gaining sense. It gave him on the spot, her failure of perception, almost a beginning of the advantage he had been planning for — that is at least if she too were not darkly dishonest. She might, he was not unaware, have made out, from some deep part of her, the bearing, in respect to herself, of the little fact he had announced; for she was after all capable of that, capable of guessing and yet of simultaneously hiding her guess. It wound him up a turn or two further, none the less, to impute to her now a weakness of vision by which he could himself feel the stronger. Whatever apprehension of his motive in shifting his abode might have brushed her with its wings, she at all events certainly did n't guess that he was giving their friend a hollow promise. That was what she had herself imposed on him; there had been in the prospect from the first a definite particular point at which hollowness, to call it by its least compromising name, would have to begin. Therefore its hour had now charmingly sounded.

Whatever in life he had recovered his old rooms for, he had not recovered them to receive Milly Theale: which made no more difference in his expression of happy readiness than if he had been — just what he was trying not to be — fully hardened and fully base. So rapid in fact was the rhythm of his inward drama that the quick vision of impossibility produced in him by his hostess's direct and unexpected appeal had the effect, slightly sinister, of positively scaring him. It gave him a measure of the intensity, the reality of his now mature motive. It prompted in him certainly no quarrel with these things, but it made them as vivid as if they already flushed with success. It was before the flush of success that his heart beat almost to dread. The dread was but the dread of the happiness to be compassed; only that was in itself a symptom. That a visit from Milly should, in this projection of necessities, strike him as of the last incongruity, quite as a hateful idea, and above all as spoiling, should one put it grossly, his game — the adoption of such a view might of course have an identity with one of those numerous ways of being a fool that seemed so to abound for him. It would remain none the less the way to which he should be in advance most reconciled. His mature motive, as to which he allowed himself no grain of illusion, had thus in an hour taken imaginative possession of the place: that precisely was how he saw it seated there, already unpacked and settled, for Milly's innocence, for Milly's beauty, no matter how short a time, to be housed with. There were things she would never recognise, never feel, never catch in the air; but this made no difference in the fact that her brushing against them would do nobody any good. The discrimination and the scruple were for *him*. So he felt all the parts of the case together, while Kate showed admirably as feeling none of them. Of course, however — when had n't it to be his last word ? — Kate was always sublime.

That came up in all connexions during the rest of these first days; came up in especial under pressure of the fact that each time our plighted pair snatched, in its passage, at the good fortune of half an hour together, they were doomed — though Densher felt it as all by *his* act — to spend a part of the rare occasion in wonder at their luck and in study of its queer character. This was the case after he might be supposed to have got, in a manner, used to it; it was the case after the girl — ready always, as we say, with the last word — had given him the benefit of her righting of every wrong appearance, a support familiar to him now in reference to other phases. It was still the case after he possibly might, with a little imagination, as she freely insisted, have made out, by the visible working of the crisis, what idea on Mrs. Lowder's part had determined it. Such as the idea was — and that it suited Kate's own book she openly professed — he had only to see how things were turning out to feel it strikingly justified. Densher's reply to all this vividness was that of course Aunt Maud's intervention had n't been occult, even for *his* vividness, from the moment she had written him, with characteristic concentration, that if he should see his way to come to Venice for a fortnight she should engage he would find it no blunder. It took Aunt Maud really to do such things in such ways; just as it took him, he was ready to confess, to do such others as he must now strike them all—did n't he?—as committed to. Mrs. Lowder's admonition had been of course a direct reference to what she had said to him at Lancaster Gate before his departure the night Milly had failed them through illness; only it had at least matched that remarkable outbreak in respect to the quantity of good nature it attributed to him. The young man's discussions of his situation—which were confined to Kate; he had none with Aunt Maud herself—suffered a little, it may be divined, by the sense that he could n't put everything off, as he privately expressed it, on other people. His ears, in solitude, were apt to burn with the reflexion that Mrs. Lowder had simply tested him, seen him as he was and made out what could be done with him. She had had but to whistle for him and he had come. If she had taken for granted his good nature she was as justified as Kate declared. This awkwardness of his conscience, both in respect to his general plasticity, the fruit of his feeling plasticity, within limits, to be a mode of life like another—certainly better than some, and particularly in respect to such confusion as might reign about what he had really come for — this inward ache was not wholly dispelled by the style, charming as that was, of Kate's poetic versions. Even the high wonder and delight of Kate could n't set him right with himself when there was something quite distinct from these things that kept him wrong.

BOOK EIGHTH

In default of being right with himself he had meanwhile, for one thing, the interest of seeing — and quite for the first time in his life — whether, on a given occasion, that might be quite so necessary to happiness as was commonly assumed and as he had up to this moment never doubted. He was engaged distinctly in an adventure — he who had never thought himself cut out for them, and it fairly helped him that he was able at moments to say to himself that he must n't fall below it. At his hotel, alone, by night, or in the course of the few late strolls he was finding time to take through dusky labyrinthine alleys and empty *campi*, overhung with mouldering palaces, where he paused in disgust at his want of ease and where the sound of a rare footstep on the enclosed pavement was like that of a retarded dancer in a banquet-hall deserted — during these interludes he entertained cold views, even to the point, at moments, on the principle that the shortest follies are the best, of thinking of immediate departure as not only possible but as indicated. He had however only to cross again the threshold of Palazzo Leporelli to see all the elements of the business compose, as painters called it, differently. It began to strike him then that departure would n't curtail, but would signally coarsen his folly, and that above all, as he had n't really "begun" anything, had only submitted, consented, but too generously indulged and condoned the beginnings of others, he had no call to treat himself with superstitious rigour. The single thing that was clear in complications was that, whatever happened, one was to behave as a gentleman — to which was added indeed the perhaps slightly less shining

183

truth that complications might sometimes have their
tedium beguiled by a study of the question of how a
gentleman would behave. This question, I hasten to
add, was not in the last resort Densher's greatest
worry. Three women were looking to him at once,
and, though such a predicament could never be, from
the point of view of facility, quite the ideal, it yet had,
thank goodness, its immediate workable law. The
law was not to be a brute — in return for amiabilities.
He had n't come all the way out from England to be a
brute. He had n't thought of what it might give him
to have a fortnight, however handicapped, with Kate
in Venice, to be a brute. He had n't treated Mrs.
Lowder as if in responding to her suggestion he had
understood her — he had n't done that either to be a
brute. And what he had prepared least of all for such
an anti-climax was the prompt and inevitable, the
achieved surrender — *as* a gentleman, oh that in-
dubitably! — to the unexpected impression made by
poor pale exquisite Milly as the mistress of a grand
old palace and the dispenser of an hospitality more
irresistible, thanks to all the conditions, than any ever
known to him.

This spectacle had for him an eloquence, an· authority, a felicity — he scarce knew by what strange
name to call it — for which he said to himself that
he had not consciously bargained. Her welcome,
her frankness, sweetness, sadness, brightness, her
disconcerting poetry, as he made shift at moments
it call it, helped as it was by the beauty of her whole
setting and by the perception at the same time, on
the observer's part, that this element gained from

her, in a manner, for effect and harmony, as much as
it gave — her whole attitude had, to his imagination,
meanings that hung about it, waiting upon her, hovering, dropping and quavering forth again, like vague
faint snatches, mere ghosts of sound, of old-fashioned
melancholy music. It was positively well for him, he
had his times of reflecting, that he could n't put it off
on Kate and Mrs. Lowder, as a gentleman so conspicuously would n't, that — well, that he had been
rather taken in by not having known in advance!
There had been now five days of it all without his
risking even to Kate alone any hint of what he ought
to have known and of what in particular therefore
had taken him in. The truth was doubtless that really,
when it came to any free handling and naming of
things, they were living together, the five of them,
in an air in which an ugly effect of "blurting out"
might easily be produced. He came back with his
friend on each occasion to the blest miracle of renewed propinquity, which had a double virtue in that
favouring air. He breathed on it as if he could
scarcely believe it, yet the time had passed, in spite
of this privilege, without his quite committing himself, for her ear, to any such comment on Milly's
high style and state as would have corresponded with
the amount of recognition it had produced in him.
Behind everything for him was his renewed remembrance, which had fairly become a habit, that he had
been the first to know her. This was what they had all
insisted on, in her absence, that day at Mrs. Lowder's;
and this was in especial what had made him feel its
influence on his immediately paying her a second

visit. Its influence had been all there, been in the high-hung, rumbling carriage with them, from the moment she took him to drive, covering them in together as if it had been a rug of softest silk. It had worked as a clear connexion with something lodged in the past, something already their own. He had more than once recalled how he had said to himself even at that moment, at some point in the drive, that he was not *there*, not just as he was in so doing it, through Kate and Kate's idea, but through Milly and Milly's own, and through himself and *his* own, unmistakeably — as well as through the little facts, whatever they had amounted to, of his time in New York.

II

THERE was at last, with everything that made for it, an occasion when he got from Kate, on what she now spoke of as his eternal refrain, an answer of which he was to measure afterwards the precipitating effect. His eternal refrain was the way he came back to the riddle of Mrs. Lowder's view of her profit — a view so hard to reconcile with the chances she gave them to meet. Impatiently, at this, the girl denied the chances, wanting to know from him, with a fine irony that smote him rather straight, whether he felt their opportunities as anything so grand. He looked at her deep in the eyes when she had sounded this note; it was the least he could let her off with for having made him visibly flush. For some reason then, with it, the sharpness dropped out of her tone, which became sweet and sincere. "'Meet,' my dear man," she expressively echoed; "does it strike you that we get, after all, so very much out of our meetings?"

"On the contrary — they're starvation diet. All I mean is — and it's all I've meant from the day I came — that we at least get more than Aunt Maud."

"Ah but you see," Kate replied, "you don't understand what Aunt Maud gets."

"Exactly so — and it's what I don't understand that keeps me so fascinated with the question. *She* gives me no light; she's prodigious. She takes everything as of a natural —!"

"She takes it as 'of a natural' that at this rate I shall be making my reflexions about you. There's every appearance for her," Kate went on, "that what she had made her mind up to as possible *is* possible; that what she had thought more likely than not to happen *is* happening. The very essence of her, as you surely by this time have made out for yourself, is that when she adopts a view she — well, to her own sense, really brings the thing about, fairly terrorises with her view any other, any opposite view, and those, not less, who represent that. I've often thought success comes to her" — Kate continued to study the phenomenon — "by the spirit in her that dares and defies her idea not to prove the right one. One has seen it so again and again, in the face of everything, *become* the right one."

Densher had for this, as he listened, a smile of the largest response. "Ah my dear child, if you can explain I of course need n't not 'understand.' I 'm condemned to that," he on his side presently explained, "only when understanding fails." He took a moment; then he pursued: "Does she think she terrorises *us*?" To which he added while, without immediate speech, Kate but looked over the place: "Does she believe anything so stiff as that you 've really changed about me?" He knew now that he was probing the girl deep — something told him so; but that was a reason the more. "Has she got it into her head that you dislike me?"

To this, of a sudden, Kate's answer was strong. "You could yourself easily put it there!"

He wondered. "By telling her so?"

188

BOOK EIGHTH

"No," said Kate as with amusement at his simplicity; "I don't ask that of you."

"Oh my dear," Densher laughed, "when you ask, you know, so little —!"

There was a full irony in this, on his own part, that he saw her resist the impulse to take up. "I'm perfectly justified in what I've asked," she quietly returned. "It's doing beautifully for you." Their eyes again intimately met, and the effect was to make her proceed. "You're not a bit unhappy."

"Oh ain't I?" he brought out very roundly.

"It does n't practically show — which is enough for Aunt Maud. You're wonderful, you're beautiful," Kate said; "and if you really want to know whether I believe you're doing it you may take from me perfectly that I see it coming." With which, by a quick transition, as if she had settled the case, she asked him the hour.

"Oh only twelve-ten" — he had looked at his watch. "We've taken but thirteen minutes; we've time yet."

"Then we must walk. We must go toward them."

Densher, from where they had been standing, measured the long reach of the Square. "They're still in their shop. They're safe for half an hour."

"That shows then, that shows!" said Kate.

This colloquy had taken place in the middle of Piazza San Marco, always, as a great social saloon, a smooth-floored, blue-roofed chamber of amenity, favourable to talk; or rather, to be exact, not in the middle, but at the point where our pair had paused by a common impulse after leaving the great mosque-like church. It rose now, domed and pinnacled, but a little way behind them, and they had in front the vast empty space, enclosed by its arcades, to which at that hour movement and traffic were mostly confined. Venice was at breakfast, the Venice of the visitor and the possible acquaintance, and, except for the parties of importunate pigeons picking up the crumbs of perpetual feasts, their prospect was clear and they could see their companions had n't yet been, and were n't for a while longer likely to be, disgorged by the lace-shop, in one of the *loggie*, where, shortly before, they had left them for a look-in — the expression was artfully Densher's — at Saint Mark's. Their morning had happened to take such a turn as brought this chance to the surface; yet his allusion, just made to Kate, had n't been an overstatement of their general opportunity. The worst that could be said of their general opportunity was that it was essentially in presence — in presence of every one; every one consisting at this juncture, in a peopled world, of Susan Shepherd, Aunt Maud and Milly. But the proof how, even in presence, the opportunity could become special was furnished precisely by this view of the compatibility of their comfort with a certain amount of lingering. The others had assented to their not waiting in the shop; it was of course the least the others could do. What had really helped them this morning was the fact that, on his turning up, as he always called it, at the palace, Milly had not, as before, been able to present herself. Custom and use had hitherto seemed fairly established; on his coming round, day after day — eight days had

been now so conveniently marked — their friends,
Milly's and his, conveniently dispersed and left him
to sit with her till luncheon. Such was the perfect
operation of the scheme on which he had been, as
he phrased it to himself, had out; so that certainly
there was that amount of justification for Kate's
vision of success. He *had*, for Mrs. Lowder — he
could n't help it while sitting there — the air, which
was the thing to be desired, of no absorption in Kate
sufficiently deep to be alarming. He had failed their
young hostess each morning as little as she had failed
him; it was only to-day that she had n't been well
enough to see him.

That had made a mark, all round; the mark was
in the way in which, gathered in the room of state,
with the place, from the right time, all bright and
cool and beflowered, as always, to receive her descent,
they — the rest of them — simply looked at each
other. It was lurid — lurid, in all probability, for
each of them privately — that they had uttered no
common regrets. It was strange for our young man
above all that, if the poor girl was indisposed to *that*
degree, the hush of gravity, of apprehension, of significance of some sort, should be the most the case —
that of the guests — could permit itself. The hush,
for that matter, continued after the party of four had
gone down to the gondola and taken their places in it.
Milly had sent them word that she hoped they would
go out and enjoy themselves, and this indeed had produced a second remarkable look, a look as of their
knowing, one quite as well as the other, what such
a message meant as provision for the alternative be-

guilement of Densher. She wished not to have spoiled his morning, and he had therefore, in civility, to take it as pleasantly patched up. Mrs. Stringham had helped the affair out, Mrs. Stringham who, when it came to that, knew their friend better than any of them. She knew her so well that she knew herself as acting in exquisite compliance with conditions comparatively obscure, approximately awful to them, by not thinking it necessary to stay at home. She had corrected that element of the perfunctory which was the slight fault, for all of them, of the occasion; she had invented a preference for Mrs. Lowder and herself; she had remembered the fond dreams of the visitation of lace that had hitherto always been brushed away by accidents, and it had come up as well for her that Kate had, the day before, spoken of the part played by fatality in her own failure of real acquaintance with the inside of Saint Mark's. Densher's sense of Susan Shepherd's conscious intervention had by this time a corner of his mind all to itself; something that had begun for them at Lancaster Gate was now a sentiment clothed in a shape; her action, ineffably discreet, had at all events a way of affecting him as for the most part subtly, even when not superficially, in his own interest. They were not, as a pair, as a "team," really united; there were too many persons, at least three, and too many things, between them; but meanwhile something was preparing that would draw them closer. He scarce knew what: probably nothing but his finding, at some hour when it would be a service to do so, that she had all the while understood him. He even had a presentiment of a juncture at which the understanding of every one else would fail and this deep little person's alone survive.

Such was to-day, in its freshness, the moral air, as we may say, that hung about our young friends; these had been the small accidents and quiet forces to which they owed the advantage we have seen them in some sort enjoying. It seemed in fact fairly to deepen for them as they stayed their course again; the splendid Square, which had so notoriously, in all the years, witnessed more of the joy of life than any equal area in Europe, furnished them, in their remoteness from earshot, with solitude and security. It was as if, being in possession, they could say what they liked; and it was also as if, in consequence of that, each had an apprehension of what the other wanted to say. It was most of all for them, moreover, as if this very quantity, seated on their lips in the bright historic air, where the only sign for their ears was the flutter of the doves, begot in the heart of each a fear. There might have been a betrayal of that in the way Densher broke the silence resting on her last words. "What did you mean just now that I can do to make Mrs. Lowder believe? For myself, stupidly, if you will, I don't see, from the moment I can't lie to her, what else there *is* but lying."

Well, she could tell him. "You can say something both handsome and sincere to her about Milly — whom you honestly like so much. That would n't be lying; and, coming from you, it would have an effect. You don't, you know, say much about her."

And Kate put before him the fruit of observation. "You don't, you know, speak of her at all."

"And has Aunt Maud," Densher asked, "told you so?" Then as the girl, for answer, only seemed to bethink herself, "You must have extraordinary conversations!" he exclaimed.

Yes, she had bethought herself. "We have extraordinary conversations."

His look, while their eyes met, marked him as disposed to hear more about them; but there was something in her own, apparently, that defeated the opportunity. He questioned her in a moment on a different matter, which had been in his mind a week, yet in respect to which he had had no chance so good as this. "Do you happen to know then, as such wonderful things pass between you, what she makes of the incident, the other day, of Lord Mark's so very superficial visit? — his having spent here, as I gather, but the two or three hours necessary for seeing our friend and yet taken no time at all, since he went off by the same night's train, for seeing any one else. What can she make of his not having waited to see *you*, or to see herself — with all he owes her?"

"Oh of course," said Kate, "she understands. He came to make Milly his offer of marriage — he came for nothing but that. As Milly wholly declined it his business was for the time at an end. He could n't quite on the spot turn round to make up to *us*."

Kate had looked surprised that, as a matter of taste on such an adventurer's part, Densher should n't see it. But Densher was lost in another thought. "Do you mean that when, turning up myself, I found him

194

leaving her, that was what had been taking place between them?"

"Did n't you make it out, my dear?" Kate enquired.

"What sort of a blundering weathercock then *is*
he?" the young man went on in his wonder.

"Oh don't make too little of him!" Kate smiled.
"Do you pretend that Milly did n't tell you?"

"How great an ass he had made of himself?"

Kate continued to smile. "You *are* in love with
her, you know."

He gave her another long look. "Why, since she
has refused him, should my opinion of Lord Mark
show it? I'm not obliged, however, to think well of
him for such treatment of the other persons I've
mentioned, and I feel I don't understand from you
why Mrs. Lowder should."

"She does n't — but she does n't care," Kate explained. "You know perfectly the terms on which
lots of London people live together even when they
're supposed to live very well. He's not committed
to us — he was having his try. May n't an unsatis-
fied man," she asked, "always have his try?"

"And come back afterwards, with confidence in
a welcome, to the victim of his inconstancy?"

Kate consented, as for argument, to be thought of
as a victim. "Oh but he has *had* his try at *me*. So
it's all right."

"Through your also having, you mean, refused
him?"

She balanced an instant during which Densher
might have just wondered if pure historic truth were

195

to suffer a slight strain. But she dropped on the right side. "I have n't let it come to that. I 've been too discouraging. Aunt Maud," she went on — now as lucid as ever — "considers, no doubt, that she has a pledge from him in respect to me; a pledge that would have been broken if Milly had accepted him. As the case stands that makes no difference."

Densher laughed out. "It is n't *his* merit that he has failed."

"It 's still his merit, my dear, that he 's Lord Mark. He 's just what he was, and what he knew he was. It 's not for me either to reflect on him after I 've so treated him."

"Oh," said Densher impatiently, "you 've treated him beautifully."

"I 'm glad," she smiled, "that you can still be jealous." But before he could take it up she had more to say. "I don't see why it need puzzle you that Milly's so marked line gratifies Aunt Maud more than anything else can displease her. What does she see but that Milly herself recognises her situation with you as too precious to be spoiled? Such a recognition as that can't but seem to her to involve in some degree your own recognition. Out of which she therefore gets it that the more you have for Milly the less you have for me."

There were moments again — we know that from the first they had been numerous — when he felt with a strange mixed passion the mastery of her mere way of putting things. There was something in it that bent him at once to conviction and to reaction. And this effect, however it be named, now broke into his tone. "Oh if she began to know what I have for you —!"

It was n't ambiguous, but Kate stood up to it. "Luckily for us we may really consider she does n't. So successful have we been."

"Well," he presently said, "I take from you what you give me, and I suppose that, to be consistent — to stand on my feet where I do stand at all — I ought to thank you. Only, you know, what you give me seems to me, more than anything else, the larger and larger size of my job. It seems to me more than anything else what you expect of me. It never seems to me somehow what I may expect of *you*. There's so much you *don't* give me."

She appeared to wonder. "And pray what is it I don't — ?"

"I give you proof," said Densher. "You give me none."

"What then do you call proof?" she after a moment ventured to ask.

"Your doing something for me."

She considered with surprise. "Am I not doing *this* for you? Do you call this nothing?"

"Nothing at all."

"Ah I risk, my dear, everything for it."

They had strolled slowly further, but he was brought up short. "I thought you exactly contend that, with your aunt so bamboozled, you risk nothing!"

It was the first time since the launching of her wonderful idea that he had seen her at a loss. He judged the next instant moreover that she did n't like it —

either the being so or the being seen, for she soon spoke with an impatience that showed her as wounded; an appearance that produced in himself, he no less quickly felt, a sharp pang of indulgence. "What then do you wish me to risk?"

The appeal from danger touched him, but all to make him, as he would have said, worse. "What I wish is to be loved. How can I feel at this rate that I *am?*" Oh she understood him, for all she might so bravely disguise it, and that made him feel straighter than if she had n't. Deep, always, was his sense of life with her — deep as it had been from the moment of those signs of life that in the dusky London of two winters ago they had originally exchanged. He had never taken her for unguarded, ignorant, weak; and if he put to her a claim for some intenser faith between them this was because he believed it could reach her and she could meet it. "I can go on perhaps," he said, "with help. But I can't go on without."

She looked away from him now, and it showed him how she understood. "We ought to be there — I mean when they come out."

"They *won't* come out — not yet. And I don't care if they do." To which he straightway added, as if to deal with the charge of selfishness that his words, sounding for himself, struck him as enabling her to make: "Why not have done with it all and face the music as we are?" It broke from him in perfect sincerity. "Good God, if you'd only *take* me!"

It brought her eyes round to him again, and he

198

could see how, after all, somewhere deep within, she felt his rebellion more sweet than bitter. Its effect on her spirit and her sense was visibly to hold her an instant. "We've gone too far," she none the less pulled herself together to reply. "Do you want to kill her?"

He had an hesitation that was n't all candid. "Kill, you mean, Aunt Maud?"

"You know whom I mean. We've told too many lies."

Oh at this his head went up. "I, my dear, have told none!"

He had brought it out with a sharpness that did him good, but he had naturally, none the less, to take the look it made her give him. "Thank you very much."

Her expression, however, failed to check the words that had already risen to his lips. "Rather than lay myself open to the least appearance of it I'll go this very night."

"Then go," said Kate Croy.

He knew after a little, while they walked on again together, that what was in the air for him, and disconcertingly, was not the violence, but much rather the cold quietness, of the way this had come from her. They walked on together, and it was for a minute as if their difference had become of a sudden, in all truth, a split — as if the basis of his departure had been settled. Then, incoherently and still more suddenly, recklessly moreover, since they now might easily, from under the arcades, be observed, he passed his hand into her arm with a force that produced for them another pause. "I'll tell any lie you want, any your idea requires, if you'll only come to me."

"Come to you?"

"Come to me."

"How? Where?"

She spoke low, but there was somehow, for his uncertainty, a wonder in her being so equal to him. "To my rooms, which are perfectly possible, and in taking which, the other day, I had you, as you must have felt, in view. We can arrange it — with two grains of courage. People in our case always arrange it." She listened as for the good information, and there was support for him — since it was a question of his going step by step — in the way she took no refuge in showing herself shocked. He had in truth not expected of her that particular vulgarity, but the absence of it only added the thrill of a deeper reason to his sense of possibilities. For the knowledge of what she was he had absolutely to *see* her now, incapable of refuge, stand there for him in all the light of the day and of his admirable merciless meaning. Her mere listening in fact made him even understand himself as he hadn't yet done. Idea for idea, his own was thus already, and in the germ, beautiful. "There's nothing for me possible but to feel that I'm not a fool. It's all I have to say, but you must know what it means. *With* you I can do it — I'll go as far as you demand or as you will yourself. Without you — I'll be hanged! And I must be sure."

She listened so well that she was really listening after he had ceased to speak. He had kept his grasp of her, drawing her close, and though they had again,

for the time, stopped walking, his talk — for others
at a distance — might have been, in the matchless
place, that of any impressed tourist to any slightly
more detached companion. On possessing himself
of her arm he had made her turn, so that they faced
afresh to Saint Mark's, over the great presence of
which his eyes moved while she twiddled her parasol.
She now, however, made a motion that confronted them
finally with the opposite end. Then only she spoke
— "Please take your hand out of my arm." He understood at once: she had made out in the shade of
the gallery the issue of the others from their place of
purchase. So they went to them side by side, and it
was all right. The others had seen them as well and
waited for them, complacent enough, under one
of the arches. They themselves too — he argued
that Kate would argue — looked perfectly ready,
decently patient, properly accommodating. They
themselves suggested nothing worse — always by
Kate's system — than a pair of the children of a su-
percivilised age making the best of an awkwardness.
They did n't nevertheless hurry — that would overdo
it; so he had time to feel, as it were, what he felt. He
felt, ever so distinctly — it was with this he faced
Mrs. Lowder — that he was already in a sense possessed of what he wanted. There was more to come
— everything; he had by no means, with his companion, had it all out. Yet what he was possessed of
was real — the fact that she had n't thrown over his
lucidity the horrid shadow of cheap reprobation. Of
this he had had so sore a fear that its being dispelled
was in itself of the nature of bliss. The danger

had dropped — it was behind him there in the great sunny space. So far she was good for what he wanted.

III

SHE was good enough, as it proved, for him to put
to her that evening, and with further ground for it,
the next sharpest question that had been on his lips
in the morning — which his other preoccupation had
then, to his consciousness, crowded out. His opportunity was again made, as befell, by his learning from
Mrs. Stringham, on arriving, as usual, with the close
of day, at the palace, that Milly must fail them again
at dinner, but would to all appearance be able to come
down later. He had found Susan Shepherd alone in
the great saloon, where even more candles than their
friend's large common allowance — she grew daily
more splendid; they were all struck with it and chaffed
her about it — lighted up the pervasive mystery of
Style. He had thus five minutes with the good lady
before Mrs. Lowder and Kate appeared — minutes
illumined indeed to a longer reach than by the number of Milly's candles.

"*May* she come down — ought she if she isn't
really up to it?"

He had asked that in the wonderment always
stirred in him by glimpses — rare as were these —
of the inner truth about the girl. There was of course
a question of health — it was in the air, it was in the
ground he trod, in the food he tasted, in the sounds
he heard, it was everywhere. But it was everywhere
with the effect of a request to him — to his very deli-

cacy, to the common discretion of others as well as
his own — that no allusion to it should be made.
There had practically been none, that morning,
on her explained non-appearance — the absence of
it, as we know, quite monstrous and awkward; and
this passage with Mrs. Stringham offered him his first
licence to open his eyes. He had gladly enough held
them closed; all the more that his doing so performed
for his own spirit a useful function. If he positively
wanted not to be brought up with his nose against
Milly's facts, what better proof could he have that his
conduct was marked by straightness? It was perhaps
pathetic for her, and for himself was perhaps
even ridiculous; but he had n't even the amount of
curiosity that he would have had about an ordinary
friend. He might have shaken himself at moments
to try, for a sort of dry decency, to have it; but that
too, it appeared, would n't come. In what therefore
was the duplicity? He was at least sure about his
feelings — it being so established that he had none
at all. They were all for Kate, without a feather's
weight to spare. He was acting for Kate — not, by
the deviation of an inch, for her friend. He was accordingly not interested, for had he been interested
he would have cared, and had he cared he would have
wanted to know. Had he wanted to know he would n't
have been purely passive, and it was his pure passivity that had to represent his dignity and his honour.
His dignity and his honour, at the same time, let us
add, fortunately fell short to-night of spoiling his little
talk with Susan Shepherd. One glimpse — it was as
if she had wished to give him that; and it was as if,

for himself, on current terms, he could oblige her by accepting it. She not only permitted, she fairly invited him to open his eyes. "I'm so glad you're here." It was no answer to his question, but it had for the moment to serve. And the rest was fully to come.

He smiled at her and presently found himself, as a kind of consequence of communion with her, talking her own language. "It's a very wonderful experience."

"Well" — and her raised face shone up at him — "that's all I want you to feel about it. If I were n't afraid," she added, "there are things I should like to say to you."

"And what are you afraid of, please?" he encouragingly asked.

"Of other things that I may possibly spoil. Besides, I don't, you know, seem to have the chance. You're always, you know, *with* her."

He was strangely supported, it struck him, in his fixed smile; which was the more fixed as he felt in these last words an exact description of his course. It was an odd thing to have come to, but he *was* always with her. "Ah," he none the less smiled, "I'm not with her now."

"No — and I'm so glad, since I get this from it. She's ever so much better."

"Better? Then she *has* been worse?"

Mrs. Stringham waited. "She has been marvellous — that's what she has been. She *is* marvellous. But she's really better."

"Oh then if she's really better —!" But he

205

checked himself, wanting only to be easy about it and above all not to appear engaged to the point of mystification. "We shall miss her the more at dinner."

Susan Shepherd, however, was all there for him. "She's keeping herself. You'll see. You'll not really need to miss anything. There's to be a little party."

"Ah I do see — by this aggravated grandeur."

"Well, it *is* lovely, is n't it? I want the whole thing. She's lodged for the first time as she ought, from her type, to be; and doing it — I mean bringing out all the glory of the place — makes her really happy. It's a Veronese picture, as near as can be — with me as the inevitable dwarf, the small blackamoor, put into a corner of the foreground for effect. If I only had a hawk or a hound or something of that sort I should do the scene more honour. The old housekeeper, the woman in charge here, has a big red cockatoo that I might borrow and perch on my thumb for the evening." These explanations and sundry others Mrs. Stringham gave, though not all with the result of making him feel that the picture closed him in. What part was there for *him*, with his attitude that lacked the highest style, in a composition in which everything else would have it? "They won't, however, be at dinner, the few people she expects — they come round afterwards from their respective hotels; and Sir Luke Strett and his niece, the principal ones, will have arrived from London but an hour or two ago. It's for *him* she has wanted to do something — to let it begin at once. We shall see more of him, because she likes him; and I'm so glad — she'll be glad too — that *you're* to see him." The good lady, in connexion with it, was urgent, was almost unnaturally bright. "So I greatly hope —!" But her hope fairly lost itself in the wide light of her cheer.

He considered a little this appearance, while she let him, he thought, into still more knowledge than she uttered. "What is it you hope?"

"Well, that you'll stay on."

"Do you mean after dinner?" She meant, he seemed to feel, so much that he could scarce tell where it ended or began.

"Oh that, of course. Why we're to have music — beautiful instruments and songs; and not Tasso declaimed as in the guide-books either. She has arranged it — or at least I have. That is Eugenio has. Besides, you're in the picture."

"Oh — I!" said Densher almost with the gravity of a real protest.

"You'll be the grand young man who surpasses the others and holds up his head and the wine-cup. What we hope," Mrs. Stringham pursued, "is that you'll be faithful to us — that you've not come for a mere foolish few days."

Densher's more private and particular shabby realities turned, without comfort, he was conscious, at this touch, in the artificial repose he had in his anxiety about them but half-managed to induce. The way smooth ladies, travelling for their pleasure and housed in Veronese pictures, talked to plain embarrassed working-men, engaged in an unprecedented sacrifice of time and of the opportunity for modest acquisition! The things they took for granted and the general misery of explaining! He could n't tell them how he had tried to work, how it was partly what he had moved into rooms for, only to find himself, almost for the first time in his life, stricken and sterile; because that would give them a false view of the source of his restlessness, if not of the degree of it. It would operate, indirectly perhaps, but infallibly, to add to that weight as of expected performance which these very moments with Mrs. Stringham caused more and more to settle on his heart. He had incurred it, the expectation of performance; the thing was done, and there was no use talking; again, again the cold breath of it was in the air. So there he was. And at best he floundered. "I'm afraid you won't understand when I say I've very tiresome things to consider. Botherations, necessities at home. The pinch, the pressure in London."

But she understood in perfection; she rose to the pinch and the pressure and showed how they had been her own very element. "Oh the daily task and the daily wage, the golden guerdon or reward? No one knows better than I how they haunt one in the flight of the precious deceiving days. Are n't they just what I myself have given up? I've given up all to follow *her*. I wish you could feel as I do. And can't you," she asked, "write about Venice?"

He very nearly wished, for the minute, that he could feel as she did; and he smiled for her kindly. "Do *you* write about Venice?"

"No; but I would — oh would n't I? — if I had n't

so completely given up. She's, you know, my princess, and to one's princess —"

"One makes the whole sacrifice?"

"Precisely. There you are!"

It pressed on him with this that never had a man
been in so many places at once. "I quite understand
that she's yours. Only you see she's not mine." He
felt he could somehow, for honesty, risk that, as he
had the moral certainty she would n't repeat it and
least of all to Mrs. Lowder, who would find in it a dis-
turbing implication. This was part of what he liked
in the good lady, that she did n't repeat, and also that
she gave him a delicate sense of her shyly wishing him
to know it. That was in itself a hint of possibilities
between them, of a relation, beneficent and elastic for
him, which would n't engage him further than he
could see. Yet even as he afresh made this out he felt
how strange it all was. She wanted, Susan Shepherd
then, as appeared, the same thing Kate wanted, only
wanted it, as still further appeared, in so different a
way and from a motive so different, even though
scarce less deep. Then Mrs. Lowder wanted, by so
odd an evolution of her exuberance, exactly what
each of the others did; and he was between them all,
he was in the midst. Such perceptions made occasions — well, occasions for fairly wondering if it
might n't be best just to consent, luxuriously, to *be*
the ass the whole thing involved. Trying not to be and
yet keeping in it was of the two things the more asin-
ine. He was glad there was no male witness; it was a
circle of petticoats; he should n't have liked a man to
see him. He only had for a moment a sharp thought

of Sir Luke Strett, the great master of the knife whom
Kate in London had spoken of Milly as in commerce
with, and whose renewed intervention at such a distance, just announced to him, required some account-
ing for. He had a vision of great London surgeons —
if this one was a surgeon — as incisive all round; so
that he should perhaps after all not wholly escape the
ironic attention of his own sex. The most he might be
able to do was not to care; while he was trying not to
he could take that in. It was a train, however, that
brought up the vision of Lord Mark as well. Lord
Mark had caught him twice in the fact — the fact of
his absurd posture; and that made a second male.
But it was comparatively easy not to mind Lord Mark.

His companion had before this taken him up, and
in a tone to confirm her discretion, on the matter of
Milly's not being his princess. "Of course she's not.
You must do something first."

Densher gave it his thought. "Would n't it be
rather *she* who must?"

It had more than he intended the effect of bringing
her to a stand. "I see. No doubt, if one takes it so."
Her cheer was for the time in eclipse, and she looked
over the place, avoiding his eyes, as in the wonder of
what Milly could do. "And yet she has wanted to be
kind."

It made him on the spot feel a brute. "Of course
she has. No one could be more charming. She has
treated me as if *I* were somebody. Call her my hostess
as I've never had nor imagined a hostess, and I'm
with you altogether. Of course," he added in the right
spirit for her, "I do see that it's quite court life."

She promptly showed how this was almost all she wanted of him. "That's all I mean, if you understand it of such a court as never was: one of the courts of heaven, the court of a reigning seraph, a sort of a vice-queen of an angel. That will do perfectly."

"Oh well then I grant it. Only court life as a general thing, you know," he observed, "is n't supposed to pay."

"Yes, one has read; but this is beyond any book. That's just the beauty here; it's why she's the great and only princess. With her, at her court," said Mrs. Stringham, "it does pay." Then as if she had quite settled it for him: "You'll see for yourself."

He waited a moment, but said nothing to discourage her. "I think you were right just now. One must do something first."

"Well, you've done something."

"No — I don't see that. I can do more."

Oh well, she seemed to say, if he would have it so! "You can do everything, you know."

"Everything" was rather too much for him to take up gravely, and he modestly let it alone, speaking the next moment, to avert fatuity, of a different but a related matter. "Why has she sent for Sir Luke Strett if, as you tell me, she's so much better?"

"She has n't sent. He has come of himself," Mrs. Stringham explained. "He has wanted to come."

"Is n't that rather worse then — if it means he may n't be easy?"

"He was coming, from the first, for his holiday. She has known that these several weeks." After which Mrs. Stringham added: "You can *make* him easy."

"*I* can?" he candidly wondered. It was truly the circle of petticoats. "What have I to do with it for a man like that?"

"How do you know," said his friend, "what he's like? He's not like any one you've ever seen. He's a great beneficent being."

"Ah then he can do without me. I've no call, as an outsider, to meddle."

"Tell him, all the same," Mrs. Stringham urged, "what you think."

"What I think of Miss Theale?" Densher stared. It was, as they said, a large order. But he found the right note. "It's none of his business."

It did seem a moment for Mrs. Stringham too the right note. She fixed him at least with an expression still bright, but searching, that showed almost to excess what she saw in it; though what this might be he was not to make out till afterwards. "Say *that* to him then. Anything will do for him as a means of getting at you."

"And why should he get at me?"

"Give him a chance to. Let him talk to you. Then you'll see."

All of which, on Mrs. Stringham's part, sharpened his sense of immersion in an element rather more strangely than agreeably warm — a sense that was moreover, during the next two or three hours, to be fed to satiety by several other impressions. Milly came down after dinner, half a dozen friends — objects of interest mainly, it appeared, to the ladies of

Lancaster Gate — having by that time arrived; and
with this call on her attention, the further call of her
musicians ushered by Eugenio, but personally and
separately welcomed, and the supreme opportunity
offered in the arrival of the great doctor, who came
last of all, he felt her diffuse in wide warm waves the
spell of a general, a beatific mildness. There was a
deeper depth of it, doubtless, for some than for others ;
what he in particular knew of it was that he seemed
to stand in it up to his neck. He moved about in it
and it made no plash; he floated, he noiselessly swam
in it, and they were all together, for that matter, like
fishes in a crystal pool. The effect of the place, the
beauty of the scene, had probably much to do with it;
the golden grace of the high rooms, chambers of art in
themselves, took care, as an influence, of the general
manner, and made people bland without making
them solemn. They were only people, as Mrs. Stringham had said, staying for the week or two at the inns,
people who during the day had fingered their Baedekers, gaped at their frescoes and differed, over frac-
tions of francs, with their gondoliers. But Milly, let
loose among them in a wonderful white dress, brought
them somehow into relation with something that made
them more finely genial; so that if the Veronese picture of which he had talked with Mrs. Stringham was
not quite constituted, the comparative prose of the
previous hours, the traces of insensibility qualified by
"beating down," were at last almost nobly disowned.
There was perhaps something for him in the accident
of his seeing her for the first time in white, but she
had n't yet had occasion — circulating with a clear-

ness intensified — to strike him as so happily pervasive. She was different, younger, fairer, with the
colour of her braided hair more than ever a not altogether lucky challenge to attention; yet he was loth
wholly to explain it by her having quitted this once,
for some obscure yet doubtless charming reason, her
almost monastic, her hitherto inveterate black. Much
as the change did for the value of her presence, she
had never yet, when all was said, made it for *him*;
and he was not to fail of the further amusement of
judging her determined in the matter by Sir Luke
Strett's visit. If he could in this connexion have felt
jealous of Sir Luke Strett, whose strong face and type,
less assimilated by the scene perhaps than any others,
he was anon to study from the other side of the saloon, that would doubtless have been most amusing
of all. But he could n't be invidious, even to profit by
so high a tide; he felt himself too much "in" it, as he
might have said: a moment's reflexion put him more
in than any one. The way Milly neglected him for
other cares while Kate and Mrs. Lowder, without so
much as the attenuation of a joke, introduced him to
English ladies — that was itself a proof; for nothing
really of so close a communion had up to this time
passed between them as the single bright look and the
three gay words (all ostensibly of the last lightness)
with which her confessed consciousness brushed by
him.

She was acquitting herself to-night as hostess, he
could see, under some supreme idea, an inspiration
which was half her nerves and half an inevitable harmony; but what he especially recognised was the

character that had already several times broken out
in her and that she so oddly appeared able, by choice
or by instinctive affinity, to keep down or to display.
She was the American girl as he had originally found
her — found her at certain moments, it was true, in
New York, more than at certain others; she was the
American girl as, still more than then, he had seen
her on the day of her meeting him in London and in
Kate's company. It affected him as a large though
queer social resource in her — such as a man, for instance, to his diminution, would never in the world
be able to command; and he would n't have known
whether to see it in an extension or a contraction of
"personality," taking it as he did most directly for a
confounding extension of surface. Clearly too it was
the right thing this evening all round: that came out
for him in a word from Kate as she approached him to
wreak on him a second introduction. He had under
cover of the music melted away from the lady toward
whom she had first pushed him; and there was something in her to affect him as telling evasively a tale of
their talk in the Piazza. To what did she want to
coerce him as a form of penalty for what he had done
to her there? It was thus in contact uppermost for
him that he had done something; not only caused her
perfect intelligence to act in his interest, but left her
unable to get away, by any mere private effort, from
his inattackable logic. With him thus in presence,
and near him — and it had been as unmistakeable
through dinner — there was no getting away for her
at all, there was less of it than ever: so she could only
either deal with the question straight, either frankly

yield or ineffectually struggle or insincerely argue, or else merely express herself by following up the advantage she did possess. It was part of that advantage for the hour — a brief fallacious makeweight to his pressure — that there were plenty of things left in which he must feel her will. They only told him, these indications, how much she was, in such close quarters, feeling his; and it was enough for him again that her very aspect, as great a variation in its way as Milly's own, gave him back the sense of his action. It had never yet in life been granted him to know, almost materially to taste, as he could do in these minutes, the state of what was vulgarly called conquest. He had lived long enough to have been on occasion "liked," but it had never begun to be allowed him to be liked to any such tune in any such quarter. It was a liking greater than Milly's — or it would be : he felt it in him to answer for that. So at all events he read the case while he noted that Kate was somehow — for Kate — wanting in lustre. As a striking young presence she was practically superseded; of the mildness that Milly diffused she had assimilated all her share; she might fairly have been dressed to-night in the little black frock, superficially indistinguishable, that Milly had laid aside. This represented, he perceived, the opposite pole from such an effect as that of her wonderful entrance, under her aunt's eyes — he had never forgotten it — the day of their younger friend's failure at Lancaster Gate. She was, in her accepted effacement — it was actually her acceptance that made the beauty and repaired the damage — under her aunt's eyes now; but whose eyes were not

effectually preoccupied? It struck him none the less
certainly that almost the first thing she said to him
showed an exquisite attempt to appear if not uncon-
vinced at least self-possessed.

"Don't you think her good enough *now?*"

Almost heedless of the danger of overt freedoms,
she eyed Milly from where they stood, noted her in
renewed talk, over her further wishes, with the members of her little orchestra, who had approached her
with demonstrations of deference enlivened by native humours — things quite in the line of old Venetian comedy. The girl's idea of music had been
happy — a real solvent of shyness, yet not drastic;
thanks to the intermissions, discretions, a general
habit of mercy to gathered barbarians, that reflected
the good manners of its interpreters, representatives
though these might be but of the order in which taste
was natural and melody rank. It was easy at all events
to answer Kate. "Ah my dear, you know how good
I think her!"

"But she's *too* nice," Kate returned with appreciation. "Everything suits her so — especially her
pearls. They go so with her old lace. I'll trouble
you really to look at them." Densher, though aware
he had seen them before, had perhaps not "really"
looked at them, and had thus not done justice to the
embodied poetry — his mind, for Milly's aspects,
kept coming back to that — which owed them part
of its style. Kate's face, as she considered them,
struck him: the long, priceless chain, wound twice
round the neck, hung, heavy and pure, down the front
of the wearer's breast — so far down that Milly's

trick, evidently unconscious, of holding and vaguely fingering and entwining a part of it, conduced presumably to convenience. "She's a dove," Kate went on, "and one somehow does n't think of doves as bejewelled. Yet they suit her down to the ground."

"Yes — down to the ground is the word." Densher saw now how they suited her, but was perhaps still more aware of something intense in his companion's feeling about them. Milly was indeed a dove; this was the figure, though it most applied to her spirit. Yet he knew in a moment that Kate was just now, for reasons hidden from him, exceptionally under the impression of that element of wealth in her which was a power, which was a great power, and which was dove-like only so far as one remembered that doves have wings and wondrous flights, have them as well as tender tints and soft sounds. It even came to him dimly that such wings could in a given case — *had*, truly, in the case with which he was concerned — spread themselves for protection. Had n't they, for that matter, lately taken an inordinate reach, and were n't Kate and Mrs. Lowder, were n't Susan Shepherd and he, was n't *he* in particular, nestling under them to a great increase of immediate ease? All this was a brighter blur in the general light, out of which he heard Kate presently going on.

"Pearls have such a magic that they suit every one."

"They would uncommonly suit you," he frankly returned.

"Oh yes, I see myself!"

As she saw herself, suddenly, he saw her — she

would have been splendid; and with it he felt more
what she was thinking of. Milly's royal ornament
had — under pressure now not wholly occult — taken
on the character of a symbol of differences, differences of which the vision was actually in Kate's face.
It might have been in her face too that, well as she
certainly would look in pearls, pearls were exactly
what Merton Densher would never be able to give
her. Was n't *that* the great difference that Milly to-
night symbolised? She unconsciously represented to
Kate, and Kate took it in at every pore, that there
was nobody with whom she had less in common than
a remarkably handsome girl married to a man unable
to make her on any such lines as that the least little
present. Of these absurdities, however, it was not
till afterwards that Densher thought. He could think
now, to any purpose, only of what Mrs. Stringham
had said to him before dinner. He could but come
back to his friend's question of a minute ago. "She 's
certainly good enough, as you call it, in the sense that
I 'm assured she 's better. Mrs. Stringham, an hour
or two since, was in great feather to me about it. She
evidently believes her better."

"Well, if they choose to call it so —!"

"And what do *you* call it — as against them?"

"I don't call it anything to any one but you. I 'm
not 'against' them!" Kate added as with just a fresh
breath of impatience for all he had to be taught.

"That 's what I 'm talking about," he said. "What
do you call it to me?"

It made her wait a little. "She is n't better. She 's
worse. But that has nothing to do with it."

"Nothing to do?" He wondered.

But she was clear. "Nothing to do with *us*. Except of course that we're doing our best for her. We're making her want to live." And Kate again watched her. "To-night she does want to live." She spoke with a kindness that had the strange property of striking him as inconsequent — so much, and doubtless so unjustly, had all her clearness been an implication of the hard. "It's wonderful. It's beautiful."

"It's beautiful indeed."

He hated somehow the helplessness of his own note; but she had given it no heed. "She's doing it for *him*" — and she nodded in the direction of Milly's medical visitor. "She wants to be for him at her best. But she can't deceive him."

Densher had been looking too; which made him say in a moment: "And do you think *you* can? I mean, if he's to be with us here, about your sentiments. If Aunt Maud's so thick with him —!"

Aunt Maud now occupied in fact a place at his side and was visibly doing her best to entertain him, though this failed to prevent such a direction of his own eyes — determined, in the way such things happen, precisely by the attention of the others — as Densher became aware of and as Kate promptly marked. "He's looking at *you*. He wants to speak to you."

"So Mrs. Stringham," the young man laughed, "advised me he would."

"Then let him. Be right with him. I don't need," Kate went on in answer to the previous question, "to deceive him. Aunt Maud, if it's necessary, will do that. I mean that, knowing nothing about me, he can see me only as she sees me. She sees me now so well. He has nothing to do with me."

"Except to reprobate you," Densher suggested.

"For not caring for *you*? Perfectly. As a brilliant young man driven by it into your relation with Milly — as all *that* I leave you to him."

"Well," said Densher sincerely enough, "I think I can thank you for leaving me to some one easier perhaps with me than yourself."

She had been looking about again meanwhile, the lady having changed her place, for the friend of Mrs. Lowder's to whom she had spoken of introducing him. "All the more reason why I should commit you then to Lady Wells."

"Oh but wait." It was not only that he distinguished Lady Wells from afar, that she inspired him with no eagerness, and that, somewhere at the back of his head, he was fairly aware of the question, in germ, of whether this was the kind of person he should be involved with when they were married. It was furthermore that the consciousness of something he had not got from Kate in the morning, and that logically much concerned him, had been made more keen by these very moments — to say nothing of the consciousness that, with their general smallness of opportunity, he must squeeze each stray instant hard. If Aunt Maud, over there with Sir Luke, noted him as a little "attentive," that might pass for a futile demonstration on the part of a gentleman who had to confess to having, not very gracefully, changed his mind. Besides, just now, he did n't care for Aunt

Maud except in so far as he was immediately to show. "How can Mrs. Lowder think me disposed of with any finality, if I'm disposed of only to a girl who's dying? If you're right about that, about the state of the case, you're wrong about Mrs. Lowder's being squared. If Milly, as you say," he lucidly pursued, "can't deceive a great surgeon, or whatever, the great surgeon won't deceive other people — not those, that is, who are closely concerned. He won't at any rate deceive Mrs. Stringham, who's Milly's greatest friend; and it will be very odd if Mrs. Stringham deceives Aunt Maud, who's her own."

Kate showed him at this the cold glow of an idea that really was worth his having kept her for. "Why will it be odd? I marvel at your seeing your way so little."

Mere curiosity even, about his companion, had now for him its quick, its slightly quaking intensities. He had compared her once, we know, to a "new book," an uncut volume of the highest, the rarest quality; and his emotion (to justify that) was again and again like the thrill of turning the page. "Well, you know how deeply I marvel at the way *you* see it!"

"It doesn't in the least follow," Kate went on, "that anything in the nature of what you call deception on Mrs. Stringham's part will be what you call odd. Why shouldn't she hide the truth?"

"From Mrs. Lowder?" Densher stared. "Why should she?"

"To please you."

"And how in the world can it please me?"

Kate turned her head away as if really at last almost tired of his density. But she looked at him again as she spoke. "Well then to please Milly." And before he could question: "Don't you feel by this time that there's nothing Susan Shepherd won't do for you?"

He had verily after an instant to take it in, so sharply it corresponded with the good lady's recent reception of him. It was queerer than anything again, the way they all came together round him. But that was an old story, and Kate's multiplied lights led him on and on. It was with a reserve, however, that he confessed this. "She's ever so kind. Only her view of the right thing may not be the same as yours."

"How can it be anything different if it's the view of serving you?"

Densher for an instant, but only for an instant, hung fire. "Oh the difficulty is that I don't, upon my honour, even yet quite make out how yours does serve me."

"It helps you — put it then," said Kate very simply — "to serve *me*. It gains you time."

"Time for what?"

"For everything!" She spoke at first, once more, with impatience; then as usual she qualified. "For anything that may happen."

Densher had a smile, but he felt it himself as strained. "You're cryptic, love!"

It made her keep her eyes on him, and he could thus see that, by one of those incalculable motions in her without which she would n't have been a quarter so interesting, they half-filled with tears from some source he had too roughly touched. "I'm taking a trouble for you I never dreamed I should take for any human creature."

Oh it went home, making him flush for it; yet he soon enough felt his reply on his lips. "Well, is n't my whole insistence to you now that I can conjure trouble away?" And he let it, his insistence, come out again; it had so constantly had, all the week, but its step or two to make. "There *need* be none whatever between us. There need be nothing but our sense of each other."

It had only the effect at first that her eyes grew dry while she took up again one of the so numerous links in her close chain. "You can tell her anything you like, anything whatever."

"Mrs. Stringham? I *have* nothing to tell her."

"You can tell her about *us.* I mean," she wonderfully pursued, "that you do still like me."

It was indeed so wonderful that it amused him. "Only not that you still like me."

She let his amusement pass. "I'm absolutely certain she would n't repeat it."

"I see. To Aunt Maud."

"You don't quite see. Neither to Aunt Maud nor to any one else." Kate then, he saw, was always seeing Milly much more, after all, than he was; and she showed it again as she went on. "*There,* accordingly, is your time."

She did at last make him think, and it was fairly as if light broke, though not quite all at once. "You must let me say I *do* see. Time for something in particular that I understand you regard as possible. Time too that, I further understand, is time for you as well."

"Time indeed for me as well." And encouraged visibly by his glow of concentration, she looked at him as through the air she had painfully made clear. Yet she was still on her guard. "Don't think, however, I'll do *all* the work for you. If you want things named you must name them."

He had quite, within the minute, been turning names over; and there was only one, which at last stared at him there dreadful, that properly fitted. "Since she's to die I'm to marry her?"

It struck him even at the moment as fine in her that she met it with no wincing nor mincing. She might for the grace of silence, for favour to their conditions, have only answered him with her eyes. But her lips bravely moved. "To marry her."

"So that when her death has taken place I shall in the natural course have money?"

It was before him enough now, and he had nothing more to ask; he had only to turn, on the spot, considerably cold with the thought that all along — to his stupidity, his timidity — it had been, it had been only, what she meant. Now that he was in possession moreover she could n't forbear, strangely enough, to pronounce the words she had n't pronounced: they broke through her controlled and colourless voice as if she should be ashamed, to the very end, to have flinched. "You'll in the natural course have money. We shall in the natural course be free."

"Oh, oh, oh!" Densher softly murmured.

"Yes, yes, yes." But she broke off. "Come to Lady Wells."

He never budged — there was too much else. "I'm
to propose it then — marriage — on the spot?"

There was no ironic sound he needed to give it; the
more simply he spoke the more he seemed ironic.
But she remained consummately proof. "Oh I can't
go into that with you, and from the moment you don't
wash your hands of me I don't think you ought to ask
me. You must act as you like and as you can."

He thought again. "I'm far — as I sufficiently
showed you this morning — from washing my hands
of you."

"Then," said Kate, "it's all right."

"All right?" His eagerness flamed. "You'll
come?"

But he had had to see in a moment that it wasn't
what she meant. "You'll have a free hand, a clear
field, a chance — well, quite ideal."

"Your descriptions" — her "ideal" was such a
touch! — "are prodigious. And what I don't make
out is how, caring for me, you can like it."

"I don't like it, but I'm a person, thank goodness,
who can do what I don't like."

It wasn't till afterwards that, going back to it, he
was to read into this speech a kind of heroic ring, a
note of character that belittled his own incapacity for
action. Yet he saw indeed even at the time the great-
ness of knowing so well what one wanted. At the time
too, moreover, he next reflected that he after all knew
what *he* did. But something else on his lips was uppermost. "What I don't make out then is how you can
even bear it."

"Well, when you know me better you'll find out

226

how much I can bear." And she went on before he could take up, as it were, her too many implications. That it was left to him to know her, spiritually, "better" after his long sacrifice to knowledge — this for instance was a truth he had n't been ready to receive so full in the face. She had mystified him enough, heaven knew, but that was rather by his own generosity than by hers. And what, with it, did she seem to suggest she might incur at his hands? In spite of these questions she was carrying him on. "All you 'll have to do will be to stay."

"And proceed to my business under your eyes?"

"Oh dear no — we shall go."

"'Go?'" he wondered. "Go when, go where?"

"In a day or two — straight home. Aunt Maud wishes it now."

It gave him all he could take in to think of. "Then what becomes of Miss Theale?"

"What I tell you. She stays on, and you stay with her."

He stared. "All alone?"

She had a smile that was apparently for his tone. "You 're old enough — with plenty of Mrs. Stringham."

Nothing might have been so odd for him now, could he have measured it, as his being able to feel, quite while he drew from her these successive cues, that he was essentially "seeing what she would say" — an instinct compatible for him therefore with that absence of a need to know her better to which she had a moment before done injustice. If it had n't been appearing to him in gleams that she would somewhere break down, he probably could n't have gone on. Still, as she was n't breaking down there was nothing for him but to continue. "Is your going Mrs. Lowder's idea?"

"Very much indeed. Of course again you see what it does for us. And I don't," she added, "refer only to our going, but to Aunt Maud's view of the general propriety of it."

"I see again, as you say," Densher said after a moment. "It makes everything fit."

"Everything."

The word, for a little, held the air, and he might have seemed the while to be looking, by no means dimly now, at all it stood for. But he had in fact been looking at something else. "You leave her here then to die?"

"Ah she believes she won't die. Not if you stay. I mean," Kate explained, "Aunt Maud believes."

"And that's all that's necessary?"

Still indeed she did n't break down. "Did n't we long ago agree that what she believes is the principal thing for us?"

He recalled it, under her eyes, but it came as from long ago. "Oh yes. I can't deny it." Then he added: "So that if I stay —"

"It won't" — she was prompt — "be our fault."

"If Mrs. Lowder still, you mean, suspects us?"

"If she still suspects us. But she won't."

Kate gave it an emphasis that might have appeared to leave him nothing more; and he might in fact well have found nothing if he had n't presently found: "But what if she does n't accept me?"

It produced in her a look of weariness that made the patience of her tone the next moment touch him. "You can but try."

"Naturally I can but try. Only, you see, one has to try a little hard to propose to a dying girl."

"She is n't for you as if she 's dying." It had determined in Kate the flash of *justesse* he could perhaps most, on consideration, have admired, since her retort touched the truth. There before him was the fact of how Milly to-night impressed him, and his companion, with her eyes in his own and pursuing his impression to the depths of them, literally now perched on the fact in triumph. She turned her head to where their friend was again in range, and it made him turn his, so that they watched a minute in concert. Milly, from the other side, happened at the moment to notice them, and she sent across toward them in response all the candour of her smile, the lustre of her pearls, the value of her life, the essence of her wealth. It brought them together again with faces made fairly grave by the reality she put into their plan. Kate herself grew a little pale for it, and they had for a time only a silence. The music, however, gay and vociferous, had broken out afresh and protected more than interrupted them. When Densher at last spoke it was under cover.

"I might stay, you know, without trying."

"Oh to stay *is* to try."

"To have for herself, you mean, the appearance of it?"

"I don't see how you can have the appearance more."

Densher waited. "You think it then possible she may *offer* marriage?"

"I can't think — if you really want to know — what she may *not* offer!"

"In the manner of princesses, who do such things?"

"In any manner you like. So be prepared."

Well, he looked as if he almost were. "It will be for me then to accept. But that's the way it must come."

Kate's silence, so far, let it pass; but she presently said: "You'll, on your honour, stay then?"

His answer made her wait, but when it came it was distinct. "Without you, you mean?"

"Without us."

"And you yourselves go at latest — ?"

"Not later than Thursday."

It made three days. "Well," he said, "I'll stay, on my honour, if you'll come to me. On *your* honour."

Again, as before, this made her momentarily rigid, with a rigour out of which, at a loss, she vaguely cast about her. Her rigour was more to him, nevertheless, than all her readiness; for her readiness was the woman herself, and this other thing a mask, a stop-gap and a "dodge." She cast about, however, as happened, and not for the instant in vain. Her eyes, turned over the room, caught at a pretext. "Lady Wells is tired of waiting: she's coming — see — to *us*."

Densher saw in fact, but there was a distance for their visitor to cross, and he still had time. "If you

decline to understand me I wholly decline to understand you. I'll do nothing."

"Nothing?" It was as if she tried for the minute
to plead.

"I'll do nothing. I'll go off before you. I'll go to-
morrow."

He was to have afterwards the sense of her having
then, as the phrase was — and for vulgar triumphs
too — seen he meant it. She looked again at Lady
Wells, who was nearer, but she quickly came back.
"And if I do understand?"

"I'll do everything."

She found anew a pretext in her approaching
friend: he was fairly playing with her pride. He had
never, he then knew, tasted, in all his relation with
her, of anything so sharp — too sharp for mere sweetness — as the vividness with which he saw himself
master in the conflict. "Well, I understand."

"On your honour?"

"On my honour."

"You'll come?"

"I'll come."

BOOK NINTH

I

IT was after they had gone that he truly felt the difference, which was most to be felt moreover in his faded old rooms. He had recovered from the first a part of his attachment to this scene of contemplation, within sight, as it was, of the Rialto bridge, on the hither side of that arch of associations and the left going up the Canal; he had seen it in a particular light, to which, more and more, his mind and his hands adjusted it; but the interest the place now wore for him had risen at a bound, becoming a force that, on the spot, completely engaged and absorbed him, and relief from which — if relief was the name — he could find only by getting away and out of reach. What had come to pass within his walls lingered there as an obsession importunate to all his senses; it lived again, as a cluster of pleasant memories, at every hour and in every object; it made everything but itself irrelevant and tasteless. It remained, in a word, a conscious watchful presence, active on its own side, for ever to be reckoned with, in face of which the effort at detachment was scarcely less futile than frivolous. Kate had come to him; it was only once — and this not from any failure of their need, but from such impossibilities, for bravery alike and for subtlety, as there was at the last no blinking; yet she had come, that once, to stay, as people called it; and what survived of her, what reminded and insisted, was something he

could n't have banished if he had wished. Luckily he
did n't wish, even though there might be for a man
almost a shade of the awful in so unqualified a consequence of his act. It had simply *worked*, his idea, the
idea he had made her accept; and all erect before him,
really covering the ground as far as he could see, was
the fact of the gained success that this represented.
It was, otherwise, but the fact of the idea as directly
applied, as converted from a luminous conception
into an historic truth. He had known it before but as
desired and urged, as convincingly insisted on for the
help it would render; so that at present, *with* the help
rendered, it seemed to acknowledge its office and to
set up, for memory and faith, an insistence of its own.
He had in fine judged his friend's pledge in advance
as an inestimable value, and what he must now know
his case for was that of a possession of the value to the
full. Was n't it perhaps even rather the value that
possessed *him*, kept him thinking of it and waiting on
it, turning round and round it and making sure of it
again from this side and that?

It played for him — certainly in this prime afterglow — the part of a treasure kept at home in safety
and sanctity, something he was sure of finding in its
place when, with each return, he worked his heavy
old key in the lock. The door had but to open for
him to be with it again and for it to be all there; so
intensely there that, as we say, no other act was possible to him than the renewed act, almost the hallu-
cination, of intimacy. Wherever he looked or sat or
stood, to whatever aspect he gave for the instant the
advantage, it was in view as nothing of the moment,

nothing begotten of time or of chance could be, or ever would; it was in view as, when the curtain has risen, the play on the stage is in view, night after night, for the fiddlers. He remained thus, in his own theatre, in his single person, perpetual orchestra to the ordered drama, the confirmed "run"; playing low and slow, moreover, in the regular way, for the situations of most importance. No other visitor was to come to him; he met, he bumped occasionally, in the Piazza or in his walks, against claimants to acquaintance, remembered or forgotten, at present mostly effusive, sometimes even inquisitive; but he gave no address and encouraged no approach; he could n't for his life, he felt, have opened his door to a third person. Such a person would have interrupted him, would have profaned his secret or perhaps have guessed it; would at any rate have broken the spell of what he conceived himself — in the absence of anything "to show" — to be inwardly doing. He was giving himself up — that was quite enough — to the general feeling of his renewed engagement to fidelity. The force of the engagement, the quantity of the article to be supplied, the special solidity of the contract, the way, above all, as a service for which the price named by him had been magnificently paid, his equivalent office was to take effect — such items might well fill his consciousness when there was nothing from outside to interfere. Never was a consciousness more rounded and fastened down over what filled it; which is precisely what we have spoken of as, in its degree, the oppression of success, the somewhat chilled state — tending to the solitary — of supreme recognition.

If it was slightly awful to feel so justified, this was by the loss of the warmth of the element of mystery. The lucid reigned instead of it, and it was into the lucid that he sat and stared. He shook himself out of it a dozen times a day, tried to break by his own act his constant still communion. It was n't still communion she had meant to bequeath him; it was the very different business of that kind of fidelity of which the other name was careful action.

Nothing, he perfectly knew, was less like careful action than the immersion he enjoyed at home. The actual grand queerness was that to be faithful to Kate he had positively to take his eyes, his arms, his lips straight off her — he had to let her alone. He had to remember it was time to go to the palace — which in truth was a mercy, since the check was not less effectual than imperative. What it came to, fortunately, as yet, was that when he closed the door behind him for an absence he always shut her in. Shut her out — it came to that rather, when once he had got a little away; and before he reached the palace, much more after hearing at his heels the bang of the greater *portone*, he felt free enough not to know his position as oppressively false. As Kate was *all* in his poor rooms, and not a ghost of her left for the grander, it was only on reflexion that the falseness came out; so long as he left it to the mercy of beneficent chance it offered him no face and made of him no claim that he could n't meet without aggravation of his inward sense. This aggravation had been his original horror; yet what — in Milly's presence, each day — was horror doing with him but virtually letting him off?

BOOK NINTH

He should n't perhaps get off to the end; there was time enough still for the possibility of shame to pounce. Still, however, he did constantly a little more what he liked best, and that kept him for the time more safe. What he liked best was, in any case, to know *why* things were as he felt them; and he knew it pretty well, in this case, ten days after the retreat of his other friends. He then fairly perceived that — even putting their purity of motive at its highest — it was neither Kate nor he who made his strange relation to Milly, who made her own, so far as it might be, innocent; it was neither of them who practically purged it — if practically purged it was. Milly herself did everything — so far at least as he was concerned — Milly herself, and Milly's house, and Milly's hospitality, and Milly's manner, and Milly's character, and, perhaps still more than anything else, Milly's imagination, Mrs. Stringham and Sir Luke indeed a little aiding: whereby he knew the blessing of a fair pretext to ask himself what more he had to do. Something incalculable wrought for them — for him and Kate; something outside, beyond, above themselves, and doubtless ever so much better than they: which was n't a reason, however — its being so much better — for them not to profit by it. Not to profit by it, so far as profit could be reckoned, would have been to go directly against it; and the spirit of generosity at present engendered in Densher could have felt no greater pang than by his having to go directly against Milly.

To go *with* her was the thing, so far as she could herself go; which, from the moment her tenure of

her loved palace stretched on, was possible but by his
remaining near her. This remaining was of course
on the face of it the most "marked" of demonstrations — which was exactly why Kate had required it;
it was so marked that on the very evening of the day
it had taken effect Milly herself had n't been able not
to reach out to him, with an exquisite awkwardness,
for some account of it. It was as if she had wanted
from him some name that, now they were to be almost alone together, they could, for their further ease,
know it and call it by — it being, after all, almost
rudimentary that his presence, of which the absence
of the others made quite a different thing, could n't
but have for himself some definite basis. She only
wondered about the basis it would have for himself,
and how he would describe it; that would quite do
for her — it even would have done for her, he could
see, had he produced some reason merely trivial, had
he said he was waiting for money or clothes, for letters or for orders from Fleet Street, without which,
as she might have heard, newspaper men never took
a step. He had n't in the event quite sunk to that;
but he had none the less had there with her, that
night, on Mrs. Stringham's leaving them alone —
Mrs. Stringham proved really prodigious — his acquaintance with a shade of awkwardness darker than
any Milly could know. He had supposed himself
beforehand, on the question of what he was doing or
pretending, in possession of some tone that would
serve; but there were three minutes of his feeling incapable of promptness quite in the same degree in which
a gentleman whose pocket has been picked feels in-

capable of purchase. It even did n't help him, oddly, that he was sure Kate would in some way have spoken for him — or rather not so much in some way as in one very particular way. He had n't asked her, at the last, what she might, in the connexion, have said; nothing would have induced him to put such a question after she had been to see him: his lips were so sealed by that passage, his spirit in fact so hushed, in respect to any charge upon her freedom. There was something he could only therefore read back into the probabilities, and when he left the palace an hour afterwards it was with a sense of having breathed there, in the very air, the truth he had been guessing.

Just this perception it was, however, that had made him for the time ugly to himself in his awkwardness. It was horrible, with this creature, to *be* awkward; it was odious to be seeking excuses for the relation that involved it. Any relation that involved it was by the very fact as much discredited as a dish would be at dinner if one had to take medicine as a sauce. What Kate would have said in one of the young women's last talks was that — if Milly absolutely must have the truth about it — Mr. Densher was staying because she had really seen no way but to require it of him. If he stayed he did n't follow her — or did n't appear to her aunt to be doing so; and when she kept him from following her Mrs. Lowder could n't pretend, in scenes, the renewal of which at this time of day was painful, that she after all did n't snub him as she might. She did nothing in fact *but* snub him — would n't that have been part of the story? — only Aunt Maud's suspicions were of the sort that had repeatedly to be dealt with. He had been, by the same token, reasonable enough — as he now, for that matter, well might; he had consented to oblige them, aunt and niece, by giving the plainest sign possible that he could exist away from London. To exist away from London was to exist away from Kate Croy — which was a gain, much appreciated, to the latter's comfort. There was a minute, at this hour, out of Densher's three, during which he knew the terror of Milly's uttering some such allusion to their friend's explanation as he must meet with words that wouldn't destroy it. To destroy it was to destroy everything, to destroy probably Kate herself, to destroy in particular by a breach of faith still uglier than anything else the beauty of their own last passage. He had given her his word of honour that if she would come to him he would act absolutely in her sense, and he had done so with a full enough vision of what her sense implied. What it implied for one thing was that to-night in the great saloon, noble in its half-lighted beauty, and straight in the white face of his young hostess, divine in her trust, or at any rate inscrutable in her mercy — what it implied was that he should lie with his lips. The single thing, of all things, that could save him from it would be Milly's letting him off after having thus scared him. What made her mercy inscrutable was that if she had already more than once saved him it was yet apparently without knowing how nearly he was lost.

These were transcendent motions, not the less blest for being obscure; whereby yet once more he was to feel the pressure lighten. He was kept on his feet in short by the felicity of her not presenting him with Kate's version as a version to adopt. He could n't stand up to lie — he felt as if he should have to go down on his knees. As it was he just sat there shaking a little for nervousness the leg he had crossed over the other. She was sorry for his suffered snub, but he had nothing more to subscribe to, to perjure himself about, than the three or four inanities he had, on his own side, feebly prepared for the crisis. He scrambled a little higher than the reference to money and clothes, letters and directions from his manager; but he brought out the beauty of the chance for him — there before him like a temptress painted by Titian — to do a little quiet writing. He was vivid for a moment on the difficulty of writing quietly in London; and he was precipitate, almost explosive, on his idea, long cherished, of a book.

The explosion lighted her face. "You'll do your book here?"

"I hope to begin it."

"It's something you have n't begun?"

"Well, only just."

"And since you came?"

She was so full of interest that he should n't perhaps after all be too easily let off. "I tried to think a few days ago that I had broken ground."

Scarcely anything, it was indeed clear, could have let him in deeper. "I'm afraid we've made an awful mess of your time."

"Of course you have. But what I'm hanging on for now is precisely to repair that ravage."

"Then you must n't mind me, you know."

"You'll see," he tried to say with ease, "how little I shall mind anything."

"You'll want" — Milly had thrown herself into it — "the best part of your days."

He thought a moment: he did what he could to wreathe it in smiles. "Oh I shall make shift with the worst part. The best will be for *you*." And he wished Kate could hear him. It did n't help him moreover that he visibly, even pathetically, imaged to her by such touches his quest for comfort against discipline. He was to bury Kate's so signal snub, and also the hard law she had now laid on him, under a high intellectual effort. This at least was his crucifixion — that Milly was so interested. She was so interested that she presently asked him if he found his rooms propitious, while he felt that in just decently answering her he put on a brazen mask. He should need it quite particularly were she to express again her imagination of coming to tea with him — an extremity that he saw he was not to be spared. "We depend on you, Susie and I, you know, not to forget we're coming" — the extremity was but to face that remainder, yet it demanded all his tact. Facing their visit itself — to that, no matter what he might have to do, he would never consent, as we know, to be pushed; and this even though it might be exactly such a demonstration as would figure for him at the top of Kate's list of his proprieties. He could wonder freely enough, deep within, if Kate's view of that especial propriety had not been modified by a subsequent occurrence; but his deciding that it was quite likely not to have been had no effect on his own preference for tact. It pleased him to think of "tact" as his present prop in doubt; that glossed his predicament over, for it was of application among the sensitive and the kind. He wasn't inhuman, in fine, so long as it would serve. It had to serve now, accordingly, to help him not to sweeten Milly's hopes. He did n't want to be rude to them, but he still less wanted them to flower again in the particular connexion; so that, casting about him in his anxiety for a middle way to meet her, he put his foot, with unhappy effect, just in the wrong place. "Will it be safe for you to break into your custom of not leaving the house ?"

"'Safe' — ?" She had for twenty seconds an exquisite pale glare. Oh but he did n't need it, by that time, to wince; he had winced for himself as soon as he had made his mistake. He had done what, so unforgettably, she had asked him in London not to do; he had touched, all alone with her here, the supersensitive nerve of which she had warned him. He had not, since the occasion in London, touched it again till now; but he saw himself freshly warned that it was able to bear still less. So for the moment he knew as little what to do as he had ever known it in his life. He could n't emphasise that he thought of her as dying, yet he could n't pretend he thought of her as indifferent to precautions. Meanwhile too she had narrowed his choice. "You suppose me so awfully bad ?"

He turned, in his pain, within himself; but by the time the colour had mounted to the roots of his hair he had found what he wanted. "I'll believe whatever you tell me."

"Well then, I'm splendid."

"Oh I don't need you to tell me that."

"I mean I'm capable of life."

"I've never doubted it."

"I mean," she went on, "that I want so to live —!"

"Well?" he asked while she paused with the intensity of it.

"Well, that I know I *can*."

"Whatever you do?" He shrank from solemnity about it.

"Whatever I do. If I want to."

"If you want to do it?"

"If I want to live. I *can*," Milly repeated.

He had clumsily brought it on himself, but he hesitated with all the pity of it. "Ah then *that* I believe."

"I will, I will," she declared; yet with the weight of it somehow turned for him to mere light and sound.

He felt himself smiling through a mist. "You simply must!"

It brought her straight again to the fact. "Well then, if you say it, why may n't we pay you our visit?"

"Will it help you to live?"

"Every little helps," she laughed; "and it's very little for me, in general, to stay at home. Only I shan't want to miss it —!"

"Yes?" — she had dropped again.

"Well, on the day you give us a chance."

It was amazing what so brief an exchange had at this point done with him. His great scruple suddenly broke, giving way to something inordinately strange, something of a nature to become clear to him only when he had left her. "You can come," he said, "when you like."

What had taken place for him, however — the drop, almost with violence, of everything but a sense of her own reality — apparently showed in his face or his manner, and even so vividly that she could take it for something else. "I see how you feel — that I'm an awful bore about it and that, sooner than have any such upset, you'll go. So it's no matter."

"No matter? Oh!" — he quite protested now.

"If it drives you away to escape us. We want you not to go."

It was beautiful how she spoke for Mrs. Stringham. Whatever it was, at any rate, he shook his head. "I won't go."

"Then *I* won't go!" she brightly declared.

"You mean you won't come to me?"

"No — never now. It's over. But it's all right. I mean, apart from that," she went on, "that I won't do anything I ought n't or that I'm not forced to."

"Oh who can ever force you?" he asked with his hand-to-mouth way, at all times, of speaking for her encouragement. "You're the least coercible of creatures."

"Because, you think, I'm so free?"

"The freest person probably now in the world. You've got everything."

"Well," she smiled, "call it so. I don't complain."

On which again, in spite of himself, it let him in. "No I know you don't complain."

As soon as he had said it he had himself heard the pity in it. His telling her she had "everything" was

247

extravagant kind humour, whereas his knowing so tenderly that she did n't complain was terrible kind gravity. Milly felt, he could see, the difference; he might as well have praised her outright for looking death in the face. This was the way she just looked *him* again, and it was of no attenuation that she took him up more gently than ever. "It is n't a merit — when one sees one's way."

"To peace and plenty? Well, I dare say not."

"I mean to keeping what one has."

"Oh that's success. If what one has is good," Densher said at random, "it's enough to try for."

"Well, it's my limit. I'm not trying for more." To which then she added with a change: "And now about your book."

"My book — ?" He had got in a moment so far from it.

"The one you're now to understand that nothing will induce either Susie or me to run the risk of spoiling."

He cast about, but he made up his mind. "I'm not doing a book."

"Not what you said?" she asked in a wonder. "You're not writing?"

He already felt relieved. "I don't know, upon my honour, what I'm doing."

It made her visibly grave; so that, disconcerted in another way, he was afraid of what she would see in it. She saw in fact exactly what he feared, but again his honour, as he called it, was saved even while she did n't know she had threatened it. Taking his words for a betrayal of the sense that he, on his side, *might* complain, what she clearly wanted was to urge on him some such patience as he should be perhaps able to arrive at with her indirect help. Still more clearly, however, she wanted to be sure of how far she might venture; and he could see her make out in a moment that she had a sort of test.

"Then if it's not for your book — ?"

"What *am* I staying for?"

"I mean with your London work — with all you have to do. Isn't it rather empty for you?"

"Empty for me?" He remembered how Kate had held that she might propose marriage, and he wondered if this were the way she would naturally begin it. It would leave him, such an incident, he already felt, at a loss, and the note of his finest anxiety might have been in the vagueness of his reply. "Oh well —!"

"I ask too many questions?" She settled it for herself before he could protest. "You stay because you've got to."

He grasped at it. "I stay because I've got to." And he couldn't have said when he had uttered it if it were loyal to Kate or disloyal. It gave her, in a manner, away; it showed the tip of the ear of her plan. Yet Milly took it, he perceived, but as a plain statement of his truth. He was waiting for what Kate would have told her of — the permission from Lancaster Gate to come any nearer. To remain friends with either niece or aunt he mustn't stir without it. All this Densher read in the girl's sense of the spirit of his reply; so that it made him feel he was lying, and he had to think of something to correct that. What he thought of was, in an instant, "Isn't it enough, whatever may be one's other complications, to stay after all for *you?*"

"Oh you must judge."

He was by this time on his feet to take leave, and was also at last too restless. The speech in question at least was n't disloyal to Kate; that was the very tone of their bargain. So was it, by being loyal, another kind of lie, the lie of the uncandid profession of a motive. He was staying so little "for" Milly that he was staying positively against her. He did n't, none the less, know, and at last, thank goodness, did n't care. The only thing he could say might make it either better or worse. "Well then, so long as I don't go, you must think of me all *as* judging!"

II

HE did n't go home, on leaving her—he did n't want to; he walked instead, through his narrow ways and his *campi* with gothic arches, to a small and comparatively sequestered café where he had already more than once found refreshment and comparative repose, together with solutions that consisted mainly and pleasantly of further indecisions. It was a literal fact that those awaiting him there to-night, while he leaned back on his velvet bench with his head against a florid mirror and his eyes not looking further than the fumes of his tobacco, might have been regarded by him as a little less limp than usual. This was n't because, before getting to his feet again, there was a step he had seen his way to; it was simply because the acceptance of his position took sharper effect from his sense of what he had just had to deal with. When half an hour before, at the palace, he had turned about to Milly on the question of the impossibility so inwardly felt, turned about on the spot and under her eyes, he had acted, by the sudden force of his seeing much further, seeing how little, how not at all, impossibilities mattered. It was n't a case for pedantry; when people were at *her* pass everything was allowed. And her pass was now, as by the sharp click of a spring, just completely his own — to the extent, as he felt, of her deep dependence on him. Anything he should do or should n't would have close reference to her life, which was thus absolutely in his hands — and ought never to have reference to anything else. It was on the cards for him that he might kill her — that was the way he read the cards as he sat in his customary corner. The fear in this thought made him let everything go, kept him there actually, all motionless, for three hours on end. He renewed his consumption and smoked more cigarettes than he had ever done in the time. What had come out for him had come out, with this first intensity, as a terror; so that action itself, of any sort, the right as well as the wrong — if the difference even survived — had heard in it a vivid "Hush!" the injunction to keep from that moment intensely still. He thought in fact while his vigil lasted of several different ways for his doing so, and the hour might have served him as a lesson in going on tiptoe.

What he finally took home, when he ventured to leave the place, was the perceived truth that he might on any other system go straight to destruction. Destruction was represented for him by the idea of his really bringing to a point, on Milly's side, anything whatever. Nothing so "brought," he easily argued, but *must* be in one way or another a catastrophe. He was mixed up in her fate, or her fate, if that should be better, was mixed up in *him*, so that a single false motion might either way snap the coil. They helped him, it was true, these considerations, to a degree of eventual peace, for what they luminously amounted to was that he was to do nothing, and that fell in after all with the burden laid on him by Kate. He was only not to budge without the girl's leave — not,

oddly enough at the last, to move without it, whether
further or nearer, any more than without Kate's.
It was to this his wisdom reduced itself — to the need
again simply to be kind. That was the same as being
still — as studying to create the minimum of vibration. He felt himself as he smoked shut up to a room
on the wall of which something precious was too pre-
cariously hung. A false step would bring it down,
and it must hang as long as possible. He was aware
when he walked away again that even Fleet Street
wouldn't at this juncture successfully touch him. His
manager might wire that he was wanted, but he could
easily be deaf to his manager. His money for the idle
life might be none too much; happily, however, Venice
was cheap, and it was moreover the queer fact that
Milly in a manner supported him. The greatest of
his expenses really was to walk to the palace to dinner. He didn't want, in short, to give that up, and
he should probably be able, he felt, to stay his breath
and his hand. He should be able to be still enough
through everything.

He tried that for three weeks, with the sense after
a little of not having failed. There had to be a delicate
art in it, for he wasn't trying — quite the contrary —
to be either distant or dull. That would not have
been being "nice," which in its own form was the real
law. That too might just have produced the vibration
he desired to avert; so that he best kept everything in
place by not hesitating or fearing, as it were, to let
himself go — go in the direction, that is to say, of
staying. It depended on where he went; which was
what he meant by taking care. When one went on

tiptoe one could turn off for retreat without betraying the manœuvre. Perfect tact — the necessity for which he had from the first, as we know, happily recognised — was to keep all intercourse in the key of the absolutely settled. It was settled thus for instance that they were indissoluble good friends, and settled as well that her being the American girl was, just in time and for the relation they found themselves concerned in, a boon inappreciable. If, at least, as the days went on, she was to fall short of her prerogative of the great national, the great maidenly ease, if she did n't diviningly and responsively desire and labour to record herself as possessed of it, this would n't have been for want of Densher's keeping her, with his idea, well up to it — would n't have been in fine for want of his encouragement and reminder. He did n't perhaps in so many words speak to her of the quantity itself as of the thing she was least to intermit; but he talked of it, freely, in what he flattered himself was an impersonal way, and this held it there before her — since he was careful also to talk pleasantly. It was at once their idea, when all was said, and the most marked of their conveniences. The type was so elastic that it could be stretched to almost anything; and yet, not stretched, it kept down, remained normal, remained properly within bounds. And he *had* meanwhile, thank goodness, without being too much disconcerted, the sense, for the girl's part of the business, of the queerest conscious compliance, of her doing very much what he wanted, even though without her quite seeing why. She fairly touched this once in saying: "Oh yes, you like us to be as we are because it's a kind of facilitation to you that we don't quite measure: I think one would have to be English to measure it!"—and that too, strangely enough, without prejudice to her good nature. She might have been conceived as doing — that is of being — what he liked in order perhaps only to judge where it would take them. They really as it went on *saw* each other at the game; she knowing he tried to keep her in tune with his conception, and he knowing she thus knew it. Add that he again knew she knew, and yet that nothing was spoiled by it, and we get a fair impression of the line they found most completely workable. The strangest fact of all for us must be that the success he himself thus promoted was precisely what figured to his gratitude as the something above and beyond him, above and beyond Kate, that made for daily decency. There would scarce have been felicity — certainly too little of the right lubricant — had not the national character so invoked been, not less inscrutably than entirely, in Milly's chords. It made up her unity and was the one thing he could unlimitedly take for granted.

He did so then, daily, for twenty days, without deepened fear of the undue vibration that was keeping him watchful. He knew in his nervousness that he was living at best from day to day and from hand to mouth; yet he had succeeded, he believed, in avoiding a mistake. All women had alternatives, and Milly's would doubtless be shaky too; but the national character was firm in her, whether as all of her, practically, by this time, or but as a part; the national character that, in a woman still so young, made of the air breathed a virtual non-conductor. It was n't till a certain occasion when the twenty days had passed that, going to the palace at tea-time, he was met by the information that the signorina padrona was not "receiving." The announcement met him, in the court, on the lips of one of the gondoliers, met him, he thought, with such a conscious eye as the knowledge of his freedoms of access, hitherto conspicuously shown, could scarce fail to beget. Densher had not been at Palazzo Leporelli among the mere receivable, but had taken his place once for all among the involved and included, so that on being so flagrantly braved he recognised after a moment the propriety of a further appeal. Neither of the two ladies, it appeared, received, and yet Pasquale was not prepared to say that either was *poco bene*. He was yet not prepared to say that either was anything, and he would have been blank, Densher mentally noted, if the term could ever apply to members of a race in whom vacancy was but a nest of darknesses — not a vain surface, but a place of withdrawal in which something obscure, something always ominous, indistinguishably lived. He felt afresh indeed at this hour the force of the veto laid within the palace on any mention, any cognition, of the liabilities of its mistress. The state of her health was never confessed to there as a reason. How much it might deeply be taken for one was another matter; of which he grew fully aware on carrying his question further. This appeal was to his friend Eugenio, whom he immediately sent for, with whom, for three rich minutes, protected from the weather, he was confronted in the

gallery that led from the water-steps to the court,
and whom he always called, in meditation, his friend;
seeing it was so elegantly presumable he would have
put an end to him if he could. That produced a relation which required a name of its own, an intimacy of
consciousness in truth for each — an intimacy of eye,
of ear, of general sensibility, of everything but tongue.
It had been, in other words, for the five weeks, far
from occult to our young man that Eugenio took a
view of him not less finely formal than essentially
vulgar, but which at the same time he could n't himself raise an eyebrow to prevent. It was all in the air
now again; it was as much between them as ever
while Eugenio waited on him in the court.

The weather, from early morning, had turned to
storm, the first sea-storm of the autumn, and Densher had almost invidiously brought him down the
outer staircase — the massive ascent, the great feature of the court, to Milly's *piano nobile.* This was to
pay him — it was the one chance — for all imputa-
tions; the imputation in particular that, clever, *tanto
bello* and not rich, the young man from London was
— by the obvious way — pressing Miss Theale's fortune hard. It was to pay him for the further ineffable
intimation that a gentleman must take the young
lady's most devoted servant (interested scarcely less
in the high attraction) for a strangely casual append-
age if he counted in such a connexion on impunity
and prosperity. These interpretations were odious to
Densher for the simple reason that they might have
been so true of the attitude of an inferior man, and
three things alone, accordingly, had kept him from

righting himself. One of these was that his critic sought expression only in an impersonality, a positive inhumanity, of politeness; the second was that refinements of expression in a friend's servant were not a thing a visitor could take action on; and the third was the fact that the particular attribution of motive did him after all no wrong. It was his own fault if the vulgar view, the view that might have been taken of an inferior man, happened so incorrigibly to fit him. He apparently was n't so different from inferior men as that came to. If therefore, in fine, Eugenio figured to him as "my friend" because he was conscious of his seeing so much of him, what he made him see on the same lines in the course of their present interview was ever so much more. Densher felt that he marked himself, no doubt, as insisting, by dissatisfaction with the gondolier's answer, on the pursuit taken for granted in him; and yet felt it only in the augmented, the exalted distance that was by this time established between them. Eugenio had of course reflected that a word to Miss Theale from such a pair of lips would cost him his place; but he could also bethink himself that, so long as the word never came — and it was, on the basis he had arranged, impossible — he enjoyed the imagination of mounting guard. He had never so mounted guard, Densher could see, as during these minutes in the damp *loggia* where the storm-gusts were strong; and there came in fact for our young man, as a result of his presence, a sudden sharp sense that everything had turned to the dismal. Something had happened — he did n't know what; and it was n't Eugenio who would tell him. What

258

Eugenio told him was that he thought the ladies — as if their liability had been equal — were a "leetle" fatigued, just a "leetle leetle," and without any cause named for it. It was one of the signs of what Densher felt in him that, by a profundity, a true deviltry of resource, he always met the latter's Italian with English and his English with Italian. He now, as usual, slightly smiled at him in the process— but ever so slightly this time, his manner also being attuned, our young man made out, to the thing, whatever it was, that constituted the rupture of peace.

This manner, while they stood a long minute facing each other over all they did n't say, played a part as well in the sudden jar to Densher's protected state. It was a Venice all of evil that had broken out for them alike, so that they were together in their anxiety, if they really could have met on it; a Venice of cold lashing rain from a low black sky, of wicked wind raging through narrow passes, of general arrest and interruption, with the people engaged in all the water-life huddled, stranded and wageless, bored and cynical, under archways and bridges. Our young man's mute exchange with his friend contained meanwhile such a depth of reference that, had the pressure been but slightly prolonged, they might have reached a point at which they were equally weak. Each had verily something in mind that would have made a hash of mutual suspicion and in presence of which, as a possibility, they were more united than disjoined. But it was to have been a moment for Densher that nothing could ease off — not even the formal propriety with which his interlocutor finally attended him to the *portone* and bowed upon his retreat. Nothing had passed about his coming back, and the air had made itself felt as a non-conductor of messages. Densher knew of course, as he took his way again, that Eugenio's invitation to return was not what he missed; yet he knew at the same time that what had happened to him was part of his punishment. Out in the square beyond the *fondamenta* that gave access to the land-gate of the palace, out where the wind was higher, he fairly, with the thought of it, pulled his umbrella closer down. It could n't be, his consciousness, un-seen enough by others — the base predicament of having, by a concatenation, just to *take* such things: such things as the fact that one very acute person in the world, whom he could n't dispose of as an interested scoundrel, enjoyed an opinion of him that there was no attacking, no disproving, no (what was worst of all) even noticing. One had come to a queer pass when a servant's opinion so mattered. Eugenio's would have mattered even if, as founded on a low vision of ap-pearances, it had been quite wrong. It was the more disagreeable accordingly that the vision of appear-ances was quite right, and yet was scarcely less low.

Such as it was, at any rate, Densher shook it off with the more impatience that he was independently restless. He had to walk in spite of weather, and he took his course, through crooked ways, to the Piazza, where he should have the shelter of the galleries. Here, in the high arcade, half Venice was crowded close, while, on the Molo, at the limit of the expanse, the old columns of the Saint Theodore and of the Lion were the frame of a door wide open to the storm. It was odd for him, as he moved, that it should have made such a difference — if the difference was n't only that the palace had for the first time failed of a welcome. There was more, but it came from that; that gave the harsh note and broke the spell. The wet and the cold were now to reckon with, and it was to Densher precisely as if he had seen the obliteration, at a stroke, of the margin on a faith in which they were all living. The margin had been his name for it — for the thing that, though it had held out, could bear no shock. The shock, in some form, had come, and he wondered about it while, threading his way among loungers as vague as himself, he dropped his eyes sightlessly on the rubbish in shops. There were stretches of the gallery paved with squares of red marble, greasy now with the salt spray; and the whole place, in its huge elegance, the grace of its conception and the beauty of its detail, was more than ever like a great drawing-room, the drawing-room of Europe, profaned and bewildered by some reverse of fortune. He brushed shoulders with brown men whose hats askew, and the loose sleeves of whose pendent jackets, made them resemble melancholy maskers. The tables and chairs that overflowed from the cafés were gathered, still with a pretence of service, into the arcade, and here and there a spectacled German, with his coat-collar up, partook publicly of food and philosophy. These were impressions for Densher too, but he had made the whole circuit thrice before he stopped short, in front of Florian's, with the force of his sharpest. His eye had caught a face within the café — he had spotted an acquaintance behind the glass. The person he had thus paused long enough to look at twice was seated, well within range, at a small table on which a tumbler, half-emptied and evidently neglected, still remained; and though he had on his knee, as he leaned back, a copy of a French newspaper — the heading of the *Figaro* was visible — he stared straight before him at the little opposite rococo wall. Densher had him for a minute in profile, had him for a time during which his identity produced, however quickly, all the effect of establishing connexions — connexions startling and direct; and then, as if it were the one thing more needed, seized the look, determined by a turn of the head, that might have been a prompt result of the sense of being noticed. This wider view showed him *all* Lord Mark — Lord Mark as encountered, several weeks before, the day of the first visit of each to Palazzo Leporelli. For it had been all Lord Mark that was going out, on that occasion, as he came in — he had felt it, in the hall, at the time; and he was accordingly the less at a loss to recognise in a few seconds, as renewed meeting brought it to the surface, the same potential quantity.

It was a matter, the whole passage — it could only be — but of a few seconds; for as he might neither stand there to stare nor on the other hand make any advance from it, he had presently resumed his walk, this time to another pace. It had been for all the world, during his pause, as if he had caught his answer to the riddle of the day. Lord Mark had simply faced him — as he had faced *him*, not placed by him, not at first — as one of the damp shuffling crowd. Recognition, though hanging fire, had then clearly

come; yet no light of salutation had been struck from
these certainties. Acquaintance between them was
scant enough for neither to take it up. That neither
had done so was not, however, what now mattered,
but that the gentleman at Florian's should be in the
place at all. He could n't have been in it long; Densher, as inevitably a haunter of the great meeting-
ground, would in that case have seen him before. He
paid short visits; he was on the wing; the question for
him even as he sat there was of his train or of his boat.
He had come back for something—as a sequel to his
earlier visit; and whatever he had come back for it had
had time to be done. He might have arrived but last
night or that morning; he had already made the difference. It was a great thing for Densher to get this answer. He held it close, he hugged it, quite leaned on
it as he continued to circulate. It kept him going and
going — it made him no less restless. But it explained
— and that was much, for with explanations he might
somehow deal. The vice in the air, otherwise, was too
much like the breath of fate. The weather had
changed, the rain was ugly, the wind wicked, the sea
impossible, *because* of Lord Mark. It was because of
him, *a fortiori*, that the palace was closed. Densher
went round again twice; he found the visitor each time
as he had found him first. Once, that is, he was star-
ing before him; the next time he was looking over his
Figaro, which he had opened out. Densher did n't
again stop, but left him apparently unconscious of his
passage — on another repetition of which Lord Mark
had disappeared. He had spent but the day; he would
be off that night; he had now gone to his hotel for

arrangements. These things were as plain to Densher as if he had had them in words. The obscure had cleared for him — if cleared it was; there was something he did n't see, the great thing; but he saw so round it and so close to it that this was almost as good. He had been looking at a man who had done what he had come for, and for whom, as done, it temporarily sufficed. The man had come again to see Milly, and Milly had received him. His visit would have taken place just before or just after luncheon, and it was the reason why he himself had found her door shut.

He said to himself that evening, he still said even on the morrow, that he only wanted a reason, and that with this perception of one he could now mind, as he called it, his business. His business, he had settled, as we know, was to keep thoroughly still; and he asked himself why it should prevent this that he could feel, in connexion with the crisis, so remarkably blameless. He gave the appearances before him all the benefit of being critical, so that if blame were to accrue he should n't feel he had dodged it. But it was n't a bit he who, that day, had touched her, and if she was upset it was n't a bit his act. The ability so to think about it amounted for Densher during several hours to a kind of exhilaration. The exhilaration was heightened fairly, besides, by the visible conditions — sharp, striking, ugly to him — of Lord Mark's return. His constant view of it, for all the next hours, of which there were many, was as a demonstration on the face of it sinister even to his own actual ignorance. He did n't need, for seeing it as evil,

seeing it as, to a certainty, in a high degree "nasty,"
to know more about it than he had so easily and so
wonderfully picked up. You could n't drop on the
poor girl that way without, by the fact, being brutal.
Such a visit was a descent, an invasion, an aggression,
constituting precisely one or other of the stupid shocks
he himself had so decently sought to spare her. Densher had indeed drifted by the next morning to the
reflexion — which he positively, with occasion, might
have brought straight out — that the only delicate
and honourable way of treating a person in such a
state was to treat her as *he*, Merton Densher, did.
With time, actually — for the impression but deepened — this sense of the contrast, to the advantage
of Merton Densher, became a sense of relief, and
that in turn a sense of escape. It was for all the world
— and he drew a long breath on it — as if a special
danger for him had passed. Lord Mark had, without
in the least intending such a service, got it straight
out of the way. It was *he*, the brute, who had stumbled into just the wrong inspiration and who had
therefore produced, for the very person he had wished
to hurt, an impunity that was comparative innocence,
that was almost like purification. The person he
had wished to hurt could only be the person so un-
accountably hanging about. To keep still meanwhile
was, for this person, more comprehensively, to keep
it all up; and to keep it all up was, if that seemed on
consideration best, not, for the day or two, to go
back to the palace.

The day or two passed — stretched to three days;
and with the effect, extraordinarily, that Densher felt

himself in the course of them washed but the more clean. Some sign would come if his return should have the better effect; and he was at all events, in absence, without the particular scruple. It would n't have been meant for him by either of the women that he was to come back but to face Eugenio. That was impossible — the being again denied; for it made him practically answerable, and answerable was what he was n't. There was no neglect either in absence, inasmuch as, from the moment he did n't get in, the one message he could send up would be some hope on the score of health. Since accordingly that sort of expression was definitely forbidden him he had only to wait — which he was actually helped to do by his feeling with the lapse of each day more and more wound up to it. The days in themselves were anything but sweet; the wind and the weather lasted, the fireless cold hinted at worse; the broken charm of the world about was broken into smaller pieces. He walked up and down his rooms and listened to the wind — listened also to tinkles of bells and watched for some servant of the palace. He might get a note, but the note never came; there were hours when he stayed at home not to miss it. When he was n't at home he was in circulation again as he had been at the hour of his seeing Lord Mark. He strolled about the Square with the herd of refugees; he raked the approaches and the cafés on the chance the brute, as he now regularly imaged him, *might* be still there. He could only be there, he knew, to be received afresh; and that — one had but to think of it — would be indeed stiff. He had gone, however — it was proved;

though Densher's care for the question either way only added to what was most acrid in the taste of his present ordeal. It all came round to what he was doing for Milly — spending days that neither relief nor escape could purge of a smack of the abject. What was it but abject for a man of his parts to be reduced to such pastimes? What was it but sordid for him, shuffling about in the rain, to have to peep into shops and to consider possible meetings? What was it but odious to find himself wondering what, as between him and another man, a possible meeting would produce? There recurred moments when in spite of everything he felt no straighter than another man. And yet even on the third day, when still nothing had come, he more than ever knew that he would n't have budged for the world.

He thought of the two women, in their silence, at last — he at all events thought of Milly — as probably, for her reasons, now intensely wishing him to go. The cold breath of her reasons was, with everything else, in the air; but he did n't care for them any more than for her wish itself, and he would stay in spite of her, stay in spite of odium, stay in spite perhaps of some final experience that would be, for the pain of it, all but unbearable. That would be his one way, purified though he was, to mark his virtue beyond any mistake. It would be accepting the disagreeable, and the disagreeable would be a proof; a proof of his not having stayed for the thing — the agreeable, as it were — that Kate had named. The thing Kate had named was not to have been the odium of staying in spite of hints. It was part of the odium as actual too that Kate was, for her comfort, just now well aloof. These were the first hours since her flight in which his sense of what she had done for him on the eve of that event was to incur a qualification. It was strange, it was perhaps base, to be thinking such things so soon; but one of the intimations of his solitude was that she had provided for herself. She was out of it all, by her act, as much as he was in it; and this difference grew, positively, as his own intensity increased. She had said in their last sharp snatch of talk — sharp though thickly muffled, and with every word in it final and deep, unlike even the deepest words they had ever yet spoken: "Letters? Never — *now*. Think of it. Impossible." So that as he had sufficiently caught her sense — into which he read, all the same, a strange inconsequence — they had practically wrapped their understanding in the breach of their correspondence. He had moreover, on losing her, done justice to her law of silence; for there was doubtless a finer delicacy in his not writing to her than in his writing as he must have written had he spoken of themselves. That would have been a turbid strain, and her idea had been to be noble; which, in a degree, was a manner. Only it left her, for the pinch, comparatively at ease. And it left *him*, in the conditions, peculiarly alone. He was alone, that is, till, on the afternoon of his third day, in gathering dusk and renewed rain, with his shabby rooms looking doubtless, in their confirmed dreariness, for the mere eyes of others, at their worst, the grinning padrona threw open the door and introduced Mrs. Stringham. That made at a bound a difference, especially when he saw that his visitor was weighted. It appeared part of her weight that she was in a wet waterproof, that she allowed her umbrella to be taken from her by the good woman without consciousness or care, and that her face, under her veil, richly rosy with the driving wind, was — and the veil too — as splashed as if the rain were her tears.

III

THEY came to it almost immediately; he was to wonder afterwards at the fewness of their steps. "She has turned her face to the wall."

"You mean she's worse?"

The poor lady stood there as she had stopped; Densher had, in the instant flare of his eagerness, his curiosity, all responsive at sight of her, waved away, on the spot, the padrona, who had offered to relieve her of her mackintosh. She looked vaguely about through her wet veil, intensely alive now to the step she had taken and wishing it not to have been in the dark, but clearly, as yet, seeing nothing. "I don't know *how* she is — and it's why I've come to you."

"I'm glad enough you've come," he said, "and it's quite — you make me feel — as if I had been wretchedly waiting for you."

She showed him again her blurred eyes — she had caught at his word. "Have you been wretched?"

Now, however, on his lips, the word expired. It would have sounded for him like a complaint, and before something he already made out in his visitor he knew his own trouble as small. Hers, under her damp draperies, which shamed his lack of a fire, was great, and he felt she had brought it all with her. He answered that he had been patient and above all that he had been still. "As still as a mouse — you'll

have seen it for yourself. Stiller, for three days together, than I've ever been in my life. It has seemed
to me the only thing."

This qualification of it as a policy or a remedy was
straightway for his friend, he saw, a light that her
own light could answer. "It has been best. I've
wondered for you. But it has been best," she said
again.

"Yet it has done no good?"

"I don't know. I've been afraid you were gone."
Then as he gave a headshake which, though slow,
was deeply mature: "You *won't* go?"

"Is to 'go,'" he asked, "to be still?"

"Oh I mean if you'll stay for me."

"I'll do anything for you. Isn't it for you alone
now I can?"

She thought of it, and he could see even more of
the relief she was taking from him. His presence,
his face, his voice, the old rooms themselves, so
meagre yet so charged, where Kate had admirably
been to him — these things counted for her, now she
had them, as the help she had been wanting: so that
she still only stood there taking them all in. With it
however popped up characteristically a throb of her
conscience. What she thus tasted was almost a personal joy. It told Densher of the three days she on
her side had spent. "Well, anything you do for me
— *is* for her too. Only, only — !"

"Only nothing now matters?"

She looked at him a minute as if he were the fact
itself that he expressed. "Then you know?"

"Is she dying?" he asked for all answer.

Mrs. Stringham waited — her face seemed to sound him. Then her own reply was strange. "She has n't so much as named you. We have n't spoken."

"Not for three days?"

"No more," she simply went on, "than if it were all over. Not even by the faintest allusion."

"Oh," said Densher with more light, "you mean you have n't spoken about *me?*"

"About what else? No more than if you were dead."

"Well," he answered after a moment, "I *am* dead."

"Then *I* am," said Susan Shepherd with a drop of her arms on her waterproof.

It was a tone that, for the minute, imposed itself in its dry despair; it represented, in the bleak place, which had no life of its own, none but the life Kate had left — the sense of which, for that matter, by mystic channels, might fairly be reaching the visitor — the very impotence of their extinction. And Densher had nothing to oppose it withal, nothing but again: "Is she dying?"

It made her, however, as if these were crudities, almost material pangs, only say as before: "Then you know?"

"Yes," he at last returned, "I know. But the marvel to me is that *you* do. I 've no right in fact to imagine or to assume that you do."

"You may," said Susan Shepherd, "all the same. I know."

"Everything?"

Her eyes, through her veil, kept pressing him. "No — not everything. That 's why I 've come."

"That I shall really tell you?" With which, as she

hesitated and it affected him, he brought out in a groan a doubting "Oh, oh!" It turned him from her to the place itself, which was a part of what was in him, was the abode, the worn shrine more than ever, of the fact in possession, the fact, now a thick association, for which he had hired it. *That* was not for telling, but Susan Shepherd was, none the less, so decidedly wonderful that the sense of it might really have begun, by an effect already operating, to be a part of her knowledge. He saw, and it stirred him, that she had n't come to judge him; had come rather, so far as she might dare, to pity. This showed him her own abasement — that, at any rate, of grief; and made him feel with a rush of friendliness that he liked to be with her. The rush had quickened when she met his groan with an attenuation.

"We shall at all events — if that's anything — be together."

It was his own good impulse in herself. "It's what I've ventured to feel. It's much." She replied in effect, silently, that it was whatever he liked; on which, so far as he had been afraid for anything, he knew his fear had dropped. The comfort was huge, for it gave back to him something precious, over which, in the effort of recovery, his own hand had too imperfectly closed. Kate, he remembered, had said to him, with her sole and single boldness — and also on grounds he had n't then measured — that Mrs. Stringham was a person who *would n't*, at a pinch, in a stretch of confidence, wince. It was but another of the cases in which Kate was always showing. "You don't think then very horridly of me?"

And her answer was the more valuable that it came
without nervous effusion — quite as if she understood what he might conceivably have believed. She
turned over in fact what she thought, and that was
what helped him. "Oh you've been extraordinary!"

It made him aware the next moment of how they
had been planted there. She took off her cloak with
his aid, though when she had also, accepting a seat,
removed her veil, he recognised in her personal ravage that the words she had just uttered to him were
the one flower she had to throw. They were all her
consolation for him, and the consolation even still
depended on the event. She sat with him at any rate
in the grey clearance, as sad as a winter dawn,
made by their meeting. The image she again evoked
for him loomed in it but the larger. "She has turned
her face to the wall."

He saw with the last vividness, and it was as if, in
their silences, they were simply so leaving what he
saw. "She does n't speak at all? I don't mean not
of me."

"Of nothing — of no one." And she went on,
Susan Shepherd, giving it out as she had had to take
it. "She does n't *want* to die. Think of her age.
Think of her goodness. Think of her beauty. Think
of all she is. Think of all she *has*. She lies there stiffen-
ing herself and clinging to it all. So I thank God —!"
the poor lady wound up with a wan inconsequence.

He wondered. "You thank God —?"

"That she's so quiet."

He continued to wonder. "*Is* she so quiet?"

"She's more than quiet. She's grim. It's what

she has never been. So you see — all these days. I
can't tell you — but it's better so. It would kill me
if she *were* to tell me."

"To tell you?" He was still at a loss.

"How she feels. How she clings. How she does n't
want it."

"How she does n't want to die? Of course she
does n't want it." He had a long pause, and they
might have been thinking together of what they could
even now do to prevent it. This, however, was not
what he brought out. Milly's "grimness" and the
great hushed palace were present to him; present
with the little woman before him as she must have
been waiting there and listening. "Only, what harm
have *you* done her?"

Mrs. Stringham looked about in her darkness. "I
don't know. I come and talk of her here with you."

It made him again hesitate. "Does she utterly
hate me?"

"I don't know. How *can* I? No one ever will."

"She'll never tell?"

"She'll never tell."

Once more he thought. "She must be magnificent."

"She *is* magnificent."

His friend, after all, helped him, and he turned it,
so far as he could, all over. "Would she see me
again?"

It made his companion stare. "Should you like
to see her?"

"You mean as you describe her?" He felt her
surprise, and it took him some time. "No."

"Ah then!" Mrs. Stringham sighed.

"But if she could bear it I'd do anything."

She had for the moment her vision of this, but it collapsed. "I don't see what you can do."

"I don't either. But *she* might."

Mrs. Stringham continued to think. "It's too late."

"Too late for her to see — ?"

"Too late."

The very decision of her despair — it was after all so lucid — kindled in him a heat. "But the doctor, all the while — ?"

"Tacchini? Oh he's kind. He comes. He's proud of having been approved and coached by a great London man. He hardly in fact goes away; so that I scarce know what becomes of his other patients. He thinks her, justly enough, a great personage; he treats her like royalty; he's waiting on events. But she has barely consented to see him, and, though she has told him, generously — for she *thinks* of me, dear creature — that he may come, that he may stay, for my sake, he spends most of his time only hovering at her door, prowling through the rooms, trying to entertain me, in that ghastly saloon, with the gossip of Venice, and meeting me, in doorways, in the sala, on the staircase, with an agreeable intolerable smile. We don't," said Susan Shepherd, "talk of her."

"By her request?"

"Absolutely. I don't do what she doesn't wish. We talk of the price of provisions."

"By her request too?"

"Absolutely. She named it to me as a subject when she said, the first time, that if it would be any comfort to me he might stay as much as we liked."

Densher took it all in. "But he is n't any comfort to you!"

"None whatever. That, however," she added, "is n't his fault. Nothing's any comfort."

"Certainly," Densher observed, "as I but too horribly feel, *I'm* not."

"No. But I did n't come for that."

"You came for *me*."

"Well then call it that." But she looked at him a moment with eyes filled full, and something came up in her the next instant from deeper still. "I came at bottom of course —"

"You came at bottom of course for our friend herself. But if it 's, as you say, too late for me to do anything?"

She continued to look at him, and with an irritation, which he saw grow in her, from the truth itself. "So I did say. But, with you here" — and she turned her vision again strangely about her — "with you here, and with everything, I feel we must n't abandon her."

"God forbid we should abandon her."

"Then you *won't?*" His tone had made her flush again.

"How do you mean I 'won't,' if she abandons *me?* What can I do if she won't see me?"

"But you said just now you would n't like it."

"I said I should n't like it in the light of what you tell me. I should n't like it only to see her as you make

277

me. I should like it if I could help her. But even then," Densher pursued without faith, "she would have to want it first herself. And there," he continued to make out, "is the devil of it. She *won't* want it herself. She *can't!*"

He had got up in his impatience of it, and she watched him while he helplessly moved. "There's one thing you can do. There's only that, and even for that there are difficulties. But there *is* that." He stood before her with his hands in his pockets, and he had soon enough, from her eyes, seen what was coming. She paused as if waiting for his leave to utter it, and as he only let her wait they heard in the silence, on the Canal, the renewed downpour of rain. She had at last to speak, but, as if still with her fear, she only half-spoke. "I think you really know yourself what it is."

He did know what it was, and with it even, as she said — rather! — there were difficulties. He turned away on them, on everything, for a moment; he moved to the other window and looked at the sheeted channel, wider, like a river, where the houses opposite, blurred and belittled, stood at twice their distance. Mrs. Stringham said nothing, was as mute in fact, for the minute, as if she had "had" him, and he was the first again to speak. When he did so, however, it was not in straight answer to her last remark — he only started from that. He said, as he came back to her, "Let me, you know, *see* — one must understand," almost as if he had for the time accepted it. And what he wished to understand was where, on the essence of the question, was the voice of Sir Luke

Strett. If they talked of not giving her up should n't *he* be the one least of all to do it ? "Are n't we, at the worst, in the dark without him ?"

"Oh," said Mrs. Stringham, "it 's he who has kept me going. I wired the first night, and he answered like an angel. He 'll come like one. Only he can't arrive, at the nearest, till Thursday afternoon."

"Well then that 's something."

She considered. "Something — yes. She likes him."

"Rather! I can see it still, the face with which, when he was here in October — that night when she was in white, when she had people there and those musicians — she committed him to my care. It was beautiful for both of us — she put us in relation. She asked me, for the time, to take him about; I did so, and we quite hit it off. That proved," Densher said with a quick sad smile, "that she liked him."

"He liked *you*," Susan Shepherd presently risked.

"Ah I know nothing about that."

"You ought to then. He went with you to galleries and churches; you saved his time for him, showed him the choicest things, and you perhaps will remember telling me myself that if he had n't been a great surgeon he might really have been a great judge. I mean of the beautiful."

"Well," the young man admitted, "that 's what he is — in having judged *her*. He has n't," he went on, "judged her for nothing. His interest in her — which we must make the most of — can only be supremely beneficent."

He still roamed, while he spoke, with his hands in

his pockets, and she saw him, on this, as her eyes sufficiently betrayed, trying to keep his distance from the recognition he had a few moments before partly confessed to. "I'm glad," she dropped, "you like him!"

There was something for him in the sound of it. "Well, I do no more, dear lady, than you do yourself. Surely *you* like him. Surely, when he was here, we all liked him."

"Yes, but I seem to feel I know what he thinks. And I should think, with all the time you spent with him, you'd know it," she said, "yourself."

Densher stopped short, though at first without a word. "We never spoke of her. Neither of us mentioned her, even to sound her name, and nothing whatever in connexion with her passed between us."

Mrs. Stringham stared up at him, surprised at this picture. But she had plainly an idea that after an instant resisted it. "That was his professional propriety."

"Precisely. But it was also my sense of that virtue in him, and it was something more besides." And he spoke with sudden intensity. "I could n't *talk* to him about her!"

"Oh!" said Susan Shepherd.

"I can't talk to any one about her."

"Except to *me*," his friend continued.

"Except to you." The ghost of her smile, a gleam of significance, had waited on her words, and it kept him, for honesty, looking at her. For honesty too — that is for his own words — he had quickly coloured: he was sinking so, at a stroke, the burden of his dis-

course with Kate. His visitor, for the minute, while
their eyes met, might have been watching him hold
it down. And he *had* to hold it down — the effort
of which, precisely, made him red. He could n't let
it come up; at least not yet. She might make what she
would of it. He attempted to repeat his statement, but
he really modified it. "Sir Luke, at all events, had
nothing to tell me, and I had nothing to tell him.
Make-believe talk was impossible for us, and —"

"And *real*" — she had taken him right up with a
huge emphasis — "was more impossible still." No
doubt — he did n't deny it; and she had straightway
drawn her conclusion. "Then that proves what I
say — that there were immensities between you.
Otherwise you 'd have chattered."

"I dare say," Densher granted, "we were both
thinking of her."

"You were neither of you thinking of any one else.
That's why you kept together."

Well, that too, if she desired, he took from her; but
he came straight back to what he had originally said.
"I have n't a notion, all the same, of what he thinks."
She faced him, visibly, with the question into which
he had already observed that her special shade of
earnestness was perpetually flowering, right and left
— "Are you *very* sure?" — and he could only note
her apparent difference from himself. "You, I judge,
believe that he thinks she 's gone."

She took it, but she bore up. "It does n't matter
what I believe."

"Well, we shall see" — and he felt almost basely
superficial. More and more, for the last five min-

utes, had he known she had brought something with her, and never in respect to anything had he had such a wish to postpone. He would have liked to put everything off till Thursday; he was sorry it was now Tuesday; he wondered if he were afraid. Yet it was n't of Sir Luke, who was coming; nor of Milly, who was dying; nor of Mrs. Stringham, who was sitting there. It was n't, strange to say, of Kate either, for Kate's presence affected him suddenly as having swooned or trembled away. Susan Shepherd's, thus prolonged, had cast on it some influence under which it had ceased to act. She was as absent to his sensibility as she had constantly been, since her departure, absent, as an echo or a reference, from the palace; and it was the first time, among the objects now surrounding him, that his sensibility so noted her. He knew soon enough that it was of himself he was afraid, and that even, if he did n't take care, he should infallibly be more so. "Meanwhile," he added for his companion, "it has been everything for me to see you."

She slowly rose at the words, which might almost have conveyed to her the hint of his taking care. She stood there as if she had in fact seen him abruptly moved to dismiss her. But the abruptness would have been in this case so marked as fairly to offer ground for insistence to her imagination of his state. It would take her moreover, she clearly showed him she was thinking, but a minute or two to insist. Besides, she had already said it. "Will you do it if *he* asks you? I mean if Sir Luke himself puts it to you. And will you give him" — oh she was earnest now! — "the opportunity to put it to you?"

"The opportunity to put what?"

"That if you deny it to her, that may still do something."

Densher felt himself — as had already once befallen him in the quarter of an hour — turn red to the top of his forehead. Turning red had, however, for him, as a sign of shame, been, so to speak, discounted: his consciousness of it at the present moment was rather as a sign of his fear. It showed him sharply enough of what he was afraid. "If I deny what to her?"

Hesitation, on the demand, revived in her, for hadn't he all along been letting her see that he knew? "Why, what Lord Mark told her."

"And what did Lord Mark tell her?"

Mrs. Stringham had a look of bewilderment — of seeing him as suddenly perverse. "I've been judging that you yourself know." And it was she who now blushed deep.

It quickened his pity for her, but he was beset too by other things. "Then *you* know — "

"Of his dreadful visit?" She stared. "Why it's what has done it."

"Yes — I understand that. But you also know — "

He had faltered again, but all she knew she now wanted to say. "I'm speaking," she said soothingly, "of what he told her. It's *that* that I've taken you as knowing."

"Oh!" he sounded in spite of himself.

It appeared to have for her, he saw the next moment, the quality of relief, as if he had supposed her thinking of something else. Thereupon, straight-

283

way, that lightened it. "Oh you thought I've known it for *true!*"

Her light had heightened her flush, and he saw that he had betrayed himself. Not, however, that it mattered, as he immediately saw still better. There it was now, all of it at last, and this at least there was no postponing. They were left with her idea — the one she was wishing to make him recognise. He had expressed ten minutes before his need to understand, and she was acting after all but on that. Only what he was to understand was no small matter; it might be larger even than as yet appeared.

He took again one of his turns, not meeting what she had last said; he mooned a minute, as he would have called it, at a window; and of course she could see that she had driven him to the wall. She did clearly, without delay, see it; on which her sense of having "caught" him became as promptly a scruple, which she spoke as if not to press. "What I mean is that he told her you've been all the while engaged to Miss Croy."

He gave a jerk round; it was almost — to hear it — the touch of a lash; and he said — idiotically, as he afterwards knew — the first thing that came into his head. "All *what* while?"

"Oh it's not I who say it." She spoke in gentleness. "I only repeat to you what he told her."

Densher, from whom an impatience had escaped, had already caught himself up. "Pardon my brutality. Of course I know what you're talking about. I saw him, toward the evening," he further explained, "in the Piazza; only just saw him — through the

glass at Florian's — without any words. In fact
I scarcely know him — there would n't have been
occasion. It was but once, moreover — he must have
gone that night. But I knew he would n't have come
for nothing, and I turned it over — what he would
have come for."

Oh so had Mrs. Stringham. "He came for exasperation."

Densher approved. "He came to let her know
that he knows better than she for whom it was she
had a couple of months before, in her fool's paradise,
refused him."

"How you *do* know!" — and Mrs. Stringham
almost smiled.

"I know that — but I don't know the good it does
him."

"The good, he thinks, if he has patience — not too
much — may be to come. He does n't know what he
has done to her. Only *we*, you see, do that."

He saw, but he wondered. "She kept from him
— what she felt?"

"She was able — I 'm sure of it — not to show anything. He dealt her his blow, and she took it without
a sign." Mrs. Stringham, it was plain, spoke by
book, and it brought into play again her appreciation
of what she related. "She 's magnificent."

Densher again gravely assented. "Magnificent!"

"And *he*," she went on, "is an idiot of idiots."

"An idiot of idiots." For a moment, on it all, on
the stupid doom in it, they looked at each other.
"Yet he 's thought so awfully clever."

"So awfully — it 's Maud Lowder's own view.

285

And he was nice, in London," said Mrs. Stringham, "to *me*. One could almost pity him — he has had such a good conscience."

"That's exactly the inevitable ass."

"Yes, but it was n't — I could see from the only few things she first told me — that he meant *her* the least harm. He intended none whatever."

"That's always the ass at his worst," Densher returned. "He only of course meant harm to me."

"And good to himself — he thought that would come. He had been unable to swallow," Mrs. Stringham pursued, "what had happened on his other visit. He had been then too sharply humiliated."

"Oh I saw that."

"Yes, and he also saw you. He saw you received, as it were, while he was turned away."

"Perfectly," Densher said — "I've filled it out. And also that he has known meanwhile for *what* I was then received. For a stay of all these weeks. He had had it to think of."

"Precisely — it was more than he could bear. But he has it," said Mrs. Stringham, "to think of still."

"Only, after all," asked Densher, who himself somehow, at this point, was having more to think of even than he had yet had — "only, after all, how has he happened to know? That is, to know enough."

"What do you call enough?" Mrs. Stringham enquired.

"He can only have acted — it would have been his sole safety — from full knowledge."

He had gone on without heeding her question; but, face to face as they were, something had none the less passed between them. It was this that, after an instant, made her again interrogative. "What do you mean by full knowledge?"

Densher met it indirectly. "Where has he been since October?"

"I think he has been back to England. He came in fact, I 've reason to believe, straight from there."

"Straight to do this job? All the way for his half-hour?"

"Well, to try again — with the help perhaps of a new fact. To make himself possibly right with her — a different attempt from the other. He had at any rate something to tell her, and he did n't know his opportunity would reduce itself to half an hour. Or perhaps indeed half an hour would be just what was most effective. It *has* been!" said Susan Shepherd.

Her companion took it in, understanding but too well; yet as she lighted the matter for him more, really, than his own courage had quite dared — putting the absent dots on several i's — he saw new questions swarm. They had been till now in a bunch, entangled and confused; and they fell apart, each showing for itself. The first he put to her was at any rate abrupt. "Have you heard of late from Mrs. Lowder."

"Oh yes, two or three times. She depends naturally upon news of Milly."

He hesitated. "And does she depend, naturally, upon news of *me*?"

His friend matched for an instant his deliberation. "I 've given her none that has n't been decently good. This will have been the first."

"'This'?" Densher was thinking.

"Lord Mark's having been here, and her being as she is."

He thought a moment longer. "What has Mrs. Lowder written about him? Has she written that he has been with them?"

"She has mentioned him but once — it was in her letter before the last. Then she said something."

"And what did she say?"

Mrs. Stringham produced it with an effort. "Well it was in reference to Miss Croy. That she thought Kate was thinking of him. Or perhaps I should say rather that he was thinking of *her* — only it seemed this time to have struck Maud that he was seeing the way more open to him."

Densher listened with his eyes on the ground, but he presently raised them to speak, and there was that in his face which proved him aware of a queerness in his question. "Does she mean he has been encouraged to *propose* to her niece?"

"I don't know what she means."

"Of course not" — he recovered himself; "and I ought n't to seem to trouble you to piece together what I can't piece myself. Only I 'guess,'" he added, "I *can* piece it."

She spoke a little timidly, but she risked it. "I dare say I can piece it too."

It was one of the things in her — and his conscious face took it from her as such — that from the moment of her coming in had seemed to mark for him, as to what concerned him, the long jump of her perception. They had parted four days earlier with

many things, between them, deep down. But these
things were now on their troubled surface, and it
was n't he who had brought them so quickly up.
Women were wonderful — at least this one was. But
so, not less, was Milly, was Aunt Maud; so, most of
all, was his very Kate. Well, he already knew what
he had been feeling about the circle of petticoats.
They were all *such* petticoats! It was just the fineness
of his tangle. The sense of that, in its turn, for us too,
might have been not unconnected with his putting
to his visitor a question that quite passed over her
remark. "Has Miss Croy meanwhile written to our
friend ?"

"Oh," Mrs. Stringham amended, "*her* friend also.
But not a single word that I know of."

He had taken it for certain she had n't — the thing
being after all but a shade more strange than his
having himself, with Milly, never for six weeks mentioned the young lady in question. It was for that
matter but a shade more strange than Milly's not having mentioned her. In spite of which, and however
inconsequently, he blushed anew for Kate's silence.
He got away from it in fact as quickly as possible, and
the furthest he could get was by reverting for a minute to the man they had been judging. "How did he
manage to get *at* her ? She had only — with what had
passed between them before — to say she could n't
see him."

"Oh she was disposed to kindness. She was easier," the good lady explained with a slight embarrassment, "than at the other time."

"Easier ?"

"She was off her guard. There was a difference."

"Yes. But exactly not *the* difference."

"Exactly not the difference of her having to be harsh. Perfectly. She could afford to be the opposite." With which, as he said nothing, she just impatiently completed her sense. "She had had *you* here for six weeks."

"Oh!" Densher softly groaned.

"Besides, I think he must have written her first — written I mean in a tone to smooth his way. That it would be a kindness to himself. Then on the spot —"

"On the spot," Densher broke in, "he unmasked? The horrid little beast!"

It made Susan Shepherd turn slightly pale, though quickening, as for hope, the intensity of her look at him. "Oh he went off without an alarm."

"And he must have gone off also without a hope."

"Ah that, certainly."

"Then it *was* mere base revenge. Has n't he known her, into the bargain," the young man asked — "did n't he, weeks before, see her, judge her, feel her, as having for such a suit as his not more perhaps than a few months to live?"

Mrs. Stringham at first, for reply, but looked at him in silence; and it gave more force to what she then remarkably added. "He has doubtless been aware of what you speak of, just as you have yourself been aware."

"He has wanted her, you mean, just *because* — ?"

"Just because," said Susan Shepherd.

"The hound!" Merton Densher brought out. He moved off, however, with a hot face, as soon as he

had spoken, conscious again of an intention in his
visitor's reserve. Dusk was now deeper, and after he
had once more taken counsel of the dreariness without he turned to his companion. "Shall we have lights
—a lamp or the candles?"

"Not for me."

"Nothing?"

"Not for me."

He waited at the window another moment and then
faced his friend with a thought. "He *will* have proposed to Miss Croy. That's what has happened."

Her reserve continued. "It's you who must
judge."

"Well, I do judge. Mrs. Lowder will have done
so too — only *she*, poor lady, wrong. Miss Croy's
refusal of him will have struck him" — Densher continued to make it out — "as a phenomenon requiring
a reason."

"And you've been clear to him *as* the reason?"

"Not too clear — since I'm sticking here and
since that has been a fact to make his descent on
Miss Theale relevant. But clear enough. He has believed," said Densher bravely, "that I may have been
a reason at Lancaster Gate, and yet at the same time
have been up to something in Venice."

Mrs. Stringham took her courage from his own.
"'Up to' something? Up to what?"

"God knows. To some 'game,' as they say. To
some deviltry. To some duplicity."

"Which of course," Mrs. Stringham observed, "is
a monstrous supposition." Her companion, after a
stiff minute — sensibly long for each — fell away

291

from her again, and then added to it another minute,
which he spent once more looking out with his hands
in his pockets. This was no answer, he perfectly knew,
to what she had dropped, and it even seemed to state
for his own ears that no answer was possible. She
left him to himself, and he was glad she had declined,
for their further colloquy, the advantage of lights.
These would have been an advantage mainly to herself. Yet she got her benefit too even from the absence of them. It came out in her very tone when at
last she addressed him — so differently, for confidence — in words she had already used. "If Sir Luke
himself asks it of you as something you can do for
him, will you deny to Milly herself what she has been
made so dreadfully to believe?"

Oh how he knew he hung back! But at last he
said: "You're absolutely certain then that she does
believe it?"

"Certain?" She appealed to their whole situation.
"Judge!"

He took his time again to judge. "Do *you* believe
it?"

He was conscious that his own appeal pressed her
hard; it eased him a little that her answer must be a
pain to her discretion. She answered none the less,
and he was truly the harder pressed. "What I believe
will inevitably depend more or less on your action.
You can perfectly settle it — if you care. I promise
to believe you down to the ground if, to save her life,
you consent to a denial."

"But a denial, when it comes to that — confound
the whole thing, don't you see! — of exactly what?"

BOOK NINTH

It was as if he were hoping she would narrow; but in fact she enlarged. "Of everything."

Everything had never even yet seemed to him so incalculably much. "Oh!" he simply moaned into the gloom.

IV

THE near Thursday, coming nearer and bringing Sir Luke Strett, brought also blessedly an abatement of other rigours. The weather changed, the stubborn storm yielded, and the autumn sunshine, baffled for many days, but now hot and almost vindictive, came into its own again and, with an almost audible pæan, a suffusion of bright sound that was one with the bright colour, took large possession. Venice glowed and plashed and called and chimed again; the air was like a clap of hands, and the scattered pinks, yellows, blues, sea-greens, were like a hanging-out of vivid stuffs, a laying-down of fine carpets. Densher rejoiced in this on the occasion of his going to the station to meet the great doctor. He went after consideration, which, as he was constantly aware, was at present his imposed, his only, way of doing anything. That was where the event had landed him — where no event in his life had landed him before. He had thought, no doubt, from the day he was born, much more than he had acted; except indeed that he remembered thoughts — a few of them — which at the moment of their coming to him had thrilled him almost like adventures. But anything like his actual state he had not, as to the prohibition of impulse, accident, range — the prohibition in other words of freedom — hitherto known. The great oddity was that if he had felt his arrival, so few weeks back, es-

pecially as an adventure, nothing could now less resemble one than the fact of his staying. It would be
an adventure to break away, to depart, to go back,
above all, to London, and tell Kate Croy he had done
so; but there was something of the merely, the almost meanly, obliged and involved sort in his going
on as he was. That was the effect in particular of
Mrs. Stringham's visit, which had left him as with
such a taste in his mouth of what he could n't do. It
had made this quantity clear to him, and yet had
deprived him of the sense, the other sense, of what,
for a refuge, he possibly *could*.

It was but a small make-believe of freedom, he
knew, to go to the station for Sir Luke. Nothing
equally free, at all events, had he yet turned over so
long. What then was his odious position but that
again and again he was afraid? He stiffened himself under this consciousness as if it had been a tax
levied by a tyrant. He had n't at any time proposed
to himself to live long enough for fear to preponderate
in his life. Such was simply the advantage it had
actually got of him. He was afraid for instance that
an advance to his distinguished friend might prove
for him somehow a pledge or a committal. He was
afraid of it as a current that would draw him too
far; yet he thought with an equal aversion of being
shabby, being poor, through fear. What finally pre-
vailed with him was the reflexion that, whatever
might happen, the great man had, after that occasion
at the palace, their young woman's brief sacrifice to
society — and the hour of Mrs. Stringham's appeal
had brought it well to the surface — shown him

marked benevolence. Mrs. Stringham's comments on
the relation in which Milly had placed them made
him — it was unmistakeable — feel things he perhaps
had n't felt. It was in the spirit of seeking a chance
to feel again adequately whatever it was he had missed
— it was, no doubt, in that spirit, so far as it went
a stroke for freedom, that Densher, arriving betimes,
paced the platform before the train came in. Only,
after it had come and he had presented himself at the
door of Sir Luke's compartment with everything that
followed — only, as the situation developed, the sense
of an anti-climax to so many intensities deprived his
apprehensions and hesitations even of the scant dignity they might claim. He could scarce have said if the
visitor's manner less showed the remembrance that
might have suggested expectation, or made shorter
work of surprise in presence of the fact.

Sir Luke had clean forgotten — so Densher read —
the rather remarkable young man he had formerly
gone about with, though he picked him up again, on
the spot, with one large quiet look. The young man
felt himself so picked, and the thing immediately
affected him as the proof of a splendid economy.
Opposed to all the waste with which he was now connected the exhibition was of a nature quite nobly
to admonish him. The eminent pilgrim, in the train,
all the way, had used the hours as he needed, thinking not a moment in advance of what finally awaited
him. An exquisite case awaited him — of which,
in this queer way, the remarkable young man was
an outlying part; but the single motion of his face,
the motion into which Densher, from the platform,

lightly stirred its stillness, was his first renewed cognition. If, however, he had suppressed the matter by leaving Victoria he would at once suppress now, in turn, whatever else suited. The perception of this became as a symbol of the whole pitch, so far as one might one's self be concerned, of his visit. One saw, our friend further meditated, everything that, in contact, he appeared to accept — if only, for much, not to trouble to sink it: what one missed was the inward use he made of it. Densher began wondering, at the great water-steps outside, what use he would make of the anomaly of their having there to separate. Eugenio had been on the platform, in the respectful rear, and the gondola from the palace, under his direction, bestirred itself, with its attaching mixture of alacrity and dignity, on their coming out of the station together. Densher did n't at all mind now that, he himself of necessity refusing a seat on the deep black cushions beside the guest of the palace, he had Milly's three emissaries for spectators; and this susceptibility, he also knew, it was something to have left behind. All he did was to smile down vaguely from the steps — they could see him, the donkeys, as shut out as they would. "I don't," he said with a sad headshake, "go there now."

"Oh!" Sir Luke Strett returned, and made no more of it; so that the thing was splendid, Densher fairly thought, as an inscrutability quite inevitable and unconscious. His friend appeared not even to make of it that he supposed it might be for respect to the crisis. He did n't moreover afterwards make much more of anything — after the classic craft, that

is, obeying in the main Pasquale's inimitable stroke
from the poop, had performed the manœuvre by
which it presented, receding, a back, so to speak,
rendered positively graceful by the high black hump
of its *felze*. Densher watched the gondola out of sight
— he heard Pasquale's cry, borne to him across the
water, for the sharp firm swerve into a side-canal, a
short cut to the palace. He had no gondola of his
own; it was his habit never to take one; and he hum-
bly — as in Venice it *is* humble — walked away,
though not without having for some time longer
stood as if fixed where the guest of the palace had left
him. It was strange enough, but he found himself
as never yet, and as he could n't have reckoned, in
presence of the truth that was the truest about Milly.
He could n't have reckoned on the force of the difference instantly made — for it was all in the air as he
heard Pasquale's cry and saw the boat disappear —
by the mere visibility, on the spot, of the personage
summoned to her aid. He had n't only never been
near the facts of her condition — which counted so
as a blessing for him; he had n't only, with all the
world, hovered outside an impenetrable ring fence,
within which there reigned a kind of expensive vagueness made up of smiles and silences and beautiful
fictions and priceless arrangements, all strained to
breaking; but he had also, with every one else, as he
now felt, actively fostered suppressions which were in
the direct interest of every one's good manner, every
one's pity, every one's really quite generous ideal.
It was a conspiracy of silence, as the *cliché* went, to
which no one had made an exception, the great smudge

of mortality across the picture, the shadow of pain
and horror, finding in no quarter a surface of spirit
or of speech that consented to reflect it. "The mere
æsthetic instinct of mankind —!" our young man had
more than once, in the connexion, said to himself;
letting the rest of the proposition drop, but touching
again thus sufficiently on the outrage even to taste involved in one's having to *see*. So then it had been —
a general conscious fool's paradise, from which the
specified had been chased like a dangerous animal.
What therefore had at present befallen was that the
specified, standing all the while at the gate, had now
crossed the threshold as in Sir Luke Strett's person
and quite on such a scale as to fill out the whole pre-
cinct. Densher's nerves, absolutely his heart-beats
too, had measured the change before he on this occasion moved away.

The facts of physical suffering, of incurable pain,
of the chance grimly narrowed, had been made, at
a stroke, intense, and this was to be the way he was
now to feel them. The clearance of the air, in short,
making vision not only possible but inevitable, the
one thing left to be thankful for was the breadth of
Sir Luke's shoulders, which, should one be able to
keep in line with them, might in some degree inter-
pose. It was, however, far from plain to Densher for
the first day or two that he was again to see his distinguished friend at all. That he could n't, on any
basis actually serving, return to the palace — this
was as solid to him, every whit, as the other feature
of his case, the fact of the publicity attaching to his
proscription through his not having taken himself off.

He had been seen often enough in the Leporelli gondola. As, accordingly, he was not on any presumption
destined to meet Sir Luke about the town, where the
latter would have neither time nor taste to lounge,
nothing more would occur between them unless the
great man should surprisingly wait upon him. His
doing that, Densher further reflected, would n't even
simply depend on Mrs. Stringham's having decided
to — as they might say — turn him on. It would
depend as well — for there would be practically some
difference to her — on her actually attempting it;
and it would depend above all on what Sir Luke would
make of such an overture. Densher had for that
matter his own view of the amount, to say nothing of
the particular sort, of response it might expect from
him. He had his own view of the ability of such a
personage even to understand such an appeal. To
what extent could he be prepared, and what importance in fine could he attach? Densher asked himself these questions, in truth, to put his own position
at the worst. He should miss the great man completely
unless the great man should come to see him, and the
great man could only come to see him for a purpose
unsupposable. Therefore he would n't come at all,
and consequently there was nothing to hope.

It was n't in the least that Densher invoked this
violence to all probability; but it pressed on him that
there were few possible diversions he could afford
now to miss. Nothing in his predicament was so odd
as that, incontestably afraid of himself, he was not
afraid of Sir Luke. He had an impression, which he
clung to, based on a previous taste of the visitor's

company, that *he* would somehow let him off. The truth about Milly perched on his shoulders and sounded in his tread, became by the fact of his presence the name and the form, for the time, of everything in the place; but it did n't, for the difference, sit in his face, the face so squarely and easily turned to Densher at the earlier season. His presence on the first occasion, not as the result of a summons, but as a friendly whim of his own, had had quite another value; and though our young man could scarce regard that value as recoverable he yet reached out in imagination to a renewal of the old contact. He did n't propose, as he privately and forcibly phrased the matter, to be a hog; but there was something he after all did want for himself. It was something — this stuck to him — that Sir Luke would have had for him if it had n't been impossible. These were his worst days, the two or three; those on which even the sense of the tension at the palace did n't much help him not to feel that his destiny made but light of him. He had never been, as he judged it, so down. In mean conditions, without books, without society, almost without money, he had nothing to do but to wait. His main support really was his original idea, which did n't leave him, of waiting for the deepest depth his predicament could sink him to. Fate would invent, if he but gave it time, some refinement of the horrible. It was just inventing meanwhile this suppression of Sir Luke. When the third day came without a sign he knew what to think. He had given Mrs. Stringham during her call on him no such answer as would have armed her faith, and the ultimatum she had de-

scribed as ready for him when *he* should be ready was
therefore — if on no other ground than her want of
this power to answer for him — not to be presented.
The presentation, heaven knew, was not what he desired.

That was not, either, we hasten to declare — as
Densher then soon enough saw — the idea with which
Sir Luke finally stood before him again. For stand
before him again he finally did; just when our friend
had gloomily embraced the belief that the limit of his
power to absent himself from London obligations
would have been reached. Four or five days, exclusive of journeys, represented the largest supposable
sacrifice — to a head not crowned — on the part of
one of the highest medical lights in the world; so that
really when the personage in question, following up
a tinkle of the bell, solidly rose in the doorway, it was
to impose on Densher a vision that for the instant cut
like a knife. It spoke, the fact, and in a single dreadful word, of the magnitude — he shrank from calling
it anything else — of Milly's case. The great man had
not gone then, and an immense surrender to her immense need was so expressed in it that some effect,
some help, some hope, were flagrantly part of the
expression. It was for Densher, with his reaction
from disappointment, as if he were conscious of ten
things at once — the foremost being that just conceivably, since Sir Luke *was* still there, she had been
saved. Close upon its heels, however, and quite as
sharply, came the sense that the crisis — plainly even
now to be prolonged for him — was to have none of
that sound simplicity. Not only had his visitor not

dropped in to gossip about Milly, he had n't dropped
in to mention her at all; he had dropped in fairly to
show that during the brief remainder of his stay, the
end of which was now in sight, as little as possible of
that was to be looked for. The demonstration, such
as it was, was in the key of their previous acquaintance, and it was their previous acquaintance that had
made him come. He was not to stop longer than the
Saturday next at hand, but there were things of interest he should like to see again meanwhile. It was for
these things of interest, for Venice and the opportunity of Venice, for a prowl or two, as he called it,
and a turn about, that he had looked his young man
up — producing on the latter's part, as soon as the
case had, with the lapse of a further twenty-four
hours, so defined itself, the most incongruous, yet
most beneficent revulsion. Nothing could in fact
have been more monstrous on the surface — and
Densher was well aware of it — than the relief he
found during this short period in the tacit drop of
all reference to the palace, in neither hearing news
nor asking for it. That was what had come out for
him, on his visitor's entrance, even in the very seconds of suspense that were connecting the fact also
directly and intensely with Milly's state. He had
come to say he had saved her — he had come, as from
Mrs. Stringham, to say how she might *be* saved —
he had come, in spite of Mrs. Stringham, to say she
was lost: the distinct throbs of hope, of fear, simul-
taneous for all their distinctness, merged their identity in a bound of the heart just as immediate and
which remained after they had passed. It simply

did wonders for him — this was the truth — that Sir Luke was, as he would have said, quiet.

The result of it was the oddest consciousness as of a blest calm after a storm. He had been trying for weeks, as we know, to keep superlatively still, and trying it largely in solitude and silence; but he looked back on it now as on the heat of fever. The real, the right stillness was this particular form of society. They walked together and they talked, looked up pictures again and recovered impressions — Sir Luke knew just what he wanted; haunted a little the dealers in old wares; sat down at Florian's for rest and mild drinks; blessed above all the grand weather, a bath of warm air, a pageant of autumn light. Once or twice while they rested the great man closed his eyes — keeping them so for some minutes while his companion, the more easily watching his face for it, made private reflexions on the subject of lost sleep. He had been up at night with her — he in person, for hours; but this was all he showed of it and was apparently to remain his nearest approach to an allusion. The extraordinary thing was that Densher could take it in perfectly as evidence, could turn cold at the image looking out of it; and yet that he could at the same time not intermit a throb of his response to accepted liberation. The liberation was an experience that held its own, and he continued to know why, in spite of his deserts, in spite of his folly, in spite of everything, he had so fondly hoped for it. He had hoped for it, had sat in his room there waiting for it, because he had thus divined in it, should it come, some power to let him off. He was *being* let off; dealt with in the only way that did n't aggravate his responsibility. The beauty was also that this was n't on system or on any basis of intimate knowledge; it was just by being a man of the world and by knowing life, by feeling the real, that Sir Luke did him good. There had been in all the case too many women. A man's sense of it, another man's, changed the air; and he wondered what man, had he chosen, would have been more to his purpose than this one. He was large and easy — that was the benediction; he knew what mattered and what did n't; he distinguished between the essence and the shell, the just grounds and the unjust for fussing. One was thus — if one were concerned with him or exposed to him at all — in his hands for whatever he should do, and not much less affected by his mercy than one might have been by his rigour. The grand thing — it did come to that — was the way he carried off, as one might fairly call it, the business of making odd things natural. Nothing, if they had n't taken it so, could have exceeded the unexplained oddity, between them, of Densher's now complete detachment from the poor ladies at the palace; nothing could have exceeded the no less marked anomaly of the great man's own abstentions of speech. He made, as he had done when they met at the station, nothing whatever of anything; and the effect of it, Densher would have said, was a relation with him quite resembling that of doctor and patient. One took the cue from him as one might have taken a dose — except that the cue was pleasant in the taking.

That was why one could leave it to his tacit dis-

cretion, why for the three or four days Densher again
and again did so leave it; merely wondering a little, at
the most, on the eve of Saturday, the announced term
of the episode. Waiting once more on this latter occasion, the Saturday morning, for Sir Luke's reappearance at the station, our friend had to recognise the
drop of his own borrowed ease, the result, naturally
enough, of the prospect of losing a support. The difficulty was that, on such lines as had served them, the
support was Sir Luke's personal presence. Would he
go without leaving some substitute for that? — and
without breaking, either, his silence in respect to his
errand? Densher was in still deeper ignorance than at
the hour of his call, and what was truly prodigious at
so supreme a moment was that — as had immediately
to appear — no gleam of light on what he had been
living with for a week found its way out of him. What
he had been doing was proof of a huge interest as well
as of a huge fee; yet when the Leporelli gondola again,
and somewhat tardily, approached, his companion,
watching from the water-steps, studied his fine closed
face as much as ever in vain. It was like a lesson, from
the highest authority, on the subject of the relevant, so
that its blankness affected Densher of a sudden almost as a cruelty, feeling it quite awfully compatible,
as he did, with Milly's having ceased to exist. And
the suspense continued after they had passed together,
as time was short, directly into the station, where
Eugenio, in the field early, was mounting guard over
the compartment he had secured. The strain, though
probably lasting, at the carriage-door, but a couple
of minutes, prolonged itself so for our poor gentle-

man's nerves that he involuntarily directed a long look at Eugenio, who met it, however, as only Eugenio could. Sir Luke's attention was given for the time to the right bestowal of his numerous effects, about which he was particular, and Densher fairly found himself, so far as silence could go, questioning the representative of the palace. It did n't humiliate him now; it did n't humiliate him even to feel that that personage exactly knew how little he satisfied him. Eugenio resembled to that extent Sir Luke — to the extent of the extraordinary things with which his facial habit was compatible. By the time, however, that Densher had taken from it all its possessor intended Sir Luke was free and with a hand out for farewell. He offered the hand at first without speech; only on meeting his eyes could our young man see that they had never yet so completely looked at him. It was never, with Sir Luke, that they looked harder at one time than at another; but they looked longer, and this, even a shade of it, might mean on his part everything. It meant, Densher for ten seconds believed, that Milly Theale was dead; so that the word at last spoken made him start.

"I shall come back."

"Then she's better?"

"I shall come back within the month," Sir Luke repeated without heeding the question. He had dropped Densher's hand, but he held him otherwise still. "I bring you a message from Miss Theale," he said as if they had n't spoken of her. "I'm commissioned to ask you from her to go and see her."

Densher's rebound from his supposition had a violence that his stare betrayed. "*She* asks me?"

Sir Luke had got into the carriage, the door of which the guard had closed; but he spoke again as he stood at the window, bending a little but not leaning out. "She told me she'd like it, and I promised that, as I expected to find you here, I'd let you know."

Densher, on the platform, took it from him, but what he took brought the blood into his face quite as what he had had to take from Mrs. Stringham. And he was also bewildered. "Then she can receive —?"

"She can receive you."

"And you're coming back —?"

"Oh because I must. She's not to move. She's to stay. I come to her."

"I see, I see," said Densher, who indeed did see — saw the sense of his friend's words and saw beyond it as well. What Mrs. Stringham had announced, and what he had yet expected not to have to face, *had* then come. Sir Luke had kept it for the last, but there it was, and the colourless compact form it was now taking — the tone of one man of the world to another, who, after what had happened, would understand — was but the characteristic manner of his appeal. Densher was to understand remarkably much; and the great thing certainly was to show that he did. "I'm particularly obliged, I'll go to-day." He brought that out, but in his pause, while they continued to look at each other, the train had slowly creaked into motion. There was time but for one more word, and the young man chose it, out of twenty, with intense concentration. "Then she's better?"

BOOK NINTH

Sir Luke's face was wonderful. "Yes, she's better." And he kept it at the window while the train receded, holding him with it still. It was to be his nearest approach to the utter reference they had hitherto so successfully avoided. If it stood for everything; never had a face had to stand for more. So Densher, held after the train had gone, sharply reflected; so he reflected, asking himself into what abyss it pushed him, even while conscious of retreating under the maintained observation of Eugenio.

BOOK TENTH

I

"THEN it has been — what do you say? a whole fortnight? — without your making a sign?"

Kate put that to him distinctly, in the December dusk of Lancaster Gate and on the matter of the time he had been back; but he saw with it straightway that she was as admirably true as ever to her instinct — which was a system as well — of not admitting the possibility between them of small resentments, of trifles to trip up their general trust. That by itself, the renewed beauty of it, would at this fresh sight of her have stirred him to his depths if something else, something no less vivid but quite separate, had n't stirred him still more. It was in seeing her that he felt what their interruption had been, and that they met across it even as persons whose adventures, on either side, in time and space, of the nature of perils and exiles, had had a peculiar strangeness. He wondered if he were as different for her as she herself had immediately appeared: which was but his way indeed of taking in, with his thrill, that — even going by the mere first look — she had never been so handsome. That fact bloomed for him, in the firelight and lamplight that glowed their welcome through the London fog, as the flower of her difference; just as her difference itself — part of which was her striking him as older in a degree for which no mere couple of months could ac-

313

count — was the fruit of their intimate relation. If she was different it was because they had chosen together that she should be, and she might now, as a proof of their wisdom, their success, of the reality of what had happened — of what in fact, for the spirit of each, was still happening — been showing it to him for pride. His having returned and yet kept, for numbered days, so still, had been, he was quite aware, the first point he should have to tackle; with which consciousness indeed he had made a clean breast of it in finally addressing Mrs. Lowder a note that had led to his present visit. He had written to Aunt Maud as the finer way; and it would doubtless have been to be noted that he needed no effort not to write to Kate. Venice was three weeks behind him — he had come up slowly; but it was still as if even in London he must conform to her law. That was exactly how he was able, with his faith in her steadiness, to appeal to her feeling for the situation and explain his stretched delicacy. He had come to tell her everything, so far as occasion would serve them; and if nothing was more distinct than that his slow journey, his waits, his delay to reopen communication had kept pace with this resolve, so the inconsequence was doubtless at bottom but one of the elements of intensity. He was gathering everything up, everything he should tell her. That took time, and the proof was that, as he felt on the spot, he could n't have brought it all with him before this afternoon. He *had* brought it, to the last syllable, and, out of the quantity it would n't be hard — as he in fact found — to produce, for Kate's understanding, his first reason.

"A fortnight, yes — it was a fortnight Friday; but I've only been keeping in, you see, with our wonderful system." He was so easily justified as that this of itself plainly enough prevented her saying she did n't see. Their wonderful system was accordingly still vivid for her; and such a gage of its equal vividness for himself was precisely what she must have asked. He had n't even to dot his i's beyond the remark that on the very face of it, she would remember, their wonderful system attached no premium to rapidities of transition. "I could n't quite — don't you know? — take my rebound with a rush; and I suppose I've been instinctively hanging off to minimise, for you as well as for myself, the appearances of rushing. There's a sort of fitness. But I knew you'd understand." It was presently as if she really understood so well that she almost appealed from his insistence — yet looking at him too, he was not unconscious, as if this mastery of fitnesses was a strong sign for her of what she had done to him. He might have struck her as expert for contingencies in the very degree of her having in Venice struck *him* as expert. He smiled over his plea for a renewal with stages and steps, a thing shaded, as they might say, and graduated; though — finely as she must respond — she met the smile but as she had met his entrance five minutes before. Her soft gravity at that moment — which was yet not solemnity, but the look of a consciousness charged with life to the brim and wishing not to overflow — had not qualified her welcome; what had done this being much more the presence in the room, for a couple of minutes, of the footman

who had introduced him and who had been interrupted in preparing the tea-table.

Mrs. Lowder's reply to Densher's note had been to
appoint the tea-hour, five o'clock on Sunday, for his
seeing them. Kate had thereafter wired him, without
a signature, "Come on Sunday *before* tea — about a
quarter of an hour, which will help us"; and he had
arrived therefore scrupulously at twenty minutes to
five. Kate was alone in the room and had n't delayed
to tell him that Aunt Maud, as she had happily
gathered, was to be, for the interval — not long but
precious — engaged with an old servant, retired and
pensioned, who had been paying her a visit and who
was within the hour to depart again for the suburbs.
They were to have the scrap of time, after the withdrawal of the footman, to themselves, and there was
a moment when, in spite of their wonderful system, in
spite of the proscription of rushes and the propriety
of shades, it proclaimed itself indeed precious. And
all without prejudice — that was what kept it noble
— to Kate's high sobriety and her beautiful self-com-
mand. If he had his discretion she had her perfect
manner, which was *her* decorum. Mrs. Stringham, he
had, to finish with the question of his delay, furthermore observed, Mrs. Stringham would have written
to Mrs. Lowder of his having quitted the place; so
that it was n't as if he were hoping to cheat them.
They 'd know he was no longer there.

"Yes, we 've known it."

"And you continue to hear?"

"From Mrs, Stringham? Certainly. By which I
mean Aunt Maud does."

"Then you've recent news?"

Her face showed a wonder. "Up to within a day or two I believe. But have n't *you?*"

"No—I've heard nothing." And it was now that he felt how much he had to tell her. "I do n't get letters. But I've been sure Mrs. Lowder does." With which he added: "Then of course you know." He waited as if she would show what she knew; but she only showed in silence the dawn of a surprise that she could n't control. There was nothing but for him to ask what he wanted. "Is Miss Theale alive?"

Kate's look at this was large. "Don't you *know?*"

"How should I, my dear — in the absence of everything?" And he himself stared as for light. "She's dead?" Then as with her eyes on him she slowly shook her head he uttered a strange "Not yet?"

It came out in Kate's face that there were several questions on her lips, but the one she presently put was: "Is it very terrible?"

"The manner of her so consciously and helplessly dying?" He had to think a moment. "Well, yes — since you ask me: very terrible to *me* — so far as, before I came away, I had any sight of it. But I don't think," he went on, "that — though I'll try — I *can* quite tell you what it was, what it is, for me. That's why I probably just sounded to you," he explained, "as if I hoped it might be over."

She gave him her quietest attention, but he by this time saw that, so far as telling her all was concerned, she would be divided between the wish and the reluctance to hear it; between the curiosity that, not unnaturally, would consume her and the opposing

317

scruple of a respect for misfortune. The more she
studied him too—and he had never so felt her closely
attached to his face—the more the choice of an attitude would become impossible to her. There would
simply be a feeling uppermost, and the feeling would
n't be eagerness. This perception grew in him fast,
and he even, with his imagination, had for a moment the quick forecast of her possibly breaking out
at him, should he go too far, with a wonderful:
"What horrors are you telling me?" It would have
the sound — would n't it be open to him fairly to
bring that out himself? — of a repudiation, for pity
and almost for shame, of everything that in Venice had
passed between them. Not that she would confess to
any return upon herself; not that she would let compunction or horror give her away; but it was in the air
for him—yes—that she would n't want details, that
she positively would n't take them, and that, if he
would generously understand it from her, she would
prefer to keep him down. Nothing, however, was
more definite for him than that at the same time he
must remain down but so far as it suited him. Something rose strong within him against his not being free
with her. She had been free enough about it all, three
months before, with *him*. That was what she was at
present only in the sense of treating him handsomely.
"I can believe," she said with perfect consideration, "how dreadful for you much of it must have
been."

He did n't however take this up; there were things
about which he wished first to be clear. "There's
no other possibility, by what you now know? I mean

for her life." And he had just to insist — she would say as little as she could. "She *is* dying?"

"She's dying."

It was strange to him, in the matter of Milly, that Lancaster Gate could make him any surer; yet what in the world, in the matter of Milly, was n't strange? Nothing was so much so as his own behaviour — his present as well as his past. He could but do as he must. "Has Sir Luke Strett," he asked, "gone back to her?"

"I believe he's there now."

"Then," said Densher, "it's the end."

She took it in silence for whatever he deemed it to be; but she spoke otherwise after a minute. "You won't know, unless you've perhaps seen him yourself, that Aunt Maud has been to him."

"Oh!" Densher exclaimed, with nothing to add to it.

"For real news," Kate herself after an instant added.

"She has n't thought Mrs. Stringham's real?"

"It's perhaps only I who have n't. It was on Aunt Maud's trying again three days ago to see him that she heard at his house of his having gone. He had started I believe some days before."

"And won't then by this time be back?"

Kate shook her head. "She sent yesterday to know."

"He won't leave her then" — Densher had turned it over — "while she lives. He'll stay to the end. He's magnificent."

"I think *she* is," said Kate.

319

It had made them again look at each other long;
and what it drew from him rather oddly was: "Oh
you don't know!"

"Well, she's after all my friend."

It was somehow, with her handsome demur, the
answer he had least expected of her; and it fanned
with its breath, for a brief instant, his old sense of
her variety. "I see. You would have been sure of
it. You *were* sure of it."

"Of course I was sure of it."

And a pause again, with this, fell upon them; which
Densher, however, presently broke. "If you don't
think Mrs. Stringham's news 'real' what do you think
of Lord Mark's?"

She did n't think anything. "Lord Mark's?"

"You have n't seen him?"

"Not since he saw her."

"You've known then of his seeing her?"

"Certainly. From Mrs. Stringham."

"And have you known," Densher went on, "the
rest?"

Kate wondered. "What rest?"

"Why everything. It was his visit that she could n't
stand — it was what then took place that simply
killed her."

"Oh!" Kate seriously breathed. But she had
turned pale, and he saw that, whatever her degree of
ignorance of these connexions, it was n't put on.
"Mrs. Stringham has n't said *that*."

He observed none the less that she did n't ask what
had then taken place; and he went on with his contribution to her knowledge. "The way it affected her was

that it made her give up. She has given up beyond
all power to care again, and that's why she's dying."

"Oh!" Kate once more slowly sighed, but with a
vagueness that made him pursue.

"One can see now that she was living by will —
which was very much what you originally told me of
her."

"I remember. That was it."

"Well then her will, at a given moment, broke
down, and the collapse was determined by that fel-
low's dastardly stroke. He told her, the scoundrel,
that you and I are secretly engaged."

Kate gave a quick glare. "But he does n't know
it!"

"That does n't matter. *She* did by the time he had
left her. Besides," Densher added, "he does know
it. When," he continued, "did you last see him?"

But she was lost now in the picture before her.
"*That* was what made her worse?"

He watched her take it in — it so added to her
sombre beauty. Then he spoke as Mrs. Stringham
had spoken. "She turned her face to the wall."

"Poor Milly!" said Kate.

Slight as it was, her beauty somehow gave it style;
so that he continued consistently : "She learned it, you
see, too soon — since of course one's idea had been
that she might never even learn it at all. And she *had*
felt sure — through everything we had done — of
there not being between us, so far at least as you were
concerned, anything she need regard as a warning."

She took another moment for thought. "It was n't
through anything *you* did — whatever that may have

321

been — that she gained her certainty. It was by the conviction she got from me."

"Oh it's very handsome," Densher said, "for you to take your share!"

"Do you suppose," Kate asked, "that I think of denying it?"

Her look and her tone made him for the instant regret his comment, which indeed had been the first that rose to his lips as an effect absolutely of what they would have called between them her straightness. Her straightness, visibly, was all his own loyalty could ask. Still, that was comparatively beside the mark. "Of course I don't suppose anything but that we're together in our recognitions, our responsibilities — whatever we choose to call them. It isn't a question for us of apportioning shares or distinguishing invidiously among such impressions as it was our idea to give."

"It wasn't *your* idea to give impressions," said Kate.

He met this with a smile that he himself felt, in its strained character, as queer. "Don't go into that!"

It was perhaps not as going into it that she had another idea — an idea born, she showed, of the vision he had just evoked. "Wouldn't it have been possible then to deny the truth of the information? I mean of Lord Mark's."

Densher wondered. "Possible for whom?"

"Why for you."

"To tell her he lied?"

"To tell her he's mistaken."

Densher stared — he was stupefied; the "possible" thus glanced at by Kate being exactly the alternat-

ive he had had to face in Venice and to put utterly
away from him. Nothing was stranger than such a
difference in their view of it. "And to lie myself, you
mean, to do it? We *are*, my dear child," he said, "I
suppose, still engaged."

"Of course we're still engaged. But to save her
life —!"

He took in for a little the way she talked of it. Of
course, it was to be remembered, she had always
simplified, and it brought back his sense of the degree in which, to her energy as compared with his
own, many things were easy; the very sense that so
often before had moved him to admiration. "Well,
if you must know — and I want you to be clear about
it — I did n't even seriously think of a denial to her
face. The question of it — *as* possibly saving her
— was put to me definitely enough; but to turn it
over was only to dismiss it. Besides," he added, "it
would n't have done any good."

"You mean she would have had no faith in your
correction?" She had spoken with a promptitude
that affected him of a sudden as almost glib; but he
himself paused with the overweight of all he meant,
and she meanwhile went on. "Did you try?"

"I had n't even a chance."

Kate maintained her wonderful manner, the manner of at once having it all before her and yet keeping it all at its distance. "She would n't see you?"

"Not after your friend had been with her."

She hesitated. "Could n't you write?"

It made him also think, but with a difference.
"She had turned her face to the wall."

This again for a moment hushed her, and they were both too grave now for parenthetic pity. But her interest came out for at least the minimum of light. "She refused even to let you speak to her?"

"My dear girl," Densher returned, "she was miserably, prohibitively ill."

"Well, that was what she had been before."

"And it did n't prevent? No," Densher admitted, "it did n't; and I don't pretend that she's not magnificent."

"She's prodigious," said Kate Croy.

He looked at her a moment. "So are you, my dear. But that's how it is," he wound up; "and there we are."

His idea had been in advance that she would perhaps sound him much more deeply, asking him above all two or three specific things. He had fairly fancied her even wanting to know and trying to find out how far, as the odious phrase was, he and Milly had gone, and how near, by the same token, they had come. He had asked himself if he were prepared to hear her do that, and had had to take for answer that he was prepared of course for everything. Was n't he prepared for her ascertaining if her two or three prophecies had found time to be made true? He had fairly believed himself ready to say whether or no the overture on Milly's part promised according to the boldest of them had taken place. But what was in fact blessedly coming to him was that so far as such things were concerned his readiness would n't be taxed. Kate's pressure on the question of what had taken place remained so admirably general that even her present enquiry kept itself free of sharpness. "So then that after Lord Mark's interference you never again met?"

It was what he had been all the while coming to. "No; we met once — so far as it could be called a meeting. I had stayed — I did n't come away."

"That," said Kate, "was no more than decent."

"Precisely" — he felt himself wonderful; "and I wanted to be no less. She sent for me, I went to her, and that night I left Venice."

His companion waited. "Would n't *that* then have been your chance?"

"To refute Lord Mark's story? No, not even if before her there I had wanted to. What did it signify either? She was dying."

"Well," Kate in a manner persisted, "why not just *because* she was dying?" She had however all her discretion. "But of course I know that seeing her you could judge."

"Of course seeing her I could judge. And I did see her! If I had denied you moreover," Densher said with his eyes on her, "I 'd have stuck to it."

She took for a moment the intention of his face. "You mean that to convince her you 'd have insisted or somehow proved —?"

"I mean that to convince *you* I 'd have insisted or somehow proved —!"

Kate looked for her moment at a loss. "To convince 'me'?"

"I would n't have made my denial, in such conditions, only to take it back afterwards."

With this quickly light came for her, and with it

also her colour flamed. "Oh you'd have broken with me to make your denial a truth? You'd have 'chucked' me" — she embraced it perfectly — "to save your conscience?"

"I could n't have done anything else," said Merton Densher. "So you see how right I was not to commit myself, and how little I could dream of it. If it ever again appears to you that I *might* have done so, remember what I say."

Kate again considered, but not with the effect at once to which he pointed. "You've fallen in love with her."

"Well then say so — with a dying woman. Why need you mind and what does it matter?"

It came from him, the question, straight out of the intensity of relation and the face-to-face necessity into which, from the first, from his entering the room, they had found themselves thrown; but it gave them their most extraordinary moment. "Wait till she *is* dead! Mrs. Stringham," Kate added, "is to telegraph." After which, in a tone still different, "For what then," she asked, "did Milly send for you?"

"It was what I tried to make out before I went. I must tell you moreover that I had no doubt of its really being to give me, as you say, a chance. She believed, I suppose, that I *might* deny; and what, to my own mind, was before me in going to her was the certainty that she'd put me to my test. She wanted from my own lips — so I saw it — the truth. But I was with her for twenty minutes, and she never asked me for it."

"She never wanted the truth" — Kate had a high

headshake. "She wanted *you*. She would have taken from you what you could give her and been glad of it, even if she had known it false. You might have lied to her from pity, and she have seen you and felt you lie, and yet — since it was all for tenderness — she would have thanked you and blessed you and clung to you but the more. For that was your strength, my dear man — that she loves you with passion."

"Oh my 'strength'!" Densher coldly murmured.

"Otherwise, since she had sent for you, what was it to ask of you?" And then — quite without irony — as he waited a moment to say: "Was it just once more to look at you?"

"She had nothing to ask of me — nothing, that is, but not to stay any longer. She did to that extent want to see me. She had supposed at first — after he had been with her — that I had seen the propriety of taking myself off. Then since I had n't — seeing my propriety as I did in another way — she found, days later, that I was still there. This," said Densher, "affected her."

"Of course it affected her."

Again she struck him, for all her dignity, as glib. "If it was somehow for *her* I was still staying, she wished that to end, she wished me to know how little there was need of it. And as a manner of farewell she wished herself to tell me so."

"And she did tell you so?"

"Face-to-face, yes. Personally, as she desired."

"And as *you* of course did."

"No, Kate," he returned with all their mutual consideration; "not as I did. I had n't desired it in the least."

"You only went to oblige her?"

"To oblige her. And of course also to oblige you."

"Oh for myself certainly I 'm glad."

"'Glad'?"—he echoed vaguely the way it rang out.

"I mean you did quite the right thing. You did it especially in having stayed. But that was all?" Kate went on. "That you must n't wait?"

"That was really all — and in perfect kindness."

"Ah kindness naturally: from the moment she asked of you such a — well, such an effort. That you must n't wait — that was the point," Kate added — "to see her die."

"That was the point, my dear," Densher said.

"And it took twenty minutes to make it?"

He thought a little. "I did n't time it to a second. I paid her the visit — just like another."

"Like another person?"

"Like another visit."

"Oh!" said Kate. Which had apparently the effect of slightly arresting his speech — an arrest she took advantage of to continue; making with it indeed her nearest approach to an enquiry of the kind against which he had braced himself. "Did she receive you — in her condition — in her room?"

"Not she," said Merton Densher. "She received me just as usual: in that glorious great *salone*, in the dress she always wears, from her inveterate corner of her sofa." And his face for the moment conveyed the scene, just as hers equally embraced it. "Do you remember what you originally said to me of her?"

328

"Ah I've said so many things."

"That she would n't smell of drugs, that she would n't taste of medicine. Well, she did n't."

"So that it was really almost happy?"

It took him a long time to answer, occupied as he partly was in feeling how nobody but Kate could have invested such a question with the tone that was perfectly right. She meanwhile, however, patiently waited. "I don't think I can attempt to say now what it was. Some day — perhaps. For it would be worth it for us."

"Some day — certainly." She seemed to record the promise. Yet she spoke again abruptly. "She'll recover."

"Well," said Densher, "you'll see."

She had the air an instant of trying to. "Did she show anything of her feeling? I mean," Kate explained, "of her feeling of having been misled."

She did n't press hard, surely; but he had just mentioned that he would have rather to glide. "She showed nothing but her beauty and her strength."

"Then," his companion asked, "what's the use of her strength?"

He seemed to look about for a use he could name; but he had soon given it up. "She must die, my dear, in her own extraordinary way."

"Naturally. But I don't see then what proof you have that she was ever alienated."

"I have the proof that she refused for days and days to see me."

"But she was ill."

"That had n't prevented her — as you yourself a

329

moment ago said— during the previous time. If it had been only illness it would have made no difference with her."

"She would still have received you?"

"She would still have received me."

"Oh well," said Kate, "if you know —!"

"Of course I know. I know moreover as well from Mrs. Stringham."

"And what does Mrs. Stringham know?"

"Everything."

She looked at him longer. "Everything?"

"Everything."

"Because you've told her?"

"Because she has seen for herself. I've told her nothing. She's a person who does see."

Kate thought. "That's by her liking you too. She as well is prodigious. You see what interest in a man does. It does it all round. So you need n't be afraid."

"I'm not afraid," said Densher.

Kate moved from her place then, looking at the clock, which marked five. She gave her attention to the tea-table, where Aunt Maud's huge silver kettle, which had been exposed to its lamp and which she had not soon enough noticed, was hissing too hard. "Well, it's all most wonderful!" she exclaimed as she rather too profusely — a sign her friend noticed — ladled tea into the pot. He watched her a moment at this occupation, coming nearer the table while she put in the steaming water. "You'll have some?"

He hesitated. "Had n't we better wait —?"

"For Aunt Maud?" She saw what he meant —

the deprecation, by their old law, of betrayals of the intimate note. "Oh you need n't mind now. We've done it!"

"Humbugged her?"

"Squared her. You've pleased her."

Densher mechanically accepted his tea. He was thinking of something else, and his thought in a moment came out. "What a brute then I must be!"

"A brute — ?"

"To have pleased so many people."

"Ah," said Kate with a gleam of gaiety, "you've done it to please *me*." But she was already, with her gleam, reverting a little. "What I don't understand is — won't you have any sugar?"

"Yes, please."

"What I don't understand," she went on when she had helped him, "is what it was that had occurred to bring her round again. If she gave you up for days and days, what brought her back to you?"

She asked the question with her own cup in her hand, but it found him ready enough in spite of his sense of the ironic oddity of their going into it over the tea-table. "It was Sir Luke Strett who brought her back. His visit, his presence there did it."

"He brought her back then to life."

"Well, to what I saw."

"And by interceding for you?"

"I don't think he interceded. I don't indeed know what he did."

Kate wondered. "Did n't he tell you?"

"I did n't ask him. I met him again, but we practically did n't speak of her."

Kate stared. "Then how do you know?"

"I see. I feel. I was with him again as I had been before —"

"Oh and you pleased him too? That was it?"

"He understood," said Densher.

"But understood what?"

He waited a moment. "That I had meant awfully well."

"Ah, and made *her* understand? I see," she went on as he said nothing. "But how did he convince her?"

Densher put down his cup and turned away. "You must ask Sir Luke."

He stood looking at the fire and there was a time without sound. "The great thing," Kate then resumed, "is that she's satisfied. Which," she continued, looking across at him, "is what I've worked for."

"Satisfied to die in the flower of her youth?"

"Well, at peace with you."

"Oh 'peace'!" he murmured with his eyes on the fire.

"The peace of having loved."

He raised his eyes to her. "Is *that* peace?"

"Of having *been* loved," she went on. "That is. Of having," she wound up, "realised her passion. She wanted nothing more. She has had *all* she wanted."

Lucid and always grave, she gave this out with a beautiful authority that he could for the time meet with no words. He could only again look at her, though with the sense in so doing that he made her more than he intended take his silence for assent.

Quite indeed as if she did so take it she quitted the table and came to the fire. "You may think it hideous that I should now, that I should *yet*" — she made a point of the word — "pretend to draw conclusions. But we've not failed."

"Oh!" he only again murmured.

She was once more close to him, close as she had been the day she came to him in Venice, the quickly returning memory of which intensified and enriched the fact. He could practically deny in such conditions nothing that she said, and what she said was, with it, visibly, a fruit of that knowledge. "We've succeeded." She spoke with her eyes deep in his own. "She won't have loved you for nothing." It made him wince, but she insisted. "And you won't have loved *me*."

II

HE was to remain for several days under the deep impression of this inclusive passage, so luckily prolonged from moment to moment, but interrupted at its climax, as may be said, by the entrance of Aunt Maud, who found them standing together near the fire. The bearings of the colloquy, however, sharp as they were, were less sharp to his intelligence, strangely enough, than those of a talk with Mrs. Lowder alone for which she soon gave him — or for which perhaps rather Kate gave him — full occasion. What had happened on her at last joining them was to conduce, he could immediately see, to her desiring to have him to herself. Kate and he, no doubt, at the opening of the door, had fallen apart with a certain suddenness, so that she had turned her hard fine eyes from one to the other; but the effect of this lost itself, to his mind, the next minute, in the effect of his companion's rare alertness. She instantly spoke to her aunt of what had first been uppermost for herself, inviting her thereby intimately to join them, and doing it the more happily also, no doubt, because the fact she resentfully named gave her ample support. "Had you quite understood, my dear, that it's full three weeks — ?" And she effaced herself as if to leave Mrs. Lowder to deal from her own point of view with this extravagance. Densher of course straightway noted that his cue for the protection of Kate was

334

to make, no less, all of it he could; and their tracks, as he might have said, were fairly covered by the time their hostess had taken afresh, on his renewed admission, the measure of his scant eagerness. Kate had moved away as if no great showing were needed for her personal situation to be seen as delicate. She had been entertaining their visitor on her aunt's behalf — a visitor she had been at one time suspected of favouring too much and who had now come back to them as the stricken suitor of another person. It was n't that the fate of the other person, her exquisite friend, did n't, in its tragic turn, also concern herself: it was only that her acceptance of Mr. Densher as a source of information could scarcely help having an awkwardness. She invented the awkwardness under Densher's eyes, and he marvelled on his side at the instant creation. It served her as the fine cloud that hangs about a goddess in an epic, and the young man was but vaguely to know at what point of the rest of his visit she had, for consideration, melted into it and out of sight.

He was taken up promptly with another matter — the truth of the remarkable difference, neither more nor less, that the events of Venice had introduced into his relation with Aunt Maud and that these weeks of their separation had caused quite richly to ripen for him. She had not sat down to her tea-table before he felt himself on terms with her that were absolutely new, nor could she press on him a second cup without her seeming herself, and quite wittingly, so to define and establish them. She regretted, but she quite understood, that what was taking place had obliged him to hang off; they had — after hearing of him from poor Susan as gone — been hoping for an early sight of him; they would have been interested, naturally, in his arriving straight from the scene. Yet she needed no reminder that the scene precisely — by which she meant the tragedy that had so detained and absorbed him, the memory, the shadow, the sorrow of it — was what marked him for unsociability. She thus presented him to himself, as it were, in the guise in which she had now adopted him, and it was the element of truth in the character that he found himself, for his own part, adopting. She treated him as blighted and ravaged, as frustrate and already bereft; and for him to feel that this opened for him a new chapter of frankness with her he scarce had also to perceive how it smoothed his approaches to Kate. It made the latter accessible as she had n't yet begun to be; it set up for him at Lancaster Gate an association positively hostile to any other legend. It was quickly vivid to him that, were he minded, he could "work" this association: he had but to use the house freely for his prescribed attitude and he need hardly ever be out of it. Stranger than anything moreover was to be the way that by the end of a week he stood convicted to his own sense of a surrender to Mrs. Lowder's view. He had somehow met it at a point that had brought him on — brought him on a distance that he could n't again retrace. He had private hours of wondering what had become of his sincerity; he had others of simply reflecting that he had it all in use. His only want of candour was Aunt Maud's wealth of sentiment. She was hugely sentimental, and the worst he did was to take it from her. He was n't so himself — everything was too real; but it was none the less not false that he *had* been through a mill.

It was in particular not false for instance that when she had said to him, on the Sunday, almost cosily, from her sofa behind the tea, "I want you not to doubt, you poor dear, that I 'm *with* you to the end!" his meeting her halfway had been the only course open to him. She was with him to the end — or she might be — in a way Kate was n't; and even if it literally made her society meanwhile more soothing he must just brush away the question of why it should n't. Was he professing to her in any degree the possession of an aftersense that was n't real? How in the world *could* he, when his aftersense, day by day, was his greatest reality? Such only was at bottom what there was between them, and two or three times over it made the hour pass. These were occasions — two and a scrap — on which he had come and gone without mention of Kate. Now that almost as never yet he had licence to ask for her, the queer turn of their affair made it a false note. It was another queer turn that when he talked with Aunt Maud about Milly nothing else seemed to come up. He called upon her almost avowedly for that purpose, and it was the queerest turn of all that the state of his nerves should require it. He liked her better; he was really behaving, he had occasion to say to himself, as if he liked her best. The thing was absolutely that she met *him* halfway. Nothing could have been broader than her vision, than her loquacity, than her sympathy. It appeared to gratify, to satisfy her to see him as he was; that too had its effect. It was all of course the last thing that could have seemed on the cards, a change by which he was completely *free* with this lady; and it would n't indeed have come about if — for another monstrosity — he had n't ceased to be free with Kate. Thus it was that on the third time in especial of being alone with her he found himself uttering to the elder woman what had been impossible of utterance to the younger. Mrs. Lowder gave him in fact, on the ground of what he must keep from her, but one uneasy moment. That was when, on the first Sunday, after Kate had suppressed herself, she referred to her regret that he might n't have stayed to the end. He found his reason difficult to give her, but she came after all to his help.

"You simply could n't stand it?"

"I simply could n't stand it. Besides you see —!" But he paused.

"Besides what?" He had been going to say more — then he saw dangers; luckily however she had again assisted him. "Besides — oh I know! — men have n't, in many relations, the courage of women."

"They have n't the courage of women."

"Kate or I would have stayed," she declared — "if we had n't come away for the special reason that you so frankly appreciated."

Densher had said nothing about his appreciation: had n't his behaviour since the hour itself sufficiently shown it? But he presently said — he could n't help going so far: "I don't doubt, certainly, that Miss Croy would have stayed." And he saw again into the bargain what a marvel was Susan Shepherd. She did

nothing but protect him — she had done nothing but
keep it up. In copious communication with the friend
of her youth she had yet, it was plain, favoured this
lady with nothing that compromised him. Milly's
act of renouncement she had described but as a change
for the worse; she had mentioned Lord Mark's descent, as even without her it might be known, so that
she must n't appear to conceal it; but she had suppressed explanations and connexions, and indeed,
for all he knew, blessed Puritan soul, had invented
commendable fictions. Thus it was absolutely that
he *was* at his ease. Thus it was that, shaking for ever,
in the unrest that did n't drop, his crossed leg, he
leaned back in deep yellow satin chairs and took such
comfort as came. She asked, it was true, Aunt Maud,
questions that Kate had n't; but this was just the
difference, that from her he positively liked them.
He had taken with himself on leaving Venice the
resolution to regard Milly as already dead to him
— that being for his spirit the only thinkable way to
pass the time of waiting. He had left her because it
was what suited her, and it was n't for him to go, as
they said in America, behind this; which imposed on
him but the sharper need to arrange himself with his
interval. Suspense was the ugliest ache to him, and
he would have nothing to do with it; the last thing
he wished was to be unconscious of her — what he
wished to ignore was her own consciousness, tortured,
for all he knew, crucified by its pain. Knowingly to
hang about in London while the pain went on —
what would that do but make his days impossible?
His scheme was accordingly to convince himself —

and by some art about which he was vague — that the
sense of waiting had passed. "What in fact," he
restlessly reflected, "have I any further to do with
it ? Let me assume the thing actually over — as it
at any moment may be — and I become good again
for something at least to somebody. I'm good, as it is,
for nothing to anybody, least of all to *her*." He consequently tried, so far as shutting his eyes and stalk-
ing grimly about was a trial; but his plan was carried
out, it may well be guessed, neither with marked success nor with marked consistency. The days, whether
lapsing or lingering, were a stiff reality; the suppression of anxiety was a thin idea; the taste of life
itself was the taste of suspense. That he *was* waiting
was in short at the bottom of everything; and it required no great sifting presently to feel that if he took
so much more, as he called it, to Mrs. Lowder this
was just for that reason.

She helped him to hold out, all the while that she
was subtle enough — and he could see her divine it
as what he wanted — not to insist on the actuality of
their tension. His nearest approach to success was
thus in being good for something to Aunt Maud, in
default of any one better; her company eased his
nerves even while they pretended together that they
had seen their tragedy out. They spoke of the dying
girl in the past tense; they said no worse of her than
that she had *been* stupendous. On the other hand,
however — and this was what wasn't for Densher
pure peace — they insisted enough that stupendous
was the word. It was the thing, this recognition, that
kept him most quiet; he came to it with her repeatedly;

talking about it against time and, in particular, we
have noted, speaking of his supreme personal impression as he had n't spoken to Kate. It was almost
as if she herself enjoyed the perfection of the pathos;
she sat there before the scene, as he could n't help
giving it out to her, very much as a stout citizen's wife
might have sat, during a play that made people cry,
in the pit or the family-circle. What most deeply
stirred her was the way the poor girl must have wanted
to live.

"Ah yes indeed — she did, she did: why in pity
should n't she, with everything to fill her world? The
mere *money* of her, the darling, if it is n't too disgust-
ing at such a time to mention that —!"

Aunt Maud mentioned it — and Densher quite
understood — but as fairly giving poetry to the life
Milly clung to: a view of the "might have been"
before which the good lady was hushed anew to
tears. She had had her own vision of these possibilities, and her own social use for them, and since
Milly's spirit had been after all so at one with her
about them, what was the cruelty of the event but a
cruelty, of a sort, to herself? That came out when
he named, as *the* horrible thing to know, the fact of
their young friend's unapproachable terror of the
end, keep it down though she would; coming out
therefore often, since in so naming it he found the
strangest of reliefs. He allowed it all its vividness,
as if on the principle of his not at least spiritually
shirking. Milly had held with passion to her dream
of a future, and she was separated from it, not shriek-
ing indeed, but grimly, awfully silent, as one might

imagine some noble young victim of the scaffold, in the French Revolution, separated at the prison-door from some object clutched for resistance. Densher, in a cold moment, so pictured the case for Mrs. Lowder, but no moment cold enough had yet come to make him so picture it to Kate. And it was the front so presented that had been, in Milly, heroic; presented with the highest heroism, Aunt Maud by this time knew, on the occasion of his taking leave of her. He had let her know, absolutely for the girl's glory, how he had been received on that occasion: with a positive effect — since she was indeed so perfectly the princess that Mrs. Stringham always called her — of princely state.

Before the fire in the great room that was all arabesques and cherubs, all gaiety and gilt, and that was warm at that hour too with a wealth of autumn sun, the state in question had been maintained and the situation — well, Densher said for the convenience of exquisite London gossip, sublime. The gossip — for it came to as much at Lancaster Gate — was n't the less exquisite for his use of the silver veil, nor on the other hand was the veil, so touched, too much drawn aside. He himself for that matter took in the scene again at moments as from the page of a book. He saw a young man far off and in a relation inconceivable, saw him hushed, passive, staying his breath, but half understanding, yet dimly conscious of something immense and holding himself painfully together not to lose it. The young man at these moments so seen was too distant and too strange for the right identity; and yet, outside, afterwards, it was his own face Den-

sher had known. He had known then at the same time
what the young man had been conscious of, and he was
to measure after that, day by day, how little he had
lost. At present there with Mrs. Lowder he knew
he had gathered all — that passed between them
mutely as in the intervals of their associated gaze they
exchanged looks of intelligence. This was as far as
association could go, but it was far enough when
she knew the essence. The essence was that something had happened to him too beautiful and too
sacred to describe. He had been, to his recovered
sense, forgiven, dedicated, blessed; but this he could
n't coherently express. It would have required an
explanation — fatal to Mrs. Lowder's faith in him
— of the nature of Milly's wrong. So, as to the wonderful scene, they just stood at the door. They had
the sense of the presence within — they felt the
charged stillness; after which, their association deepened by it, they turned together away.

That itself indeed, for our restless friend, became
by the end of a week the very principle of reaction:
so that he woke up one morning with such a sense
of having played a part as he needed self-respect
to gainsay. He had n't in the least stated at Lancaster
Gate that, as a haunted man — a man haunted with
a memory — he was harmless; but the degree to
which Mrs. Lowder accepted, admired and explained
his new aspect laid upon him practically the weight
of a declaration. What he had n't in the least stated
her own manner was perpetually stating; it was as
haunted and harmless that she was constantly putting him down. There offered itself however to his

purpose such an element as plain honesty, and he had embraced, by the time he dressed, his proper corrective. They were on the edge of Christmas, but Christmas this year was, as in the London of so many other years, disconcertingly mild; the still air was soft, the thick light was grey, the great town looked empty, and in the Park, where the grass was green, where the sheep browsed, where the birds multitudinously twittered, the straight walks lent themselves to slowness and the dim vistas to privacy. He held it fast this morning till he had got out, his sacrifice to honour, and then went with it to the nearest post-office and fixed it fast in a telegram; thinking of it moreover as a sacrifice only because he had, for reasons, felt it as an effort. Its character of effort it would owe to Kate's expected resistance, not less probable than on the occasion of past appeals; which was precisely why he — perhaps innocently — made his telegram persuasive. It had, as a recall of tender hours, to be, for the young woman at the counter, a trifle cryptic; but there was a good deal of it in one way and another, representing as it did a rich impulse and costing him a couple of shillings. There was also a moment later on, that day, when, in the Park, as he measured watchfully one of their old alleys, he might have been supposed by a cynical critic to be reckoning his chance of getting his money back. He was waiting — but he had waited of old; Lancaster Gate as a danger was practically at hand — but she had risked that danger before. Besides it was smaller now, with the queer turn of their affair; in spite of which indeed he was graver as he lingered and looked out.

Kate came at last by the way he had thought least likely, came as if she had started from the Marble Arch; but her advent was response — that was the great matter; response marked in her face and agreeable to him, even after Aunt Maud's responses, as nothing had been since his return to London. She had not, it was true, answered his wire, and he had begun to fear, as she was late, that with the instinct of what he might be again intending to press upon her she had decided — though not with ease — to deprive him of his chance. He would have of course, she knew, other chances, but she perhaps saw the present as offering her special danger. This, in fact, Densher could himself feel, was exactly why he had so prepared it, and he had rejoiced, even while he waited, in all that the conditions had to say to him of their simpler and better time. The shortest day of the year though it might be, it was, in the same place, by a whim of the weather, almost as much to their purpose as the days of sunny afternoons when they had taken their first trysts. This and that tree, within sight, on the grass, stretched bare boughs over the couple of chairs in which they had sat of old and in which — for they really could sit down again — they might recover the clearness of their prime. It was to all intents however this very reference that showed itself in Kate's face as, with her swift motion, she came toward him. It helped him, her swift motion, when it finally brought her nearer; helped him, for that matter, at first, if only by showing him afresh how terribly well she looked. It had been all along, he certainly remembered, a phenomenon of no rarity that he had felt her, at particular moments, handsomer than ever before; one of these for instance being still present to him as her entrance, under her aunt's eyes, at Lancaster Gate, the day of his dinner there after his return from America; and another her aspect on the same spot two Sundays ago — the light in which she struck the eyes he had brought back from Venice. In the course of a minute or two now he got, as he had got it the other times, his apprehension of the special stamp of the fortune of the moment. Whatever it had been determined by as the different hours recurred to him, it took on at present a prompt connexion with an effect produced for him in truth more than once during the past week, only now much intensified. This effect he had already noted and named: it was that of the attitude assumed by his friend in the presence of the degree of response on his part to Mrs. Lowder's welcome which she could n't possibly have failed to notice. She *had* noticed it, and she had beautifully shown him so; wearing in its honour the finest shade of studied serenity, a shade almost of gaiety over the workings of time. Everything of course was relative, with the shadow they were living under; but her condonation of the way in which he now, for confidence, distinguished Aunt Maud had almost the note of cheer. She had so by her own air consecrated the distinction, invidious in respect to herself though it might be; and nothing, really, more than this demonstration, could have given him had he still wanted it the measure of her superiority. It was doubtless for that matter this superiority alone that on the winter noon gave smooth decision to her step and charming courage to her eyes — a courage that deepened in them when he had presently got to what he did want. He had delayed after she had joined him not much more than long enough for him to say to her, drawing her hand into his arm and turning off where they had turned of old, that he would n't pretend he had n't lately had moments of not quite believing he should ever again be so happy. She answered, passing over the reasons, whatever they had been, of his doubt, that her own belief was in high happiness for them if they would only have patience; though nothing at the same time could be dearer than his idea for their walk. It was only make-believe of course, with what had taken place for them, that they could n't meet at home; she spoke of their opportunities as suffering at no point. He had at any rate soon let her know that he wished the present one to suffer at none, and in a quiet spot, beneath a great wintry tree, he let his entreaty come sharp.

"We 've played our dreadful game and we 've lost. We owe it to ourselves, we owe it to our feeling *for* ourselves and for each other, not to wait another day. Our marriage will — fundamentally, somehow, don't you see? — right everything that 's wrong, and I can't express to you my impatience. We 've only to announce it — and it takes off the weight."

"To 'announce' it?" Kate asked. She spoke as if not understanding, though she had listened to him without confusion.

"To accomplish it then — to-morrow if you will;

do it and announce it as done. That's the least part of it — after it nothing will matter. We shall be so right," he said, "that we shall be strong; we shall only wonder at our past fear. It will seem an ugly madness. It will seem a bad dream."

She looked at him without flinching — with the look she had brought at his call; but he felt now the strange chill of her brightness. "My dear man, what has happened to you?"

"Well, that I can bear it no longer. *That's* simply what has happened. Something has snapped, has broken in me, and here I am. It's *as* I am that you must have me."

He saw her try for a time to appear to consider it; but he saw her also not consider it. Yet he saw her, felt her, further — he heard her, with her clear voice — try to be intensely kind with him. "I don't see, you know, what has changed." She had a large strange smile. "We've been going on together so well, and you suddenly desert me?"

It made him helplessly gaze. "You call it so 'well'? You've touches, upon my soul —!"

"I call it perfect — from my original point of view. I'm just where I was; and you must give me some better reason than you do, my dear, for *your* not being. It seems to me," she continued, "that we're only right as to what has been between us so long as we do wait. I don't think we wish to have behaved like fools." He took in while she talked her imperturbable consistency; which it was quietly, queerly hopeless to see her stand there and breathe into their mild remembering air. He had brought her there to be

348

moved, and she was only immoveable — which was not moreover, either, because she did n't understand. She understood everything, and things he refused to; and she had reasons, deep down, the sense of which nearly sickened him. She had too again most of all her strange significant smile. "Of course if it's that you really *know* something — ?" It was quite conceivable and possible to her, he could see, that he did. But he did n't even know what she meant, and he only looked at her in gloom. His gloom however did n't upset her. "You do, I believe, only you've a delicacy about saying it. Your delicacy to me, my dear, is a scruple too much. I should have no delicacy in hearing it, so that if you can *tell* me you know —"

"Well?" he asked as she still kept what depended on it.

"Why then I'll do what you want. We need n't, I grant you, in that case wait; and I can see what you mean by thinking it nicer of us not to. I don't even ask you," she continued, "for a proof. I'm content with your moral certainty."

By this time it had come over him — it had the force of a rush. The point she made was clear, as clear as that the blood, while he recognised it, mantled in his face. "I know nothing whatever."

"You've not an idea?"

"I've not an idea."

"I'd consent," she said — "I'd announce it to-morrow, to-day, I'd go home this moment and announce it to Aunt Maud, for an idea: I mean an idea straight *from* you, I mean as your own, given me in good faith. There, my dear!"—and she smiled again. "I call that really meeting you."

If it *was* then what she called it, it disposed of his appeal, and he could but stand there with his wasted passion — for it was in high passion that he had from the morning acted — in his face. She made it all out, bent upon her — the idea he did n't have, and the idea he had, and his failure of insistence when it brought up *that* challenge, and his sense of her personal presence, and his horror, almost, of her lucidity. They made in him a mixture that might have been rage, but that was turning quickly to mere cold thought, thought which led to something else and was like a new dim dawn. It affected her then, and she had one of the impulses, in all sincerity, that had before this, between them, saved their position. When she had come nearer to him, when, putting her hand upon him, she made him sink with her, as she leaned to him, into their old pair of chairs, she prevented irresistibly, she forestalled, the waste of his passion. She had an advantage with his passion now.

III

HE had said to her in the Park when challenged on
it that nothing had "happened" to him as a cause
for the demand he there made of her — happened he
meant since the account he had given, after his return,
of his recent experience. But in the course of a few
days — they had brought him to Christmas morning
— he was conscious enough, in preparing again to
seek her out, of a difference on that score. Something
had in this case happened to him, and, after his taking
the night to think of it he felt that what it most, if not
absolutely first, involved was his immediately again
putting himself in relation with her. The fact itself
had met him there — in his own small quarters — on
Christmas Eve, and had not then indeed at once
affected him as implying that consequence. So far
as he on the spot and for the next hours took its
measure — a process that made his night mercilessly
wakeful — the consequences possibly implied were
numerous to distraction. His spirit dealt with them,
in the darkness, as the slow hours passed; his intelligence and his imagination, his soul and his sense,
had never on the whole been so intensely engaged.
It was his difficulty for the moment that he was
face to face with alternatives, and that it was
scarce even a question of turning from one to the
other. They were not in a perspective in which they
might be compared and considered; they were, by

351

a strange effect, as close as a pair of monsters of whom he might have felt on either cheek the hot breath and the huge eyes. He saw them at once and but by looking straight before him; he would n't for that matter, in his cold apprehension, have turned his head by an inch. So it was that his agitation was still — was not, for the slow hours, a matter of restless motion. He lay long, after the event, on the sofa where, extinguishing at a touch the white light of convenience that he hated, he had thrown himself without undressing. He stared at the buried day and wore out the time; with the arrival of the Christmas dawn moreover, late and grey, he felt himself somehow determined. The common wisdom had had its say to him — that safety in doubt was *not* action; and perhaps what most helped him was this very commonness. In his case there was nothing of *that* — in no case in his life had there ever been less: which association, from one thing to another, now worked for him as a choice. He acted, after his bath and his breakfast, in the sense of that marked element of the rare which he felt to be the sign of his crisis. And that is why, dressed with more state than usual and quite as if for church, he went out into the soft Christmas day.

Action, for him, on coming to the point, it appeared, carried with it a certain complexity. We should have known, walking by his side, that his final prime decision had n't been to call at the door of Sir Luke Strett, and yet that this step, though subordinate, was none the less urgent. His prime decision was for another matter, to which impatience, once he was on the way, had now added itself; but he remained sufficiently aware that he must compromise with the perhaps excessive earliness. This, and the ferment set up within him, were together a reason for not driving; to say nothing of the absence of cabs in the dusky festal desert. Sir Luke's great square was not near, but he walked the distance without seeing a hansom. He had his interval thus to turn over his view — the view to which what had happened the night before had not sharply reduced itself; but the complexity just mentioned was to be offered within the next few minutes another item to assimilate. Before Sir Luke's house, when he reached it, a brougham was drawn up — at the sight of which his heart had a lift that brought him for the instant to a stand. This pause wasn't long, but it was long enough to flash upon him a revelation in the light of which he caught his breath. The carriage, so possibly at such an hour and on such a day Sir Luke's own, had struck him as a sign that the great doctor was back. This would prove something else, in turn, still more intensely, and it was in the act of the double apprehension that Densher felt himself turn pale. His mind rebounded for the moment like a projectile that has suddenly been met by another: he stared at the strange truth that what he wanted *more* than to see Kate Croy was to see the witness who had just arrived from Venice. He wanted positively to be in his presence and to hear his voice — which was the spasm of his consciousness that produced the flash. Fortunately for him, on the spot, there supervened something in which the flash went out. He became aware within this minute that the coachman on the box of the brougham had a face known to him, whereas he had never seen before, to his knowledge, the great doctor's carriage. The carriage, as he came nearer, was simply Mrs. Lowder's; the face on the box was just the face that, in coming and going at Lancaster Gate, he would vaguely have noticed, outside, in attendance. With this the rest came: the lady of Lancaster Gate had, on a prompting not wholly remote from his own, presented herself for news; and news, in the house, she was clearly getting, since her brougham had stayed. Sir Luke *was* then back — only Mrs. Lowder was with him.

It was under the influence of this last reflexion that Densher again delayed; and it was while he delayed that something else occurred to him. It was all round, visibly — given his own new contribution — a case of pressure; and in a case of pressure Kate, for quicker knowledge, might have come out with her aunt. The possibility that in this event she might be sitting in the carriage — the thing most likely — had had the effect, before he could check it, of bringing him within range of the window. It was n't there he had wished to see her; yet if she *was* there he could n't pretend not to. What he had however the next moment made out was that if some one was there it was n't Kate Croy. It was, with a sensible shock for him, the person who had last offered him a conscious face from behind the clear plate of a café in Venice. The great glass at Florian's was a medium less obscure, even with the window down, than the air of the London Christmas; yet at present also, none the less, between the two men, an exchange of recognitions

354

could occur. Densher felt his own look a gaping arrest — which, he disgustedly remembered, his back as quickly turned, appeared to repeat itself as his special privilege. He mounted the steps of the house and touched the bell with a keen consciousness of being habitually looked at by Kate's friend from positions of almost insolent vantage. He forgot for the time the moment when, in Venice, at the palace, the encouraged young man had in a manner assisted at the departure of the disconcerted, since Lord Mark was not looking disconcerted now any more than he had looked from his bench at his café. Densher was thinking that *he* seemed to show as vagrant while another was ensconced. He was thinking of the other as — in spite of the difference of situation — more ensconced than ever; he was thinking of him above all as the friend of the person with whom his recognition had, the minute previous, associated him. The man was seated in the very place in which, beside Mrs. Lowder's, he had looked to find Kate, and that was a sufficient identity. Meanwhile at any rate the door of the house had opened and Mrs. Lowder stood before him. It was something at least that *she* was n't Kate. She was herself, on the spot, in all her affluence; with presence of mind both to decide at once that Lord Mark, in the brougham, did n't matter and to prevent Sir Luke's butler, by a firm word thrown over her shoulder, from standing there to listen to her passage with the gentleman who had rung. "*I'll* tell Mr. Densher; you need n't wait!" And the passage, promptly and richly, took place on the steps.

"He arrives, travelling straight, to-morrow early. I could n't not come to learn."

"No more," said Densher simply, "could I. On my way," he added, "to Lancaster Gate."

"Sweet of you." She beamed on him dimly, and he saw her face was attuned. It made him, with what she had just before said, know all, and he took the thing in while he met the air of portentous, of almost functional, sympathy that had settled itself as her medium with him and that yet had now a fresh glow. "So you *have* had your message?"

He knew so well what she meant, and so equally with it what he "*had* had" no less than what he had n't, that, with but the smallest hesitation, he strained the point. "Yes — my message."

"Our dear dove then, as Kate calls her, has folded her wonderful wings."

"Yes — folded them."

It rather racked him, but he tried to receive it as she intended, and she evidently took his formal assent for self-control. "Unless it's more true," she accordingly added, "that she has spread them the wider."

He again but formally assented, though, strangely enough, the words fitted a figure deep in his own imagination. "Rather, yes — spread them the wider."

"For a flight, I trust, to some happiness greater—!"

"Exactly. Greater," Densher broke in; but now with a look, he feared, that did a little warn her off.

"You were certainly," she went on with more reserve, "entitled to direct news. Ours came late last night: I'm not sure otherwise I should n't have gone to you. But you're coming," she asked, "to *me?*"

He had had a minute by this time to think further, and the window of the brougham was still within range. Her rich "me," reaching him moreover through the mild damp, had the effect of a thump on his chest. "Squared," Aunt Maud? She was indeed squared, and the extent of it just now perversely enough took away his breath. His look from where they stood embraced the aperture at which the person sitting in the carriage might have shown, and he saw his interlocutress, on her side, understand the question in it, which he moreover then uttered. "Shall you be alone?" It was, as an immediate instinctive parley with the image of his condition that now flourished in her, almost hypocritical. It sounded as if he wished to come and overflow to her, yet this was exactly what he did n't. The need to overflow had suddenly — since the night before — dried up in him, and he had never been aware of a deeper reserve.

But she had meanwhile largely responded. "Completely alone. I should otherwise never have dreamed; feeling, dear friend, but too much!" Failing on her lips what she felt came out for him in the offered hand with which she had the next moment condolingly pressed his own. "Dear friend, dear friend!" — she was deeply "with" him, and she wished to be still more so: which was what made her immediately continue. "Or would n't you this evening, for the sad Christmas it makes us, dine with me *tête-à-tête?*"

It put the thing off, the question of a talk with her — making the difference, to his relief, of several hours; but it also rather mystified him. This however did n't diminish his need of caution. "Shall you mind if I don't tell you at once?"

"Not in the least — leave it open: it shall be as you may feel, and you need n't even send me word. I only *will* mention that to-day, of all days, I shall otherwise sit there alone."

Now at least he could ask. "Without Miss Croy?"

"Without Miss Croy. Miss Croy," said Mrs. Lowder, "is spending her Christmas in the bosom of her more immediate family."

He was afraid, even while he spoke, of what his face might show. "You mean she has left you?"

Aunt Maud's own face for that matter met the enquiry with a consciousness in which he saw a reflexion of events. He was made sure by it, even at the moment and as he had never been before, that since he had known these two women no confessed nor commented tension, no crisis of the cruder sort would really have taken form between them: which was precisely a high proof of how Kate had steered her boat. The situation exposed in Mrs. Lowder's present expression lighted up by contrast that superficial smoothness; which afterwards, with his time to think of it, was to put before him again the art, the particular gift, in the girl, now so placed and classed, so intimately familiar for him, as her talent for life. The peace, within a day or two — since his seeing her last — had clearly been broken; differences, deep down, kept there by a diplomacy on Kate's part as deep, had been shaken to the surface by some exceptional jar; with which, in addition, he felt Lord

Mark's odd attendance at such an hour and season
vaguely associated. The talent for life indeed, it at
the same time struck him, would probably have
shown equally in the breach, or whatever had occurred; Aunt Maud having suffered, he judged, a
strain rather than a stroke. Of these quick thoughts,
at all events, that lady was already abreast. "She
went yesterday morning — and not with my approval, I don't mind telling you — to her sister:
Mrs. Condrip, if you know who I mean, who lives
somewhere in Chelsea. My other niece and her affairs — that I should have to say such things to-day!
— are a constant worry; so that Kate, in consequence
— well, of events! — has simply been called in. My
own idea, I'm bound to say, was that with *such* events
she need have, in her situation, next to nothing to
do."

"But she differed with you?"

"She differed with me. And when Kate differs
with you —!"

"Oh I can imagine." He had reached the point
in the scale of hypocrisy at which he could ask himself why a little more or less should signify. Besides,
with the intention he had had he *must* know. Kate's
move, if he did n't know, might simply disconcert
him; and of being disconcerted his horror was by
this time fairly superstitious. "I hope you don't
allude to events at all calamitous."

"No — only horrid and vulgar."

"Oh!" said Merton Densher.

Mrs. Lowder's soreness, it was still not obscure,
had discovered in free speech to him a momentary

balm. "They've the misfortune to have, I suppose you know, a dreadful horrible father."

"Oh!" said Densher again.

"He's too bad almost to name, but he has come upon Marian, and Marian has shrieked for help."

Densher wondered at this with intensity; and his curiosity compromised for an instant with his discretion. "Come upon her — for money?"

"Oh for that of course always. But, at *this* blessed season, for refuge, for safety: for God knows what. He's *there*, the brute. And Kate's with them. And that," Mrs. Lowder wound up, going down the steps, "is her Christmas."

She had stopped again at the bottom while he thought of an answer. "Yours then is after all rather better."

"It's at least more decent." And her hand once more came out. "But why do I talk of *our* troubles? Come if you can."

He showed a faint smile. "Thanks. If I can."

"And now — I dare say — you'll go to church?"

She had asked it, with her good intention, rather in the air and by way of sketching for him, in the line of support, something a little more to the purpose than what she had been giving him. He felt it as finishing off their intensities of expression that he found himself to all appearance receiving her hint as happy. "Why yes — I think I will": after which, as the door of the brougham, at her approach, had opened from within, he was free to turn his back. He heard the door, behind him, sharply close again and the vehicle move off in another direction than his own.

360

He had in fact for the time no direction; in spite
of which indeed he was at the end of ten minutes
aware of having walked straight to the south. That,
he afterwards recognised, was, very sufficiently, because there had formed itself in his mind, even while
Aunt Maud finally talked, an instant recognition of
his necessary course. Nothing was open to him but
to follow Kate, nor was anything more marked than
the influence of the step she had taken on the emotion itself that possessed him. Her complications,
which had fairly, with everything else, an awful
sound — what were they, a thousand times over, but
his own ? His present business was to see that they
did n't escape an hour longer taking their proper
place in his life. He accordingly would have held
his course had n't it suddenly come over him that he
had just lied to Mrs. Lowder — a term it perversely
eased him to keep using — even more than was necessary. To what church was he going, to what church,
in such a state of his nerves, *could* he go ? — he pulled
up short again, as he had pulled up in sight of Mrs.
Lowder's carriage, to ask it. And yet the desire
queerly stirred in him not to have wasted his word.
He was just then however by a happy chance in the
Brompton Road, and he bethought himself with a
sudden light that the Oratory was at hand. He had
but to turn the other way and he should find himself
soon before it. At the door then, in a few minutes,
his idea was really — as it struck him — consecrated :
he was, pushing in, on the edge of a splendid service
— the flocking crowd told of it — which glittered and
resounded, from distant depths, in the blaze of altar-

lights and the swell of organ and choir. It did n't match his own day, but it was much less of a discord than some other things actual and possible. The Oratory in short, to make him right, would do.

IV

THE difference was thus that the dusk of afternoon
— dusk thick from an early hour — had gathered
when he knocked at Mrs. Condrip's door. He had
gone from the church to his club, wishing not to present himself in Chelsea at luncheon-time and also
remembering that he must attempt independently to
make a meal. This, in the event, he but imperfectly
achieved: he dropped into a chair in the great dim
void of the club library, with nobody, up or down, to
be seen, and there after a while, closing his eyes,
recovered an hour of the sleep he had lost during
the night. Before doing this indeed he had written —
it was the first thing he did — a short note, which,
in the Christmas desolation of the place, he had managed only with difficulty and doubt to commit to a
messenger. He wished it carried by hand, and he was
obliged, rather blindly, to trust the hand, as the messenger, for some reason, was unable to return with a
gage of delivery. When at four o'clock he was face to
face with Kate in Mrs. Condrip's small drawing-room
he found to his relief that his notification had reached
her. She was expectant and to that extent prepared;
which simplified a little — if a little, at the present
pass, counted. Her conditions were vaguely vivid to
him from the moment of his coming in, and vivid
partly by their difference, a difference sharp and suggestive, from those in which he had hitherto con-

stantly seen her. He had seen her but in places comparatively great; in her aunt's pompous house, under
the high trees of Kensington and the storied ceilings
of Venice. He had seen her, in Venice, on a great
occasion, as the centre itself of the splendid Piazza:
he had seen her there, on a still greater one, in his
own poor rooms, which yet had consorted with her,
having state and ancientry even in their poorness;
but Mrs. Condrip's interior, even by this best view of
it and though not flagrantly mean, showed itself as
a setting almost grotesquely inapt. Pale, grave and
charming, she affected him at once as a distinguished
stranger — a stranger to the little Chelsea street —
who was making the best of a queer episode and a
place of exile. The extraordinary thing was that at
the end of three minutes he felt himself less ap-
pointedly a stranger in it than she.

A part of the queerness — this was to come to him
in glimpses — sprang from the air as of a general
large misfit imposed on the narrow room by the scale
and mass of its furniture. The objects, the orna-
ments were, for the sisters, clearly relics and sur-
vivals of what would, in the case of Mrs. Condrip at
least, have been called better days. The curtains that
overdraped the windows, the sofas and tables
that stayed circulation, the chimney-ornaments that
reached to the ceiling and the florid chandelier that almost dropped to the floor, were so many mementoes
of earlier homes and so many links with their unhappy mother. Whatever might have been in itself
the quality of these elements Densher could feel the
effect proceeding from them, as they lumpishly

blocked out the decline of the dim day, to be ugly almost to the point of the sinister. They failed to accommodate or to compromise; they asserted their differences without tact and without taste. It was truly having a sense of Kate's own quality thus promptly to see them in reference to it. But that Densher had this sense was no new thing to him, nor did he in strictness need, for the hour, to be reminded of it. He only knew, by one of the tricks his imagination so constantly played him, that he was, so far as her present tension went, very specially sorry for her — which was not the view that had determined his start in the morning; yet also that he himself would have taken it all, as he might say, less hard. *He* could have lived in such a place; but it was n't given to those of his complexion, so to speak, to be exiled anywhere. It was by their comparative grossness that they could somehow make shift. His natural, his inevitable, his ultimate home — left, that is, to itself — was n't at all unlikely to be as queer and impossible as what was just round them, though doubtless in less ample masses. As he took in moreover how Kate would n't have been in the least the creature she was if what was just round them had n't mismatched her, had n't made for her a medium involving compunction in the spectator, so, by the same stroke, that became the very fact of her relation with her companions there, such a fact as filled him at once, oddly, both with assurance and with suspense. If he himself, on this brief vision, felt her as alien and as ever so unwittingly ironic, how must they not feel her and how above all must she not feel them ?

365

Densher could ask himself that even after she had presently lighted the tall candles on the mantel-shelf. This was all their illumination but the fire, and she had proceeded to it with a quiet dryness that yet left play, visibly, to her implication between them, in their trouble and failing anything better, of the presumably genial Christmas hearth. So far as the genial went this had in strictness, given their conditions, to be all their geniality. He had told her in his note nothing but that he must promptly see her and that he hoped she might be able to make it possible; but he understood from the first look at her that his promptitude was already having for her its principal reference. "I was prevented this morning, in the few minutes," he explained, "asking Mrs. Lowder if she had let you know, though I rather gathered she had; and it's what I've been in fact since then assuming. It was because I was so struck at the moment with your having, as she did tell me, so suddenly come here."

"Yes, it was sudden enough." Very neat and fine in the contracted firelight, with her hands in her lap, Kate considered what he had said. He had spoken immediately of what had happened at Sir Luke Strett's door. "She has let me know nothing. But that does n't matter — if it's what *you* mean."

"It's part of what I mean," Densher said; but what he went on with, after a pause during which she waited, was apparently not the rest of that. "She had had her telegram from Mrs. Stringham; late last night. But to me the poor lady has n't wired. The event," he added, "will have taken place yester-

day, and Sir Luke, starting immediately, one can see,
and travelling straight, will get back to-morrow
morning. So that Mrs. Stringham, I judge, is left
to face in some solitude the situation bequeathed to
her. But of course," he wound up, "Sir Luke
could n't stay."

Her look at him might have had in it a vague betrayal of the sense that he was gaining time. "Was
your telegram from Sir Luke?"

"No — I 've had no telegram."

She wondered. "But not a letter — ?"

"Not from Mrs. Stringham — no." He failed
again however to develop this — for which her forbearance from another question gave him occasion.
From whom then had he heard? He might at last,
confronted with her, really have been gaining time;
and as if to show that she respected this impulse she
made her enquiry different. "Should you like to
go out to her — to Mrs. Stringham?"

About that at least he was clear. "Not at all.
She 's alone, but she 's very capable and very courage-
ous. Besides —!" He had been going on, but he
dropped.

"Besides," she said, "there 's Eugenio? Yes, of
course one remembers Eugenio."

She had uttered the words as definitely to show
them for not untender; and he showed equally every
reason to assent. "One remembers him indeed, and
with every ground for it. He 'll be of the highest value
to her — he 's capable of anything. What I was going
to say," he went on, "is that some of their people
from America must quickly arrive."

On this, as happened, Kate was able at once to satisfy him. "Mr. Someone-or-other, the person principally in charge of Milly's affairs — her first trustee, I suppose — had just got there at Mrs. Stringham's last writing."

"Ah that then was after your aunt last spoke to me — I mean the last time before this morning. I'm relieved to hear it. So," he said, "they'll do."

"Oh they'll do." And it came from each still as if it wasn't what each was most thinking of. Kate presently got however a step nearer to that. "But if you had been wired to by nobody what then this morning had taken you to Sir Luke?"

"Oh something else — which I'll presently tell you. It's what made me instantly need to see you; it's what I've come to speak to you of. But in a minute. I feel too many things," he went on, "at seeing you in this place." He got up as he spoke; she herself remained perfectly still. His movement had been to the fire, and, leaning a little, with his back to it, to look down on her from where he stood, he confined himself to his point. "Is it anything very bad that has brought you?"

He had now in any case said enough to justify her wish for more; so that, passing this matter by, she pressed her own challenge. "Do you mean, if I may ask, that *she*, dying — ?" Her face, wondering, pressed it more than her words.

"Certainly you may ask," he after a moment said. "What has come to me is what, as I say, I came expressly to tell you. I don't mind letting you know," he went on, "that my decision to do this took for

me last night and this morning a great deal of thinking of. But here I am." And he indulged in a smile
that could n't, he was well aware, but strike her as
mechanical.

She went straighter with him, she seemed to
show, than he really went with her. "You did n't
want to come?"

"It would have been simple, my dear" — and he
continued to smile — "if it had been, one way or the
other, only a question of 'wanting.' It took, I admit it, the idea of what I had best do, all sorts of
difficult and portentous forms. It came up for me
really — well, not at all for my happiness."

This word apparently puzzled her — she studied
him in the light of it. "You look upset — you 've
certainly been tormented. You 're not well."

"Oh — well enough!"

But she continued without heeding. "You hate
what you 're doing."

"My dear girl, you simplify" — and he was now
serious enough. "It is n't so simple even as that."

She had the air of thinking what it then might be.
"I of course can't, with no clue, know what it is."
She remained none the less patient and still. "If
at such a moment she could write you one 's inevitably quite at sea. One does n't, with the best will
in the world, understand." And then as Densher
had a pause which might have stood for all the
involved explanation that, to his discouragement,
loomed before him: "You *have n't* decided what to
do."

She had said it very gently, almost sweetly, and he

did n't instantly say otherwise. But he said so after a look at her. "Oh yes — I have. Only with this sight of you here and what I seem to see in it for you — ! " And his eyes, as at suggestions that pressed, turned from one part of the room to another.

"Horrible place, is n't it ?" said Kate.

It brought him straight back to his enquiry. "Is it for anything awful you 've had to come ?"

"Oh that will take as long to tell you as anything *you* may have. Don't mind," she continued, "the 'sight of me here,' nor whatever — which is more than I yet know myself — may be 'in it' for me. And kindly consider too that, after all, if you 're in trouble I can a little wish to help you. Perhaps I can absolutely even do it."

"My dear child, it 's just because of the sense of your wish —! I suppose I 'm in trouble — I suppose that 's it." He said this with so odd a suddenness of simplicity that she could only stare for it — which he as promptly saw. So he turned off as he could his vagueness. "And yet I ought n't to be." Which sounded indeed vaguer still.

She waited a moment. "Is it, as you say for my own business, anything very awful ?"

"Well," he slowly replied, "you 'll tell me if you find it so. I mean if you find my idea —"

He was so slow that she took him up. "Awful ?" A sound of impatience — the form of a laugh — at last escaped her. "I can't find it anything at all till I know what you 're talking about."

It brought him then more to the point, though it did so at first but by making him, on the hearthrug before her, with his hands in his pockets, turn awhile to and fro. There rose in him even with this movement a recall of another time — the hour in Venice, the hour of gloom and storm, when Susan Shepherd had sat in his quarters there very much as Kate was sitting now, and he had wondered, in pain even as now, what he might say and might n't. Yet the present occasion after all was somehow the easier. He tried at any rate to attach that feeling to it while he stopped before his companion. "The communication I speak of can't possibly belong — so far as its date is concerned — to these last days. The postmark, which is legible, does; but it is n't thinkable, for anything else, that she wrote —!" He dropped, looking at her as if she 'd understand.

It was easy to understand. "On her deathbed?" But Kate took an instant's thought. "Are n't we agreed that there was never any one in the world like her?"

"Yes." And looking over her head he spoke clearly enough. "There was never any one in the world like her."

Kate, from her chair, always without a movement, raised her eyes to the unconscious reach of his own. Then when the latter again dropped to her she added a question. "And won't it further depend a little on what the communication is?"

"A little perhaps — but not much. It 's a communication," said Densher.

"Do you mean a letter?"

"Yes, a letter. Addressed to me in her hand — in hers unmistakeably."

Kate thought. "Do you know her hand very well?"

"Oh perfectly."

It was as if his tone for this prompted — with a slight strangeness — her next demand. "Have you had many letters from her?"

"No. Only three notes." He spoke looking straight at her. "And very, very short ones."

"Ah," said Kate, "the number does n't matter. Three lines would be enough if you 're sure you remember."

"I 'm sure I remember. Besides," Densher continued, "I 've seen her hand in other ways. I seem to recall how you once, before she went to Venice, showed me one of her notes precisely *for* that. And then she once copied me something."

"Oh," said Kate almost with a smile, "I don't ask you for the detail of your reasons. One good one 's enough." To which however she added as if precisely not to speak with impatience or with anything like irony: "And the writing has its usual look?"

Densher answered as if even to better that description of it. "It 's beautiful."

"Yes — it *was* beautiful. Well," Kate, to defer to him still, further remarked, "it 's not news to us now that she was stupendous. Anything 's possible."

"Yes, anything 's possible" — he appeared oddly to catch at it. "That 's what I say to myself. It 's what I 've been believing you," he a trifle vaguely explained, "still more certain to feel."

She waited for him to say more, but he only, with his hands in his pockets, turned again away, going this time to the single window of the room, where in the absence of lamplight the blind had n't been drawn. He looked out into the lamplit fog, lost himself in the small sordid London street — for sordid, with his other association, he felt it — as he had lost himself, with Mrs. Stringham's eyes on him, in the vista of the Grand Canal. It was present then to his recording consciousness that when he had last been driven to such an attitude the very depth of his resistance to the opportunity to give Kate away was what had so driven him. His waiting companion had on that occasion waited for him to say he *would;* and what he had meantime glowered forth at was the inanity of such a hope. Kate's attention, on her side, during these minutes, rested on the back and shoulders he thus familiarly presented — rested as with a view of their expression, a reference to things unimparted, links still missing and that she must ever miss, try to make them out as she would. The result of her tension was that she again took him up. "You received — what you spoke of — last night?"

It made him turn round. "Coming in from Fleet Street — earlier by an hour than usual — I found it with some other letters on my table. But my eyes went straight to it, in an extraordinary way, from the door. I recognised it, knew what it was, without touching it."

"One can understand." She listened with respect. His tone however was so singular that she presently added: "You speak as if all this while you *had n't* touched it."

"Oh yes, I 've touched it. I feel as if, ever since,

I'd been touching nothing else. I quite firmly," he pursued as if to be plainer, "took hold of it."

"Then where is it?"

"Oh I have it here."

"And you've brought it to show me?"

"I've brought it to show you."

So he said with a distinctness that had, among his other oddities, almost a sound of cheer, yet making no movement that matched his words. She could accordingly but offer again her expectant face, while his own, to her impatience, seemed perversely to fill with another thought. "But now that you've done so you feel you don't want to."

"I want to immensely," he said. "Only you tell me nothing."

She smiled at him, with this, finally, as if he were an unreasonable child. "It seems to me I tell you quite as much as you tell me. You haven't yet even told me how it is that such explanations as you require don't come from your document itself." Then as he answered nothing she had a flash. "You mean you haven't read it?"

"I haven't read it."

She stared. "Then how am I to help you with it?"

Again leaving her while she never budged he paced five strides, and again he was before her. "By telling me *this*. It's something, you know, that you wouldn't tell me the other day."

She was vague. "The other day?"

"The first time after my return — the Sunday I came to you. What's he doing," Densher went on, "at that hour of the morning with her? What does his having been with her there mean?"

"Of whom are you talking?"

"Of that man — Lord Mark of course. What does it represent?"

"Oh with Aunt Maud?"

"Yes, my dear — and with you. It comes more or less to the same thing; and it's what you did n't tell me the other day when I put you the question."

Kate tried to remember the other day. "You asked me nothing about any hour."

"I asked you when it was you last saw him — previous, I mean, to his second descent at Venice. You would n't say, and as we were talking of a matter comparatively more important I let it pass. But the fact remains, you know, my dear, that you have n't told me."

Two things in this speech appeared to have reached Kate more distinctly than the others. "I 'would n't say'? — and you 'let it pass'?" She looked just coldly blank. "You really speak as if I were keeping something back."

"Well, you see," Densher persisted, "you're not even telling me now. All I want to know," he nevertheless explained, "is whether there was a connexion between that proceeding on his part, which was practically — oh beyond all doubt! — the shock precipitating for her what has now happened, and anything that had occurred with him previously for yourself. How in the world did he know we're engaged?"

V

KATE slowly rose; it was, since she had lighted the candles and sat down, the first movement she had made. "Are you trying to fix it on me that I must have told him?"

She spoke not so much in resentment as in pale dismay — which he showed he immediately took in. "My dear child, I'm not trying to 'fix' anything; but I'm extremely tormented and I seem not to understand. What has the brute to do with us anyway?"

"What has he indeed?" Kate asked.

She shook her head as if in recovery, within the minute, of some mild allowance for his unreason. There was in it — and for his reason really — one of those half-inconsequent sweetnesses by which she had often before made, over some point of difference, her own terms with him. Practically she was making them now, and essentially he was knowing it; yet inevitably, all the same, he was accepting it. She stood there close to him, with something in her patience that suggested her having supposed, when he spoke more appealingly, that he was going to kiss her. He had n't been, it appeared; but his continued appeal was none the less the quieter. "What's he doing, from ten o'clock on Christmas morning, with Mrs. Lowder?"

Kate looked surprised. "Did n't she tell you he's staying there?"

"At Lancaster Gate?" Densher's surprise met it. "'Staying'? — since when?"

"Since day before yesterday. He was there before I came away." And then she explained — confessing it in fact anomalous. "It's an accident — like Aunt Maud's having herself remained in town for Christmas, but it is n't after all so monstrous. *We* stayed — and, with my having come here, she's sorry now — because we neither of us, waiting from day to day for the news you brought, seemed to want to be with a lot of people."

"You stayed for thinking of — Venice?"

"Of course we did. For what else? And even a little," Kate wonderfully added — "it's true at least of Aunt Maud — for thinking of you."

He appreciated. "I see. Nice of you every way. But whom," he enquired, "has Lord Mark stayed for thinking of?"

"His being in London, I believe, is a very commonplace matter. He has some rooms which he has had suddenly some rather advantageous chance to let — such as, with his confessed, his decidedly proclaimed want of money, he has n't had it in him, in spite of everything, not to jump at."

Densher's attention was entire. "In spite of everything? In spite of what?"

"Well, I don't know. In spite, say, of his being scarcely supposed to do that sort of thing."

"To try to get money?"

"To try at any rate in little thrifty ways. Apparently however he has had for some reason to do what he can. He turned at a couple of days' notice out of

377

his place, making it over to his tenant; and Aunt Maud, who's deeply in his confidence about all such matters, said: 'Come then to Lancaster Gate — to sleep at least — till, like all the world, you go to the country.' He was to have gone to the country — I think to Matcham — yesterday afternoon: Aunt Maud, that is, told me he was."

Kate had been somehow, for her companion, through this statement, beautifully, quite soothingly, suggestive. "Told you, you mean, so that you need n't leave the house?"

"Yes — so far as she had taken it into her head that his being there was part of my reason."

"And *was* it part of your reason?"

"A little if you like. Yet there's plenty here — as I knew there would be — without it. So that," she said candidly, "does n't matter. I'm glad I am here: even if for all the good I do —!" She implied however that that did n't matter either. "He did n't, as you tell me, get off then to Matcham; though he may possibly, if it *is* possible, be going this afternoon. But what strikes me as most probable — and it's really, I'm bound to say, quite amiable of him — is that he has declined to leave Aunt Maud, as I've been so ready to do, to spend her Christmas alone. If moreover he has given up Matcham for her it's a *procédé* that won't please her less. It's small wonder therefore that she insists, on a dull day, in driving him about. I don't pretend to know," she wound up, "what may happen between them; but that's all I see in it."

"You see in everything, and you always did," Densher returned, "something that, while I'm with you at least, I always take from you as the truth itself."

She looked at him as if consciously and even carefully extracting the sting of his reservation; then she spoke with a quiet gravity that seemed to show how fine she found it. "Thank you." It had for him, like everything else, its effect. They were still closely face to face, and, yielding to the impulse to which he had n't yielded just before, he laid his hands on her shoulders, held her hard a minute and shook her a little, far from untenderly, as if in expression of more mingled things, all difficult, than he could speak. Then bending his head he applied his lips to her cheek. He fell, after this, away for an instant, resuming his unrest, while she kept the position in which, all passive and as a statue, she had taken his demonstration. It did n't prevent her, however, from offering him, as if what she had had was enough for the moment, a further indulgence. She made a quiet lucid connexion and as she made it sat down again. "I 've been trying to place exactly, as to its date, something that did happen to me while you were in Venice. I mean a talk with him. He spoke to me — spoke out."

"Ah there you are!" said Densher who had wheeled round.

"Well, if I 'm 'there,' as you so gracefully call it, by having refused to meet him as he wanted — as he pressed — I plead guilty to being so. Would you have liked me," she went on, "to give him an answer that would have kept him from going?"

It made him a little awkwardly think. "Did you know he was going?"

"Never for a moment; but I'm afraid that — even if it does n't fit your strange suppositions — I should have given him just the same answer if I had known. If it's a matter I have n't, since your return, thrust upon you, that's simply because it's not a matter in the memory of which I find a particular joy. I hope that if I've satisfied you about it," she continued, "it's not too much to ask of you to let it rest."

"Certainly," said Densher kindly, "I'll let it rest." But the next moment he pursued: "He saw something. He guessed."

"If you mean," she presently returned, "that he was unfortunately the one person we had n't deceived, I can't contradict you."

"No — of course not. But *why*," Densher still risked, "was he unfortunately the one person —? He's not really a bit intelligent."

"Intelligent enough apparently to have seen a mystery, a riddle, in anything so unnatural as — all things considered and when it came to the point — my attitude. So he gouged out his conviction, and on his conviction he acted."

Densher seemed for a little to look at Lord Mark's conviction as if it were a blot on the face of nature. "Do you mean because you had appeared to him to have encouraged him?"

"Of course I had been decent to him. Otherwise where *were* we?"

"'Where' — ?"

"You and I. What I appeared to him, however,

had n't mattered. What mattered was how I appeared to Aunt Maud. Besides, you must remember that he has had all along his impression of *you*. You can't help it," she said, "but you're after all — well, yourself."

"As much myself as you please. But when I took myself to Venice and kept myself there — what," Densher asked, "did he make of that?"

"Your being in Venice and liking to be — which is never on any one's part a monstrosity — was explicable for him in other ways. He was quite capable moreover of seeing it as dissimulation."

"In spite of Mrs. Lowder?"

"No," said Kate, "not in spite of Mrs. Lowder now. Aunt Maud, before what you call his second descent, had n't convinced him — all the more that my refusal of him did n't help. But he came back convinced." And then as her companion still showed a face at a loss: "I mean after he had seen Milly, spoken to her and left her. Milly convinced him."

"Milly?" Densher again but vaguely echoed.

"That you were sincere. That it was *her* you loved." It came to him from her in such a way that he instantly, once more, turned, found himself yet again at his window. "Aunt Maud, on his return here," she meanwhile continued, "had it from him. And that's why you're now so well with Aunt Maud."

He only for a minute looked out in silence — after which he came away. "And why *you* are." It was almost, in its extremely affirmative effect between them, the note of recrimination; or it would have been perhaps rather if it had n't been so much more the note of truth. It was sharp because it was true, but its truth appeared to impose it as an argument so conclusive as to permit on neither side a sequel. That made, while they faced each other over it without speech, the gravity of everything. It was as if there were almost danger, which the wrong word might start. Densher accordingly at last acted to better purpose: he drew, standing there before her, a pocket-book from the breast of his waistcoat and he drew from the pocket-book a folded letter to which her eyes attached themselves. He restored then the receptacle to its place and, with a movement not the less odd for being visibly instinctive and unconscious, carried the hand containing his letter behind him. What he thus finally spoke of was a different matter. "Did I understand from Mrs. Lowder that your father's in the house?"

If it never had taken her long in such excursions to meet him it was not to take her so now. "In the house, yes. But we need n't fear his interruption" — she spoke as if he had thought of that. "He's in bed."

"Do you mean with illness?"

She sadly shook her head. "Father's never ill. He's a marvel. He's only — endless."

Densher thought. "Can I in any way help you with him?"

"Yes." She perfectly, wearily, almost serenely, had it all. "By our making your visit as little of an affair as possible for him — and for Marian too."

"I see. They hate so your seeing me. Yet I could n't — could I? — not have come."

"No, you could n't not have come."

"But I can only, on the other hand, go as soon as possible?"

Quickly it almost upset her. "Ah don't, to-day, put ugly words into my mouth. I've enough of my trouble without it."

"I know — I know!" He spoke in instant pleading. "It's all only that I'm as troubled *for* you. When did he come?"

"Three days ago — after he had n't been near her for more than a year, after he had apparently, and not regrettably, ceased to remember her existence; and in a state which made it impossible not to take him in."

Densher hesitated. "Do you mean in such want —?"

"No, not of food, of necessary things — not even, so far as his appearance went, of money. He looked as wonderful as ever. But he was — well, in terror."

"In terror of what?"

"I don't know. Of somebody — of something. He wants, he says, to be quiet. But his quietness is awful."

She suffered, but he could n't not question. "What does he do?"

It made Kate herself hesitate. "He cries."

Again for a moment he hung fire, but he risked it. "What *has* he done?"

It made her slowly rise, and they were once more fully face to face. Her eyes held his own and she was paler than she had been. "If you love me — now — don't ask me about father."

He waited again a moment. "I love you. It's because I love you that I'm here. It's because I love
you that I've brought you this." And he drew from
behind him the letter that had remained in his hand.

But her eyes only — though he held it out — met
the offer. "Why you've not broken the seal!"

"If I had broken the seal — exactly — I should
know what's within. It's for *you* to break the seal
that I bring it."

She looked — still not touching the thing — inordinately grave. "To break the seal of something to
you from *her?*"

"Ah precisely because it's from her. I'll abide by
whatever you think of it."

"I don't understand," said Kate. "What do you
yourself think?" And then as he didn't answer:
"It seems to me *I* think you know. You have your
instinct. You don't need to read. It's the proof."

Densher faced her words as if they had been an accusation, an accusation for which he was prepared
and which there was but one way to face. "I have
indeed my instinct. It came to me, while I worried
it out, last night. It came to me as an effect of the
hour." He held up his letter and seemed now to insist more than to confess. "This thing had been
timed."

"For Christmas Eve?"

"For Christmas Eve."

Kate had suddenly a strange smile. "The season
of gifts!" After which, as he said nothing, she went
on: "And had been written, you mean, while she
could write, and kept to *be* so timed?"

Only meeting her eyes while he thought, he again did n't reply. "What do *you* mean by the proof?"

"Why of the beauty with which you 've been loved. But I won't," she said, "break your seal."

"You positively decline?"

"Positively. Never." To which she added oddly: "I know without."

He had another pause. "And what is it you know?"

"That she announces to you she has made you rich."

His pause this time was longer. "Left me her fortune?"

"Not all of it, no doubt, for it 's immense. But money to a large amount. I don't care," Kate went on, "to know how much." And her strange smile recurred. "I trust her."

"Did she tell you?" Densher asked.

"Never!" Kate visibly flushed at the thought. "That would n't, on my part, have been playing fair with her. And I did," she added, "play fair."

Densher, who had believed her — he could n't help it — continued, holding his letter, to face her. He was much quieter now, as if his torment had somehow passed. "You played fair with me, Kate; and that 's why — since we talk of proofs — I want to give *you* one. I 've wanted to let you see — and in preference even to myself — something I feel as sacred."

She frowned a little. "I don't understand."

"I 've asked myself for a tribute, for a sacrifice by which I can peculiarly recognise — "

"Peculiarly recognise what?" she demanded as he dropped.

"The admirable nature of your own sacrifice. You were capable in Venice of an act of splendid generosity."

"And the privilege you offer me with that document is my reward?"

He made a movement. "It's all I can do as a symbol of my attitude."

She looked at him long. "Your attitude, my dear, is that you're afraid of yourself. You've had to take yourself in hand. You've had to do yourself violence."

"So it is then you meet me?"

She bent her eyes hard a moment to the letter, from which her hand still stayed itself. "You absolutely *desire* me to take it?"

"I absolutely desire you to take it."

"To do what I like with it?"

"Short of course of making known its terms. It must remain — pardon my making the point — between you and me."

She had a last hesitation, but she presently broke it. "Trust me." Taking from him the sacred script she held it a little while her eyes again rested on those fine characters of Milly's that they had shortly before discussed. "To hold it," she brought out, "is to know."

"Oh I *know!*" said Merton Densher.

"Well then if we both do —!" She had already turned to the fire, nearer to which she had moved, and with a quick gesture had jerked the thing into the flame. He started — but only half — as to undo her action: his arrest was as prompt as the latter had been decisive. He only watched, with her, the paper burn; after which their eyes again met. "You'll have it all," Kate said, "from New York."

VI

IT was after he had in fact, two months later, heard
from New York that she paid him a visit one morning at his own quarters — coming not as she had
come in Venice, under his extreme solicitation, but
as a need recognised in the first instance by herself,
even though also as the prompt result of a missive
delivered to her. This had consisted of a note from
Densher accompanying a letter, "just to hand," addressed him by an eminent American legal firm, a
firm of whose high character he had become conscious while in New York as of a thing in the air
itself, and whose head and front, the principal ex-
ecutor of Milly Theale's copious will, had been duly
identified at Lancaster Gate as the gentleman hurry-
ing out, by the straight southern course, before the
girl's death, to the support of Mrs. Stringham. Densher's act on receipt of the document in question —
an act as to which and to the bearings of which his
resolve had had time to mature — constituted in strictness, singularly enough, the first reference to Milly,
or to what Milly might or might not have done, that
had passed between our pair since they had stood
together watching the destruction, in the little vulgar
grate at Chelsea, of the undisclosed work of her hand.
They had at the time, and in due deference now, on
his part, to Kate's mention of her responsibility for
his call, immediately separated, and when they met
again the subject was made present to them — at all

events till some flare of new light — only by the intensity with which it mutely expressed its absence. They were not moreover in these weeks to meet often, in spite of the fact that this had, during January and a part of February, actually become for them a comparatively easy matter. Kate's stay at Mrs. Condrip's prolonged itself under allowances from her aunt which would have been a mystery to Densher had he not been admitted, at Lancaster Gate, really in spite of himself, to the esoteric view of them. "It's her idea," Mrs. Lowder had there said to him as if she really despised ideas — which she did n't; "and I 've taken up with my own, which is to give her her head till she has had enough of it. She *has* had enough of it, she had that soon enough; but as she's as proud as the deuce she'll come back when she has found some reason — having nothing in common with her disgust — of which she can make a show. She calls it her holiday, which she's spending in her own way — the holiday to which, once a year or so, as she says, the very maids in the scullery have a right. So we're taking it on that basis. But we shall not soon, I think, take another of the same sort. Besides, she's quite decent; she comes often — whenever I make her a sign; and she has been good, on the whole, this year or two, so that, to be decent myself, I don't complain. She has really been, poor dear, very much what one hoped; though I need n't, you know," Aunt Maud wound up, "tell *you*, after all, you clever creature, what that was."

It had been partly in truth to keep down the opportunity for this that Densher's appearances under the good lady's roof markedly, after Christmas, interspaced themselves. The phase of his situation that on his return from Venice had made them for a short time almost frequent was at present quite obscured, and with it the impulse that had then acted. Another phase had taken its place, which he would have been painfully at a loss as yet to name or otherwise set on its feet, but of which the steadily rising tide left Mrs. Lowder, for his desire, quite high and dry. There had been a moment when it seemed possible that Mrs. Stringham, returning to America under convoy, would pause in London on her way and be housed with her old friend; in which case he was prepared for some apparent zeal of attendance. But this danger passed — he had felt it a danger, and the person in the world whom he would just now have most valued seeing on his own terms sailed away westward from Genoa. He thereby only wrote to her, having broken, in this respect, after Milly's death, the silence as to the sense of which, before that event, their agreement had been so deep. She had answered him from Venice twice, and had had time to answer him twice again from New York. The last letter of her four had come by the same post as the document he sent on to Kate, but he had n't gone into the question of also enclosing that. His correspondence with Milly's companion was somehow already presenting itself to him as a feature — as a factor, he would have said in his newspaper — of the time whatever it might be, long or short, in store for him; but one of his acutest current thoughts was apt to be devoted to his not having yet mentioned it to Kate.

She had put him no question, no "Don't you ever hear?" — so that he had n't been brought to the point. This he described to himself as a mercy, for he liked his secret. It was as a secret that, in the same personal privacy, he described his transatlantic commerce, scarce even wincing while he recognised it as the one connexion in which he was n't straight. He had in fact for this connexion a vivid mental image — he saw it as a small emergent rock in the waste of waters, the bottomless grey expanse of straightness. The fact that he had on several recent occasions taken with Kate an out-of-the-way walk that was each time to define itself as more remarkable for what they did n't say than for what they did — this fact failed somehow to mitigate for him a strange consciousness of exposure. There was something deep within him that he had absolutely shown to no one — to the companion of these walks in particular not a bit more than he could help; but he was none the less haunted, under its shadow, with a dire apprehension of publicity. It was as if he had invoked that ugliness in some stupid good faith; and it was queer enough that on his emergent rock, clinging to it and to Susan Shepherd, he should figure himself as hidden from view. That represented no doubt his belief in her power, or in her delicate disposition to protect him. Only Kate at all events knew — what Kate did know, and she was also the last person interested to tell it; in spite of which it was as if his *act*, so deeply associated with her and never to be recalled nor recovered, was abroad on the winds of the world. His honesty, as he viewed it with Kate, was the very element of that menace:

to the degree that he saw at moments, as to their final impulse or their final remedy, the need to bury in the dark blindness of each other's arms the knowledge of each other that they could n't undo.

Save indeed that the sense in which it was in these days a question of arms was limited, this might have been the intimate expedient to which they were actually resorting. It had its value, in conditions that made everything count, that thrice over, in Battersea Park — where Mrs. Lowder now never drove — he had adopted the usual means, in sequestered alleys, of holding her close to his side. She could make absences, on her present footing, without having too inordinately to account for them at home — which was exactly what gave them for the first time an appreciable margin. He supposed she could always say in Chelsea — though he did n't press it — that she had been across the town, in decency, for a look at her aunt; whereas there had always been reasons at Lancaster Gate for her not being able to plead the look at her other relatives. It was therefore between them a freedom of a purity as yet untasted; which for that matter also they made in various ways no little show of cherishing as such. They made the show indeed in every way but the way of a large use — an inconsequence that they almost equally gave time to helping each other to regard as natural. He put it to his companion that the kind of favour he now enjoyed at Lancaster Gate, the wonderful warmth of his reception there, cut in a manner the ground from under their feet. He was too horribly trusted — they had succeeded too well. He could n't in short

make appointments with her without abusing Aunt
Maud, and he could n't on the other hand haunt that
lady without tying his hands. Kate saw what he
meant just as he saw what she did when she admitted
that she was herself, to a degree scarce less embarrassing, in the enjoyment of Aunt Maud's confidence.
It was special at present — she was handsomely used;
she confessed accordingly to a scruple about misapply-
ing her licence. Mrs. Lowder then finally had found —
and all unconsciously now — the way to baffle them.
It was n't however that they did n't meet a little,
none the less, in the southern quarter, to point for
their common benefit the moral of their defeat. They
crossed the river; they wandered in neighbourhoods
sordid and safe; the winter was mild, so that, mounting to the top of trams, they could rumble together
to Clapham or to Greenwich. If at the same time
their minutes had never been so counted it struck Densher that by a singular law their tone — he scarce
knew what to call it — had never been so bland. Not
to talk of what they *might* have talked of drove them
to other ground; it was as if they used a perverse
insistence to make up what they ignored. They concealed their pursuit of the irrelevant by the charm
of their manner; they took precautions for the court-
esy they had formerly left to come of itself; often,
when he had quitted her, he stopped short, walking
off, with the aftersense of their change. He would
have described their change — had he so far faced it
as to describe it — by their being so damned civil.
That had even, with the intimate, the familiar at the
point to which they had brought them, a touch almost

of the droll. What danger had there ever been of their becoming rude — after each had long since made the other so tremendously tender? Such were the things he asked himself when he wondered what in particular he most feared.

Yet all the while too the tension had its charm — such being the interest of a creature who could bring one back to her by such different roads. It was her talent for life again; which found in her a difference for the differing time. She did n't give their tradition up; she but made of it something new. Frankly moreover she had never been more agreeable nor in a way — to put it prosaically — better company: he felt almost as if he were knowing her on that defined basis — which he even hesitated whether to measure as reduced or as extended; as if at all events he were admiring her as she was probably admired by people she met "out." He had n't in fine reckoned that she would still have something fresh for him; yet this was what she had — that on the top of a tram in the Borough he felt as if he were next her at dinner. What a person she would be if they *had* been rich — with what a genius for the so-called great life, what a presence for the so-called great house, what a grace for the so-called great positions! He might regret at once, while he was about it, that they were n't princes or billionaires. She had treated him on their Christmas to a softness that had struck him at the time as of the quality of fine velvet, meant to fold thick, but stretched a little thin; at present, however, she gave him the impression of a contact multitudinous as only the superficial can be. She had throughout

never a word for what went on at home. She came
out of that and she returned to it, but her nearest
reference was the look with which, each time, she
bade him good-bye. The look was her repeated prohibition: "It's what I *have* to see and to know — so
don't touch it. That but wakes up the old evil, which
I keep still, in my way, by sitting by it. I go now —
leave me alone! — to sit by it again. The way to pity
me — if that's what you want — is to believe in me.
If we could really *do* anything it would be another
matter."

He watched her, when she went her way, with the
vision of what she thus a little stiffly carried. It was
confused and obscure, but how, with her head high,
it made her hold herself! He really in his own person
might at these moments have been swaying a little
aloft as one of the objects in her poised basket. It
was doubtless thanks to some such consciousness as
this that he felt the lapse of the weeks, before the day
of Kate's mounting of his stair, almost swingingly
rapid. They contained for him the contradiction that,
whereas periods of waiting are supposed in general
to keep the time slow, it was the wait, actually, that
made the pace trouble him. The secret of that anomaly, to be plain, was that he was aware of how, while
the days melted, something rare went with them.
This something was only a thought, but a thought
precisely of such freshness and such delicacy as made
the precious, of whatever sort, most subject to the
hunger of time. The thought was all his own, and his
intimate companion was the last person he might have
shared it with. He kept it back like a favourite pang;

left it behind him, so to say, when he went out, but came home again the sooner for the certainty of finding it there. Then he took it out of its sacred corner and its soft wrappings; he undid them one by one, handling them, handling *it*, as a father, baffled and tender, might handle a maimed child. But so it was before him — in his dread of who else might see it. Then he took to himself at such hours, in other words, that he should never, never know what had been in Milly's letter. The intention announced in it he should but too probably know; only that would have been, but for the depths of his spirit, the least part of it. The part of it missed for ever was the turn she would have given her act. This turn had possibilities that, somehow, by wondering about them, his imagination had extraordinarily filled out and refined. It had made of them a revelation the loss of which was like the sight of a priceless pearl cast before his eyes — his pledge given not to save it — into the fathomless sea, or rather even it was like the sacrifice of something sentient and throbbing, something that, for the spiritual ear, might have been audible as a faint far wail. This was the sound he cherished when alone in the stillness of his rooms. He sought and guarded the stillness, so that it might prevail there till the inevitable sounds of life, once more, comparatively coarse and harsh, should smother and deaden it — doubtless by the same process with which they would officiously heal the ache in his soul that was somehow one with it. It moreover deepened the sacred hush that he could n't complain. He had given poor Kate her freedom.

BOOK TENTH

The great and obvious thing, as soon as she stood there on the occasion we have already named, was that she was now in high possession of it. This would have marked immediately the difference — had there been nothing else to do it — between their actual terms and their other terms, the character of their last encounter in Venice. That had been *his* idea, whereas her present step was her own; the few marks they had in common were, from the first moment, to his conscious vision, almost pathetically plain. She was as grave now as before; she looked around her, to hide it, as before; she pretended, as before, in an air in which her words at the moment itself fell flat, to an interest in the place and a curiosity about his "things"; there was a recall in the way in which, after she had failed a little to push up her veil symmetrically and he had said she had better take it off altogether, she had acceded to his suggestion before the glass. It was just these things that were vain; and what was real was that his fancy figured her after the first few minutes as literally now providing the element of reassurance which had previously been his care. It was she, supremely, who had the presence of mind. She made indeed for that matter very prompt use of it: "You see I've not hesitated this time to break your seal."

She had laid on the table from the moment of her coming in the long envelope, substantially filled, which he had sent her enclosed in another of still ampler make. He had however not looked at it — his belief being that he wished never again to do so; besides which it had happened to rest with its addressed side up. So he "saw" nothing, and it was only into her eyes that her remark made him look, declining any approach to the object indicated. "It's not 'my' seal, my dear; and my intention — which my note tried to express — was all to treat it to you as not mine."

"Do you mean that it's to that extent mine then?"

"Well, let us call it, if we like, theirs — that of the good people in New York, the authors of our communication. If the seal is broken well and good; but we *might*, you know," he presently added, "have sent it back to them intact and inviolate. Only accompanied," he smiled with his heart in his mouth, "by an absolutely kind letter."

Kate took it with the mere brave blink with which a patient of courage signifies to the exploring medical hand that the tender place is touched. He saw on the spot that she was prepared, and with this signal sign that she was too intelligent not to be, came a flicker of possibilities. She was — merely to put it at that — intelligent enough for anything. "Is it what you're proposing we *should* do?"

"Ah it's too late to do it — well, ideally. Now, with that sign that we *know* —!"

"But you don't know," she said very gently.

"I refer," he went on without noticing it, "to what would have been the handsome way. Its being dispatched again, with no cognisance taken but one's assurance of the highest consideration, and the proof of this in the state of the envelope — *that* would have been really satisfying."

She thought an instant. "The state of the envelope proving refusal, you mean, not to be based on the insufficiency of the sum?"

Densher smiled again as for the play, however whimsical, of her humour. "Well yes — something of that sort."

"So that if cognisance *has* been taken — so far as I'm concerned — it spoils the beauty?"

"It makes the difference that I'm disappointed in the hope — which I confess I entertained — that you'd bring the thing back to me as you had received it."

"You did n't express that hope in your letter."

"I did n't want to. I wanted to leave it to yourself. I wanted — oh yes, if that's what you wish to ask me — to see what you'd do."

"You wanted to measure the possibilities of my departure from delicacy?"

He continued steady now; a kind of ease — from the presence, as in the air, of something he could n't yet have named — had come to him. "Well, I wanted — in so good a case — to test you."

She was struck — it showed in her face — by his expression. "It *is* a good case. I doubt whether a better," she said with her eyes on him, "has ever been known."

"The better the case then the better the test!"

"How do you know," she asked in reply to this, "what I'm capable of?"

"I don't, my dear! Only with the seal unbroken I should have known sooner."

"I see" — she took it in. "But I myself should n't

399

have known at all. And you would n't have known, either, what I do know."

"Let me tell you at once," he returned, "that if you 've been moved to correct my ignorance I very particularly request you not to."

She just hesitated. "Are you afraid of the effect of the corrections? Can you only do it by doing it blindly?"

He waited a moment. "What is it that you speak of my doing?"

"Why the only thing in the world that I take you as thinking of. Not accepting — what she has done. Is n't there some regular name in such cases? Not taking up the bequest."

"There 's something you forget in it," he said after a moment. "My asking you to join with me in doing so."

Her wonder but made her softer, yet at the same time did n't make her less firm. "How can I 'join' in a matter with which I 've nothing to do?"

"How? By a single word."

"And what word?"

"Your consent to my giving up."

"My consent has no meaning when I can't prevent you."

"You can perfectly prevent me. Understand that well," he said.

She seemed to face a threat in it. "You mean you won't give up if I *don't* consent?"

"Yes. I do nothing."

"That, as I understand, is accepting."

Densher paused. "I do nothing formal."

"You won't, I suppose you mean, touch the money."

"I won't touch the money."

It had a sound — though he had been coming to it — that made for gravity. "Who then in such an event *will*?"

"Any one who wants or who can."

Again a little she said nothing: she might say too much. But by the time she spoke he had covered ground. "How can I touch it but *through* you?"

"You can't. Any more," he added, "than I can renounce it except through you."

"Oh ever so much less! There's nothing," she explained, "in my power."

"I'm in your power," Merton Densher said.

"In what way?"

"In the way I show — and the way I've always shown. When have I shown," he asked as with a sudden cold impatience, "anything else? You surely must feel — so that you need n't wish to appear to spare me in it — how you 'have' me."

"It's very good of you, my dear," she nervously laughed, "to put me so thoroughly up to it!"

"I put you up to nothing. I did n't even put you up to the chance that, as I said a few moments ago, I saw for you in forwarding that thing. Your liberty is therefore in every way complete."

It had come to the point really that they showed each other pale faces, and that all the unspoken between them looked out of their eyes in a dim terror of their further conflict. Something even rose between them in one of their short silences — some-

thing that was like an appeal from each to the other
not to be too true. Their necessity was somehow
before them, but which of them must meet it first?
"Thank you!" Kate said for his word about her
freedom, but taking for the minute no further action
on it. It was blest at least that all ironies failed them,
and during another slow moment their very sense
of it cleared the air.

There was an effect of this in the way he soon
went on. "You must intensely feel that it's the
thing for which we worked together."

She took up the remark, however, no more than if
it were commonplace; she was already again occupied with a point of her own. "Is it absolutely true
— for if it is, you know, it's tremendously interesting — that you haven't so much as a curiosity about
what she has done for you?"

"Would you like," he asked, "my formal oath
on it?"

"No — but I don't understand. It seems to me
in your place —!"

"Ah," he couldn't help breaking in, "what do
you know of my place? Pardon me," he at once
added; "my preference is the one I express."

She had in an instant nevertheless a curious thought.
"But won't the facts be published?"

"'Published'?" — he winced.

"I mean won't you see them in the papers?"

"Ah never! I shall know how to escape that."

It seemed to settle the subject, but she had the next
minute another insistence. "Your desire is to escape
everything?"

"Everything."

"And do you need no more definite sense of what it is you ask me to help you to renounce?"

"My sense is sufficient without being definite. I'm willing to believe that the amount of money's not small."

"Ah there you are!" she exclaimed.

"If she was to leave me a remembrance," he quietly pursued, "it would inevitably not be meagre."

Kate waited as for how to say it. "It's worthy of her. It's what she was herself — if you remember what we once said *that* was."

He hesitated — as if there had been many things. But he remembered one of them. "Stupendous?"

"Stupendous." A faint smile for it — ever so small — had flickered in her face, but had vanished before the omen of tears, a little less uncertain, had shown themselves in his own. His eyes filled — but that made her continue. She continued gently. "I think that what it really is must be that you're afraid. I mean," she explained, "that you're afraid of *all* the truth. If you're in love with her without it, what indeed can you be more? And you're afraid — it's wonderful! — to be in love with her."

"I never was in love with her," said Densher.

She took it, but after a little she met it. "I believe that now — for the time she lived. I believe it at least for the time you were there. But your change came — as it might well — the day you last saw her; she died for you then that you might understand her. From that hour you *did*." With which Kate slowly rose. "And I do now. She did it *for* us." Densher rose to face her, and she went on with her thought. "I used to call her, in my stupidity—for want of anything better — a dove. Well she stretched out her wings, and it was to *that* they reached. They cover us."

"They cover us," Densher said.

"That's what I give you," Kate gravely wound up. "That's what I've done for you."

His look at her had a slow strangeness that had dried, on the moment, his tears. "Do I understand then —?"

"That I do consent?" She gravely shook her head. "No — for I see. You'll marry me without the money; you won't marry me with it. If I don't consent *you* don't."

"You lose me?" He showed, though naming it frankly, a sort of awe of her high grasp. "Well, you lose nothing else. I make over to you every penny."

Prompt was his own clearness, but she had no smile this time to spare. "Precisely — so that I must choose."

"You must choose."

Strange it was for him then that she stood in his own rooms doing it, while, with an intensity now beyond any that had ever made his breath come slow, he waited for her act. "There's but one thing that can save you from my choice."

"From your choice of my surrender to you?"

"Yes" — and she gave a nod at the long envelope on the table — "your surrender of that."

"What is it then?"

"Your word of honour that you're not in love with her memory."

"Oh — her memory!"

"Ah" — she made a high gesture — "don't speak of it as if you could n't be. *I* could in your place; and you're one for whom it will do. Her memory's your love. You *want* no other."

He heard her out in stillness, watching her face but not moving. Then he only said: "I'll marry you, mind you, in an hour."

"As we were?"

"As we were."

But she turned to the door, and her headshake was now the end. "We shall never be again as we were!"

THE END